THEIR FESTIVE ISLAND ESCAPE

NINA SINGH

THEIR UNEXPECTED CHRISTMAS GIFT

SHIRLEY JUMP

MILLS & BOON

First Published in Great Britain 2019
by Mills & Boon, an imprint of HarperCollinsPublishers,
1 London Bridge Street, London, SE1 9GF

Their Festive Island Escape © 2019 Nilay Nina Singh
Their Unexpected Christmas Gift © 2019 Shirley Kawa-Jump, LLC

ISBN: 978-0-263-27270-3

1119

MIX

Paper from
responsible sources

FSC C007454
www.fsc.org

This book is produced from independently certified FSC™
paper to ensure responsible forest management.

For more information visit: www.harpercollins.co.uk/green

Printed and bound in Spain
by CPI, Barcelona

Nina Singh lives just outside Boston, USA, with her husband, children and a very rambunctious Yorkie. After several years in the corporate world she finally followed the advice of family and friends to 'give the writing a go, already'. She's oh-so-happy she did. When not at her keyboard she likes to spend time on the tennis court or golf course. Or immersed in a good read.

New York Times and *USA TODAY* bestselling author **Shirley Jump** spends her days writing romance so she can avoid the towering stack of dirty dishes, eat copious amounts of chocolate and reward herself with trips to the shopping centre. Visit her website at shirleyjump. com for author news and a book list, and follow her at Facebook.com/ shirleyjump.author for giveaways and deep discussions about important things like chocolate and shoes.

THEIR FESTIVE ISLAND ESCAPE

NINA SINGH

To my children,
you make every vacation and holiday
nothing less than a gift.

CHAPTER ONE

HER SISTER JUST didn't get it. But then again, Celeste had never really been able to get through to her when it came to the holidays. Or through to her mother, for that matter. Her family would never understand. Not that she really understood them in return.

"I can't believe you haven't moved on yet," Tara declared, throwing her hands up in the air. "Your wedding was three years ago. Get over it already."

Tara wasn't often accused of being overly sensitive. For the wedding her sister had so callously just referred to had never actually happened. Celeste bit down on a frustrated groan. She really was in no mood to talk about this. She didn't even want to think about the day she'd been so humiliatingly left at the altar, waiting for a groom who had never bothered to show up.

The humiliation still haunted her nightmares—dozens of pitying eyes staring at her as the minutes ticked by.

She was supposed to have been a Christmas bride. Instead she'd been a jilted one.

How did Tara not understand that she wanted nothing to do with the holiday now? How did she not see that the best thing to do for her mental health was just to get away from the city until the whole season was over?

Her sister's next question only proved that she didn't understand Celeste at all.

"How can you leave your family and just take off to the islands every year? Christmas just isn't the same without you here."

Celeste couldn't help the pang of guilt that landed in her gut. Perhaps one day she'd be able to put all of it behind her. Maybe she'd even enjoy the holidays again at some future point in time. She just wasn't there yet. Nowhere near, in fact. Every street decoration, every holiday jingle, every sidewalk corner Santa only reminded her of Jack and the days leading up to her abject humiliation.

Not to mention, her sister's seeming disappointment held a secondary layer. On the surface, Tara sounded like a caring, loving sibling who just wanted to spend the holidays with her older sister. But there was more to it than that. At the age of twenty-six, Tara was much too dependent on her older sister financially. And so was their mother, for that matter.

Celeste knew she should have curbed that dependence long before. Especially given all that it had cost her three years ago. But her sense of duty and responsibility as the only financially stable member of her family often overrode her good sense. Something had broken in her mother when their father had abandoned them over a decade ago, leaving nothing behind but his debts. Wendy had never fully recovered. And Tara had taken it just as hard. It had been left to Celeste as the older sibling to try to pick up the pieces.

She was still doing so. By now it was second nature. Which wasn't exactly a sound reason to keep doing it, but she couldn't exactly turn her back on either of them. Especially considering Tara was a mother herself now. Besides, wasn't one of the reasons Celeste had worked so hard to be able to help out her always cash-strapped family members?

"I thought for sure you'd stay around this year, sis." Tara's voice was petulant and whiny.

"Why would you think that?"

"Because your usual resort is nothing but a pile of damaged debris."

She spoke the truth. The last hurricane season had nearly destroyed the island that housed Celeste's yearly destination spot. After her devastating non-wedding, Celeste had chosen to continue on and attend her already-paid-for Caribbean honeymoon on a luxe tropical resort. She'd been going back to the same location every December since. This year, that island was sadly not an option.

Celeste had been heartbroken thinking of the usual staff and how they'd lost their livelihoods. She'd been regularly donating to various charities in charge of rebuilding, wished she could do more. In the meantime, she'd had to choose an unfamiliar resort on a different island. Apparently, her family had been counting on her canceling the trip altogether.

Never mind that she'd called weeks ago to tell both her sister and her mother of her exact plans.

Honestly, it was as if they didn't know her at all.

It would take more than a natural disaster to keep her in Manhattan over the holidays. She wanted nothing to do with Christmas, would skip the entire month of December if she possibly could. The non-stop carols, the sparkling decorations all over the city, the hustling and bustling crowds within a mile of any shopping center. It all overwhelmed and irritated her to no end. Even the usually quiet and cozy café they sat in was now a crowded mess of harried shoppers carrying all manner of bags and parcels.

And none of that even had anything to do with the bad memories of her broken engagement. That only added a whole other layer of distaste.

Bah humbug and all that.

Across the square wooden table, Tara's lower lip actually did a little quiver. For the briefest moment, Celeste couldn't help but feel touched. Tara had her faults, but Celeste knew deep down that her little sister really did miss her over the holidays. Tara just wasn't one to show much emotion. No wonder, given the way they'd had to grow up. Though that quality had seemed to be slowly softening since she'd become a mother.

"I was hoping we could go in on Mom's gift together," Tara continued. "You know, split the cost." She glanced downward toward the floor. "Money's a little tight for me right now, and you just got that promotion…"

The usual hint of guilt tugged within her chest.

Celeste wasn't going to bother to point out that "going in together" most often meant she would be footing the whole cost of their mother's gift and the holiday dinner. But what was there to do? The truth was, Celeste really was much better off than her sister. As was usually the case. Still, it was a fact that couldn't exactly be ignored.

Besides, Celeste didn't have it in her to discuss it much further. She had to get home and start packing. She reached for her purse and pulled out her checkbook, started scribbling after deciding on an amount, then handed it to her only sibling.

"Here, this should cover the cost of Mom's gift and a nice dinner out for the two of you. As well as a little extra so that you can pick up something for yourself," she added, despite the fact that she'd already handed Tara the holiday gift she'd purchased for her as soon as they'd sat down—a pair of fourteen-karat gold teardrop earrings she'd meticulously wrapped herself in bright, colorful paper and ribbons. Looked like Tara's guilt trip about her leaving to go on holiday was indeed working.

Tara's lips quivered ever so slightly and her eyes grew shiny as she reached for the check. "Thanks, sis. I'm going to find a way to pay you back one of these days. Once I figure out how to get on my own two feet."

Celeste gave her hand a squeeze. "I know you will," she reassured, despite her own doubt.

Tara smiled. "Hope you have a good trip. See you when you get back."

Even under the bulky, stuffed red flannel suit, it was clear the man who wore it was no regular Santa. No, this man was definitely not old, rotund or particularly jolly. Though Celeste could tell he was trying hard to fit the part. Couldn't the resort have found a better-fitting actor to play the role? Even from this distance where she sat on her lounge chair, she could tell Santa was tall and fit. His piercing dark eyes held no jolly old twinkle, though they did seem to catch the sunlight as he shifted his gaze from one child to the next as he handed out presents from his burly, oversize sack. An odd sensation of déjà vu nagged at her. Something about the pretend Santa seemed oddly familiar. Probably just her imagination.

The kids didn't seem to notice how ill-suited he was for the role, they were all laughing loudly and scurrying to open the gifts they'd just been handed.

Celeste flipped the page of the paperback she'd picked up at the airport and returned her attention to the story. Or she tried to, anyway. The kids were pretty noisy. The scene before her was charming and sweet—Santa sent to the beach to entertain and bestow gifts upon the youngest guests. It reminded her of everything she'd once so foolishly longed for. Exactly the kind of scene she was trying to get away from when she jetted out to the Caribbean every December. She was here for warm and tropical. Not stark reminders of all she'd lost three years ago when the man she'd loved, the man she'd dreamed of having children with like the ones currently in front of her, had so callously deserted her at the worst possible moment.

This resort was definitely geared more toward families than the one she was used to. She might have to find a more remote section of beach in order to avoid such scenes for the rest of her stay. Her heart couldn't take it.

A shadow suddenly fell over the pages of her book. "Ho-ho-ho."

Santa appeared to be strolling the beach closer and closer to where she sat, the children following close behind him. Now they all stood just a couple of feet from her chair. She watched as St. Nicholas leaned down to tousle the hair of one particularly excited young boy who'd clearly just received some type of toy car based on the wrapped shape.

It was futile. There was no way to even try to concentrate on her romantic suspense novel now. As charming as the children were, and they really were adorable, she couldn't take much more Christmas cheer. Glancing down the expanse of sand, she searched in vain for another empty beach chair farther away from this main part of the resort. They all appeared taken. With a resigned sigh, Celeste dropped the book and stood, wrapping her silky sarong around her midsection. Might as well get another cup of coffee or perhaps a latte until all the commotion quieted.

A squealing toddler darted past her to get to the faux Santa and she nearly toppled over in her effort to avoid the collision. This was so far from the relaxing morning she'd envisioned. Not that the kids weren't cute. They really were, with all their excitement and near tangible anticipation to receive a present. They were just so... loud. Loud, boisterous reminders of all she'd be missing out on in life. Look at how her one attempt to start a family had turned out; nothing more than an abject lesson in humiliation and hurt.

No, she wouldn't be having children. Or her own family. The one she'd been born into took up more than enough of her time and emotional energy.

She leaned down to retrieve her flip-flops from beneath the lounge chair and stopped short when she straightened. A wall of bright red topped by a cotton white beard suddenly filled her view.

"Ho-ho-ho. Well, hello there, young lady." Santa smiled at her.

"Um...hi."

"We appear to have disturbed your morning, miss. A big jolly apology for the nuisance."

His words were cordial enough. But Celeste had the clear impression that he was somehow mocking her.

"No apology necessary, St. Nick," she said with a slight salute, then tried to step around him, only to have him block her path. Of all the nerve.

The smile grew wider under the thick fake beard. "Really? I mean, you practically have a circular thought bubble above your head that screams 'bah humbug.'"

The same strange sensation of familiarity nagged at her yet again. He was clearly deepening his voice for the role but something about the tone and inflection rang a bell. And the eyes. As she studied their golden depths she couldn't help but sense that she'd somehow gazed upon those eyes before.

Had she met him before in a professional capacity?

Her position as VP of marketing for a luxury goods firm had her regularly working on advertising campaigns with various agencies. Maybe Santa had done work previously as a character actor for a project she'd worked on in the past.

What were the chances?

Not that it mattered. Right now all that mattered was that she find some peace and quiet.

But St. Nick seemed to have other plans.

"Excuse me."

Reid knew he should have stepped away the first time she'd said it. But he couldn't seem to help himself. He'd recognized her immediately. She clearly didn't remember Reid in return. He wondered if her cutting look of utter disdain would change at all if she did recall who he was. No doubt it would intensify. They hadn't exactly been on the best of terms the last time they'd seen each other.

Well, the feeling was mutual.

The children scattered all at once, clearly bored with the conversation the adults were having above their heads.

"I didn't realize they'd hired someone to play the part of Scrooge this morning," he goaded her, not even sure why he was doing so. There really was no reason to try to get a rise out of her. Other than for his pure entertainment.

She sucked in a breath. "I'm sorry. I somehow missed the part where my holiday spirit was any of your business."

He shrugged. "We just aim to please every guest, is all."

She folded her arms across her chest. "And this is how you go about doing so? Aren't you overstepping your responsibility just a bit? You're here simply to hand out some presents to the children." She pointed to the empty fleece sack he held. "Clearly your task is over."

Wow, she really was something else. She may as well have flicked him away like a royal princess dismissing a lowly jester. Not that he didn't look the part in this ridiculous suit.

"Furthermore, I fail to see how my satisfaction is the responsibility of the resort Santa." She studied him up and down. Clearly, he came up lacking in her summation. He should have walked away long before. Or never approached her in the first place. Life was too short to deal with the likes of Miss Frajedi. He had too much on his plate trying to get this place in order.

Still, Reid found himself studying her closely. The past three years had been extremely kind to her, she was still strikingly attractive. Dark, wavy hair framed a strong face with high cheekbones and hazel eyes the color of a Caribbean sunset. No wonder Jack had fallen for her so hard, the poor man. Luckily, he'd come to his senses in time. Though Reid had never approved of the way his friend had ultimately ended things. So last-minute. So hurtful. It was never right to leave a lady at the altar. Not even one like Celeste Frajedi. He'd made sure to share that sentiment with his friend, resulting in a now strained relationship between the men.

Her eyes suddenly narrowed on his face. "Do I know you?" she demanded.

Reid hesitated. For the briefest moment, he debated telling her exactly who he was. The look on her face when she found out would be a sight to see.

Ultimately, he decided against it. What would be the point? She was a paying guest after all. She was entitled to the tropical vacation she had paid for. The resort was large and expansive. The beach alone covered over a mile. If he played his cards right, they would never have to run into each other again for the duration of her stay. In fact, he vowed to make sure of it.

He shrugged. "Everyone knows me. I'm Santa Claus."

She studied him some more. Part of him wanted her to figure it out. Finally, she blew out a deep breath. "Right. Well, Santa. I'd like to go get a cup of coffee." With that, she brushed against his arm in her haste to get past him. An enticing scent of coconut and sun-kissed skin tickled his nose. Some kind of static electricity shot through his elbow and clear down his side.

"Merry Christmas, princess."

He spoke to her back as she stormed off. Her gait hastened as she walked past the breakfast cabana and instead veered toward the residential suite area. Apparently, she'd lost her appetite for the cup of coffee. That thought sent a tingle of guilt through his center.

Reid rubbed a hand down his face as he watched her walk away. Damn it. What had he just done? He thought about going after her to apologize. Now that he thought about it, he had to admit he'd been less than professional just now. As the newly minted co-owner of the Baja Majestic Resort on the beautiful island of Jamaica, he owed it to all of his guests to treat them well, regardless of any past history. He had no excuse. He'd just been so surprised to see her lying there, the recognition had thrown him off.

But he had to make sure not to slip up like that again. He couldn't forget how important his role was here. No one else was going to get this place up to the standards that the Evanson clientele expected. His father certainly wasn't up to the task. In fact, his father seemed to be doing everything possible to run the family hospitality business into the ground. A gambler through and through, his fraternal parent took way too many chances, risked too many valuables. The cleanup always fell to Reid. This current project being no exception.

He couldn't allow himself to forget how much responsibility he bore. An entire conglomerate of employees, contract workers, and their dependents relied on Evanson Hotels and Resorts for their livelihoods and their future. Not to mention his own parents.

And he'd just gone and insulted a valuable, paying guest.

As much as he hated to admit it, he would have to make up for his behavior. He had to somehow atone for the way he'd just treated Celeste Frajedi.

Merry Christmas, princess.

The derisive words repeatedly echoed through her head as Celeste fled to her deluxe suite and slammed the door behind her. Walking over to the glass screen door leading to the third-floor balcony, she pulled aside the curtains to let the bright sunshine in. He hands were shaking, she realized with no small amount of dismay. He'd rattled her. When was the last time she'd actually felt thrown by a man? Or anyone else, for that matter? Her mother notwithstanding.

Perhaps a better question was why had she let the likes of a pretend Santa Claus in an ill-fitting suit and a side-skewed beard get to her so badly?

There was something about the way he'd looked at her. He clearly hadn't liked what he'd seen. Had her feelings regarding the noisy children been so obvious? She hadn't realized she'd shown any outward signs that she'd been bothered by them but clearly the man had picked up something. He'd called her a scrooge!

Never mind that his labeling of her as such was perilously close to the truth. Still, her attitude to Christmas was none of his business. How dare he treat her the way he had? Her ire and irritation shot up even further as she thought of the derision in his eyes as he'd studied her.

His negative view of her seemed way out of proportion to whatever imagined slight he'd witnessed. It was as if he'd disliked her on sight. Which brought back the question: Why had he seemed so familiar to her?

Celeste shook off the query. The answer hardly mattered. She had no doubt the upper-level management in charge of the resort would be appalled if they knew of the actions of their character actor employee. She was in the very business of appealing to consumers as a professional marketer. The faux Santa's behavior would be considered a nightmare to any business leader. That was no way to treat any customer.

Still, the encounter shouldn't have shaken her up as much as it had. She was a professional, after all. And she'd certainly suffered through worse humiliation. The best thing to do would be to try to just forget about the whole incident and put it completely behind her. She would chalk it up to yet one more instance of a negative holiday memory. As if she needed any more of those.

With a calming inhalation of breath, she sank to the carpeted floor. She would meditate until the whole interaction with the wayward St. Nick was nothing more than a mere ghost of a thought in her head. Relaxing all her muscles, she began to count down from ten. Then she did nothing but clear her mind.

It wasn't easy.

Knock. Knock. Knock.

Celeste had no idea how much time had passed before the annoying knocking roused her out of her deep state of meditative trance. Was it too much to ask for just some calming time after the morning she'd had? Apparently, this day was just going to be one irritation after another.

"Room service," came a soft, feminine voice from the other side of her door.

It took a moment to reorient as Celeste forced herself to stand from her cross-legged sitting position on the floor. Her leg muscles screamed in protest at the abrupt movement as she walked to the door.

"There's been some kind of mistake," she said to the petite uniformed woman standing outside with a cart. "I haven't ordered any room service."

The woman smiled as she shook her head. "This is on the house, madam." Without waiting for acknowledgment, she wheeled the cart toward the center of the room.

"I don't understand?"

The woman's smile didn't falter as she answered. "No charge, madam. Compliments of the resort." She handed her an envelope that had sat in the middle of the tray. With that, she pivoted on her heel and left the room.

Celeste blinked in confusion at the shut door before understanding dawned. Sure enough, when she read the note, her suspicion was confirmed.

Please accept this complimentary gesture as a token of appreciation and regret that you may have been inconvenienced in any way this morning.
Sincerely, The Baja Majestic Resort.

Someone in upper management must have witnessed the unpleasantness between her and Santa earlier this morning. She studied the goodies before her on the food service cart. They'd certainly made an effort to appease her. A silver carafe of steaming hot coffee sat in the center of the tray. A chilled bottle of champagne sent a curl of frost into the air. Orange juice and a variety of pastries rounded out the offerings. Not bad at all as a conciliatory gesture. Someone was trying hard to make things up to her. A foolish part of her felt guilty that perhaps bad Santa might have been chastised harshly by his superiors. Or even worse, that he'd been fired.

He may have been an overbearing clod, but he didn't deserve to have his livelihood jeopardized. She would have to look into that. The desk attendant in the concierge lounge would surely know exactly what had transpired and the ultimate outcome that had led to the enticing cart she'd just had delivered. A visit later this afternoon wouldn't hurt. If he had been let go, it was probably not too late for her to intervene. Not that he deserved her good will. Still, she would be the bigger person if needed.

It was a role she'd been well groomed for her whole life, after all.

CHAPTER TWO

"ONE OF THE guests would like to see you, *mi paadie*."

Reid looked up from the spreadsheet he'd been studying to the man who had just entered his office without
knocking. Alex was co-owner of the property and Reid
felt grateful every day for that fact. He wasn't sure what
he would have done without the other man's intimate
knowledge of the island and its customs. Not to mention
his sharp head for business.

Though Alex definitely had one flaw: a clear aversion
to knocking before entering a closed door. Not that Reid
had been doing much in the way of concentrating just
now. A set of light hazel eyes and tumbling dark hair had
interrupted his thoughts unwanted and unbidden throughout the morning. He wondered if she'd liked the tray of
goodies he'd had sent to her room. Would she find it all
an adequate apology? Or had she huffed in disgust and
pushed the tray aside. He suspected the latter. Not that
he could really blame her if she had.

"And hello to you too, Alex," he answered his partner
without looking away from the screen he hadn't really
been focusing on.

"Did you hear what I said, man?"

He nodded. "It appears I'm being summoned by one
of the guests, is that it?"

Alex smiled at him. "You wanted to be hands-on, did you not? She's asking for you specifically."

Wasn't it enough that he'd been commandeered into playing Santa this morning when the actor originally hired to play the part had called in sick? The entertainment manager had run to him in a panic. No one else was available to do it. And the resort had announced the event weeks in advance. In the end it was easier just to don the suit and get the whole fiasco over with.

Only he'd come face-to-face with a woman he hadn't ever expected to see again.

Now he apparently had to go smooth the ruffles of a guest who no doubt felt slighted somehow or was trying to finagle a room upgrade.

"I tried to take care of it myself. Explained to her that I was co-owner of the resort. But like I said, the guest insists on seeing you specifically."

Reid sighed and stood. The guest in question had to be one of those checking in this morning who he'd greeted. Apparently, they'd taken it to heart when he'd said that he'd personally see to any detail regarding their stay that they weren't completely happy with. Though why Alex hadn't just taken care of it by partially crediting the guest or explaining that they were at full capacity and had no upgrade to give out was lost on him.

Again, it was probably best to simply go get it over with. It was just clearly going to be one of those days.

Celeste shook her head and tried to blink away the image she was sure she had to be imagining. But when she opened her eyes again, the unwanted vision stood clear as day in front of her still.

This couldn't be happening. "You're the nasty Santa?"

Her words came out harsher and louder than she'd

intended. Every eye currently in the concierge lounge turned to stare at her. She distinctly heard a giggle of feminine laughter from behind her somewhere.

To his credit, Reid Evanson looked as shocked as she was at the unexpected turn. Suddenly, the events of the morning seemed to make much more sense. She definitely hadn't been imagining the waves of dislike emanating from the man playing jolly ol' St. Nick.

Well, the feeling went both ways.

"What are you doing here?" she demanded.

He thrust his hands into his pockets before answering. "You're the one who asked for me."

He was being deliberately obtuse. Celeste tried to summon some semblance of calm. It didn't help that the gentleman she'd spoken to earlier was shifting his amused gaze from one of them to the other. None of this was the least bit amusing.

"I mean, what are you doing here on this resort?"

"You two know each other?" the other man wanted to know.

"We were acquainted once," Reid answered briefly.

Despite herself, she found herself studying him. He'd aged well. Clean shaven before, he currently sported a close-cropped beard slightly darker than the sandy blond hair on his head. He wore said hair longer, nearly touching his shoulders. Instead of the Santa suit from earlier, he now wore a formfitting T-shirt tucked into pleated khaki pants. It all showed off the physique of a man who clearly took care of himself. Had he always been so muscular?

"Why did you ask for me?" Reid wanted to know.

"I didn't. I asked to see Santa Claus." This time, the person behind her didn't even bother to try to hide her laughter. Heaven help her, she knew how ridiculous she sounded. She had half a mind to let out a giggle herself.

Without another word, he stepped around the long, highly polished counter and gently took her by the elbow.

"Let's discuss all this in my office."

His office? The room he led her to, if it held human emotions, would have no doubt been insulted to be referred to as such. Floor-to-ceiling glass walls overlooked a scenic beach with a majestic view of the crystal-blue ocean into the horizon. Plush carpeting had her feet sinking in her flip-flops. A grand desk with three large monitors sat in the center of it all.

"You run the resort," she commented as he shut the door behind him.

"I own it. Along with my partner, Alex Wiliston. "He was the gentleman you were speaking with earlier."

The pieces started to fall into place. She remembered now that Reid came from a wealthy family of hoteliers. Though the family business had suffered some losses recently, Reid had taken the helm from his father and turned things around. Last she'd heard, Evanson Properties had not only returned to a profitable enterprise, the company had expanded, all thanks to the prodigal son.

"You decided to expand into the resort business, I take it," Celeste said.

Something flickered behind his eyes. He gave a small nod before answering. "The Caribbean specifically."

"I see. But earlier this morning…when I saw you…" Now she was just rambling.

"Just filling in for an employee who couldn't make it at the last minute."

"I see," she repeated uselessly.

Suddenly, it was all too much. Far from fleeing her unpleasant associations with the holiday as it related to her failed relationship, she'd somehow ended up face-to-face with someone who'd played a major role in the whole fiasco.

Reid had been her ex-fiancé's best man. And she knew he'd never thought her good enough for his buddy.

"Can I get you something to drink?" Reid asked, for lack of anything better to say. How exactly did one proceed with this conversation? The scenario was so completely unexpected in so many myriad ways.

She shook her head. "No. Thank you. I just had some coffee and a mimosa to wash down several pastries." She took in a shaky breath. "But I'm guessing you already know that. Seeing as you were probably behind the delivery to my room."

"I was. Did you enjoy them?"

Her eyes grew wide. "Are we really doing this?"

"Doing what?"

"Pretending I'm just another one of your regular guests?"

The feeling of guilt from earlier blossomed once again in Reid's chest. Celeste was indeed his guest. A paying customer. He hadn't meant to come off as boorish as he had out on the beach. But he'd just been so thoroughly disconcerted at seeing her again after all this time. If he was being honest with himself, he'd imagined encountering Celeste Frajedi more than a few times over the years. Not that he'd ever been able to explain to himself exactly why that was so. He had no reason to be thinking of her at all.

"But that's exactly what you are," he answered. "An appreciated guest. Hence, my desire to apologize for my behavior earlier. I hope the gesture served as an adequate apology. I should never have let…our history, so to speak…affect in any way how I treat a guest at my establishment. There's no excuse for my having done so," he added with complete sincerity. He really didn't have any kind of excuse. Not even considering the morning he'd had. On top of the missing Santa and the shock of seeing Celeste again, he'd started the day with another aggravating, infuriating phone call with his father, who was once again trying to take over the company he'd almost single-handedly destroyed.

Celeste looked far from convinced by his words.

"I can assure you such behavior on my part won't happen again," he told her. "In fact, you can forget I'm even here."

The skeptical look she speared him with clearly said he hadn't done much to convince her any further.

You can forget I'm even here.

Hah! As if she could forget his presence for even a moment. What a mistake it had been to come here. Of all the resorts she could have chosen as a substitute for her regular vacation spot, how in the world had she landed on this one? The cruel fates were clearly laughing at her.

Celeste flopped herself down on the wide king bed back in her suite and draped an arm across her face. No, she couldn't so easily forget that Reid Evanson was right here on this very island. Nor could she forget the way he'd made her feel three years ago. As if she could never be enough for the likes of his best friend. Never mind that Jack had turned out to be a reckless, disloyal excuse for a fiancé who had eventually left her stranded at the very altar where they were to have made their vows. Sure, now she realized just how much of a favor he'd done her. Aside from saving her from what could have been years of betrayal and heartbreak, he'd helped her come to a conclusion about herself. She clearly wasn't the type of woman who was meant for a family or a steady relationship. He'd enabled her to avoid the mistake of a lifetime.

A mistake that could have led her straight down the same path her mother had traveled.

But that knowledge hadn't stopped the sting of rejection, nor the burn of embarrassment as she'd faced down a whole church full of wedding guests to tell them that the ceremony had been suddenly called off.

Reid had been there every step of the way. He'd witnessed her humiliation in its entirety. And she'd received the distinct impression that he felt she'd only gotten what she'd deserved.

An incoming message on her phone pulled her out of her thoughts. The screen lit up with the profile picture of her sister smiling as she held her toddler niece. Celeste groaned and debated whether to answer. On the one hand, she felt drained and conversations with her sister could often be one-sided; Tara's side. On the other hand, Celeste could really use someone to talk to right about now.

With no small amount of doubt, she pressed her thumb on the icon to answer.

"Hey, Tara."

"Hey, sis." The sound of a musical children's show could be heard playing loudly in the background.

"What's up?"

"Just calling to see how things are in paradise. Still can't believe you're there and not here." Ah, so this was the routine guilt-trip call. Cynical as it sounded, Celeste couldn't help the thought given past experience.

Celeste sighed deeply as she shifted to a seated position on the edge of the bed. "Well, it just so happens, I'm beginning to doubt my decision to come."

Tara's sudden exhalation came through loud and clear across the tiny speaker. "What's happened? Spill!"

"Let's just say there's someone here I didn't expect to see. Ever."

"Details, please. Is it a man?"

"Yes, as a matter of fact. But that's not the import—"

But Tara cut her off. "Ooh, this is getting interesting. Is it someone you had a previous fling with? Can you have another one? Hot and heavy with no strings attached! You could so use that, you know."

Celeste rubbed a hand across her tense forehead. Honestly, Tara didn't know her in the least. "I don't do flings."

"Well, maybe you should start. Heaven knows your serious relationships don't turn out so great." She grunted a laugh. "They don't turn out at all."

Ouch. So much for a sisterly conversation to make her feel better. Foolish of her to even entertain the notion. Celeste found herself wondering if she should have answered the phone after all.

"So, who is it?" her sister asked after a heavy pause.

"Never mind. It's not important. Forget I brought it up. How's Mom? And little Nat?"

It wasn't often any of them referred to her niece by her full given name, Natalie.

"They're all fine," Tara answered. But she wasn't having it with the attempted change in topic. "And no way you're going to try to drop the matter of this mystery man. Tell me who you ran into. And tell me what he means to you."

Celeste opened her mouth to respond with a resounding and emphatic denial that Reid Evanson meant absolutely anything to her whatsoever. That she'd hardly thought about him over the past three years.

But the lie wouldn't form on her tongue.

CHAPTER THREE

ALEX STILL STOOD in the middle of Reid's office studying him like a lab specimen. "Is there something I can do for you?" Reid finally asked, ultimately losing the game of visual chicken.

"Yeah. Neither you nor the young lady really answered me earlier when I asked if you two knew each other. It appears you do."

Reid pretended to type on his keyboard. "Then you seem to have answered your own question."

"I have more."

Reid gave up all pretense of trying to get any work done. Leaning back in his leather desk chair, he tried to stretch out some of the tension that seemed to have tied a knot in the back of his neck right at the base of his skull. "Somehow, I knew you would."

"I do. One of them being, exactly how do you know our esteemed guest? I couldn't help but notice she's traveling alone."

"So?"

Alex grinned. "So does that fact have anything to do with you?"

"What? No! Of course not." *Not directly, anyway.*

He hadn't realized he'd mumbled the last part under his breath until Alex questioned him.

"What does that mean, Reid? Not directly?"

Alex sighed, the tension in his neck traveling farther down his spine. He might have to hit the spa later for some kind of back treatment massage. Though he'd been meaning to do that for weeks, ever since he'd arrived at the start of the season.

"It's not what you're thinking, partner."

"Then what is it? You two obviously have some kind of history and not all of it is positive.

Reid almost laughed at that. Less than positive would be an understatement.

"Celeste was almost the wife of a friend of mine. Let's just say he hasn't been the same ever since their relationship ended."

Alex nodded slowly. "Oh. So she dumped him."

Reid rubbed his jaw. "Not exactly."

"Then I don't understand."

Reid ran a hand down his face. He hadn't been sleeping well. There was always something that needed to be done, some detail to attend to. He also had his father's ill-formed takeover attempt to contend with. Now he'd been thrown another curveball in the form of Celeste Frajedi and he wasn't sure how to explain to his partner exactly what had gone down three years ago. It hadn't really had anything to do with him. So it was hard to explain why he'd taken it all so personally back then. Even when it came to explaining it to himself.

"Well, on the surface, Jack was the one who actually did the dumping."

His friend gave him a blank look. "On the surface?"

"She wasn't in the relationship for the right reasons. He told me all about it."

Alex raised an eyebrow.

Reid felt a sensation of discomfort meander down his

spine. As if he was betraying a confidence somehow. Though he'd be hard-pressed to identify whose privacy he was uneasy about. Celeste's or Jack's?

"Celeste is a shrewd businesswoman. She's very well known in the industry as one of the most successful marketing executives in New York. The business sites have regular profiles on her. She can be ruthless when she doesn't get what she wants."

"You said your friend hasn't been the same ever since the disastrous wedding that didn't happen."

Reid nodded. "That's right. He's still traipsing all over Europe, partying in different cities. Living with various women." Some of those women being wealthy, married socialites looking for a good time on the side.

"Huh. And he didn't behave like that before he met Celeste?" Alex wanted to know.

The uneasy feeling grew from tingling sensation to an all-out burning down his back as Reid sought for a truthful way to answer. If he was being completely honest, Jack had always had a propensity to be a bit of a partier, something of a Lothario. If anything, his relationship with Celeste had seemed to temper that side of him.

"It's just different. Trust me. I heard all about it before he called off the wedding. Celeste worked long hours, was never around for him. He said he felt single most of the time."

"Sounds like she's just ambitious."

"I agree that's a commendable trait. But for people like her, it's never enough," Reid answered quickly, though the uneasiness was now sitting like a boulder at the base of his spine. Damn it, why hadn't he scheduled that massage? Maybe they could fit him in between clients.

Alex went on, "She also happens to have booked our

most exclusive and pricey deluxe suite for an extended stay. So clearly her ambitions have served her well."

Reid shrugged. "I guess. Again, some people can't seem to have enough." He couldn't even tell anymore if he was talking from personal experience about his father or if he was still referring wholly to Celeste.

"You sound like a man who's only considered one side of a story."

"What's that supposed to mean?"

"You sure you're not confusing cause and effect, partner?"

But his friend didn't give him a chance to answer, just turned and left the office. Apparently, the question was a rhetorical one. Good thing, too. Reid would be hard-pressed to come up with an answer.

Had he been completely unfair in his assessment of Celeste three years ago? Of course, it had occurred to him more than once over the years that he'd only heard one side of the story. But Jack had been his friend since they'd been roommates at university. He was a loyal friend and he'd come through for Reid more than a few times over the years. Reid's father's recklessness and wandering eye had started right around that time, too.

Jack had genuinely seemed shaken when he'd confided in Reid as his nuptials had fast approached. He'd talked about how cold and critical Celeste had suddenly gotten when a couple of Jack's business ventures hadn't panned out. How demanding she'd been that he get back on his feet in all haste.

Reid slammed his laptop shut in frustration.

What did any of it matter now anyhow? It was all past history. Jack had moved on, even if some of his current behavior bordered on self-destructive. He was a grown-up who could make his own choices. Even if everything

Jack had told him about her was the absolute truth, Celeste couldn't be faulted for her ex-groom's behavior three years after the fact.

That thought had him feeling like a heel again for the way he'd behaved earlier when he'd first seen her. And also for the assumptions he'd made about her judging him.

In all fairness, Reid had been nothing less than judgmental himself.

Bouncy reggae music greeted her as Celeste made her way down the beach to the seaside cabana she planned to visit for her first dinner here. Her paperback tucked under her arm, she was looking forward to a relaxing evening with a nice glass of wine and a tasty meal of local seafood. Her morning plans had gone woefully astray. The least she deserved right now was a satisfying meal followed by a peaceful stroll on the beach. Then she'd spend the rest of the evening tucked in under her bedcovers, enjoying some further reading. To most women her age, such plans might sound boring and flat. To her, it all sounded like heaven. Exactly what she was looking for during her evening hours on this vacation.

Her step faltered as she approached the cabana. It was already packed and hopping. Every table appeared full. She approached the hostess manning the front entrance.

"Hi, it's just me. Table for one please."

The young lady gave her a sympathetic look before motioning toward the bar area where couples sat sharing various appetizers. Several bartenders stepped around each other mixing drinks and taking orders.

"I'm afraid all we have available right now is bar seating, miss. And those spots are going fast."

Celeste released a sigh of disappointment and made

her way to one of the few open bar stools. Squeezing herself in between a burly older man in a Hawaiian shirt and a bikinied brunette, she reached for the drinks menu.

One of the bartenders appeared in front of her within moments. His gold name tag said Phillipe in black lettering. "What can I get for the lovely lady?" He asked her with a wide grin. "And I do mean lovely."

Celeste tried to smile back. He wasn't doing any harm but she really wasn't in any kind of mood for a flirtation. And she had no doubt the young man was flirting. The way he was looking at her left no question about it.

She almost wanted to tell him his efforts were hardly necessary. She always tipped well and if this was sympathy flirting simply because she was sitting at a bar alone in a popular resort, she had no need for it. She placed her order for a glass of sparkling wine and a plate of fish tacos without acknowledging the compliment.

She'd gotten through several pages of her book before her meal arrived.

Phillipe winked at her as he placed the plate in front of her on the bar.

Maybe she should have ordered room service. Now she would have to spend the entire time eating trying to avoid his gaze. And a quick cursory glance in his direction confirmed he was indeed staring at her. Oh, yeah, she couldn't wait to submit an online review about this place after her stay. She'd normally go straight to the owner with her complaints, but he'd been a part of the problem.

Phillipe appeared as soon as she'd taken her last bite. "So, I have a break coming up in a couple of hours. Can I treat you to another drink then?"

She didn't get a chance to answer as a thick baritone

voice suddenly sounded from behind her. "Miss Frajedi, I hope you enjoyed your meal."

She didn't need to turn around, recognized the voice immediately as belonging to Reid. Unlike earlier, he wasn't speaking in the low husky voice of a makeshift Santa.

Phillipe immediately took a step back. "Oh. Hey, boss."

Celeste darted a glance over her shoulder. Reid stood only an inch behind her. Arms crossed in front of his chest, his chin tight. He didn't look happy. He merely nodded in a curt acknowledgment of Phillipe's greeting.

Then, to her surprise, he held her hand out to help her up off her stool.

"I haven't settled my bill," she protested.

Reid didn't take his eyes off Phillipe when he answered. "It's on the house."

"Yes, boss," Phillipe immediately responded. She could have sworn he clicked his heels behind the bar.

For lack of anything else to do, Celeste wiped her mouth with her cloth napkin and took Reid's hand before standing. He gently led her away from the crowded bar toward the sand.

"I take it there's a rule about the workers fraternizing with the guests," she ventured after they'd made their way to the beach. The sun was slowly setting across the horizon, throwing brilliant shades of red and orange across the evening sky.

"Not yet, there isn't. Though I've made a mental note to get one drafted ASAP."

His voice sounded strained and tight. If there wasn't any such policy, why did he seem so bothered by Phillipe's behavior? Could it possibly have anything to do with her?

And how many times in one day could she wonder

about whether her behavior was going to affect someone else's livelihood, for heaven's sake?

"I'm sorry if you were made to feel uncomfortable during your dinner. We strive to make everyone feel completely at ease at all times. I'll have a word with the staffing manager to make sure it doesn't happen again."

So that was it. She'd been foolish to even feel tempted to look further into it than what lay on the surface.

"Another apology from the top man," she commented, kicking off her sandals to feel the silky soft sand underneath her feet. Reid paused while she nudged them off to the side.

He exhaled. "It appears we are off to a bad start."

She knew he meant the resort, but she took the opportunity to address the proverbial elephant in the room. "Or we're simply continuing along the same path as we were three years ago."

His step didn't falter but she could have sworn she felt him stiffening ever so slightly beside her. "I thought your intention on this trip was to forget all about it."

"Believe me, I see the irony in all of this." An exotic-looking bird flew past them at eye level, a myriad of colors along its wing.

"Tell me something," Celeste began. "You never did appear to be on board with my and Jack's wedding." Or with her, for that matter.

"You didn't seem right for each other," he answered simply.

She couldn't be offended. For he was completely right. Still, his words held enough of a sting that she wondered if she should have even started this conversation.

She could guess what he meant. She and her ex-fiancé were from two different worlds. Celeste had grown up struggling to merely survive while Jack was a trust fund baby who'd always known wealth and privilege.

Much like the man beside her now. Though she'd have to admit, if one were to look closely, the two men didn't really have all that much in common besides factors visible on the surface.

While Reid had worked incredibly hard to make a name for himself in the hospitality business, Jack was a mere figurehead for the yachting company his family owned and operated. Reid had taken all that had been handed to him and then grown and expanded it, becoming an industry titan in the process.

Celeste gave a shake of her head. What good did it do to compare the two men? There was no reason for it. In fact, there was no reason to give Jack another thought. Why had she even brought up his name?

Still, something tugged at her to get to the bottom of Reid's statement, she couldn't seem to help herself. "What do you mean? That we didn't seem right for each other?"

He gave a small shrug. "You're very different personalities. He's not as…ambitious, I guess. You're much more driven. Yet, there's a side of you—" He stopped abruptly. "You know what? Never mind. None of this is my place."

Celeste halted in her tracks and gently nudged him to stop walking. His gaze dropped to where she'd touched him on the elbow. She ignored the way his eyes darkened and quickly dropped her hand. "Please finish what you were going to say. There's a side of me that's what?"

Reid released a deep sigh and looked off into the distance at the horizon. "Just that there's a side of you which must have overwhelmed a man like him. An untamed, stormy quality just underneath your surface. A side a man like Jack wouldn't be able to handle." His eyes seemed to add the words *unlike me*.

Celeste's gasp was audible over the crashing waves behind them. She wouldn't challenge his words, couldn't. For he spoke the very truth. Celeste did everything she could to hide the wild inner-city kid she'd grown up as behind a highly polished professional veneer. She'd made certain to bury the hardscrabble teen who'd bartered, begged and stole simply to survive when the three of them had found themselves homeless on the streets for close to a year.

Then there was her ancestry. She'd fully studied her absent father's Persian roots, intrigued by all she'd learned about the culture. But she'd never explored that part of herself, hadn't so much as looked into visiting that area of the world. Though she'd had plenty of opportunity.

Somehow Reid had seen through all those layers three years ago when they were barely more than strangers.

"I'm not sure how to take what you've just said, Reid," she said once she found her voice again. "That I was somehow too much for Jack to handle."

He turned to fully face her then. "You should take it as a compliment."

Reid had no intention of stopping by the bar when he left his office behind the concierge lounge. He wanted nothing more after a long frustrating day than to head to his suite in the main quarters and pop open a bottle of cabernet and order a thick juicy burger.

But then he'd seen Celeste sitting at the bar by herself. He didn't even want to examine what had made him stop and just watch her for a while. She was alone, but she'd made it clear solitude was what she was after.

She'd seemed perfectly content with her book and sea-food plate. He'd been ready to move on, get going with the rest of his evening, but then he'd seen the way the bartender had been watching her. He'd found himself moving toward her then. So much for having her forget he was here.

Some strange emotion lodged in his chest when he heard the other man ask to buy her a drink. He didn't even know his intention until he reached her side. And what had possessed him to ask her to walk with him? He probably should have bidden her good-night right after intervening then went about his business. For now, they seemed to be awkwardly strolling along the beach, neither one managing to say anything much by way of conversation after the awkward words about their past.

He shouldn't have told her all the things he'd just shared, didn't even realize he was going to until the words were leaving his mouth.

Celeste cleared her throat. "So, you mentioned you'd recently acquired this place?" She was clearly looking to change the subject.

"Yeah. Last summer. I'd been looking to expand into the Caribbean resort business for a while. Luckily, it was one of the few islands that came through the hurricane season unscathed."

She humphed out a small laugh.

"What?"

"That happens to be the only reason I'm here. My usual spot is in shambles." The faraway look in her eyes told him she missed it. "This was one of the few places left to book."

Reid clapped his hand to his chest in mock offense. "You wound me. You mean to tell me the only reason you chose my resort was for lack of other options?"

She smiled just as a slight breeze blew a dark tendril of hair along her cheek. How silly that his fingers itched to gently tuck it back behind her ear for her.

"I'm afraid so. I rather miss the other place. No offense."

"I'm not so much offended as I am concerned as a business owner. What does it say about this place that you only booked it as a backup?" How many other potential clients were doing the same? The resort could face losing all sorts of business further down the line once the other resorts were back up and running.

"Would you like my professional opinion?"

"Can I afford it?" he teased. "You do have a reputation for being the best."

"Consider this a freebie."

He tilted his head for her to continue. "Well, to put it plainly, your marketing and advertising is somewhat subpar. Frankly, it's garbage. Rubbish."

Double ouch. "Hey, don't get technical now."

She laughed out loud. "Seriously. There's nothing on the website to compel me to click Book Now. Aside from a few pretty pictures of the beach, you don't really say anything very enticing about attractions, nearby landmarks, activities for the guests…"

"Yet you booked it anyway."

"Like I said, I was running out of options and grew concerned everything would sell out. It's competitive enough around Christmas under the best of circumstances. And it's really important to me to get away from the city around the holidays."

He could guess why. It was hard to forget that she and Jack had planned their nuptials around the holiday season. A wedding during Christmas in Manhattan. It was supposed to have been so romantic. Until it had all come crumbling down.

He'd been so quick to take Jack's word for everything and toss the full brunt of responsibility for the mess on her shoulders. Alex's words echoed through his mind. *Are you sure you're not confusing cause and effect, partner?*

Perhaps he had been. All this time.

She continued, bringing his focus back to the matter at hand—his resort's lack of a real media presence that would draw more potential guests. "And I have to be honest, now that I'm here, nothing really compels me to consider returning. Our mutual history aside."

Sighing, he answered her. "You're actually not telling me anything I don't already know. But you have awakened me to the urgency of it all. It's just one more thing on the list. We've been interviewing various marketing firms. None seem to fit the bill."

"If I were you, I would make a decision fairly quick."

She wasn't wrong. The implications of the failure to do so weren't lost on him. This was all so new. Not for the first time, Reid wondered if he'd bitten off more than he could chew. The differences between running a high-rise hotel in a metropolitan city and running a tropical resort were surprisingly vast.

He'd be even more lost if he didn't have Alex by his side. But clearly it wasn't enough.

"Any suggestions?"

"Are you asking for me to work on my vacation?" she asked, a teasing whimsical tone in her voice.

He couldn't help but laugh. "I'm shameless."

They'd reached the pier that moored the excursion boats. A couple of them were still out, it seemed. He was due to participate in a few of the outings himself, to get a feel for the experiences as the owner. He rested his arms over the steel railing and let his hands dangle over the side. Several blue-gold fish could be seen swimming right under the surface of the water.

"You're absolutely right," he told her. "About communicating better regarding all that we have to offer." The excursions were a prime example. Sure, there were chalkboards and newsletters written up daily detailing the outings available to their guests. But they were only that, mere announcements. Nothing describing the thrilling adventures waiting for those looking for extra experiences, more than just beach volleyball or swim aerobics.

A glimmer of an idea began to form in his head. Reid knew he was too tired and too distracted—a fact that had everything to do with the woman standing next to him—to voice the notion aloud just yet.

But he certainly had some thinking to do. And when he did think it all through, he could only hope Celeste would be on board with his suggestion.

CHAPTER FOUR

CELESTE AWOKE TO the sound of a piece of paper being shuffled under her door.

What the…?

It couldn't be the bill. She wasn't due to check out for several days still. Honestly, if they had confused her with another guest, Reid was going to get an earful about the way his resort was run. A glance at the clock told her it was past nine thirty. That was surprising. She never usually slept this late. But she'd had a restless night. Every time she'd closed her eyes, she'd been met with a set of bright golden ones. Visions of Reid's smile as they walked along the beach. The way he'd glowered at the flirty bartender when he'd approached her after her dinner.

When was the last time she'd taken a walk with a man? She couldn't recall. Had she and Jack visited any beaches? She didn't think so. Probably the reason she preferred to be on a tropical island this time of year.

For that matter, when was the last time she'd simply been with a man? Out on a date? Or in a capacity that wasn't strictly professional? Too long. With groggily heavy limbs, she climbed out of bed, suppressing a groan of frustration. Such thoughts were only going to make her miserable, thinking about all she didn't have in her life.

There's a side of you a man like Jack can't handle.

Celeste shook her head to push thoughts of yesterday's conversation aside.

The item slid under her door turned out to be an envelope with a card inside. Curiouser and curiouser. Her heart thumped in her chest as she removed the card and read its contents.

Please join me for breakfast if you haven't eaten already. I have a few matters I'd like to discuss. It will be worth your time. I'll be in my office until you're ready.
Reid

What in the world could he have in mind? A cry of warning screamed in her head. His cell number was printed on the top half of the card. She should just call him and tell him she had indeed eaten already. Or that she wasn't available. Or just outright tell him she wasn't interested in seeing him or in anything he may have to say. Though that would be a lie. She was more than intrigued. And more than a little excited at the prospect of seeing him again today. She could hardly get him out of her mind last night. And all the things he'd told her.

As if that wasn't reason enough right there to turn him down.

The man was her ex-fiancé's good friend for heaven's sake. Two short days ago, he practically cornered her on the beach and accused her of being a scrooge. No doubt he still harbored suspicions that she'd ruined her ex's life. After all, what else could he have meant when he'd said she was too much for someone like Jack to handle? Most likely that he thought her too uncultured, too unpolished to sully someone like Jack. Or Reid Evanson, for that matter. Somehow, Reid must have seen straight through her three years ago.

No. There was no reason to go see him.

So why had she walked over to the closet and taken out her prettiest sundress? The red one she knew brought out the hue of her olive skin. With thread-thin straps and a flowy skirt that accented her curves.

The warning cry sounded again, telling her to put the dress back and crawl back into bed if she knew what was good for her.

She lay the dress out on the bureau instead and walked to the shower stall.

It wouldn't hurt to just ask her, Reid thought as he waited impatiently in his office for Celeste's response to his written invite. He'd long ago given up any pretense of trying to get work done and now just stood staring at the tropical scene before him. A line had formed at the main dining hut for breakfast. He made a mental note to address the wait time in the mornings for food. But his thoughts immediately returned to the woman he'd spent the evening with. He couldn't remember the last time he'd simply walked with a lady along a sandy beach, just talking and enjoying the sunset. He had to admit he'd enjoyed it.

Celeste was already sporting the beginnings of a golden tan, her hair had lightened since the first day she'd arrived. She'd looked like a tempting goddess standing next to him as they stood on the marina pier.

He'd been thinking about her all night.

But none of that had anything to do with his invite asking her to join him for breakfast. That was strictly professional.

The door suddenly flung open and Reid didn't need to

look up to know it was Alex. He was the only one who never knocked. "Morning, partner."

Reid merely nodded.

"Your father keeps calling the main office," Alex informed him. "Says you're not returning his calls when he phones you directly."

Reid tried to bridle the surge of irritation that shot through his core. His father. The man was determined to ruin himself at this golden stage of his life. And he'd nearly driven Evanson Properties to the brink of ruin as well until Reid had stepped in and taken over as CEO. All because of a woman. A much younger woman.

Reid rubbed his forehead. "I missed one call from him last night. Not that there's a real need to call him back, in any case. I have no interest in what he has to say."

"Maybe he just wants to talk about his upcoming nuptials."

Reid threw his pen onto his desk. "Ha. If anything, I should be calling my mother about that wedding. Make sure she's all right." His mother had not deserved the way she'd been treated after three decades of marriage to the same man.

"I'll be sure to call him," Reid assured his partner. "Tell him to stop bothering the staff." He made a mental note to reach out to his mother first, however.

Alex gave him a mini salute and turned to leave.

Reid knew exactly why his father was trying to contact him. Now that the company was finally out of the red, Dale Reid was trying desperately to regain the power he'd initially handed over to his only son once the trouble had started.

Which was why he could use Celeste's help. He needed his latest acquisition to be a resounding success. There could be no questioning of his competence or abilities from the board, or anyone else, for that matter. Her marketing expertise could go a long way to establishing this place as a prime vacation spot.

Nope, nothing to do with wanting to see her again. His slight reflection in the glass mocked him even as his brain formed the denial. The truth was, the lines were becoming a bit blurred. Yes, he really was interested in her professional feedback, had no qualms about asking her for it and trying to make some sort of business deal to benefit both of them.

But he couldn't deny he'd been sorely tempted to seek her out this morning even without the business incentive. Something about her called to him, intrigued him like no other woman he'd ever met. The brief time they'd spent together had familiarized him with a woman far different from the one Jack had so often described. "Complained about" would be a more accurate description, though.

He wanted to learn more.

Half an hour after Alex left, a sharp knock on the door had him turning around so swiftly that he sloshed some of the now lukewarm coffee he held onto his desk behind him.

"Come in."

Biting out a curse, he wiped away the spill with the palm of his hand, leaving an unseemly streak of liquid across his highly polished desk. But it was just his office assistant with the latest island tax and duty figures.

He repeated the curse after she'd walked out again. Maybe his invitation had been a mistake. After all, almost an hour had passed.

Looked like Celeste was going to ignore him.

Celeste didn't get a chance to knock on Reid's door before it flung open. In the next moment, she found herself face-to-face with the man himself.

Oomph!

Reid had clearly been in the process of rushing out of the room. He couldn't stop his momentum in time. The crash was unavoidable. She wasn't sure which one of them appeared more taken aback by the collision. A set of strong arms suddenly gripped her around the middle and steadied her back onto her feet before she could topple backward.

"Are you all right?" he asked above her head.

She wasn't sure. Physically she was fine. But a curl of heat seemed to be simmering in the pit of her stomach. The scent of his skin surrounded her, a heady mix of mint, spicy aftershave and pure male. "I'm fine."

"I'm sorry. I wasn't expecting you."

She blinked up at him in confusion. He was the one who had asked her to come see him. But it was hard to think. Her hands itched to reach up and run her fingers through his wavy hair, then move lower and feel the silkiness of his beard. His nearness coupled with her confusion at his words made speaking difficult. "I…uh…got your card."

He had yet to let her go. Heaven help her, she couldn't bring herself to make a move to step out of his embrace. Their faces were inches apart, his breath felt hot against her cheek and lips.

"That was quite a while ago, princess. I wouldn't have pegged you for a late sleeper. Like to linger in bed, do you?"

It wasn't her imagination, his voice had definitely lowered to a huskier, deeper baritone as he uttered the last phrase. But her imagination did rev upward in response. A slew of images flooded her brain. She was in bed in all of them, all right. Only she wasn't alone. And she certainly wasn't sleeping.

His knowing smirk of a smile told her his words had had the intended effect. She shook off the oh-so-dangerous thoughts. What in the world was wrong with her? Two days ago, she would have named Reid Evanson as one the few people on earth she'd be content to never run into again throughout her lifetime. Now, here she was fantasizing about him as he held her in a viselike grip.

"I didn't notice the envelope right away," she lied. What was one small fib in an attempt at saving face? His eyes narrowed on her before traveling down the length of the dress she wore. He wasn't convinced. The truth was she'd agonized over whether to come or not. She'd stood so long in the shower trying to decide, her skin would probably stay pruned into next week.

"I can come back," she managed to say. With some reluctance, she moved out of his arms. He hesitated for the briefest moment before letting her go. "You were obviously on your way out."

"No. Come in," he said then stepped aside, motioning her into the room. "My errand can wait."

Celeste had to take a steadying breath as she moved past him into the spacious office.

"Have you eaten?" he asked as he followed her in. "The offer was to treat you to breakfast, after all."

The answer was no. She hadn't had a bite to eat this morning, just some coffee brewed in the room. But she didn't think she'd be able to summon an appetite right now. Her heart was still stammering in her chest. Her pulse hadn't slowed yet. And she certainly didn't need any more of the strong island coffee in the state she was in.

"Maybe just some tea."

He nodded then fired off a text. Before she'd even had

a chance to sit down, a young woman appeared carrying a tray with a steaming carafe and various tea bags.

"Help yourself."

"What did you want to see me about, Reid?" she asked as she poured herself a cup of steaming water and dunked two bags of English breakfast in.

He sat down in the large leather desk chair across from her. The massive mahogany desk between them served as a makeshift barrier and calmed her somewhat. But not completely. Why was she finding herself so affected by this man? She remembered there had always been a strange kind of awareness between them when she'd been engaged to Jack. But she'd chalked it up to conflicting personalities. She certainly hadn't realized all he'd observed about her, the things he'd shared last night.

Reid began to speak. "You mentioned last night that we don't call enough attention to the various activities and attractions that the resort has to offer."

"That's right."

"I know you have no reason to, but I wanted to ask if you'd help me with that."

The successful businesswoman in her suddenly stood at attention. Celeste couldn't deny she was intrigued. "Help you how?"

He shrugged. "It's what you're known for professionally. Developing and running marketing campaigns that appeal to as large a target audience as possible. Tell me how to appeal to potential vacationers about all we have to offer. I'm prepared to pay you for your time. Or, since I'm guessing you don't need the money, I'm willing to offer you a lifetime of free stays with us. As long as we have space, you can come spend a week here completely complimentary."

"I can afford vacations, Reid. Like you said, I don't need the money and I don't need freebie getaways."

"But you have to admit, it would be a nice option to have at your disposal."

His statement reminded her just how far she'd come in life. The girl she'd been, the one who'd grown up with hardly enough to get by let alone the means to travel, would never have believed the opportunity before her now. Hard to believe that girl had grown into the woman who was about to turn such an offer down.

"I'm on vacation. I really wasn't expecting to do any kind of work."

He smiled and tapped a finger against his temple. Had she found that smile so dazzling three years ago when he'd been a member of her wedding party? No wonder she'd done her best to avoid the man. That smile was dangerous. Perhaps she should be avoiding him now, too.

"That's the best part," Reid continued. "What I'm proposing will only enhance your vacation experience."

Now her curiosity was definitely piqued.

"Hear me out," Reid prodded further.

Despite herself, she tilted her head in agreement. What did she have to lose to just listen for a few minutes? Celeste took a sip of the hot, soothing tea then settled in her chair and waited for Reid to begin.

He was perilously close to the verge of babbling nonsensically. Reid knew he wasn't explaining his proposal as well as he could. But it was hard to focus. He still felt Celeste's warmth down the length of his body. The smell of her shampoo lingered in his nose. Her hair was slightly damp, hanging in loose freshly washed waves down her sun-kissed shoulders. She must have come down to see him right after a shower. The sudden, unbidden image of her naked under a stream of steamy water led immediately to yet another much more vivid one. In this next vision, he was under the water with her, running his hands down her skin. Rubbing soapy bubbles over her shoulders and moving his hands lower... That image had him tripping over his words again.

Get a grip.

She was here at his request so that he could run a business proposition by her. He had no business fantasizing about joining her in a steamy shower.

For heaven's sake, he was an accomplished businessman. He had given talks and presentations to world leaders and titans of industry. There was no reason to act so flustered now.

But then again, he had never before imagined anyone in his audiences naked in the shower.

Luckily, Celeste seemed to be getting the gist of what he was trying to say.

She cleared her throat. "Let me get this straight," she began. "You want me to go on the resort's offered excursions, with you. So that I can offer you some suggestions on how to market them to potential guests?"

"Exactly. What do you say? I'd planned to go by myself. But I could use another set of eyes."

"With you?" she repeated, seemingly hung up on that variable. Would she prefer to go by herself? He felt his fists clench at his sides.

"Yes," he answered simply.

"I thought you said you had a business partner?"

"Alex needs to stay here and run things while I'm gone all day. And besides, as someone who lives and grew up on the island, his isn't exactly the vantage point I'm after."

"What kind of excursions are we talking about, exactly?" she asked cautiously. He wasn't surprised that she was trying to ascertain all the details.

"The best Jamaica has to offer. We'd be climbing up a rushing waterfall, visiting a beautiful botanical garden, driving ATV's over some rugged terrain."

Celeste bit her lip. "I'd really intended to just lie on the beach and read for the next several days."

"You're here for what? Over a week? You'll have plenty of opportunity to do so in the coming days."

"How many days exactly are you asking me for?"

"Three, max. We should be able to cover all the excursions in that amount of time. I've already booked for myself, I'll just add your name."

She held her hands up. "Hold on. I haven't said yes yet."

"But you haven't said no." He paused for effect. "Come on, there are worse ways to spend three days on an island like Jamaica."

It occurred to him that he was trying too hard. With anyone else, he would have laid his offer on the table then walked away. He'd always been known as a tough negotiator, not willing to budge or cajole. For some reason, with Celeste, he was intent on making his case. Not like him at all.

He would have to think about why that was so. After all, this was nothing more than another smart business decision.

Everything he said made perfect sense, Celeste had to admit as she took in exactly what Reid was suggesting. In fact, his proposal was so logical that a small part of her felt a slight tickle of disappointment. Reid was strictly all business at the moment. He was dressed in black slacks this morning, a white button-down shirt accenting the contours of his hardened chest and torso. The shiny gold watch on his wrist caught the sunlight as he gestured with his hands occasionally while speaking.

An appealing, successful, handsome man was asking to spend time with her on various island adventures but his only objective was her business acumen.

That shouldn't have bothered her as much as it did. But that was a silly notion, it wasn't like she and Reid were friends or anything. In fact, a few short days ago, she would have listed him as one of the few people on earth who actually may not even like her.

"Why me?" she asked. There had to be other individuals he could ask. A man like Reid was unlikely to be lacking in female companionship. No doubt he had a girlfriend. Hadn't she just recently stumbled upon a social media posting of Reid accompanying a famous international pop star to some Hollywood gala event? In the photo, he'd had his arm wrapped around her waist as she looked up at him adoringly, clearly smitten. What would *she* think about another woman spending the whole day traipsing around a beautiful island with her man? If their roles were reversed, Celeste didn't think she'd appreciate the circumstances one bit.

Then again, any woman lucky enough to snare Reid was probably more than secure with herself and her status as his girlfriend.

That wayward thought led her to other unwanted ones. She imagined what it would be like to date a man like him. What it would mean if he was sitting here asking her to do these things with her simply because he wanted to spend time with her.

What his lips would feel against hers if he ever were to kiss her.

Dear saints! What in the world was wrong with her?

Was it simply because she'd been without a man for so long? Perhaps it was the romantic, exotic location. Something had to be causing such uncharacteristic behavior on her part.

Why hadn't she just said no already? Was she really even entertaining the idea?

She wasn't exactly the outdoors type. Or much of an athlete, for that matter. Sure, she'd scaled countless fences during her youth trying to outrun the latest neighborhood bully after defending her younger sister. And she'd developed some really quick reflexes averting touchy men in city shelters. But that was about the extent of it.

Reid answered her, breaking into the dangerous thoughts. "Think about it. Between your professional credentials and the fact that you take frequent tropical vacations, you're actually the perfect person to accompany me."

Again, nothing but logic behind his reasoning. On the surface, she'd be a fool to turn down such an exciting opportunity; the chance to experience so much more of what the island had to offer and, in the process, acquire a host of memories she'd hold for a lifetime. It was as if he really was Santa and he had just handed her a gift most women would jump at.

Still, she couldn't bring herself to say yes. Not right away.

"I'll need to, Reid. Think about it, that is."

His eyes clouded with disappointment but he gave her a small nod. "As you wish."

She could think of nothing else.

Celeste vowed she would take her time and weigh all the pros and cons before getting back to Reid with her decision. So why did she now find herself in the resort's retail surf shop? Why was she eyeing water shoes that someone would need if she were to go waterfall climbing? And why was there a one-piece swimsuit draped over her arm? She'd only packed two-pieces or tankinis and those wouldn't be terribly conducive to water sports or rock climbing.

So many questions. Like had she imagined it, or had Reid indeed held her just a smidge longer than necessary when they'd collided in his office? That lingering uncertainty was what had her debating the merits of accepting his offer.

Her unexpected attraction to him was throwing her off balance. Reid represented everything in her life that she'd vowed to move on from. He and her ex weren't terribly similar below the surface but they were cut from the same cloth; wealthy, privileged, carefree. They'd been lifelong friends, for heaven's sake.

Reid may be a successful hospitality industry tycoon but men like him didn't understand women like her. They didn't get what it took to succeed in life when you'd literally started with nothing. Or what it was like to try to hold a near full-time job during high school and still maintain your grades well enough. Or when your single parent couldn't earn enough to make ends meet, which meant that you and your younger sister often went hungry. Or without adequate shelter.

None of that however had anything to do with the matter at hand currently. She couldn't keep Reid waiting for long.

A sales clerk approached her from across the aisle. The young woman had a dazzling smile and long, tight braids cascading down her back.

"Can I be of assistance, miss?"

Celeste returned her smile. "I'm just being indecisive, that's all." In so many ways.

She pointed to the water shoes Celeste held. "Well, if you're going on the tour tomorrow to climb Dunn's River, you'll need sturdier protection than those for your feet."

That was indeed one of the excursions Reid had asked her to attend.

"Follow me," the clerk said, then turned to lead her to a different shelf. "These are a bit thicker in the sole. Better to grip the slippery rocks."

Just how slippery were those rocks? Maybe this was a sign. The universe had sent this pretty sales clerk to warn her not to try to do anything so perilous as climbing up a waterfall. She liked to think she was fit. But her exercise regimen mainly consisted of meditation and yoga. Though the latter could be strenuous and muscle straining, Celeste was no rock climber.

The sales clerk suddenly laughed. "You look very concerned."

"I am a bit," Celeste admitted. "I've never climbed up a waterfall before."

"Trust me, you will love it. It's an experience of a lifetime. There are professional, knowledgeable guides to help you every step of the way. You'll do fine."

"I'm not so sure. Sounds like it could be very dangerous." Part of her was referring to so much more than the climb. She'd be opening herself up to danger on so many other fronts. She could no longer deny her attraction to her ex-fiancé's best man. An attraction which was wrong on so many levels.

The more Jack had learned about her background, the more distant he'd grown. Ultimately, he'd walked away.

What made her think Reid would be any different?

"This isn't an opportunity you want to miss. What if you never get the chance again?" the smiling clerk asked, breaking into her thoughts.

That was certainly something to consider.

"It's just not an activity I would normally do," Celeste admitted.

The woman's smile grew. "What better time than on vacation to take a chance and try something new?"

Celeste didn't bother to explain. She wasn't usually the type to take chances. Too many things could go wrong. Life ran so much smoother when every detail was attended to and risky endeavors were steadfastly avoided. The only time she'd been remiss in that regard had resulted in humiliation and heartbreak.

Climbing up some slippery rocks as a waterfall cascaded over your body certainly wasn't on the same scale as agreeing to marry a man you had many reservations about. But still, risk was risk. What would happen to her mother if anything were to happen to Celeste? Or to her sister and young niece, for that matter? She knew they'd be taken care of financially, she'd seen to that years ago. But they needed her so much more than just monetarily.

Then again, maybe she was just flattering herself. Maybe Tara and her mom would figure out how to move forward without her, especially as long as the checks kept on coming.

Plus, how dangerous could these excursions really be? It wasn't like she was putting her life in danger. From what Reid had explained, dozens of tourists a day participated in this particular activity. Even young children.

She'd spent countless days on vacation lying on lounge chairs with her nose in the pages of a book. Maybe it was time to try something different.

"Also," the clerk continued, "your man is going to love the way you look in that." She pointed to the swimsuit Celeste held. "That shade of blue will look great with your skin tone and dark hair."

"Oh! I'm not— I mean, we don't—"

The other woman quirked an eyebrow at her. "Are you going alone? That's all right, too. Many people do."

"No. I won't be alone. I am going with a man. It's just that—well, he isn't *my* man. Just a man, you see. And we're not even going as friends. Not really. It's more a business thing."

For Pete's sake. Now she was just a rambling, incoherent mess. Hard to believe she made her living the way she did.

Not surprisingly, the clerk stood staring at her with a look of utter confusion on her face.

"You'll be climbing the falls for business?" she asked.

Celeste nodded. "Something like that. It's hard to explain."

"I see."

She lifted the items in her arms and gestured to the shoes the clerk held. "I'd like to charge these to the room, please."

There it was. Somehow, without even realizing, it appeared she'd come to a decision after all.

She could only hope she wouldn't regret it.

CHAPTER FIVE

HER PHONE VIBRATED in her dress pocket just as Celeste slid her keycard into the door lock slot. So much for giving her time to get back to him. Assuming it had to be Reid, she fished it out of her pocket and clicked before checking to be sure.

She was mistaken. It was her mother's voice that greeted her on the other end.

"Are you on the beach, enjoying some fruity frou-frou drink with a paper umbrella?" The question was asked in a mean-spirited and mocking tone.

Celeste took a fortifying breath. The way her mother's words slurred and rolled into one another gave all the indications that she was the one indulging in drink at the moment. And Wendy's choice of beverage would never be described as frou-frou. Conversations with her mother were always beyond draining under the best of circumstances. When she was drinking, they bordered on traumatic.

Though she could be a caring and nurturing parent when sober, Wendy Frajedi was a mean drunk.

"Hello, Mother. I just walked into my room after picking up some things from the resort shop, as a matter of fact."

"Huh. Must be nice. Do you know how much I need

around the house? If only I had a daughter who was willing to help out with some shopping for me." Wendy put extra emphasis on the last word.

Celeste pinched the bridge of her nose and kicked the door shut behind her. "I left a sizable amount of cash in the jar last time I was there, Mom."

"That doesn't mean you're around to help me shop and put the stuff away now, does it?"

She wanted to tell her parent that she was perfectly capable of getting her own groceries or whatever else might be needed. But opposing her mother in any way when she was like this only led to long, drawn-out arguments that merely served to frustrate and demoralize her, sometimes to the brink of tears. As much as she hated to admit it, Wendy Frajedi was the one person on the planet who could make her feel like she hadn't done anything right in her life, even when she knew it was 99 percent the vodka talking. It was just that the 1 percent delivered a mountain of hurt.

Celeste had long ago given up trying push back when her mother was in her cups. The tension only escalated if she did so. No. Her mom would have to get off her chest all that she felt compelled to say. Then she would sleep off the bender until a pounding hangover headache woke her up. At which point a different kind of misery would befall her. The woman refused treatment as she insisted she didn't have a problem, that she only drank once in a while.

"How come you never invite me or your sister on some fancy-schmancy vacation?" Wendy now demanded to know.

Like déjà vu. The two of them went through this every year. More accurately, they went through it every time Celeste traveled. "You know you don't like airplanes,

Mom. Tara can hardly be expected to travel with the baby. And last year she was pregnant."

Her mother grunted in disgust at her response. "There are plenty of places we can drive to together, aren't there?"

Celeste couldn't think of anything less relaxing than driving long-distance with her sibling and parent in order to spend several days together. Of course, she didn't bother to say so.

"I needed to get away, Mom. I'll make it up to you."

Her mother's peal of laughter screeched loudly into the phone. "Yeah, right. Like I'd believe that."

"Is there somewhere specific you'd like to visit?" Celeste threw out the question, just to play devil's advocate. Her mother had no real desire to travel. Right now, she just wanted to chastise her daughter for doing so.

"How should I know? You're the smarty pants in the family."

And her mother would never forgive her for being smart. Or driven. Or successful. She would never understand her older child's fierce desire to escape the cloud of destitution their family had been born under. Celeste sighed. Her mother usually took longer to get to this point in the conversation. Next would come the tirade; the outlining of all the things that were wrong with Wendy's life and how impossible it was to better any of it.

"I'm a little too old to be watching that baby, you know," her mother began, describing Tara's nine-month-old daughter. Her only grandchild. "Since you're not around, I've had to do it more times than I'd like to think."

Celeste didn't bother to remind her mother that she'd only been gone for about three days. Wendy couldn't have babysat more than once or twice since then.

But logic wasn't the point of these conversations. "Sorry, Mother. How is little Nat?" she asked in an attempt to change the subject.

"Loud. Cries a lot. Must be teething or somethin'. I tell ya, I couldn't wait to get outta there."

Celeste bit back the surge of anger that suddenly rose to the surface. Tara's daughter was the sweetest, most loving baby, despite the lineage of women she came from. Celeste uttered a prayer to heaven at least once a day that the pleasant nature the child had been born with somehow carried through as she grew up. She'd do everything she could to ensure that happened.

One thing was for certain, Celeste would have to arrange for a professional babysitter for the child the next time she traveled. She might even have to look into hiring one now long-distance. She didn't want Wendy around the child if she was growing resentful of the responsibility. Celeste was completely confident that Wendy wouldn't drink around the baby. She preferred to drink alone in the privacy of her own apartment, without judging eyes advising her to slow down or stop.

But it simply wasn't worth the risk.

Celeste made a mental note to look into a sitter first thing tomorrow morning and tell Tara.

But Wendy's next words made the issue a moot one. "Thank goodness I won't have to watch her anymore. Not anytime soon. Looks like your sister was let go again."

Celeste didn't even know why she was surprised. It was a wonder her sister ever got hired at all. She tended to arrive late to work and then slacked off once she got there. No doubt Tara's latest setback had something of a hand in her mother's afternoon of binge drinking.

"That was her third job this year, wasn't it?"

Her mother pounced. "Well, I guess we can't all be as

perfect as you." Bingo. Her mother had now hit all the usual notes. Celeste hoped she felt some semblance of relief now that it was out of her system. For the moment and until next time.

Celeste resisted the urge to ask her outright. *Feel better now, Mom?*

Sadly enough, the answer was still no. And Wendy would feel awful once she woke up and remembered how she'd spoken to her eldest daughter. Then the barrage of apologies would start.

Until it all happened again.

By the time he'd walked the entirety of the resort for the third time, Reid had to admit that he was trying to seek Celeste out. It galled him that she hadn't responded yet to his proposal.

He also had to admit that he'd be profoundly disappointed if she ultimately turned him down. Which was sort of funny if one thought about it. Before he'd laid eyes on her, he had a determined set plan in place to attend the excursions by himself and then meet with a marketing team to see how best to advertise them. Now, the thought of going by himself held absolutely zero appeal.

He was doing this for the sake of expanding resort bookings. He wanted this place to be the first resort people thought of when they decided to vacation in Jamaica. Celeste could really help him toward that goal. That was the only purpose behind him asking her to accompany him.

So why did a surge of pleasure shoot through his chest when he finally did spot her? Until he approached, that is. The closer he got to where she sat, the more he could see something was wrong.

She sat alone at a tall table at the outdoor pub by the

stage. A plate of French fries sat untouched in front of her. She was staring at the glass she held which must have once been a frozen drink but now appeared to be a mixture of icy slush and dark rum.

An unfamiliar sensation of concern settled in his gut.

"Something wrong with the fries? Do I have to speak to the chefs?"

She blinked up at him in confusion, holding her hand to her forehead to block the sun in her eyes. "Reid." She gave him a smile that didn't seem quite genuine enough to reach her eyes.

"Were the fries not done to your liking?"

She looked down at her plate in surprise, as if she'd forgotten it was there. Maybe she had. She'd certainly been deep in thought when he'd approached her.

"I guess I wasn't all that hungry."

"May I?" he gestured to the other empty stool at her high top table.

"By all means."

She began to speak as soon as he sat down. "I know I still owe you an answer."

It surprised him that her failure to respond to his proposal was the furthest thing from his mind at the moment. His first concern was why she appeared so, well, sad.

"This is going to sound like the worst kind of pickup line, but…" he hesitated. Maybe probing would be overstepping his bounds.

"Yes?"

"It really is such a shame to look so down on such a beautiful day in paradise."

She let out a small laugh. "You're right. That does sound like a bad pickup line. And here I thought you would have a better game. Given your reputation as such a player and all."

He laughed in return, ducked his head in mock embarrassment. "I might be out of practice. I've been a little busy with this place."

"Fair enough."

What little there was of the smile on her face faltered then disappeared completely.

"Is everything all right?" he asked, now downright worried for her.

"Just fine." He definitely didn't believe her. Was debating whether to push when she spoke again. "And I'd like to say yes, by the way."

For the briefest moment, he wasn't sure what she was referring to. Then understanding dawned. She was agreeing to help him with the marketing ideas.

But right now, all he felt was concern. Celeste looked far from a woman on vacation. Rather, she looked forlorn and melancholy.

Not that it was any of his business.

"Did you hear me?" she asked.

He summoned a pleased grin. "Glad to hear it. You won't regret this. Let's shake on it," he suggested, holding out his hand.

Her hand felt small and dainty in his large palm. He could probably wrap his thumb and forefinger around her tiny wrist. It occurred to him just how vulnerable she looked. Formidable businesswoman or not, Celeste Frajedi had a softness about her that set his protective instincts at high guard status. As backward and downright Neanderthal as that sounded.

He wondered if a man was behind her current state of sadness. That thought had him reeling with an unreasonable degree of anger. She'd been hurt enough romantically for one lifetime.

Celeste had so much going for her. Any man would

be a fool to treat her poorly in any way. How shameful that he hadn't seen that three years ago. Something had blinded him then to Jack's faults.

He'd been told more than once that he could be loyal to a fault. Next time he and Jack crossed paths, he would have a few words he'd like to share with the other man.

Not that it would be any time soon. The two of them had certainly grown apart since the ill-fated wedding. Reid couldn't even recall the last time the two of them had spoken to each other live. For all he knew, Celeste and Jack were still in touch. Maybe Jack was the reason for her current state of sorrow. He felt his neck muscles tighten at the thought. After all, the last time he'd witnessed such sorrow on her face, Jack had been the precise cause.

Without thinking, he blurted out the pesky question that had been lurking in his brain. "So, what exactly went down that day?"

Celeste didn't even pretend to not know what he was referring to.

Her lips tightened into an ironic smile. "You'd like to ask me about my failed wedding. Now of all times."

He wasn't sure what that last part meant, decided to push on anyway. "Only if you'd like to talk about it." She certainly appeared as if she could use the excuse to get something off her mind.

"You said yourself that he and I seemed to be incompatible. Turns out you were right. As I'm sure you heard from the man himself."

"I'd like to hear your take on it," he prompted.

She shrugged ever so slightly, trailed a finger over the condensation down the side of her glass before she finally spoke. "Jack gave me a final ultimatum as a test. And I failed miserably."

* * *

Celeste couldn't bring herself to look up away from her glass. But she could feel Reid's questioning eyes on her nevertheless. He remained silent at her cryptic remark, simply waited for her to continue. But she'd be hard pressed to decide exactly where to begin. The troublesome signs that her engagement was doomed had grown more and more frequent as the wedding day had approached. She'd just chosen to ignore them.

"What kind of test?" Reid wanted to know.

This was all so difficult to talk about, Celeste thought. She'd done her best to try to put it all behind her. To try to forget. What kind of woman was left behind at the altar? How could she ever trust in her feelings again when she'd fallen for a man who had been cruel enough to do such a thing?

Visions of that nightmarish day flooded her brain. Her coworkers seated in the pews, her friends from school, various other invitees. All of them giving her looks of unmitigated pity. The disappointment flooding her mother's face. She'd never felt such a strong desire to sink into the floor and disappear. There'd been no father to walk her down the aisle. Celeste had asked a former mentor to do her the honor. The look on the man's face as they'd waited and waited for a groom who'd never appeared had nearly crushed her soul. Bless him, he'd been the one to finally make the announcement as she'd fled, trying to squelch the flood of tears before she could get away. She'd vowed never to give her heart to another man unless she was absolutely sure of his love and commitment.

"Celeste? What kind of test?" Reid repeated.

She forced herself to shake off the thoughts. "A week before the wedding, Jack decided he wanted to elope."

Reid's eyebrows lifted in surprise. She'd always wondered if Reid had been in on the idea as best man. His reaction just now made it clear he hadn't been.

"I see," Reid answered, clearly confused.

He didn't really. And there was no way to explain it to him, Celeste thought. Jack's sudden decision to forgo a traditional ceremony had had nothing to do with wanting a private event between the two of them.

It had everything to do with being embarrassed in front of his friends and loved ones about the kind of family she came from. Eloping would keep Tara and her mother out of sight. The love Jack supposedly felt for her wasn't enough to overcome the shame he felt about her family.

She'd called his bluff. And he'd walked away.

"I take it you weren't keen on the idea," Reid said.

She shrugged. "I wanted a traditional wedding," she answered simply, leaving out the more relevant part—mainly that her fiancé had been too much of a snob to accept her for who she was and where she came from. In hindsight, Jack's strategy was all too clear. He'd wanted a cowardly way out of marrying her. So he'd given her a choice that wasn't really a choice. How could she have turned her back on the two most important people in her life on the biggest day of her life?

Reid's expression held every indication that he suspected there was far more to the story than she was telling. Well, this was as much as she was willing to divulge. As much as her heart could take to reveal.

"I've known Jack for most of my life," Reid finally spoke after a long bout of silence, one where she couldn't quite meet his questioning gaze. "I've seen him act downright reckless all too often." He paused to take a deep breath and looked away off to the side. "But losing you has to be the most foolish thing he's ever done."

His words hung heavy and loaded in the air. Reid watched as Celeste's eyes grew wide. He didn't regret what he'd just said, but decided not to push the conversation any further. Celeste also appeared to have said all she was willing to say. For now.

She slowly pushed her glass away before standing. "Now that that's all out of the way, I should go back to my room and try to get an early night. I'm guessing we have quite the day ahead of us tomorrow. It won't do for me to be tired and sluggish."

Reid gently grasped her arm. "I have a better idea."

Her gaze dropped to where he touched her. For the briefest moment, neither one of them moved. Electricity seemed to crackle through the early evening air.

Finally, Celeste slowly sat back down and broke the silence. "What would that be?"

He motioned to her full plate. "Well, you clearly haven't eaten. We'll have to remedy that. Aside from not being tired tomorrow, we can't have you malnourished."

"Hardly a danger, but what did you have in mind?"

"Dinner to start with?"

Her eyebrows lifted in question. "Just to start? What then?"

He couldn't help but grin. "It happens to be Thursday."

"So?"

"Don't you read the daily newsletter? Thursdays are karaoke nights on the beach. Tonight's theme is Christmas carols."

Celeste's spine stiffened. "I don't think that's really—"

But he stopped her. "Karaoke happens to be one of the activities we'd like to highlight when advertising. We had a deal that you just agreed to, remember?"

Her look of horror told him she wanted badly to forget.

She really needed to head this development off at the pass. The steely set of determination in Reid's eyes only upped her panic. He couldn't possibly see her as a karaoke kind of gal in any way, shape, or form.

"Uh. I don't do public singing. And I certainly don't do Christmas carols."

He shook his head real slow. "This is all about you experiencing everything the Baja Majestic has to offer. That includes karaoke."

Celeste rubbed a weary hand across her forehead. What had she gotten herself into here? "Listen, I don't so much as sing in the shower."

Something darkened behind his gaze at her words. "I'm certainly not going to do it in front of a beach full of strangers," she added.

Reid glanced at his shiny, expensive watch. She'd been speculating that it was a Rolex. "There's plenty of time to discuss it. Let's go get some real food." He picked up a fry and popped it in his mouth even as he declared her discarded snack fake.

"There's nothing to discuss, Reid."

He stood and took her by the elbow, nudging her to join him. "Sure there is. First, we figure out dinner. Hibachi's always good. My favorite chef's on tonight. Or we could do the Mediterranean restaurant. The kebabs melt in your mouth. Something to do with the marinade."

She wanted to deny that she was hungry, but her stomach had other plans. An audible rumble sounded from her midsection when he mentioned the word kebab.

Reid let out a short but hearty laugh. "Mediterranean it is. Let's go."

He didn't give her a chance to argue. A few minutes later, they were climbing a spiral cement staircase to a building fashioned to appear like an ancient Greek cathedral complete with Ionic columns and goddess statues. The petite blonde maître d' approached them as soon as they entered. Her eyes lit up as she greeted Reid. Her crush was nearly visible. Not that she could be blamed for it.

"Hey, boss. You haven't been in for a while."

Reid returned her smile with a much more platonic one.

"My friend here would like to try the kebab, Michelle. Table for two please."

Michelle spared a glance in her direction, clearly appraising. She wondered if she passed some sort of Reid-worthy test as far as the other woman was concerned. Probably not.

"Of course, right this way."

They were seated at an elegant table with ivory-white table settings, a crisply laundered tablecloth, and tall lit candles. All in all, the atmosphere in the dining area could only be described as highly romantic. That notion frayed her nerves a bit further. She absolutely could not be having any thoughts of romance whatsoever. Despite how much she'd shared of herself with Reid earlier. He'd simply caught her at a vulnerable moment. Phone calls with her mother when she was drunk tended to bring out that vulnerability.

She forced herself to focus on the menu. Every entrée and salad description made her mouth water. To think, she'd been convinced she wasn't hungry at first. But the aroma of spices in the air combined with what she read on the menu had her stomach grumbling once more. How very ladylike. Good heavens, it hadn't been that long since she'd enjoyed male companionship. Why was she coming off as such an awkward neophyte?

A white-jacketed waiter took their order within minutes. Clearly, every worker in the restaurant had been made aware that the co-owner was in attendance. Another waiter soon appeared and placed a small glass jug with clear liquid in the center of the table.

Celeste stared at it in confusion. "Is that all the water we're getting?"

Reid looked up from his menu. "Darling, that's not water. And if you're not familiar with it, I would definitely not drink it as if it were."

It was hard not to react internally to the endearment. Reid hadn't really meant anything with the affectionate word, but something curled deep in her belly nonetheless.

She figured out what he was getting at as far as the small pitcher was concerned. Greek architecture, Mediterranean cuisine. "It's ouzo, isn't it?"

"That it is. I'm guessing you've never had it?"

"Never," she answered. "And I probably shouldn't start today."

He nodded. "It's potent stuff. If you change your mind, start with a really small sip. Or we could have it watered down for you."

She shook her head. The last thing she needed in his presence was anything else throwing her off balance in any way. She felt enough out of her element as it was.

"I'll stick to the simple white wine, thanks."

He ordered her a chardonnay then poured himself a small amount of the ouzo into a shot glass that the waiter returned with. By the time their food arrived, the crisp, fruity wine had done a great deal to smooth her frazzled nerves. Between the disastrous phone call with her mother and the sheer magnitude of Reid's presence, she found it rather surprising that she was finally starting to relax.

Until Reid brought up the matter of karaoke again.

"I just thought you were a woman open to trying new things." He was clearly goading her. Unfortunately, she fell for the trap. In a way she was too tipsy to realize she'd quickly regret.

"I am about certain things. See, look."

Reaching for the remaining sliver of ouzo that sat in the mini pitcher. It was barely more than half a tablespoon. How strong could it be? She downed it in one swift gulp. Then gasped in shock as liquid fire shot through her midsection.

Reid sat staring at her wide-eyed. What had possessed her to do something so reckless? Suddenly, he threw his head back and barked out in laughter. He then gave a mini seated salute.

"I'm gonna need some more water."

Her belly felt like she'd swallowed a lit match. A rush of heat shot through to her cheeks. The room seemed to have tilted slightly. None of that was particularly funny.

So she wasn't quite sure why she returned Reid's laugh with a hearty one of her own.

Reid had stopped speculating what might have led to the scene he'd come across earlier this evening when he'd found Celeste so forlorn and defeated at the outside pub. But there was no question she seemed to be enjoying herself now. If her wide smile was any indication.

A trove of pleasure blossomed in his chest at the

thought that he'd helped put that smile on her face. As they left the restaurant and headed toward the beach, he took the opportunity to study her, the way he had through most of dinner.

She was unlike anyone he'd ever met. How could Jack have ever described her as standoffish and guarded? No doubt she'd tried to present herself that way in response to Jack's stilted demeanor.

He wished he'd bothered to ask three years ago. Maybe he could have talked some sense into his friend. Then again, he wouldn't be sitting with her here now if he'd done so. Selfish or not, he didn't feel sorry that the turn of events had led to this current moment.

"How do you feel?" he asked as they reached the sand.

"Surprisingly all right. But I don't think I'll be looking to do any more shots of ouzo this evening. Or ever again," she added after the slightest pause.

"Probably a wise decision."

A speaker suddenly sounded from near the water with a bouncy rendition of "Holly Jolly Christmas."

"We're headed to the karaoke event, aren't we?" she asked, a note of resignation laced in her voice.

"Trust me, you don't want to miss it."

She sighed and continued walking. "I suppose it can't hurt to watch for a bit. There are worse ways to spend the evening."

Reid hung his head low in mock offense. "Wow, not the most enthusiastic response I've gotten to the prospect of spending time with me, but I guess I'll take it."

"Trust me, it's nothing less than a compliment. I can't think of one other person who could convince me to go near an event featuring amateur singing of Christmas carols."

There was no reason for her comment to cause the rush of pleasure in him that it did.

"You sure it's me? It might be the ouzo," he teased.

She groaned out loud. "I can't believe I did that."

They'd reached the area by the wooden stage, the music growing louder by the second. The slow crashing of the waves behind them grew more and more muted. An impressive crowd had gathered. Two staffers sat at a table, surrounded by laptops and sound equipment. They each had Santa hats on. Another staffer dressed as an elf walked around passing out the same hats to guests.

Reid realized he was taking it all in more as a participant rather than the co-owner of the resort. He couldn't recall when that had ever happened before on one of his properties. He risked a glance at the woman next to him. She had to be the reason he was suddenly viewing things through different eyes. Though for the life of him he wouldn't be able to explain why. What manner of effect did she have on him?

"Mr. Evanson," the hat deliverer had reached them. Without asking, she reached up and placed one atop his head. Then she turned and did the same to Celeste.

Reid noticed her hat was different. It had a floral design instead of plain white at the base. The lettering said You've Been Chosen.

The hat elf clapped her hands. "You've been chosen, madam!"

Celeste blinked at her in confusion. She looked at him for some clarity. Damned if he knew what was going on.

"Chosen?"

"You have one of the special hats," the elf answered.

"Special how?"

"It's our version of mistletoe. But you have a choice. You can perform a song onstage."

Celeste's hand flew to her mouth in horror. "What's the other option?"

The elf laughed in response. "You kiss someone, silly. That's how mistletoe works, right?"

The staffer looked pointedly at Reid as she explained. Her coworkers had all turned their focus on the three of them. Several of the revelers turned to watch, as well. So, his employees were taking the opportunity to have a little fun at their boss's expense. Nothing malicious, he knew. Harmless fun.

But Celeste looked as if she'd swallowed a raw conch.

He discreetly drew the staffer's attention and gave a slight, almost imperceptible shake of his head. *Drop it.*

The elf immediately nodded in agreement. But it was too late. The crowd had now gotten involved. Chants of encouragement had begun.

"I'm not up for either of those options," Celeste said in a low voice. Enough of the crowd heard her that the encouraging cheers started to switch to long, exaggerated boos.

This was his fault, Reid thought as he tried to find the quickest path out of the crowd. He'd never forgive himself if she was humiliated.

"Come on," a man urged her to their left. "Pick one."

Reid clenched his hand by his side. His fingers itched to shove the man aside and away from her but it wouldn't do to accost one of his guests.

He grabbed Celeste by the wrist and began to lead her away. The boos grew louder.

She surprised him by halting them both to a stop. When he turned in question, she'd gone pale.

"It's okay. I'll do it," she declared, breathless, her voice aquiver.

He pivoted to face her fully. "You don't have to, Celeste. I'll get you out of here," he said on a low whisper against her ear so that only she could hear.

She nodded slowly. "I'm sure. I don't run from things," she offered with a shaky smile. "Then again, that might just be the ouzo talking."

Without waiting for his response, she turned toward the stage and stepped toward it. Reid shook off his shock and quickly followed her up the steps onto the platform.

The crowd erupted in cheers and applause once more. Reid placed his hand gently on her waist at the base of her spine. Bowing slightly to the crowd, he took the mike.

"What are you doing?" Celeste asked him.

He shrugged. "Can't let you have all the fun, can I? What are we singing?"

CHAPTER SIX

If SHE HAD somehow managed to sing in front of a throng of beach partygoers last night, the task before her should be a piece of cake.

Celeste took Reid's hand as he helped her off the charter boat onto the smooth beach they'd spent half an hour sailing to after leaving the Baja Majestic earlier this morning.

She could do this. Besides, part of her was looking forward to it maybe just a little. The waterfall they were to climb up couldn't be that tall, could it? She got her answer soon enough.

The falls was tall, all right. But it didn't seem terribly steep. She took a steadying breath, reminding herself that she'd signed up for this. There would be no backing out now. Just like last night onstage.

Hard to believe but she felt a quiver of a smile tug her lips at the memory. She and Reid had butchered "Jingle Bells" so badly, it was a wonder they hadn't been escorted off stage. To think she could laugh about it now, when at the time she'd thought she might faint with nervousness. What choice had she had? She wasn't going to hightail it and run away in front of all those people. And what was the other option? To kiss Reid.

She'd thought about it, she really had. In fact, she'd found herself oh-so-tempted to just lean into him, even in front of all those people, and find out once and for all what his lips would taste like, how they would feel up against her own.

Singing in front of strangers had absolutely been the safer choice.

Though *singing* might be too generous a word. Reid had stayed onstage with her and "sung" too.

"You ready?" he asked her now.

"I suppose." She followed him to the base where two guides were waiting for them. After a brief summary of safety measures and what to expect, they began the climb by stepping on the first big boulder.

So far so good.

Granted, it was literally the first step. But she'd take any encouragement where she could get it. They were both absolutely soaked in no time. Reid seemed unfazed by the sheer physicality required. Lithe and agile, she got the feeling he'd be bounding upward boulder to boulder if he wasn't hampered by her. Despite the early-morning heat, there was enough of a breeze and shaded areas that she found herself shivering with cold.

In response, Reid rubbed his palms absent-mindedly over her arms when they came to a brief stop before scaling the next large boulder. More than once, she lost her footing on the slippery rocks and he was there to catch and steady her. She'd always prided herself on her independence. Even after her broken engagement, Celeste defined herself by her own successes, for being her own person. But something about the way Reid kept rescuing her from slips and falls awakened a side of her she didn't recognize. It was nice for once to literally have someone to fall back on.

The noise of the gushing water made conversation impossible. Not that she would have known what to say. His touch sent electricity over her skin.

Forty-five minutes later, they'd finally reached the top. Her muscles quivered with exhaustion. But that wasn't all she felt. She was elated. She'd done it. She'd conquered the phenomenal task—to her, anyway—of climbing up a one-hundred-and-fifty-foot waterfall.

Their guides congratulated them with a round of high fives. Reid reached for his waterproof wallet and handed several wilted bills to the two men.

He turned to her with a wide grin. "You did it!"

She didn't get a chance to respond as he lifted her by the waist and twirled her around in a tight embrace.

Celeste didn't even bother to try to suppress her squeal of laughter. She *had* done it! She'd successfully conquered a feat she wouldn't have even attempted a week ago. All because Reid was by her side throughout it all.

She would have to examine at some point what that meant for her going forward. But right now, she was due a bit of a celebration.

When he sat her back on her feet, an unknown heaviness hung in the air between them. She could have sworn he was going to touch her again. Instead, he clenched his hands into tight fists and squeezed his eyes shut.

Heavens. Maybe she should have asked for that kiss last night when she'd had an excuse.

"Reid?" she wasn't even sure what she was asking of him. Just then, another couple cleared the top of the waterfall and ran past them laughing. Several feet away, they stopped to embrace and indulge in a long and ardent kiss. A stab of longing hit Celeste deep in her core and she couldn't look away. She wanted what that couple had. That intimacy, that closeness. The clear passion between the two of them.

Heaven help her, Celeste had thought she'd given up on that longing three years ago. She realized she'd been fooling herself. She'd simply fallen for the wrong man.

She turned to see Reid watching the other couple also. His fist seemed to clench even tighter at his side.

"We should get cleaned up and dried off," he told her, gesturing to the building behind them that housed the shower and spa facilities.

But her feet wouldn't move. She didn't want this moment to end. The world around them seemed to fall away. Her vision zeroed in on one thing only—the man standing before her. The hunger in his eyes was as clear as the sunny sky above. Could he see that same hunger in her own?

"Lunch will be waiting for us soon," he reminded her. "We can use the time to go over your thoughts on ways to advertise this as part of the resort package."

It took a moment for her to register exactly what he was saying. How could she have forgotten even for a moment? She was only here because Reid was after her professional feedback.

While she stood here like a fool entertaining all sorts of romantic fantasies, Reid was simply utilizing her for her marketing expertise. His only concern was for his business.

The realization was like more cold water splashing over her skin. How could she have not learned her lesson? Technically, she was nothing more than Reid's employee.

Celeste certainly cleaned up well.

Reid watched as she found him at the wooden table where they'd be eating an authentic Jamaican lunch. She wore leather sandals, lace-covered shorts that showed off her long shapely legs and a thin-strapped tank top. She hadn't bothered to dry her hair and wore it in a loose pile atop her head.

She was a breathtakingly stunning woman.

It wasn't easy, but Reid was trying hard to ignore the sudden awkwardness that had developed between them. He could pinpoint exactly when it had happened. That darned couple with the passionate kiss atop the waterfall. Usually, the PDA of other people didn't bother him or so much as give him pause. He worked at a tropical resort that hosted numbers of couples, after all. But watching that kiss made him realize how badly he wanted to kiss Celeste.

That was unacceptable.

She was essentially working for him. After she left the resort, their paths may never cross again.

Oh, and there was also that whole other part where she'd been engaged to one of his closest friends. All that, on top of where he was in his life right now, Reid knew better than to acknowledge his growing attraction to a woman so clearly off-limits.

He cursed under his breath as she reached the table and sat down across from him. The smile she flashed him seemed forced and uncertain. She was aware of the awkwardness between them also.

Damn.

They still had a whole afternoon together. Not to mention all the activities scheduled for tomorrow. And the day after.

Maybe this whole thing hadn't been such a good idea. There was something developing between them that he hadn't expected or been prepared for.

Maybe he was deluding himself, but he was certain whatever was happening between them was mutual. That fact only made it all the worse.

He had a company to run, a devastated mother to look after, and he had to protect the family business from his reckless and disloyal father.

Nowhere in the scenario was there room to pursue any kind of relationship, let alone with a woman who'd once been engaged to one of his best friends.

"You look none worse for the wear," he said in a rather lame attempt at conversation.

Lord, he could use some of the rum punch this place was known for. Unfortunately, the next leg of this particular package happened to involve driving an ATV.

The waitress appeared with two loaded plates and a couple bottles of water before Celeste had a chance to respond.

"Hope you like hot and spicy."

She shrugged. "Depends on the heat level. Too much makes me uncomfortable."

He really couldn't read anything into that statement. Though he was sorely tempted to ask her if they were still speaking about the jerk chicken.

"I'll have a write-up ready for you before the morning. I made sure to dictate some notes into my phone before showering just now," she said.

She had turned all business.

Probably for the best anyway. But he found he'd lost some of his appetite. For her part, Celeste was barely picking at her own plate.

Reid took another bite and relished the punishing heat of the scotch bonnet pepper on his tongue. The silence between them grew. Finally, he threw his napkin down on his plate. Shameful waste of authentic jerk chicken but he didn't want any more.

"Something the matter?" Celeste asked.

This was ridiculous. They were both mature adults. Maybe it was time to address the proverbial elephant in the room. Yet another one.

"Yeah, I happen to have something on my mind," he admitted.

She raised an eyebrow in question.

"About what happened back there," he continued. "After we were done climbing."

Her eyes grew wide.

"Maybe we should talk about it," he added.

"Maybe we should. What would you like to say?" Her question sounded like a dare.

Well, he could play the game as well anyone. "I think we got caught up in an exciting moment. What about you?"

Her lips tightened into a thin line before she answered him. "I see. That's the conclusion you came to then?"

He nodded. "I'm interested in your opinion, however."

A glimmer sparked in her eyes before she leaned in closer to him over the table. "By that you mean you'd like me to confirm your convenient take on the matter so that you can rest easy."

"What?"

"Don't worry, Reid. We can forget the moment even happened. And ignore everything else too, for that matter. We'll play our roles as contract employee and boss man. That's the way you want things, isn't it?"

"Yes!" he said without taking the time to think. "I mean, no," he then corrected after a beat. "I mean, I don't know."

They were starting to attract the attention of the other diners.

The waitress approached, a look of concern as she eyed their still-full plates. "Is the food not to your liking, sir? Madam?"

"It's very good," he answered, not taking his eyes off the woman who had him so vexed at the moment.

"It's delicious, thank you," Celeste answered, somehow summoning a smile.

He'd been wrong. This was not the time or place to try to have this conversation. What did she want him to say anyway? It wasn't as if he could admit there was some kind of attraction there.

What good would that do either of them?

"Unfortunately, we're short on time," he explained to the waitress who didn't look any less concerned after their exchange. "If we could settle the bill. We'll be sure to come back another time," he lied. The chances of him coming back here with Celeste seemed slim to none right about now.

In fact, he'd be lucky if she didn't ditch the whole idea of his proposal and leave him to his own devices. That thought settled like a brick of disappointment in his chest. And though he was loath to admit it, the feeling had nothing to do with his professional goals.

At least the next activity would be on dry land.

Celeste followed Reid through the tree line down the dirt path where they were to meet their ATV driving guide. At least out of the water she wouldn't be tempted to look at Reid's chiseled chest and tanned, muscular arms. And she wouldn't notice how strikingly dark his sandy blond hair turned when it was wet. Nor the way his tanned skin glistened when wet.

He'd almost kissed her.

But he'd made himself stop, as if he'd immediately regretted the near lapse. She didn't want to acknowledge just how much that wounded her. Or why.

For then she'd have to admit what a glutton for punishment she was. She'd gone down this route before. Men like Reid and Jack knew exactly how to shut down their attraction or even affection for a woman when they realized she wasn't good enough for them.

She'd let her guard down and fooled herself into thinking that Reid might be different from Jack. Would she ever learn?

Finally, they reached a convoy of parked all-terrain vehicles, some of them were caked over almost completely with mud. Clearly, she'd overdressed for the occasion. By contrast, Reid had changed into dark green camouflage canvas shorts and a black T-shirt. His attire seemed much more appropriate. Looked like she should have gone over the details more carefully.

A guide came out of one of the banana-leaf roofed huts and the two men shook hands. After another safety lecture and being fitted with helmets, they climbed into one of the vehicles.

"You sure you don't want to drive one yourself?" Reid asked her, though they'd gone over this on the charter boat this morning.

"I'm sure. I have no desire to race down muddy embankments and treacherous curves in an open-top vehicle barely larger than a golf cart." She knew she sounded overly critical but she wasn't in the best of moods currently. This definitely wasn't an activity she would choose for herself when picking out an itinerary. In fact, she wasn't sure how to write about it in a way that might make it sound enticing.

"Let's go then."

With that, Reid revved the engine and peeled out into the wooded terrain. Celeste gritted her teeth. She'd been on smoother roller coasters. Reid was pushing the vehicle to the top edge of the speedometer. Trees and bushes zipped past her line of vision, her whole body jostled and bounced in the seat. He was driving perilously close to the edge of the cliff and she had to focus on her breathing as if in meditation to avoid a full-fledged panic attack. She thought for sure he'd slow down as they approached a hairpin turn, but if anything, he seemed to accelerate.

Celeste could have sworn they were riding on only the two side wheels for a brief moment.

Without warning, he suddenly veered into a more densely wooded area. Branches and brush whipped at the face mask of her helmet. Her panic grew by several notches.

The petrifying drive seemed to be having an opposite effect on Reid. Laughing and completely at ease, he was fully enjoying this. The next bump lifted her clear off the seat despite the tight seat belt. She landed back down with a thud that rattled her spine. Good thing she hadn't eaten much of the lunch earlier. No doubt it would have come up and lodged in her throat. Or worse.

An eternity seemed to go by before they turned back onto the beaten path. Reid started to slow the car and eventually came to a blessed stop. Reid let out another excited whoop and put the car in gear at the end of the line of the others.

Celeste uttered a small prayer of thanks to whichever deity was listening then wasted no time removing her helmet and jumping out of the car. Running to the nearest tree, she braced herself against the trunk and sucked in some much-needed air.

It wasn't long before she heard his footsteps behind her. "Uh…are you all right?"

Celeste summoned all the effort she could in order to try to keep her voice steady. She failed. "Did you have to go quite so fast? And you left the path. In fact, you ignored it altogether!" she blurted out, all too aware of the accusatory tone of her voice.

"Going fast is sort of the point," he countered. "And the guide said the path was a recommendation only. That more experienced drivers could use their best judgment."

"You consider yourself experienced, then, do you?"

She hated the high pitch of her voice. But, rational or not, she'd really been scared back there.

A muscle twitched in his jaw. "I do, as a matter of fact. I grew up riding such vehicles. As well as snowmobiles."

Of course he had. Was there nothing he wasn't good at? Or didn't have experience with? Whereas this was the first time she'd so much as sat on an ATV. The closest she'd come was the subway. Yet another example of how different they were, how their worlds had nothing in common. History repeating itself.

"Well, did you think about what might have happened if you'd lost control, even for a split second? I have a mother, a sister and a niece who need me alive to provide for them!" she almost shouted, then forced herself to calm down and take a breath. "I just need a minute to regain some balance here," she told him unevenly.

Reid took a step closer to her and frowned. "Take your time. You do look a little pale."

"I'll be fine." Once her pulse finally settled. Only that didn't seem like it was going to be anytime soon.

Just breathe.

"Why didn't you say anything?" he wanted to know.

Celeste didn't bother to answer. The fact was, she'd wanted to. But she hated that she'd gotten so panicky, that she'd felt so weak. She hated the idea of having to admit it to him. She'd just prayed that he'd eventually slow the cursed vehicle down. Only he hadn't.

As if reading her thoughts, Reid continued, "Look, I'm sorry if you were nervous or scared during the ride. And I'm even more sorry that I didn't notice. But I assure you that you were never in any danger. I knew exactly what I was doing."

That made one of them, Celeste thought.

CHAPTER SEVEN

THE FOLLOWING MORNING Celeste decided she was going to do absolutely nothing that day. Reid didn't have anything booked for them until tomorrow. Thank heavens for that small mercy. She punched her fluffy pillow and turned over in bed to stare at the ceiling.

So why did she miss seeing him so much already? Why had last night seemed so empty and boring? Barely twelve hours had passed since she'd seen him last and it wasn't as if they'd parted on the most positive note. Even after the awkward boat ride back to the resort where neither one had so much as spoken a word to the other, she wondered if that strained silence would have been preferable to the solitary dinner she'd had on her balcony before retiring early.

She'd somehow grown used to his company. That did not bode well at all.

Her phone screen lit up with a text on the bedside table next to her. She didn't need to look to know that it was Tara. She and her mother had been trying to get a hold of her all day yesterday. Celeste had no intention of returning the call just yet. Whatever it was could wait. She needed some downtime to process everything that had happened in the last twenty-four hours. The last thing that would allow her to do that would be to have any kind of toxic conversation with her family. If it was a true emergency, she knew they'd move all manner of heaven and earth to contact her.

No. Today she was going to linger in bed, then quietly meditate. Maybe afterward she'd take one of the yoga classes offered at the resort gym. Then she may or may not spend the afternoon in a lounge chair by the pool. Or back in her room with the gripping book she'd been neglecting.

Her idea of utopia. Usually, anyway.

Though she'd be alone the whole time. Normally, that would not have given her pause. In fact, it was the way she preferred to spend time on vacation.

She uttered a curse under her breath. The only reason she was questioning that now was because of one sandy blond masculine CEO with eyes the color of the deep ocean at sunrise and a dark beard. Celeste had never even liked facial hair before this. But on Reid, all she could think about was running her fingers through it. Or how it might feel against her skin.

She bolted upright before that thread of thought could go any further. Maybe her wayward thoughts about him were simply a result of her self-imposed celibacy these past few years. Maybe she'd do well to find a random single man on the beach and invite him back to her room for a no-strings-attached fun-filled afternoon.

Tara would be delighted for her.

Ha! As if she'd manage to let go of her inhibitions to ever allow that. As if she'd ever be so carefree. No. That was more her sister's style. That would take a level of lightheartedness Celeste had never achieved in her life. Plus, she didn't think it would do any good toward ridding her brain of Reid Evanson imaginings.

The ring of her room landline jarred her out of her

musings. Now she was concerned. Maybe there was some kind of emergency back home if her mother and Tara were trying to reach her through the hotel phone service. She grabbed the receiver.

"Hello?"

"Ms. Frajedi. Good morning. This is Prita at the front desk."

"Is everything all right?"

"Absolutely," Prita answered cheerfully with the slightest creole accent.

A wave of relief washed over her at the announcement.

"I'm just calling to let you know that you have a spa package waiting for you. You can come in anytime today."

"The spa? I didn't book anything at the spa."

"This is complimentary, Ms. Frajedi."

"I don't understand."

"It was booked at the direction of Mr. Evanson."

"I see."

"The package includes a full massage, facial, followed by a manicure and pedicure. It will take a few hours if you'd like to decide on a time."

"Thank you, Prita. I'd like to think about it and get back to you."

"Certainly, Ms. Frajedi. I'll give you the line to the spa and you can contact them directly."

Celeste made note of the number and disconnected the call. Reid had set her up with a day of luxurious pampering. She'd be a fool to turn it down.

Why had he done it?

Was this some manner of apology for the way things had turned out yesterday? Or was she to approach it as his employee and give him feedback on her spa experience? Perhaps he'd simply wanted to do something nice for her?

The latter was the least likely possibility.

So many lines were blurred between them now. They were former enemies but now she was technically working for him. She'd been engaged to one of his good friends.

She couldn't get the thought of kissing him out of her head. Or the way his touch had warmed her skin every time he'd caught her while climbing the falls. How it had felt to be embraced in his arms when he'd congratulated her afterward.

Enough already! What a pointless waste of brain cells to go over all of it repeatedly in her head. What was the use?

So much for staying in bed all day. Suddenly, she was too restless and wired up to just lay there. A day at the spa wasn't such a bad idea.

With a deep sigh, Celeste got up and made her way to the shower. She had some pampering to prepare herself for.

Thanks to Reid.

Reid's focus was completely shot. For what had to be the umpteenth time during their morning meeting, he tried to lure his concentration back to what Alex was saying. Instead, his mind kept wandering to thinking about what Celeste might be doing at this very moment. Had she taken him up yet on the spa offer? Was she there even now, lying on a massage table having some of the tension kneaded out of her muscles?

Would she accept his overture as the apology that it was intended to be?

Alex was making another point. "And I've spoken with the entertainment committee to put together a showing of *The Nutcracker* ballet with you dancing the major roles."

Reid nodded. "That's good, thank—"

Wait a minute.

Reid dropped his pen on the desk. "Ha-ha. That's really funny, partner."

"Just checking to see if you were paying attention. Where is your head at this morning, man?"

If he only knew. "I have a lot on my mind."

"Including the woman who's been helping you pull together a potential marketing campaign?"

Reid quirked his eyebrow. "Why do you ask that?"

"Let's just say you haven't quite been the same since she arrived on the island."

So it was that obvious.

Luckily, his partner wasn't the type to delve into his personal life. Not usually, anyway. "How's that whole project going anyway?" Alex asked, reverting back to business matters.

Reid wasn't quite sure how to answer. Where exactly did things stand now between Celeste and himself? "We just started yesterday."

Alex tilted his head. "And?"

"And we have a couple more excursions on the schedule tomorrow. She'll provide a written analysis and suggestions for each one we take."

Though, after the way yesterday had turned out, Reid wasn't even sure if Celeste was even still on board with it. He was half-afraid she'd already made the decision to end their agreement. Something told him she wouldn't do that. That she took her professional commitments far too seriously.

In fact, he was banking on it.

Still, she hadn't called to thank him or so much as acknowledge the spa day he'd arranged for her. An image of her lying on a massage table with only a narrow towel draped around her luscious curves flashed in his mind.

His partner was staring at him expectantly. Oh, yeah. He'd asked him a question, hadn't he?

Something about what he and Celeste were working on together. Reid decided to stick the truth. For the most part, anyway.

"Things are complicated between Celeste and me," he admitted, rubbing his forehead. "There's a bit of a history."

"I see," Alex responded. "And is that the only complication?"

"Absolutely," Reid lied. It wasn't an egregiously big lie however. Because he'd made something of a decision last night. As he'd lain there thinking about Celeste and the way she'd felt in his arms, he'd come to the conclusion that his dealings with her had to change.

From this point forward, he would maintain a safer distance. He would be at his utmost professional as they worked together. Though not technically his direct employee, Celeste was indeed doing work for him. He would treat her like the contractor that she was. No more touching, no more teasing. And definitely no more imagining her naked on a massage table or in the shower.

"Good," Alex interrupted that risky train of thought. "I'm interested to see what the two of you come up with. What's next?"

If Celeste didn't withdraw from the project altogether, they were due for a rather sublime activity tomorrow. "We're scheduled to visit the flower garden in St. Anne's Parish." An activity that would require no physical contact whatsoever, Reid thought with no small amount of gratefulness. The family owned and run botanical garden attracted tourists from all over the world to admire the striking flora that graced so much of the island. After a tour of the flower beds and exotic plants and trees, the excursion included some light shopping and a home-cooked meal.

Surely, he could get through something like that without laying his hands on Celeste's tempting body?

Piece of cake.

To make matters even better, they'd be fully clothed. No swimsuits involved for this outing. He wouldn't have to force his gaze away from the tiny dimple in Celeste's luscious thigh. Or the way her suit fit her like a glove and accentuated all those glorious curves.

"You just drifted off again, my friend."

Reid uttered a small curse. Thank heavens Alex had no idea exactly where his mind had drifted off to.

Who was he kidding? Celeste wasn't even here and he couldn't get her out of his head. He had his work cut out for him if he was going to maintain a professional distance tomorrow.

"Sorry. I was just mentally going over my to-do list." Another fib. He hadn't been this slippery with his friend and partner at any other time before this. He was behaving uncharacteristically in so many ways, he'd lost count.

Alex suddenly stood, apparently giving up on any kind of productive meeting given the state of Reid's mental sharpness at the moment.

"I should go get started on mine," he said, then turned to leave. He stopped at the door and turned back with a playful smile. "You sure you won't reconsider the *Nutcracker* gig now?"

"I'm sure, my man. No one needs to see me in tights."

Alex released a bark of laughter before exiting.

Reid turned to stare out at the glass wall behind his desk. In the distance, the ocean sparkled like a sea of precious gems. The sun shone bright in a clear, azure-blue sky. Another beautiful day in paradise.

The building that housed the spa could be seen at the edge of the property. Was she there now?

Reid stood and closed the lid of his laptop. Nothing wrong with taking a walk in that direction. He hadn't even been outside yet today. Some fresh Caribbean air would do him some good right now. He definitely wasn't trying to seek Celeste out. And if he did run into her merely by chance, what would be wrong with that?

No harm, no foul, he reassured himself. He'd simply be checking on a contract employee. Fifteen minutes later, after catching no sign of her, Reid resigned himself to acknowledging that their paths would not be crossing this morning. He also had to acknowledge the disappointment he felt.

CHAPTER EIGHT

RIGHT ON TIME.

Celeste's cell phone screen lit up with a text message as she was walking down the concrete pathway to the entrance of the resort property.

I'm here a couple minutes early. See you soon. R

She'd be arriving right at the time they'd agreed to meet at the bellhop desk to board the shuttle bus that would take them to the Flower Forest. Looked like Reid didn't want to take any chances that she'd be late. Or that she wouldn't show. If she was being fair, she would admit he couldn't be blamed for being uncertain. She hadn't so much as dropped him a thank-you text for the extravagant day of decadence he'd treated her to yesterday.

Even worse, she'd seen him approaching the spa building as she was leaving but had ducked for cover and turned the other way. Not that she'd meant to avoid him. But she had just needed one full day away from him to regain her equilibrium.

Truth be told, she was also a little embarrassed. Her reaction to the ATV ride weighed on her. Reid probably saw her as weak and fearful of new activities. It galled her to appear that way to anyone, let alone a man like him. The temperature dropped several degrees as she entered the air-conditioned concierge lobby. She spotted Reid right away, but then he was particularly hard to miss. A head taller than most of the people in the room, he was dressed in khaki shorts and another formfitting T-shirt, blue this time. She had no doubt the rich color would serve to heighten the golden hue of his eyes.

Her conclusion was confirmed when she reached him. Yep, a girl could get lost in those beautiful golden depths if she didn't check herself.

Celeste would have to make sure to check herself.

"You made it."

She wasn't imagining the relief in his voice. He'd been afraid she wasn't going to show.

"All refreshed and ready to go," she answered with a smile. "Thank you for my day of pampering yesterday. I feel like a new woman."

His responding smile sent a bolt of awareness through her core.

"I'm glad you enjoyed it."

"Shall we?" Celeste prompted, before another one of those awkward silences could ensue that seemed to be so very frequent between them.

Reid nodded and led her outside to the waiting town car and held the back door open for her before climbing in the other side. Within moments they were pulling out of the long stone driveway and onto the main road. It always took Celeste a moment to adjust to the sensation of being driven on the opposite side of the street than what she was used to in the States.

Reid flipped open a console between their feet to reveal an assortment of drinks and snacks. "Can I get you anything?"

Celeste accepted some water and a rich chocolate bar

that seemed to melt in her mouth when she bit into it. Between hours at the spa yesterday and this luxurious ride, she could get used to this lifestyle. City life was overrated.

"So, tell me about this flower garden," she said between bites.

Reid uncapped a bottle of iced tea as he answered. "It's called the Flower Forest. It's one of the first excursions we contracted out after acquiring the resort. Owned and operated by the same family for generations. Now it's just the matriarch and her son and daughter. All three are delightful people. A bit on the traditional side. You'll enjoy meeting them."

"I look forward to it." She realized she was looking forward to the whole day, in fact. Unlike the adventurous feats of the previous excursions, this one sounded low-key and relaxing.

She'd have a chance to spend some time with Reid without a constant stream of adrenaline clouding her judgment. Maybe they'd even enjoy each other's company.

No. That was hardly the goal for today. She had to keep that fact in mind. They weren't a couple out enjoying an island getaway. They were barely friends, if one were to be completely accurate. Boundaries were important here.

Half an hour later, they pulled onto a gravel road and eventually came to a thick, green tree line.

Celeste had to suck in a breath when she exited the car at the sheer amount of color that greeted her. A flowing river could be heard behind the trees. The fragrant scent of exotic flowers filled the air. The entire scene could have been painted by a talented landscape artist.

Oh, yeah. This was much more up her alley than a jostling ride in an open-air vehicle as it straddled a cliff edge.

"Oh! It's so beautiful, Reid. Just lovely." This would be the easiest write-up she'd ever done.

A rotund woman who appeared to be in her early sixties appeared from behind a wooden gate and approached them. She was trailed by a young man and woman. Each had the same facial structure and eye shape. It was clear they were siblings.

"Mr. Reid. So nice to see you again," the woman said, giving Reid a hug and a small peck on the cheek.

"Uma, the pleasure's all mine," Reid answered over her head.

"You remember my son and daughter, Rinna and Theo," Uma added. The siblings nodded in acknowledgment.

"Of course." Reid motioned to where Celeste stood behind them.

"And I'd like you all to meet Celeste. She's a colleague of mine. She's going to help us bring some more attention and visitors to this lovely slice of paradise you have here."

Celeste reached out her hand but Uma ignored it and hugged her instead, as well. She mustered a smile as she returned the older woman's embrace but it was forced.

The word *colleague* had never sounded so disappointing.

"I have a confession to make," Reid said in a low voice as they trailed behind Rinna and Theo, their tour guides. Uma had left for the kitchen to start preparing the meal.

"What's that?" Celeste asked, her curiosity peaked. What in the world could he be referring to?

"I was a little concerned you'd back out of coming along today. After you know…the last time."

So he had been worried. Celeste felt a pang of regret. She had a stellar reputation as a competent and efficient businesswoman. To think that she'd given Reid the impression of unreliability would weigh heavily on her for some time to come.

Her professional reputation was a matter she took very seriously and an accomplishment she had worked very hard for over the years. Just made for another reason why she had to suppress whatever this attraction was between her and Reid. She had too much at stake. Theo stopped in front of a tree and turned to face them.

"This is Frangipani," Theo explained, pointing to the small tree adorned with white flowers. Celeste could smell the rich perfume of the petals where she stood.

They moved on. Theo and Rinna took turns pointing out and naming various flowers, bushes, and trees. Celeste was fascinated by the hibiscus flowers, which she'd seen on countless tea bag label ingredients but now had a picture of what the plant looked like.

All in all, it was a fascinating stroll. The weather was perfect, warm yet not muggy. A gentle breeze fanned her skin. By the time their tour ended, she felt both entertained and educated. A perfect tagline to advertise the attraction.

They'd reached the banks of the river when Uma came out to summon them to lunch. In moments, they were seated at a wooden picnic table by the water enjoying a mouthwatering meal of fried fish, rice and plantain.

"You were right," Celeste remarked between bites. "They are a delightful family. And Uma's a wonderful cook."

"Do you think you have a good idea of how to frame the description of this place?"

There it was again. Reid's sole focus was on the mission at hand. She wanted to kick herself for feeling any disappointment at his remark. It wasn't Reid's fault that she kept forgetting the true objective here. If anything, she should be thanking him for leading her back on track.

She nodded in response to his question. "I think so. The delicious food will play a major role."

Reid put his fork down and leaned toward her over the table. "Tell me something."

"Yes?" Celeste was fully expecting a question about her thoughts on the Flower Forest and what sort of features she would highlight in any summary she put together for him. So, his next words threw her completely off guard.

"Have you moved on? From your engagement to Jack and how it ended?"

Whoa. She had definitely not seen that coming.

Reid had an almost uncanny knack for throwing her off her feet. She swallowed the last bite she'd taken quickly, before she risked having it lodged in her throat.

She wasn't sure how to answer his question. If Reid was asking her if she'd met someone else in the past three years, the answer was no. But in every other sense, she'd moved on.

He suddenly looked away, out toward the water. "I'm sorry. I shouldn't have asked you that. It's none of my business."

"But you did ask. Why?"

"I'm not sure." He gave her a tight smile. "Like I said. I shouldn't have. I have no excuse for asking it."

Theo approached them before she could respond. He carried a sleek-looking professional camera. "Reid. Celeste. I hoped I might be able to take a few photos of the two of you."

Celeste couldn't decide if she was relieved or annoyed at the interruption. A little bit of both probably, she'd have to admit.

"I'm trying to do my own little bit of publicity for Mom. Just some photos to add to our website."

Reid looked at her in question. "That okay with you?"

Celeste shrugged. "Sure. Why not?"

They turned and smiled for Theo who snapped several shots in rapid succession.

"Let's do some by the water, yeah?" Theo suggested, and led them to the riverbank. "And I hate to ask…"

Reid gave him an indulgent smile. "Anything for you, Theo. What is it?"

"It's just that we're trying to appeal to a wider audience. Mainly couples. We seem to only get families with children. I was thinking it couldn't hurt to emphasize the romantic aspects of this place." He gestured around him.

Uh-oh. Celeste could guess where Theo was headed. He confirmed her suspicions. "You two mind posing like you're a real couple? You know, just so the photos look authentic?"

Neither one of them could seem to come up with an answer. Theo must have sensed their mutual discomfort. "Uh… Never mind. Forget I asked."

A pang of guilt settled in Celeste's stomach. What was the harm in a couple of photos? Theo, his mom and his sister had been the most perfect of hosts; gracious and accommodating. The least she and Reid could do was playact for a couple of stills.

"I'm okay with it if you are," she uttered, not quite able to look Reid in the eyes as she spoke.

Reid gave a slight shrug. "Sure. Go for it, Theo."

Theo flashed them a wide smile. "Thanks! So, just step together closer and, Reid, put your arm around Celeste's shoulders."

Reid did as instructed and Theo snapped away.

"That's great, you two. You both are naturals at this." He looked at the camera screen with a pleased smile. "It looks real. Like you guys are really together."

Celeste had to suppress an internal groan. Then things went from bad to worse.

"How about a pretend kiss?" Theo suggested.

CHAPTER NINE

Reid had every intention of simply dropping the slightest peck on Celeste's cheek. At the most, he might have softly brushed his lips along the corner of her mouth.

But somehow, after Theo made his suggestion, Reid's lips found hers and he seemed to have lost control of his intentions.

She tasted of berries and chocolate, her lips soft and luscious under his. Someone sighed heavily. He couldn't even tell which one of them it was. Her arms went up around his neck and it was all the invite he needed to pull her closer, deepen the kiss. Time seemed to stand still, their audience forgotten. Nothing of the outside mattered for him now. His one and only focus was the woman in his arms and how it felt to hold her, to kiss her.

He'd been imagining this, he had to admit. He'd had dreams at night where he held her, touched her, took her mouth with his exactly as he was doing now. The reality of it was so much more than he could have guessed. The clicking of Theo's camera suddenly registered in his brain. He couldn't be sure which one of them broke the contact first. Only that he felt the loss like a physical pang as Celeste pulled back and looked up at him. Her cheeks were flushed, her lips reddened from his mouth. It excited him to think that he'd been the one to put that color into her face, and her reaction to him only served to heighten his own desire.

"Reid?" she whispered softly, low enough so that he was sure Theo couldn't hear her question over the noise of his picture taking.

He wanted desperately to answer her. Not verbally but by kissing her again, he wanted to show her how much he desired her, how much of an effect she was having on him.

Theo's voice charged through his desire-fogged mind. "That's perfect, you two. These will work great. Let's move onto a different location, yeah?"

Reid couldn't seem to make his limbs work. He knew he should let her go. He knew they should turn around and follow Theo who had already stepped away and was walking toward the garden. But he couldn't so much as tear his gaze from Celeste's face.

Her breath had gone shallow. The one word question she'd uttered as simply his name still hung heavily in the air.

He couldn't help it, he touched his finger to her bottom lip and trailed it lower to her jaw.

Confusion grew in her eyes. "Uh. Theo's left. You don't have to keep pretending now."

The words felt like ice water thrown at him. They served just as effectively to pull him out of his desire-filled daze.

How foolish of him. Looked like only one of them had simply been pretending.

She'd never been good at pretending. The lines always became blurry for her. They certainly had just now. How much of Reid's kiss was real? How much was fake?

Dear heavens. She had to admit that everything she'd

felt as soon as his lips touched hers felt one hundred percent real. Well, she'd do well to snap out of it. Reid had already moved forward. He turned to see if she was following him.

"Coming?" he asked, completely nonchalant. Unlike her, he seemed far from affected in any way by the kiss they'd shared.

The fake kiss.

Celeste forced her feet to move and reached his side. Together they walked over to where Theo stood waiting for them by the Frangipani tree he'd told them about earlier when they'd first arrived. He motioned for them to go stand in front of it.

"How about you two hold hands?" Theo suggested after they'd complied with his request. Reid reached for her and she swore a bolt of electricity shot through her arm as she took his hand.

She had to clamp down on all this emotion. She couldn't let herself continue this way. She was only here in Jamaica for a few more short days. Soon, this whole adventure of a vacation would be over. She'd go back to her old life, her demanding job, and her draining family. She had neither the time nor the energy to spend her days pining over a man from her past. A man who was tied to her one majorly disastrous failed relationship. That life was her reality, those were the things waiting for her back home. A life full of responsibility and consequences. This was all a fantasy, a fake portrait that was meant to go into brochures and on websites.

It wouldn't do for her to forget that for even the slightest moment.

"You're not really smiling," Reid informed her through the side of his mouth. By contrast, he looked like a man thoroughly enjoying the day.

"Sorry. I'm not really good at this acting thing." Celeste forced her mouth to curve into a smile.

"Really? You could have fooled me."

What was that supposed to mean? She probably didn't even want to know.

"Let's just get this over with," Reid added. His grip against her palm lightened ever so slightly.

Well, that comment certainly cemented it. If she'd harbored any illusions that Reid was in any way as moved by their kiss earlier as she was, she could rest assured that he wasn't.

If only she could be like the tree behind her, Celeste thought, feigning another smile for Theo's camera. If only she could completely shed her unwanted feelings like they were discarded leaves. And then start anew. A whole new beginning, completely leaving the past behind.

The first metaphorical leaf she would drop would be her fraught and complicated feelings toward the man currently holding her hand.

Rinna approached them as they wrapped up the last few photos. It had taken some effort but somehow Celeste had willed her breath to return to a normal pace.

Well, as normal as she'd ever experienced while in Reid's presence.

"Momma asks that you two stay for dinner," the young woman announced when she reached them. "She says there's some type of holiday parade blocking the roads near the city. So you may as well wait it out."

As if on cue, Reid's phone lit up and he blew out a frustrated sigh when he glanced at it. "My driver has just confirmed exactly that." He turned to her. "Looks like we'll be here a bit longer than intended. Did you have any plans?"

Celeste shook her head. Of course, she didn't. She was here solo, after all. A warring flurry of uncertainty tightened her chest. Part of her didn't want this day to end. Another more sensible part warned her that any prolonging of time spent with Reid was a lethal threat to her inner peace.

"Excellent." Rinna clapped her hands in front of her chest. "I'll go let Momma know. She loves having company. We'll eat in about half an hour."

"This is good," Theo added after his sister left. "This will give you two a chance to see the holiday lights we set up this year. We decorated many of the trees. It's beautiful after dark."

"I'm looking forward to it," Celeste answered. She'd always been a sucker for Christmas trees and the sparkling lights during the season. One of the few aspects of the holidays she hadn't grown to resent.

Theo lifted his camera. "I'm going to go upload these images. You two take your time. See you at the house in a bit."

"Sorry about this," Reid said after the other man had left. "Things work differently on the islands. Holiday parades sometimes pop up without advance warning."

"It's all right, Reid," she answered. "Like I said, I didn't have any plans." She wondered if he thought that was pathetic.

"Well, good. If you'll excuse me, I should make a few phone calls given the change in my return time. I'm afraid I was due to meet someone who'll be arriving on the island tonight. Alex will have to take over."

Of course, unlike her, Reid would have a full schedule. No doubt this delay caused all sorts of disruption for him. A business owner like him had all sorts of demands on his time.

She wondered if one of the phone calls he was making was a personal one. Did it have anything to do with whoever he was expecting to fly in? He'd never mentioned being involved with a woman but why would he? It wasn't like it was any of her business. And though Celeste had never actually seen him with a lady so far on this trip, that meant nothing. She'd only been on the island a few days. While she'd spent a considerable amount of time during those days fantasizing and thinking about him, she'd steadfastly avoided wondering about his social life.

Now that she'd been confronted with the possibility he was attached, she felt even more foolish for pining for him for even a moment. Seemed she was a magnet for rejection. To imagine that someone like Reid would ever see her as anything like a romantic girlfriend was downright folly. She'd fallen for that fantasy once before, only to have reality come straight back and slap her into the truth. Men like Reid didn't end up with women like her.

No doubt the mysterious arrival was a beautiful, successful, and accomplished gem of a woman. Perhaps she was the model from the magazine cover she'd seen at the airport. Or maybe an actress. She vaguely recalled seeing a different photo several months back of Reid at some movie awards ceremony, attending as the guest of a Hollywood starlet.

She glanced at Reid's back now as he spoke into his cell phone, braced against one of the trees a few feet away. Slowly, she made her way toward the river. Watching the water stream by might be a soothing way to iron out her frazzled nerves. The whole day had been an emotional roller coaster. Correction, her whole trip had been a harrowing series of ups and downs. Definitely not what she'd expected to be in store for her. Just one more curve thrown at her. To think, she'd been so excited to leave the city behind her for several days.

Maybe this should have been the one year she stayed home for the holidays. The sadness the season always invoked in her might have actually been preferable to the assault to her peace that had been this trip so far.

She heard his footsteps behind her and instinctively took another step forward in a futile attempt at creating some distance between them. She really could use some time to think alone.

"Careful," Reid's voice warned from behind her. "You're awfully close to the edge there. The ground can be slippery. Unless you're looking for an impromptu swim."

An illogical surge of annoyance speared through her. She was a grown woman. One who certainly didn't need to be told what to do. In sheer defiance born of rebellion, she took another step.

Only to prove the worth of Reid's word of warning. Her foot slid out from underneath her as it landed on a slick patch of mud. She felt the shocking splash of water an instant later. Reid's shouted curse was immediately followed by another splash as he jumped in after her. Why in the world would he do that? She could swim, for heaven's sake. Now they'd both be a soaked, river-slimed mess. She opened her lips to tell him so only to have her mouth flooded with said slimy water. That couldn't be good.

"Hang on," Reid shouted over the splash of the water.

Even in the shock of her fall, only one thought crammed through her mind.

She hated that he'd been right. And that he was now attempting to rescue her.

* * *

Reid bit out another curse as he landed in the steadily flowing river. Grabbing Celeste by the waist, he began to hoist her onto the edge of the riverbank. Was she actually resisting? What the...?

He lifted her out of the water and followed her onto the land. "Are you all right? You didn't hurt yourself, did you?"

She ignored his question, posing one of her own. "Why did you do that?" she demanded to know crossly. "You did not need to jump in after me."

Well, if that didn't take the cake. "You have a funny way of saying thank you." Swiping the moisture off his face, he then ran his fingers through his hair.

Celeste was shooting fire at him. For helping her out of the water she'd fallen into, despite him having warned her.

He would never understand this woman, probably shouldn't even try. So he wanted to kick himself for the direction his next thoughts took him in. No woman should look that enticing dripping wet after a drenching in a green tinged, mossy body of water.

For that's exactly what she was. Enticing.

Her hair had turned a shade darker after the drenching, accenting the golden hue of her tanned skin. Her soaked white lace dress clung to her like a caress in all the right places. He had a clear view of her undergarments through the wet fabric of her clothes. Reid made himself avert his gaze. It wasn't easy.

He longed to slowly strip her of the dress, then rub his hands over every inch of her soaked skin to warm it up. His breath caught in his throat at the image. He couldn't deny it any longer. He wanted her. And he wanted her so badly it made him ache inside. How or when it had happened, he couldn't even try to place. Maybe it had all started that first day he'd seen her sprawled on a lounger on the beach. Perhaps it went back even further than that.

Not something he really wanted to examine at the moment. The better question was what he was going to do about it.

"Honestly, Reid," she huffed as she stepped around him. "Now we're both a mess."

He blinked. "Are you actually upset that I helped you out of the water?"

"I didn't need rescuing," she declared and tried to push past him.

Without thinking, he reached out to take her by the elbow and turned her around to face him.

"What is your deal?"

Her chin lifted in defiance. "I thought I already explained. I didn't need you to jump in after me. I'm perfectly capable of swimming out of a body of water."

He gave his head a shake. "Have you always been this difficult? I can't seem to remember."

It was the wrong thing to say. Celeste's eyes darkened with anger. "Is that what Jack told you?" she demanded to know. "That I'm difficult? That I'm hardly worth the effort? Did you two have fun talking about me and how sad and downright pathetic I looked waiting for him at the altar? Do you two get together at the bar on weekends and make fun of how ridiculous I looked on what should have been the happiest day of my life?"

Reid felt his jaw drop. Such an accusation was the last thing he'd been expecting. "What? Of course not."

"What exactly are you denying, Reid? That you think I'm difficult? Or that I'm a pathetic, dejected discard? Or that you and Jack get a kick out of recalling my humiliation?"

He couldn't seem to find the words to respond. The things she was saying were downright preposterous. Little did she know, he thought Jack's behavior was inexcusable that day. Friend or not, it had been a cowardly and treacherous way to treat a woman. Let alone someone like Celeste.

She pulled her arm free from his grasp. "Never mind. I'm going to ask for a towel."

With that she trudged away toward the house. He caught up to her in mere strides, though he didn't dare reach for her again. For he was far too tempted to shake some sense into her. Then he would tell her how ridiculous a notion it was to hint that she'd been at all responsible for the way Jack had treated her. That she was far too good for him and always had been. And then he would quiet any further protest by crushing his lips to hers and tasting her again the way he wanted to so badly.

"For the record," he bit out. "Jack and I never discussed you after that day. Not once. Even when the subject of his averted wedding came up. The conversation never turned to talk about you specifically." Mainly because Reid wouldn't allow it, he added silently. "And we certainly don't laugh at you over beers at the local pub!"

"Yeah, right," she answered, not breaking her stride. He had several inches on her and much longer legs, but somehow it was an effort to keep pace with her. Her anger seemed to be propelling her forward. Or her desire to get away from him.

"What reason would I have to lie about that?"

She shrugged, still moving ahead. "I don't know. Some misplaced sense of loyalty your friend perhaps? I know how charming and convincing Jack can be."

Reid rubbed a frustrated hand down his face. "Why

are we arguing about this? Now of all times?" But the answer occurred to him before he got the last word out.

She was thinking of Jack. She wanted to know if he asked about her, talked about her. And apparently, the answer mattered to her. Why else would she be so upset?

One thing was certain. The reverse was absolutely true. Even if Jack didn't think of her, Celeste still thought about her former fiancé. Jack was on her mind even at this very moment. Even after she'd spent the morning with Reid. After he'd kissed her under the native tree, held her hand and smiled with her at Theo and his camera.

A fireball of anger seemed to ignite in his gut. His vision turned gray and he had to bite back a curse. He stopped in his tracks and let her continue forward. He would have to meet her at the house later. Right now he needed to be alone. He needed to try to think straight.

A task he couldn't seem to do well whenever Celeste was near.

"Oh, my!" Rinna cried out when she saw the state Celeste was in. "I see you fell into the water."

"We both did," Celeste announced and climbed up the porch steps. "Well, to be more accurate, I fell in. Then Reid jumped in after me. For some inexplicable reason."

"I see," Rinna said simply. She glanced in the distance behind where Celeste stood. "Where is Reid?"

Celeste was vaguely aware that he'd stopped following her at some point. Thank heavens he had. Or she might have turned to him then and there and asked him exactly what he thought of her. How he *felt* about her. She might have run the risk of having him come and say straight out what she suspected—that he liked her enough as a person. But that there could never be anything between them. Hence, she'd be making a fool of herself over a man yet again.

"Um…could I borrow a towel?" Celeste asked just Uma stepped out onto the porch from behind the screen door.

The older woman clapped a hand to her face. "Of course, dear. Come in and let's get you dry."

Celeste went up the stairs gratefully and went to step inside, only to have her ankle give out.

Uma and Rinna both jointly caught her just before she could hit the ground. "Are you all right, dear? Did you hurt yourself in the river?"

Celeste gave her head a shake. "I didn't think so. But I must have sprained it somehow during the fall. And then the walk to the house must have aggravated it." She rubbed a hand down her foot, which was starting to swell and bruise right before her eyes.

"Let's get you to the couch," Rinna suggested. "Theo's gone back out for more pictures. Can you try to stand without putting any weight on that foot?"

She didn't get a chance to answer. A deep masculine voice sounded from behind the three of them.

"I've got her."

A set of strong, muscular arms suddenly wrapped around her waist and under her bottom. The next instant she felt herself lifted into Reid's masculine embrace. Heaven help her, she took a moment to simply inhale the scent of him. The same mixture of citrus and sandalwood combined with mint, somehow still present despite the river water soaking his skin. Without giving herself a chance to think, she rested her forehead against his broad chest, taking comfort in the warmth of his skin against her cheek. Reid nuzzled his jaw against the top of her head. She didn't dare try to read anything into his action. He probably just felt bad for her.

"Does it hurt badly?" he asked, his voice smooth above her head.

"No. Not really. Just a little achy."

"Sorry about all this," he spoke low into her ear as he carried her farther inside and toward the couch.

Great. Now he was trying to take responsibility for her fall. "I'm not sure why you're apologizing."

"You're only here in the first place because of me."

"That may be. But I fell into the water on my own. Due to my own carelessness."

He exhaled deeply as he set her down on the couch. "Anyone ever tell you that you can be stubborn?" he asked.

Was it her imagination or did his hands linger around her body just a bit longer than was necessary after he set her down on the cushions? She looked up to find the smallest hint of a smile on his face.

"As a matter of fact, I do hear that from time to time."

The smile grew. "I'll bet."

A strange sensation tugged at her heart. The warmth of his touch still lingered over her wet skin. The man did something to her insides she couldn't recall feeling with anyone else ever. Not even the man she'd been prepared to marry.

Rinna appeared from behind them with a couple of pillows. She placed one behind her back and the other under the offending foot. Reid leaned over her. "May I?" he asked, gesturing to her leg.

She reluctantly agreed and he ran a gentle finger along the arch of her foot and around her ankle. Then he went up higher, toward her knee. Totally innocuous as it was, tingles of awareness rippled up her skin at his touch.

Full-out kisses by other men had elicited less of a reaction from her than Reid simply examining her sore ankle. She had to suppress a shudder of reaction.

"It doesn't appear to be broken," he announced. "Just a sprain."

"You think so?"

"I'd place a wager on it if I had to." He nodded and gave her a teasing wink. "I've broken enough bones in my lifetime to be able to speak with some authority on the subject."

Celeste thanked the other woman for the pillows and allowed herself a groan of frustration. What a burden she was being to these people. And Reid, for that matter. All because she had been a careless klutz. She had no one else to blame but herself. Truth be told, she'd been distracted and dazed since that first day when she'd gone to find Santa only to discover Reid Evanson in his stead.

"Do you have any ice?" Reid asked Rinna.

"We do. But we can do even better than that. Momma has gone out to gather the plants she needs to mix up a medicinal balm." She laughed and shook her head. "I've had it applied to my various scrapes and bruises countless times over the years. She'll be back to prepare it soon. You'll start healing in no time," she reassured.

Celeste resisted the urge to ask if Uma might be able to come up with a balm to ease the ache in her heart.

CHAPTER TEN

THEY ALL ATE in the living room so that Celeste could remain lying on the sofa with her foot propped up. True to Rinna's word, Uma had wrapped a cloth around her ankle after applying the homemade poultice. Whatever the concoction was, it smelled heavenly. Miraculously, her foot started to feel better within minutes. Celeste didn't think it was the placebo effect. She could feel the swelling go down and the throbbing sensation had almost completely stopped. Between the filling meal and the relief from pain, she found herself drifting off into a comfortable sleep.

When she opened her eyes again, she was shocked that two hours had passed. She slowly roused herself to a seated position. Reid sat across from her at a wooden dining table, typing away at the keyboard of a laptop. He appeared to have showered and had changed into clean clothes. Oh, to be so lucky.

He glanced up when he realized she'd awakened. "You're up."

"It's dark out."

"That it is."

"Shouldn't our car have been here by now?"

"I asked for it to be delayed."

"Why?"

He shrugged. "You looked like you could use the rest. I didn't want to disturb you."

Great. Yet another misstep she could feel guilty about. "But I know you had to get back to the resort." And to finally meet whoever had been due to arrive earlier, she added silently.

Reid motioned to the computer in front of him. "It's okay. Theo was nice enough to lend me his laptop so I could get some stuff done remotely. How does your foot feel?"

Celeste wiggled her toes and moved her ankle from side to side. The pain had mostly subsided. Only a slight ache remained in the joint. "Much better. Rinna was right. Uma's potion has some sort of magical healing properties."

She huffed out a breath. "I feel so foolish for going and hurting myself like that. It must have been a terrible inconvenience for them to have to take care of me this whole time." And for him, too.

"Accidents happen. You're not at fault." He stood and walked over to stand in front of her. "If you're up for it, I can call for the car to come for us."

Uma entered the room at that precise moment. "It's much too late to try to make that drive," the older woman argued. "You two stay here for the night. We have an extra room."

Reid gave Celeste a questioning look. He was waiting for her to make the decision. "I don't want to inconvenience anyone," Celeste said to the room in general.

Uma waved her hand in dismissal. "It's not a bother. Everything is ready for you. The bed stays made as we have overnight guests quite often. And the sofa down here is large and comfortable enough for you to sleep on, Reid."

Reid turned from the older woman to address Celeste. "Uma's offer makes sense. I'd feel better if you stayed completely off that ankle at least for the night. Also, I'd hate to make the driver leave his house this late just to drive us across the island and then have to drive back home again."

Well, how could she argue with any of that? She'd already been enough of a burden to the people currently under this roof. She certainly didn't want to further inconvenience the poor nameless driver.

"Thank you, Uma. You're far too kind," she told her, vowing to come up with a way to thank the woman at some future date. She'd never experienced such hospitality from strangers she'd met only hours before.

"That settles it then," Reid announced before turning to Uma. "We'll take you up on your generous offer. Thank you."

Uma patted his cheek and left the room. Celeste made an effort to get up off the coach. Reid was by her side in an instant. "Whoa there. What do you think you're doing?"

Embarrassingly enough, she needed to use the washroom, for one. "Uh, I could use to freshen up a little."

He wordlessly leaned down and lifted her off the sofa. It was hard not to savor the feel of being in his arms again, despite the circumstances that had led her there. He carried her to the nearest bathroom.

"Just holler when you're done."

Celeste shut the door and took a moment to study herself in the bathroom mirror. She looked as if she'd gone toe to toe with some kind of swamp creature. Her hair was a tangled mess, dark circles framed her eyes and her clothes were in a wrinkled state of disarray. Oh, yeah, compared to the gorgeous models and actresses Reid was used to dating, she would definitely fall far short.

With a resigned sigh, she cleaned up as best she could, helping herself to some of the mouthwash sitting on the bureau behind her.

She may not look great, but by the time she opened the door, she at least felt better. Reid remained in the same spot, waiting for her.

"All set?"

She nodded, trying to maintain her balance on the one foot. With what seemed to be little effort, he picked her up and carried her once more. "This can't be good for your back," she commented.

"You wound me. Are you questioning my masculine strength?"

She had to smile. "I wouldn't dream of it."

To her surprise, rather than plant her back on the sofa, he walked toward the front porch.

"Where are we going?"

"You'll see." Kicking the door open with his foot, he took her out onto the porch.

Once they stepped outside, the sight before her took her breath away. The lights that Theo had referred to earlier were now lit up. The whole garden looked like a magical holiday light display. Several Christmas trees, a few bushes decorated like presents, glowing lights along the path leading to the river. She couldn't help her squeal of delight at the festive scene.

"It's beautiful, Reid! I'm so glad I got to see it." She knew it was silly, but part of her was almost grateful for the accidental fall that had led her to be able to be here for this sight.

Reid set her down gently on one of the outdoor patio chairs then took a seat of his own. The night was balmy with just enough wind to offer a refreshing breeze once in a while. A silver-gray moon floated above them in a velvet navy blue sky. Celeste couldn't guess how long the two of them wordlessly sat there simply admiring the view.

Her awareness of the man next to her was near tangible, so she felt it instinctively when his mood seemed to shift. A tenseness suddenly appeared in the set of his shoulders. His chin hardened. His shoulders slumped ever so slightly, yet enough for Celeste to notice. No doubt he was thinking of all the responsibilities waiting for him back at the resort.

"I'm sorry we got stuck here. Due to my carelessness."

He turned to her, surprise flickering in his gaze. "Don't apologize, Celeste. You had an accident." He gestured around him. "Besides, how can I possibly be upset about spending time here amidst all this beauty and calm? I dare say I needed the peace and quiet for an evening."

Did that include spending time with her? Silly question.

"But you seem quite distracted. I imagine you're thinking of all you need to get done."

He shook his head, turned back to stare at the navy blue horizon in the distance. "Just thinking about a phone call I have to make when I get back."

"Must be some phone call." The tension was practically vibrating off his skin as he talked about it. "Business or personal? If you don't mind my asking."

He crossed his arms in front of his chest. "Both. That's the problem."

"Want to tell me about it?"

He shrugged. "I have the very unpleasant task of dispelling the notion my father has that he can retake control of Evanson Properties."

Celeste didn't know much about Reid's company, nothing beyond what she'd read in the business papers. But his statement confused her, based on those reports. "I don't understand. I thought the company was on the brink of bankruptcy until you took over as CEO and turned it around." He'd done so in an astonishingly brief period of time, too.

"He's not exactly thinking straight. His motivation has more to do with an outside party. A woman."

Understanding dawned. She'd also read about the messy, bitter divorce of the elder Evansons. "I see."

He let out a grunt of a laugh. "My future stepmother has made it clear to him that she fell in love with a CEO, so she'd fully expected to marry a CEO."

"Sounds like a compromise might be difficult."

His eyebrows drew together. "Compromise?"

Celeste nodded. "There has to be a way for both you and your father to come to some kind of agreement."

He blinked at her. "Why would I bother? This is the man who let an uninformed, inexperienced outsider talk him into all sorts of bad investments. Everything from hiring social media influencers who simply took advantage of complimentary stays at our hotels, to investing in a failed music festival which resulted in countless lawsuits." He inhaled an agitated breath. "Lawsuits I'm still dealing with."

The underlying hurt in his tone was as clear as the flickering neon lights before them. His father's business failings were the least of the complicated scenario Reid was dealing with. No wonder he dreaded talking to the man.

"You feel betrayed," she supplied.

"How can I not? Evanson Properties was founded by my grandfather, it employs countless employees all over the globe. The Evanson name has been associated with luxury hotels for nearly a century. My father nearly destroyed all that with a few strokes of his pen. And for what? A midlife crisis?"

"But that's not all, is it?" she prompted.

"What else?"

Celeste bit the inside of her cheek. There was a chance she was overstepping here. But Reid was staring at her with expectation for an answer. "You also feel betrayed as his son."

Something seemed to have dislodged in his chest, some type of tight knot he hadn't even been aware of. He hadn't sat down and really discussed the disastrous events of the past couple of years or the hurtful actions of his father with anyone before this. He certainly wasn't about to burden his mother with any of it, she was a big part of the reason he'd worked so hard to rectify it all.

And his relationship with his closest male friend was far too strained and had been for the past three years. Unloading some of it simply by talking about it with Celeste felt like a bit of the burden being lifted off his shoulders.

You feel betrayed as his son.

He hadn't been able to come up with a response when she'd uttered those words. Her demeanor told him no response was needed.

Now they were both sitting in the balmy Caribbean air, enjoying a comfortable silence. He couldn't recall the last time he'd simply sat outside, chatting with someone. Someone who wasn't afraid to tell him what he needed to hear.

But it was getting late. And Celeste had had quite a day. Uma, Theo and Rinna had bidden them good-night several minutes ago and explained that the light display would turn off soon based on the timer system running it. Looked like the evening was coming to an end. And he'd already said more than he probably should have shared with her. He stood and stretched out his back.

"Guess we should head inside, huh?" Celeste asked.

"Guess so. Here, I'll help you upstairs to the spare bedroom."

Even in the relative darkness he could see her grimace. She didn't like being indebted to anyone. She might have read his thoughts based on her next statement. "I hate that you have to carry me, Reid. And I hate that you felt you needed to jump in after me when I fell." She inhaled deeply, her chest rising. "I'm not used to being dependent on anyone. It makes me uncomfortable. I'm afraid that's why I...lashed out...after my fall. I regret that. And I'd like to say I'm sorry for the way I behaved."

Huh. Reid couldn't recall the last time someone had directly come clean and apologized to him after making a mistake. Certainly not his father after the countless times he'd jeopardized the family business empire. And certainly not any of the women he'd dated in the recent past after a quarrel or spat. He'd always been the one to take responsibility and accept fault, regardless of whether it was deserved or not.

He checked his thoughts. It was way too late and the day had been way too long to become this pensive.

"Well, if it makes you feel better, you're probably one of the least dependent people I've ever come across," he told her with absolute sincerity. In fact, based on what she'd told him after the incident with the ATV, she'd made herself responsible not only for herself, but also for those she cared for. He hadn't known her that well three years ago, certainly hadn't been aware of the situation with her sister and mother. The knowledge now definitely shed some light on some of the mysteries he'd wondered about when it came to Celeste. In fact, if he'd been a betting man like his father, he would guess Celeste's family had been the real reason Jack had ultimately got cold feet over marrying her. He wasn't one to share. And he wasn't the type to appreciate a woman who came with that kind of baggage. Even a woman like Celeste.

Jack really could be incredibly selfish.

Reid couldn't help feeling somewhat sorry for him. The man had no idea what he'd had then foolishly lost. If Reid were in any kind of position to be with a woman like her, he'd hold on tight and refuse to let her go.

"Thank you for that," Celeste said. "It means a lot to hear you say so."

"You're welcome." Walking over to her chair, he cradled her in his arms and lifted her up. "Now I'm gonna get you to bed, beautiful."

He felt more than heard her sharp intake of breath, and couldn't decide whether she was reacting to the endearment or the loaded statement. He hadn't meant either, truth be told. He certainly hadn't meant to sound so provocative. "I'm sure you're ready to get some sleep," he quickly added.

Using his toe to nudge the door open, he carried her inside the house and up the stairs. He could get used to this, the feel of her in his arms. She was light and soft against his chest. Her shapely legs draped over his arms. The scent of her filling his senses. She belonged there, snuggled into him up against his chest.

Reid didn't bother with the light switch when they reached the room, the moonlight and glow of the still-lit display outside afforded just enough light to see. Reid stepped over to the bed to gently set her down. But two things happened at once. First, the bed was much lower than he was used to. Second, the lights outside suddenly went out right at that very moment. Rather than gently set her down, Reid lost his footing and they both stumbled onto the mattress.

"We have to stop meeting like this," he quipped as they both landed unceremoniously onto the soft surface. Her lips were inches from his, he could feel her hot, sweet breath against his jaw. His skin felt afire everywhere her body touched his; the softness of her chest, her long legs up against his.

Her response was to tilt her face up toward his. Reid didn't even know who moved first. But suddenly he was tasting her, devouring her the way he'd so often imagined doing. He thrust his hands into her hair, pulled her tighter against him and deepened the kiss. She tasted like fruit and honey and enticing spice. She tasted like home.

Her hands found his shoulders, then moved over his biceps, toward his back. She wrapped her arms around his neck and deepened the kiss. But it wasn't enough. He would never get enough of her touch, the taste of her.

The sound of a door shutting from somewhere down the hall served as a warning bell. Though it hurt like a physical blow, he made himself break the kiss and pull away. He had to suck in a breath to try to steady his pounding pulse.

Celeste's cry of protest nearly undid him. But as much as he wanted to continue kissing and exploring her, this wasn't the time or the place.

One thing was unarguable. He wanted her. And she wanted him. There was no doubt in his mind judging by the way she'd reacted just now and the shallowness of her breathing as she stared up at him in confusion. He'd had to fight hard the strong urge to throw all care aside and simply join her where she lay on the bed.

Instead, he leaned down and dropped a gentle, soft

kiss to her forehead. "Good night, Celeste." Then he forced himself to turn and walk away.

One and only one thought hammered his brain as he left the room to make his way down to the sofa on the first floor; he could make her forget she'd ever been committed to another man. Hell, he could make her forget that other man even existed.

There was no question of attraction. Not after what had just happened between them in that room and the way Celeste had melted in his arms. Under better circumstances, they could explore whatever this was between them and see where it might lead. If they were two completely different people, Reid would have no doubt in his mind about finding out once and for all.

No, the only question was whether he had any right to want her the way he did.

CHAPTER ELEVEN

THEIR TRIP TO the flower garden seemed like forever ago. Hard to believe only one day had passed. Celeste sank deeper into the Italian marble bath and took a deep breath. The hot water and luxurious fizziness of the scented bath bomb was doing wonders for her anxious nerves. But a dip in the bathtub could only do so much. She hadn't seen Reid all day yesterday once they'd arrived back at the resort, nor this morning or afternoon.

But she was due to spend the evening with him in a couple of short hours. The next item he had her writing up was a formal dinner cruise followed by live music and dancing aboard the boat.

What a fun, romantic evening it would have been if only it was all real. She had no idea what they would say to each other. The only words they'd spoken had been awkward and forced during their mostly silent drive back to the hotel yesterday morning after bidding Uma and her children goodbye. And then Reid had disappeared without a word to her except a brief text this morning confirming the time of the cruise. She'd been tempted to feign illness, to say that she wasn't up for it. But any fool would see right through that excuse.

Maybe he was avoiding her after what had happened in Uma's spare bedroom. Or perhaps he was busy with whoever had arrived that evening when the two of them couldn't return to the resort as expected. A pang of hurt she didn't want to identify as jealousy lodged in her chest.

The most probable explanation was that he was indeed avoiding her. He was no doubt embarrassed that things had gone so far between them that night. Heaven help her, she would have let things go even further if he hadn't suddenly stopped their kiss and walked out.

But he *had* walked out.

Reid had been the one to come to his senses. They had nothing in common, a shared brief past history which only complicated things further, and the chances that they would run into each other again once this trip was over were slim to none.

Unless, of course, she took him up on the free lifetime vacations he'd offered in return for her services. But she wouldn't. Her heart wouldn't be able to handle doing it. Seeing him every year, being tempted by a man she could never have.

A glance at the ornate clock on the wall above the sink counter told her she only had about half an hour left to get ready. With a sigh of regret, she stood and stepped out of the tub. There was no avoiding the inevitable. She could do this. She could dress the part, paste a fake smile on her face, and act like the all-business marketing professional that she was.

Toweling off, she walked over to the closet and removed the one formal dress that she'd packed. A silky black number that reached midthigh with red spaghetti straps and trim. Red leather high-heeled sandals and ruby earrings would complete the look. She'd included the outfit just in case when she'd packed, convinced she'd actually have no occasion to wear it.

If she'd only known.

About twenty minutes later, she was dressed and walk-

ing out the door of her suite to meet the man she'd somehow developed a devastatingly shocking attraction to.

This was a disaster in the making. The evening would
no doubt be a lesson in self-torture. How was she going
to playact the part of objective observer when the whole
night all she'd be thinking about was how much she
wanted him?

And heaven help her, she did want him. So much that
she'd been aching inside ever since the other night. If she
were honest with herself and looked deep within, she'd
have to acknowledge something much more worrisome
and disturbing: beyond the physical attraction, she'd developed feelings for him. Somehow, in the course of a
few short days, she'd started falling for a man who was
completely wrong for her. How many times in her life
could she make the same mistake?

There was no denying that mistake when she reached
the resort marina and found him waiting for her by the
water. Celeste had to remind herself to breathe. Dressed
in pressed dark pants and a midnight black fitted jacket
with a collared shirt, he took her breath away. Against the
backdrop of the luxury yacht and sparkling water, Reid
could have been posing for a men's cologne ad. In fact,
if she ever worked on a cologne campaign, this scene before her would serve as ample inspiration. She might find
a way to use this image in the very project she was working on for the resort.

That's it, girl. Stay focused on the business aspect.
Steady now.

Some protective instinct must have kicked into gear
in her head. The survival skills she'd built and developed
as an inner-city latchkey child were coming through for
her as they so often had throughout her life. She could
do this, she could get through this evening as an unemo-

tional, unaffected, driven businesswoman who was simply attending this event as part of a job commitment.

And for all intents and purposes, the man standing before her was simply her boss.

Never mind that she wanted nothing more at this moment than to run into his arms.

Reid had to clench his fists by his sides in order to keep himself from pulling Celeste tight against him and into his arms when she reached his side. He'd come close to canceling this evening. That option would have been the wisest course of action. But he couldn't bring himself to do it. He needed this marketing project completed and he needed it completed successfully. Distractions and delays wouldn't do.

Or so he told himself. If pushed, he would have to concede that he hadn't called it off because he hadn't wanted to. He'd wanted to see her. Avoiding her this past day and a half had been nothing short of painful. And what did that say about the sad state he currently found himself in? He'd been missing a woman he had no claim to. A woman who would walk out of his life in a few short days and most likely never return.

Given the way she looked right now, he knew he wasn't likely to stop wanting what he couldn't have anytime soon. The silky black-and-red dress she wore complemented her ever-deepening tan. Strappy red high heeled shoes accented her shapely legs, she'd worn her hair down cascading like an ebony dark curtain over her satin smooth shoulders.

He swallowed hard.

"Hey there," she greeted him when she reached his side.

Somehow, he got his mouth to work. "Hey yourself." He handed her the rose he'd thought to pick up on his way. Fake date or not, he knew when an occasion called for a flower.

She seemed surprised as she took it and inhaled deeply
of the petals. He wanted to do the same. Only he would
prefer to nuzzle his face against the gentle curve of her
neck and inhale deeply of her now oh-so-familiar scent.

"Thanks. This was very thoughtful."

"You're welcome," he replied, then motioned toward
the boat behind them. "Shall we?"

Celeste took the hand he'd extended and followed him
on board. A group of uniformed crew members greeted
them and they made their way below deck. A few other
couples were already seated at elegant, candlelit tables.
Yet others strolled in behind them.

A white tuxedoed crew member led them to their table
and pulled out their chairs.

"How's your foot?" Reid asked.

"Completely healed, it seems." She took a sip of her
water. "Uma's poultice is a wonder drug. She should bottle that stuff and sell it worldwide."

"I might have to suggest that idea next time I'm at the
flower garden." It occurred to him that on his next stop
there he'd mostly likely be by himself. Or with Alex. He'd
never be able to visit the place again without remembering the time he'd spent there with Celeste. Just one of the
many marks she'd be leaving on him when she left the
resort for good shortly.

The waiter reappeared with a fruity, frosted cocktail
complete with a swirly straw and placed it in front of Celeste. "The bartender's specialty drink, miss. Please enjoy."

He placed a shorter glass full of amber liquid in front
of Reid. Top-shelf Jamaican dark rum. "Your usual, sir."

Reid made a mental note to sip the drink much more
slowly than usual tonight. He couldn't risk a repeat of the
other night when he'd completely lost control and practically ravished Celeste in Uma's spare bedroom. Though

he'd been stone-cold sober then. Still, he didn't want to take the chance of lessening his inhibitions in any way.

Celeste took a sip of her drink and closed her eyes in pleasure. "Mmm, this tastes heavenly. Definitely something to note when writing about this outing."

Good for her for keeping her mind on the task at hand, Reid thought. At least one of them had their head in the right place. So why was a small part of him just a touch disappointed?

"I've also got some great things to say about the light show at Uma's place," she continued, then looked down at her drink.

Their thoughts must have drifted in the same direction; what had transpired between them after they'd admired said light display that evening.

Reid cleared his throat, trying to summon exactly what he wanted to say. They had to acknowledge what had happened. Or this awkwardness was simply going to continue to grow.

"Celeste, I'm not sure where to begin, but maybe we should be talking—"

But she held an elegantly manicured hand up to stop him. "Please, Reid. If it's just as well with you, I'd like to focus on the here and now. I need to if I'm going to be effective in what I'm trying to do here tonight."

All right. He would have to respect her wishes if that's the way she wanted to play things.

He sighed and took the slightest sip of his drink. "If that's what you'd prefer. But we're going to run out of small talk at some point. And you can only do so much observation and analysis."

She leaned over the table, resting her elbows on the surface. "Let's discuss some fun things then," she suggested.

"Fun?"

She nodded with enthusiasm. "What does the man I'm working for do to have fun?"

The man she was working for. He wanted to correct her description of him. He'd been so much more than that the other night, hadn't he? But again, he would respect her wishes. He would play her small-talk game.

"What do you do outside of work, Reid? Do you have any hobbies? What happens when you finally have some free time and want to enjoy yourself?" She paused to take a sip of her drink. "And who do you spend that free time with?"

So, that's what this was about. She was asking if there was a woman in his life. Celeste wasn't as unaffected by their mutual attraction as she pretended. A selfish part of him couldn't help but feel pleased. And if that didn't make him self-centered, he didn't know what would.

He took another swig of his rum and focused his gaze on her face. "Celeste, I believe you're asking me if I'm attached to anyone. Do I have that right?"

Celeste wanted to kick herself. She was usually much more subtle. In her defense, she hadn't realized that she planned to ask him that question. It had just come blurting out of her lips. Now it was too late to take it back.

"Just trying to learn more about you, that's all."

He flashed her a knowing smile. "All right, I'll bite," he stated. "I don't have much time for hobbies. But when I can get away, I enjoy a good getaway to the mountains for downhill skiing. In warmer climates, I'm an avid scuba enthusiast. Been certified since my teens. It's one of the reasons I started looking into the Caribbean as an investment opportunity."

So he was going to start with the less loaded questions. Then again, maybe he wouldn't answer her last question at all. Served her right. His personal life was none of her business, not really.

What did it matter that they'd lost control with each other on a couple different occasions? They'd simply both been carried away by the romantic setting and the adrenaline rush afforded by all the activities they'd done together. The strong possibility was that he probably had several girlfriends. He probably dated someone different in every city he traveled to. That was the impression she'd first gotten of him when they'd met three years ago at Jack's introduction. As a matter of fact, she distinctly remembered a conversation about which lucky lady Reid would bring to the wedding as his companion. Her bridesmaids had certainly fallen over each other trying to get his attention. She'd thought it rather amusing at the time. Not so much now. Now that he could also count her as one of the many females who had a thing for him.

They were interrupted by another server who appeared with a platter of cold shellfish. Everything from oysters, to clams, to chilled lobster garnished with lemons and capers sat on a bed of ice. Simultaneously, a sommelier appeared with a bottle of red wine and handed the cork to Reid. He simply nodded at the man after taking a small sniff. Another bottle of white wine was also placed alongside the table in a standing silver bucket sweaty with condensation.

Good thing she hadn't eaten all day. This was only the first course. Not that she had much of an appetite. Her frazzled nerves were wreaking havoc on her stomach.

Think of this as a straightforward business meeting.

Her own words mocked her. The way Reid looked in his suit and the romantic mood of the setting made that darn near impossible.

She vowed to try. "I've never been scuba diving," she

said, resuming their conversation after the servers had left. "I do ski occasionally. Nothing more than bunny trails. That's all I have the courage or the balance for, I'm afraid. I'm not much of an athlete." Unlike him.

His gaze dropped to her shoulders then traveled down and Celeste had to suppress a shiver of awareness. "If you don't mind my saying," he began. "You're clearly quite fit."

It was downright silly to feel as giddy as she did about that compliment.

"I do a lot of yoga. It helps center me. I started in college." Thank goodness she had. Between the stress of her job, the long hours, and the continuous mess that was her family life, she needed the release and quiet peacefulness of the practice.

"Makes sense." Reid offered her one of the lobster tails. "I've never tried it, but I hear some of the poses can be very physically demanding."

"Oh, yes. Definitely. Some of the more challenging ones can have me breathless with my muscles screaming and sweat pouring over my skin while I hold the pose."

"Sounds athletic to me."

She shrugged. "I guess."

He leaned back in his chair, studied her. "You do that a lot, don't you?"

"Do what?"

"Discount yourself. What you're capable of."

His statement surprised her. "I—I didn't realize I did."

"You were certain climbing the falls was going to be too much for you. Yet you handled it just fine."

"I had you there to guide and catch me."

He ignored that. "And the way you disparaged your karaoke performance."

Now he had to be teasing her. "Do you blame me? I sounded horrible. Pitchy and completely off key."

"Is that your takeaway from that night?"

"It's the truth! Please don't pretend I have any talent whatsoever as a singer."

"No. I won't."

She had to laugh at that quick response acknowledging her lack of singing ability. "Thank you."

"Does that mean you should never sing karaoke?" he asked with all seriousness. Celeste was beginning to wonder if this might be one of the most vexing conversations she'd ever had. To top it off, they were supposed to be talking about *him*.

"I dunno. I might say that's exactly what it means."

"You'd be wrong. You may be bad at singing. But you're great at karaoke."

Okay. Now he was making zero sense. "Uh… Come again?"

"You were magnificent up there when we sang together," he declared.

Magnificent? "Um… I was?"

He nodded with zero hesitation.

"How do you figure?"

"You were engaging and endearing, despite being scared out of your mind. Most important, you had the crowd entertained. Off key or not, they were with you through the whole song, some singing along. Others simply bouncing to the beat of the song."

Huh. Had that really been the way that whole scene had played out? She'd been so nervous, all she'd thought about was getting through the song and fleeing off the stage.

"I was?" she stammered, completely shocked at what he was telling her.

"Yes. You were. Everyone who witnessed it saw how amazing you were that night. Everyone but you."

CHAPTER TWELVE

HE'D IMPLIED THAT he found her amazing. Celeste couldn't seem to get that thought out of her head. They'd finished their dinner of salt fish and grilled vegetables moments ago and were now on the upper deck of the boat admiring the star-filled night sky and the tranquility of the Caribbean waters as they sailed over the surface.

For a conversation that had started out all about Reid, he'd certainly given her a lot to think of about herself. All her life she'd been told that she wasn't enough, that she had to try harder, be better, simply to be enough. Her mother certainly found her lacking. As did her younger sister. Her fiancé had left her emotionally bruised and publicly humiliated.

Yet here was this charming, enigmatic man trying to tell her the exact opposite—that she didn't give herself enough credit.

They'd carried their wine goblets up with them and Celeste took a sip of her drink as she admired the view. The band due to perform was setting up a few feet away toward the stern as she and Reid stood portside. They couldn't have asked for a more perfect evening for a dinner cruise. She couldn't deny that she was enjoying herself. Despite the somewhat awkward start to the evening, she and Reid had managed to lapse into an easy state of camaraderie and friendly conversation. But she couldn't get some of the things he'd just said about her out of her mind.

"You appear to have drifted off. Penny for your thoughts?" he asked, not looking away from the horizon.

Celeste gave a small shake of her head. "Just admiring the beautiful evening, I guess."

It occurred to her that he still hadn't answered her earlier question. This time, she'd take a different approach. "You were worried the other night about missing someone who was due to fly onto the island," she ventured. "Were they upset that you weren't there to greet them when they arrived?"

Perfectly innocent question. But maybe it would give her some kind of hint as to his relationship status. But Reid only shook his head. "No, they were perfectly understanding."

That told her absolutely nothing about who he was supposed to meet that night. Maybe a more direct approach was necessary after all. Though heaven knew she should just drop the entire matter altogether. But she couldn't seem to let it go.

Reid gave her a chance at an opening with his next question. "So, tell me. Is there no one at home upset that you aren't there with them to celebrate the holidays?"

"Not really. What about you? Is anyone unhappy that you're here, essentially working through the holidays?"

He smiled at her. "You first. I don't consider 'not really' much of an answer."

She blew out a long sigh. "Yes. My mother and sister are upset that I left the city for the holidays. But they're upset for all the wrong reasons." Celeste fought to find the exact right way to explain. She didn't particularly want to get into the whole matter of her family and all their dysfunction. It would only spoil the evening.

"I don't understand," Reid prompted.

"Christmas wasn't particularly a joyous occasion for me as a child. I grew up with a single mother who couldn't always make ends meet. Most years, she would have to work over the holiday, she usually waitressed. And I'd end up having to babysit my younger sister, who was usually upset and cranky that Mommy was gone and she was stuck at home with just her sister. Not much celebrating happened."

He'd turned to face her fully, listening intently to her every word.

"So, you see," she continued. "Christmastime wasn't exactly festive to begin with."

"And then your Christmas wedding happened," he supplied for her.

"Or didn't happen, to be more accurate. There's really nothing I find celebratory about it. Better to just take off for several days of fun and sun."

He reached for her hand over the railing, held it gently in his. "I'm sorry, Celeste. You didn't deserve that. Any of it."

Oh, no, they were not going to discuss Jack. Not here, not now. "Don't be!" she quickly countered before things headed in that direction. "I'd say I'm lucky. Nothing wrong with spending the holidays in paradise on a tropical island."

He looked less than convinced but didn't push. "Your turn," she prompted.

Reid let go of her hand and took a sip of his wine. Was it wrong that she wanted to reach for him again?

"No. My parents split wasn't terribly amicable. My mother's active with a lot of charities that ramp up their activity during the holiday season. And my father is in Aspen currently to spend the holidays skiing with his newly found love, a woman he left his wife of thirty years for."

"I see," was all Celeste could manage in response. For all the people the world over who looked forward to Christmas every year, there had to be just as many who dreaded it. "I'm sorry too, Reid."

He gave a small shrug. "No need. I have plenty that keeps me occupied during the holidays. The hospitality industry doesn't exactly slow down at Christmas. If anything, things are even busier. Then there's all the effort still required to clean up the mess made by Father's recent business decisions." He lifted his glass in mock salute before taking a long swig.

The resentment in Reid's voice was as clear as the starry sky above them.

"So, I guess you and I are a lot alike in many regards," he added, taking another sip of cabernet.

"How so?"

He turned to her once more. "Isn't it obvious? It appears neither one of us will be reveling in yuletide cheer anytime soon."

This conversation was becoming way too heavy. Reid shook off the melancholy that suddenly threatened the atmosphere between him and Celeste. He took the opportunity of a passing waiter to unburden them of their now empty wineglasses. Enough deep talk for now.

The band had finished setting up and began to play a reggae version of "Holly Jolly Christmas." The happy tune immediately lured several couples up and onto the dance floor.

"You think your foot might be up to a dance?" he asked Celeste.

At her somewhat hesitant nod, he gently took her by the elbow and they joined the other dancers. The tempo was just bouncy enough that they could sway easily to the beat. "I see you have yet another talent, Mr. Evanson. Consider me impressed with your footwork."

"Mother insisted on years of dance lessons. Said I needed to be cultured," he answered over the loud music. "You're not so bad yourself."

He couldn't recall going dancing with a woman and actually enjoying himself this much. Celeste seemed to be able to bring a level of energy and fun to whatever she was doing. It was infectious. The dance floor grew more and more crowded as the band started the next number. Celeste was a natural, her movements fluid and in tune with the music. He noticed several pairs of appreciative male eyes on her and reflexively stepped closer. Their bodies brushed against each other as they both moved. Hot, sharp need seared through him every time they made contact. When the band launched into a much slower song, Reid didn't give himself a chance to think. Her wrapped his arms around her and pulled her tight up against him. She didn't protest or make any effort to pull away. Thank the gods for he wasn't sure if he'd be able to let her go.

One of the band members began to speak through the mike over the music. "We're going to make sure everyone has a good time tonight," he announced to responding applause and cheers. He went on, "I hear there are a lot of couples here celebrating."

More cheers sounded. "Raise your hands if you're here to celebrate an anniversary."

Several sets of hands went up.

"How many of you are here on your honeymoon?" The bandmate asked.

Another round of hands responded along with raucous cheers, including from the young blonde woman and her companion who were dancing right next to them.

Celeste gave the couple a warm smile. "Congratulations," she said over all the noise around them.

"Thank you!" The woman responded with a grin. "We got married two days ago." She wagged a finger between him and Celeste. "How long have you two been together?"

"Oh, we're not—" Celeste began.

Reid decided to spare her the awkwardness. "We've known each other for about three years," he answered truthfully. The lady didn't need to know the details.

"That's lovely!" the other woman declared. "We only met last year. But it was love at first sight, you know? We've been inseparable ever since. When it's the right person, you just know. All the signs are there. I had no doubt he's the man I'm meant to spend my life with the moment I met him."

Her spouse nodded enthusiastically in agreement next to her as they continued to dance.

"That's really wonderful," Celeste said, her tone wistful enough that Reid instinctively pulled her closer against him.

"Thanks! I hope we're having as much fun in three years as you two are together."

Celeste seemed to deflate in his arms. He figured she could use a drink. "Why don't we head below deck for some refreshments?" he suggested.

She didn't hesitate, following him off the dance floor and to the bar down the starboard steps. He ordered them more wine once they were seated on the bar stools. But once their glasses arrived, Celeste didn't so much as take a sip. She merely rubbed her finger around the rim, deep in thought.

Reid cursed the loss of the easy companionship they'd been enjoying before running into the newlyweds. He could only guess what Celeste was thinking. She was wondering if she'd ever have what that couple had. If she'd experience the thrill of a honeymoon, or dancing with her new husband above deck aboard a dinner boat cruising over the Caribbean waters.

It was the strangest thing, but he was thinking along those same lines for himself. Definitely not something he'd ever considered before. He shook off the useless thoughts. He already had his hands more than full. Between the family holdings and his father's self-destructive behavior, Reid didn't have it in him to commit to any other kind of relationship.

His gaze fell on the woman sitting next to him.

No. He couldn't even go there, couldn't allow himself to think those thoughts. Celeste had been hurt enough in her lifetime. The last thing she needed was someone like him toying with her affections further.

But they had the rest of this trip. At the least, they had the rest of tonight. There was nothing wrong with enjoying each other's company.

Though Celeste looked far from joyful at the moment. He would have to do something about that. He couldn't have her this forlorn. The evening was much too beautiful to let it go to waste. They were the only people downstairs at the bar, with everyone else still at the dance party above.

He stood and took her by the hand. "Here, follow me." Acknowledging the sole bartender, he walked her behind the bar and led her to the kitchen area behind it.

Several cooks and servers waved as they entered. Reid walked over to the freezer in the center of the room and reached inside.

Celeste blinked at the carton he'd pulled out. "Ice cream?"

"Chocolate."

Her confusion grew into a wide smile. "Where do we find spoons?"

Five minutes later they stood at the hull of the boat with his jacket thrown over Celeste's shoulders and the wind blowing around them, spooning chocolate ice cream straight out of its container.

She didn't want the night to end. And it was just silly to think that way. It wasn't as if she and Reid were walking back to her room after any kind of real date. Foolish, really.

Reid's suit jacket still hung over her shoulders, the smell of him enveloping her, reminding her of the way it had felt to be in his arms on the dance floor. Not to mention, all those other times when they'd been alone.

A shiver ran over her skin. He must have noticed. "Are you still cold? I can call for a beach cart to drive you back to your room," he offered.

No. That wasn't what she wanted. She wanted to continue walking with him, to delay the inevitable. When they would part for the night. What then? Reid didn't mention any other activity he wanted her to attend, no other excursions were planned. For all she knew, this was it.

There would be no more opportunities to spend any time alone with him. Celeste felt an ache of pain in the center of her chest.

"I'm actually enjoying the night air. Thank you for walking me back."

"What kind of gentleman would I be if I left you to head back to your suite by yourself?"

"The kind that serves a girl chocolate ice cream on the hull of a boat during a dinner cruise?"

He laughed at that. The rest of their stroll continued on in pleasant silence, the night air balmy and comfortable. Celeste indulged in a slight fantasy and just let herself pretend. Just for these few short moments, she would make believe that she had what that couple on that boat had. That she'd found the man she was meant to be with and had known right away. And that, fanciful as it was, Reid happened to be that man.

Never mind that her reality was the complete opposite. By contrast, the one time she'd been engaged, it had been a mistake of epic proportions. And with Reid... She sighed. She honestly didn't know the true reality when it came to Reid. He was obviously attracted to her. But what did that mean when he was so quick to step back from her before things could go anywhere? The answer should be obvious, she figured. He knew they had no business being together, so he wasn't going to let things get too far. Wise of him. Unlike her, he was thinking straight.

Maybe she was done with having to do the wise thing, though. Maybe this one time she wanted more. Even if it was just temporary. It might shatter her inside afterward when it all ended and she had to leave, but in her heart she knew it would be worth it.

She just had to know. Without giving herself a chance to think, she blurted out one of the questions that had been on her mind. "I know it's getting late. Do you have to rush to get back? Is someone waiting for you?"

He turned and lifted an eyebrow in question. "What?"

"You were due to meet someone that day when we got stranded at the flower garden. You appeared upset to have to miss them. Are they waiting for you right now?"

The eyebrow lifted ever so higher. "My spirits supplier?"

She clasped a hand to her mouth. "Oh. You were due to meet your spirits supplier that night?"

He nodded once. "That's right. Who did you think it might have been?"

Celeste felt heat rush to her cheeks. Well, at least now she knew. And she couldn't help the sense of relief and giddiness that washed over her at the newfound knowledge. But it had all come at a price. Reid was on to her. He'd be stupid not to have figured out what she was getting at.

They'd reached her building and made their way to her door on the second floor. Celeste turned to face him, not even sure what she was going to say. The only thing she was certain of was that she wasn't ready to walk through that door just yet.

Her heart hammered in her chest as Reid stepped closer to her. She felt the wooden door up against her back as the warmth of his body seeped into the front of hers.

"Why did you want to know?" he asked on a strained whisper.

Her nerves completely on edge and with Reid standing so close, it was hard to think of an answer. The truth. She would go with the truth. She was done with the pretenses. "I think you know why."

"Spell it out for me, Celeste. I don't want to jump to any conclusions here."

Celeste sucked in a deep breath for courage. She was really doing this. "Go ahead and jump. You'd be correct."

Heat darkened his eyes and he visibly stiffened.

And then she couldn't take it anymore. Moving fully up against him, she slid her arms around his neck and brought her face up to his.

It was all the invitation he needed.

He hauled her tight into him and crushed his mouth to hers. He tasted of wine and chocolate and pure, unfiltered male. It was a taste she would never get enough of. The scent of him rushed her senses. His hands moved over her hips and up to her rib cage. All the while, his mouth continued pleasuring her lips, his kiss growing deeper.

"Reid, yes," she managed to whisper against his mouth.

She'd never been so wanton, so in need. But that was the only way to describe the state she was in. She *needed* this man. She needed his arms around her, and to have him hold her all night. And there was no reason not to give in to that primal desire.

Not for this one night, anyway.

Morning would come soon enough.

CHAPTER THIRTEEN

HE WAS GONE.

Celeste could feel his absence without even having to open her eyes. He must have left her bed in the middle of the night. Tears formed behind her lids and she opened them slowly to glance at the bedside clock. Just past midnight. There was no way she would be getting any sleep. Her body felt languid, the heat of Reid's touch still lingered on her skin. He'd brought her to a feeling of euphoria she'd never experienced before.

It was highly unlikely she would ever experience it again. Her eyes stung further before she shoved the sorrow aside. She was a big girl; she'd made her decision and would learn to live with it somehow.

A shadow moved outside on her balcony.

Celeste rubbed her eyes to make sure she wasn't seeing things. A surge of hope shot through her chest when she looked again. Reid hadn't left, he was standing on her balcony, arms draped over the railing, staring out at the ocean in the distance. He was still here. But everything about his stance told her that something was off.

Celeste stood and walked to the closet where the terry cloth robe hung on a hanger. Throwing it on, she took a deep breath. If she was smart, she'd go back to bed and feign that she was still asleep. But something about the rigid set to

Reid's back, the way his head hung forward, called to her. She just had to hope he wanted her to go to him right now.

Well, she was about to find out.

Sliding the glass door open slowly, she stepped out onto the concrete in her bare feet.

"Hey, there," she said softly.

He didn't turn to her. "Sorry if I woke you."

"I awoke on my own. Weren't you able to sleep, either?"

He shook his head. "Happens sometimes."

"I thought at first that you'd left."

"Would you like me to?"

Her answer was immediate. "No! Don't." *Please stay*, she added silently, hating herself for the despair flooding her insides at the threat of him walking out right now.

He simply shrugged. "Okay."

Okay? That was all he was going to say?

She sucked in a breath. "Would you like to be alone?"

He remained silent so long that Celeste was convinced he wasn't going to answer her. Which was answer enough in itself, she figured. But then he finally turned to her, reached for her hands.

"No. I've been alone long enough. Stay with me."

She wouldn't allow herself to look too deeply into his words. They'd just been intimate with each other, as close as two people could get. And heaven help her, she only wanted desperately to be back in his arms again, snuggled up against him in her bed. The next time she woke up, she wanted to be nestled in his embrace with his warmth surrounding her body.

Right now, she stepped into his open arms and let him hold her. After several moments, he exhaled deeply and turned her to face the ocean, her back up against his front.

She could feel his chest rise and fall with each breath he took. His strong, muscular arms held her tightly around her waist.

"It's beautiful out there, isn't it?" he asked, his breath hot up against her ear.

She nodded under his chin. "The whole resort is a sight to behold. You've really done well here, Reid."

He continued, "It's times like this when I wish I could simply take it all in and just enjoy this place. Rather than worry about how it's run. Or if we'll turn enough of a profit. It's all just so new."

He had a huge burden on his shoulders, she knew. She hadn't realized just how heavily it all must have weighed on him.

"I wish there was a way I could help."

"You are helping. You're helping me put the marketing plan together to help sell this place. I couldn't have asked for a better contractor."

Celeste tried not to bristle at the reminder that she was essentially his temporary employee. He had to see her as more than that after what they'd just shared.

Or was it simply wishful thinking on her part to think so?

"I'll do my best, Reid. But something tells me you would have figured out the marketing approach with or without me."

He turned her to face him then, dropped a soft kiss along the base of her neck. Red-hot desire had her shuddering all over. It was quite a marvel how the smallest peck of a kiss from him could make her insides burn with want.

"I'm glad it was with you," he said then took her lips in a hungry kiss. "So very glad."

Any thought of profits or marketing strategies completely fled her mind as soon as his lips touched hers. Her only focus was the man holding her, kissing her, making her *want*. Her arms instantly went around his neck as his hands found her skin underneath the robe.

The next instant she was lifted off her feet and carried inside.

Where he set her further aflame.

Reid woke up to find Celeste sprawled over his chest. She was still sound asleep. Her breath was hot against his chest, hair spread out fanlike over his skin. He took the opportunity to run his fingers over their silken strands, remembering the way he'd thrust his hands through them last night and the way she'd melted in his arms over and over again.

Morning had come all too soon. A glance at the tableside clock told him that it was much later than he usually started the day. Alex was probably wondering where he was.

Yep, reality had dawned just as clearly as the morning sun. He couldn't shove it aside any longer. Unwilling to let her go just yet, he pulled Celeste ever so slightly up against him. They would have some talking to do later. Though he had no real idea where he would start the conversation. He couldn't risk mucking it all up by trying before he'd even figured things out.

He had nothing to offer her. His world was hotels and resorts and meetings and investments. And somehow consoling his betrayed mother. Not to mention preparing for the fight he was certain was coming from his father. Dale Evanson wanted to regain control of the company he'd almost run into the ground. And he had enough cronies on the board who were ready to help him get what he was after.

A woman like Celeste had no room in her life for so many complications. Especially when she had enough of her own to contend with. Oh, and there was that whole former-fiancée-of-a-good-friend thing hanging above their heads, as well. He couldn't let himself forget that.

Yeah, reality could land a real kick to the gut sometimes.

Reid swore softly under his breath and made an effort to gently remove himself from bed without rousing her. She stirred but didn't open her eyes. It took a few more tries before he was able to disengage out of their embrace. He reached for his shirt and pants lying over the back of the leather chair. He had to go start his day. He would have to leave her a note or try calling her later.

But there would be no need to do either of those things. Celeste slowly opened her eyes and sat halfway up. She looked so alluring with her hair in complete disarray and her lips still swollen from his kisses. He could see the minor redness on her shoulders and around her chest where he'd rubbed his beard over her skin. He had to close his eyes to keep from crawling back into bed and joining her once more.

"You're up."

He nodded. "I have to get going. There's a lot happening today." *On and off the resort*, he added under his breath.

"Does that mean breakfast together is out of the question?" The look of longing in her eyes nearly undid him. He had to hold firm.

"I'm afraid so. I have one meeting after another." Starting with the business partner who was probably wondering where the devil he was at this very moment.

"I see."

He leaned over the bed, brushed a soft kiss across her temple. "You go back to sleep. No need for both of us to leave the warmth and comfort of the bed."

"It's not quite as warm anymore," she countered.

Reid ignored that, just turned to throw his pants on. Then he pulled his shirt over his shoulders. He had to turn away, if he continued looking at the enticing picture she made—with the sheet pulled up over the roundness of her breasts—he wasn't sure how much resolve he could muster. He wasn't made of stone, after all.

"I have to get you my written recommendations," Celeste said behind him as he sat in the chair to tie his shoes. "I've already got most of it written up on my tablet. I can use the business office to get it all printed once I finish."

"No need to do that," Reid threw over his shoulder. "Would you mind sending it via text? As an attachment. I'll look at it when I get a chance."

She sat studying him as he finished the last knot and stood. "Sure. I can do that," she answered.

"Thanks. I'm really looking forward to seeing what you have to say."

"Reid…"

"Yes?"

She opened her mouth but shut it again without speaking. Instead, she dropped back onto the pillow behind her and flung her arm over her face. "Never mind. It's not important."

Reid fought the urge to go to her side and indulge in another kiss, this time to her lips. But it would be dangerous to risk tasting her again. The sooner he walked out of this room, the better for both of them.

"Bye, sweetheart," he said and pulled the door open.

She didn't answer before he walked out.

She had no one but herself to blame.

Celeste turned the nozzle of the shower to the very end of the hot setting, allowing the punishing heat of the water to wash over her until she could stand it no longer. It did nothing to scorch away her internal anguish. What had she been expecting? To spend the day with Reid holding hands and walking along the beach? She'd understood last night exactly what she was getting into.

The fact that she was hurt and disappointed by the way he'd left this morning was no one's fault but her own.

She'd been naive, fooling no one except herself. She knew how ill-equipped she was for meaningless flings. She'd gone ahead and spent the night with Reid anyway. Worse yet, she'd fooled herself into thinking she could somehow conveniently forget that she'd fallen for him. It had only been a few days since she'd arrived on the island and run into him again. But it was like the newlywed on the dinner cruise had said last night—when you're with the right person, you just know.

Celeste just knew.

Though they hadn't been on the best of terms three years ago when she'd first met him, she'd noted Reid's determination and quiet strength. How hard he seemed to work as chairman of his family business. He'd always been a good friend to Jack, coming through for him with countless errands to help with the responsibilities of the would-be groom. Of all Jack's friends, it was only Reid whom she'd grown to admire.

And the time she'd spent with him these past few days had grown that admiration into so much more. Celeste bit back a sob.

She stayed under the spray until the water turned cold and her skin started to prune. Then she made herself take a deep breath and shake off the useless, defeatist thoughts. Celeste Frajedi had learned long ago that the best way to overcome any stumble or setback was to keep busy and work hard. Stepping out of the stall, she toweled off, threw on shorts and a tank top, then ordered coffee and breakfast from room service. Then she pulled up her tablet and got to work. She had a marketing report to complete.

CHAPTER FOURTEEN

HER SCRAMBLED EGGS sat cold and untouched an hour later when Celeste started putting the final touches to her write-up. Though the entire pot of coffee was gone. The next pot she ordered could be enjoyed relaxing on the balcony and watching the beach scene outside, now that she had the file mostly completed. And she'd done a good job with it too, if she did say so herself. There was a part of the report that could prove risky. A professional should never allow personal feelings to affect a business project, but she'd decided to take the chance. There wasn't much left to lose.

The ring of her cell phone pulled her focus.

Reid.

Her hand immediately reached for the device. Without stopping to glance at the screen, she immediately clicked the answer button, didn't even care how anxious she'd appear at having answered so quickly.

She was wrong. The voice that greeted her over the line was a husky feminine one. The first words spoken were slurred.

"Hope you're having fun lying on the beach while the rest of us are stuck here."

Her mother.

Celeste tried to clamp down on the alarm rising within

her core. This was twice in a matter of days. Wendy's problems appeared to be escalating. So far, this was turning into one sucker punch of a day.

"Hello, Mother. Is something the matter back at home?"

Her mother grunted in clear disgust. "Better believe there is."

An icicle of fear dropped into Celeste's stomach. "Is everything okay with the baby? What is it?"

"The baby's fine," her mother huffed. Celeste allowed herself a moment of relief before her mother continued. "Your sister needs to start looking for another job, ya know."

Celeste grasped for patience. What she did know for certain was that Tara wasn't in any rush to do any kind of job search. Especially now, mere days away from Christmas. "Mother, please tell me why you're calling. You said something was wrong."

"I'll have you know they're threatening to shut off my power. It's below freezing here. Not like that sunny, warm place you're at. And they're gonna try to cut my heat off."

Alarm tightened Celeste's muscles. "What? Why?"

"I don't know. They're saying the bill wasn't paid."

"Are they saying that because it's true? Did you neglect to pay the bill?"

"I don't remember."

"Just send the check out now. Pay it as soon as you can."

"I got nothing to pay it with, do I?"

Celeste rubbed a weary hand over her forehead. Her mother's account must be seriously overdue for the utility to be threatening to shut off supply. Which meant Wendy hadn't paid the bill for several months.

"Momma, I deposited more than enough money in

your account to cover all the expenses and utilities." And she'd done so consistently every month. "Why didn't you pay the bill?"

A muffled sound echoed from the tiny speaker. Was that a sob? Celeste's earlier alarm turned into an icy brick of fear in the pit of her stomach. "I kept trying to win the money, Celeste," Wendy said on a loud hiccup. "And I came so close, but then the table would turn the other way." There was no doubt now that Wendy was indeed crying.

"Have you been gambling?"

Another hiccup followed by a sniffle. "I was just tryin' a get some money to buy the baby some extra-special Christmas presents. Wanted to do it on my own, without help from nobody."

Celeste leaned back in her chair, her surprise almost too much to contain. Her mother had actually wanted to feel the pride of getting her first grandchild a holiday gift without asking for money from anyone else. Mainly her.

Celeste couldn't help but feel touched. But Wendy had gone about it in an oh-so-wrong way.

One thing was clear. Her mother needed to get help. It couldn't be put off any longer. Not only did her occasional alcohol benders seem to be growing more frequent, she now ran the very real risk of acquiring a gambling addiction, too.

"Mother, stop crying. I'll take care of the electricity bill, okay?"

"Th-thank you," Wendy was no longer trying to hold back the wails. "I didn't want to freeze."

"You won't. And we'll be sure to get Nat a wonderful present when I get back, okay? But you have to stop trying to win the money."

"Okay."

"Promise me, Mother."

"I promise," Wendy answered, and another loud sniffle followed.

Celeste squeezed her eyes shut and counted her breath for several beats after her mother hung up. It took some time, but finally her pulse started to slow and some of the tension left her midsection. She would need a full and long meditation session soon to try to take the edge off her frayed emotions. Given her day already, the session would have to be a marathon one.

She had so much to take care of once she returned to New York City.

But first things first. Saving the document she was working on, she switched browsers and called up her mother's electricity bill. The sum in arrears made her gasp. It was a wonder the electricity company hadn't shut her off already. With resignation and sadness, Celeste transferred the amount out of her own checking account to cover the debt.

This was her truth. Her reality.

Incidents like this were the reason she shouldn't have forgotten herself last night. Worse, they were the reason she should have never let herself fall for a man like Reid Evanson in the first place. Why hadn't she learned her lesson the first time?

For his reality was so very different from the one she lived in.

Alex made a show of glancing at his watch when Reid finally made it into the office later that morning. Reid braced himself for the inevitable ribbing that was sure to be headed his way.

"Yeah. I know I'm late, partner. How about giving

me some slack this one time, huh?" he asked, his arms spread out and his palms up.

Alex rubbed his jaw. The serious playacting he was attempting was severely undercut by the quiver of a smile at the corners of his mouth. "I don't know, man. I mean, you've been the one out enjoying yourself on all these various excursions with a beautiful woman by your side who you say is 'helping you.'" He added air quotes with his fingers as he spoke the last two words.

Reid had to groan out loud at the mention of Celeste. Alex noticed, of course. He immediately turned serious.

"What's happened?"

He really didn't want to get into any of this. Not ever. He didn't want to discuss Celeste at all. In fact, he didn't even want to think about her. Because doing that would undoubtedly tempt him to seek her out and drag her back to her room where they could run a replay of last night.

Just. Stop.

It was a risk he couldn't take.

"Nothing happened," he fibbed to his business partner. "I just overslept." That part was at least the truth.

Alex's eyes narrowed on him, clearly questioning whether to accept his answer as the whole truth. Reid knew he was too sharp and would see through it without effort. He was right. "I can't recall another time you've ever overslept."

"It was bound to happen sometime."

Alex gave a slight shrug of his shoulder. "Suit yourself. Don't tell me, then."

"What did I miss around here?" Reid asked, in a blatantly obvious move to change the subject.

Luckily, Alex was going to play along. "The usual," he answered. "A few minor guest complaints. The tennis pro asked that the courts be redone. And we're running low on chardonnay."

Reid gave him a nod. "Got it. I'll go make some phone calls." He pivoted toward his office.

"And then there's your father," Alex called out after him.

Reid stopped in his tracks and turned back to face his friend. "What about him?"

"He's been calling the office all morning. Says he got tired of leaving you messages on your cell just to have you ignore him."

Of course his father would say that. The truth was, Reid had given him every opportunity to change the course of the disastrous path they currently found themselves on.

"How's that whole thing going anyway?" Alex asked.

"About as well as can be expected. He wants full control of the company back." What made it so much worse was that Reid knew his father was ready to retire. The only reason he was doing this was to please his new bride-to-be.

"Any chance of that happening?" Alex wanted to know.

Reid shrugged. "He has some cronies on the board who are ready to vote as he wants." Reid would risk an all-out battle before he let that vote go his father's way—if it ever came to a vote.

Alex let out a low whistle. "Hostile takeover attempts can be brutal under any circumstances."

"Let alone amongst family," Reid finished his thought for him.

"I'm here if you want to talk," Alex said to his back as Reid walked into his office.

Once there, with the door shut, he finally let out the full brunt of the frustration he'd been feeling since leaving Celeste's bed this morning, by launching his priceless signed Red Sox vintage baseball across the room. It hit the wall with a loud thud and sent chips of paint flying.

Great. One more thing to have to fix. This time, he'd done it to himself.

If Alex heard the noise outside in the foyer, he was too astute to knock and ask him about it. Not that he ever actually knocked.

The angry calls from his father served as a reminder that he was right to leave Celeste this morning without lingering any further the way he'd wanted to. He'd so badly wanted to. The right thing to do was to leave her alone.

It wouldn't be easy, and it would take a great deal of effort, but eventually, he might even stop thinking about the way she'd felt in his arms last night.

An internal voice immediately mocked him. *Yeah, right.* He'd be thinking about her touch for the rest of his natural life. He could only hope to stop missing her at some point during it. Forty or fifty years apart might do it.

But she deserved to be able to move on. He didn't have the right to stand in her way.

He was going stir-crazy in this office. Reid cursed and threw his pen down on the desk blotter so hard it bounced off and landed on the carpet. He had to get out for a while. There were a dozen more calls to be made. Several documents to be signed and countless emails to answer. But he couldn't concentrate. Before the start of this week he might have boasted about his superior focus skills. It didn't help that he kept checking his phone to see if Celeste had sent him the text yet. As of three minutes ago, she had not. The short time frame didn't stop him from checking yet again. Nothing.

Not from her, anyway. By cruel contrast, his phone was buzzing with texts and voice mails left by his father.

He stood up and stormed out of his office. The desk attendant in the concierge area smiled at him when he approached. "Reid. I was just about to come knock. Someone left a file for you."

She handed him an envelope. He removed the papers within. Celeste's report. But she was supposed to have sent it electronically.

"How long ago was this dropped off?"

"Just a couple of minutes. The young lady used the business office to print it then dropped it off here. She said you were expecting it."

She couldn't have gotten far. Reid knew he shouldn't do it, but he found himself following the path she would take if she were to head back to her room from the concierge lobby. The least he could do was thank her.

The mocking voice reemerged. As if that's the reason you're trying to catch her.

He saw her moments later on the path by the kiddie pool. She stopped to retrieve and toss back an inflatable ball to a toddler when it rolled by her feet. The action stalled her long enough for him to catch up.

"Celeste." She froze.

"Reid?"

"Hey." He lifted the envelope in his hand. "Thanks for bringing this by."

"The text I attached it to kept bouncing back. The file must have been too big."

That explained the printout. He could release any notion that she might have come by the office hoping to run into him. He should have discounted that possibility in the first place. She had left it for him at the counter after all.

"Oh. Thanks for taking the time to print it out, then." How many times could he thank her in one conversation? He had no reason to be this tongue-tied around her. He had to get a grip already.

"You're welcome."

The toddler threw the ball back at her. Celeste flashed the child a bright smile and tossed the toy back once more.

"I'm looking forward to reading it," he told her when she'd turned back to him.

"I hope it helps."

"There's still the matter of your compensation. I can have papers drawn up—"

She held a hand up before he could continue. "That won't be necessary. I won't accept any type of payment from you."

A boulder settled in his chest. Part of him was convinced she'd take him up on the free annual vacations. That he would at least be able to see her again once every year. Though he'd feel gutted every time she left. "I don't understand. I don't feel right having you do all this work for nothing."

The ball landed between their feet again. They both turned to find the same toddler boy giggling.

Come on, pal, Reid thought, groaning inside. This was hard enough without a toothless lothario intent on a game of catch with his woman.

His woman?

He cleared his throat. "I'd like to talk about this."

She gave a slight lift of her shoulder. "If you wish. Sure, we can talk. But I won't change my mind."

Reid quickly took her by the elbow and led her to the poolside cabana bar before the beach ball reappeared. Celeste allowed him to guide her onto one of the stools. He motioned for the bartender and ordered two rum punches. He never drank during the day when he was working. But this was an extenuating circumstance if ever he'd encountered one.

He'd missed her. It had only been a few hours since he'd left her this morning. But he couldn't deny that he'd spent those hours wishing she was still by his side. He missed her smile, her wit. The way she smelled.

"Tell me why," he said once their icy drinks had arrived.

Celeste took a swig from her paper straw and his gaze immediately fell to her lips.

"I thought we had an agreement," he added.

"I've changed my mind. Consider it professional courtesy on my part. As your resort guest."

So that's all she was going to classify herself as. He had no business being disappointed. He wanted this distance, didn't he? It's why he had fled her room after the night they'd spent together.

For such a hot, pleasant day, they were the only two people seated at the bar. The bartender was busy at work several feet away with his back to them organizing bottles and tidying.

If they were a real couple, Reid might take the opportunity to kiss her.

His cell phone started to vibrate in his shirt pocket before he took that thought any further. He quickly removed the device and set it to do not disturb, ignoring the risk of missing an important business call. And if it was his father calling yet again…well, he'd had enough of his father's interruptions for a lifetime.

"I don't mind," Celeste said, pointing to his phone on the bar. "You can answer that, if you want."

"I don't want."

She lifted an eyebrow in question. "Oh?"

Reid blew out a deep breath. "I'm in the middle of something rather unpleasant. It involves my father. He wants to talk about it. Only there's nothing left to talk about."

"Ah." Celeste took another sip of her drink. "If it makes you feel better, I wish I hadn't received a call from my own parent this morning."

He laughed. "Yeah?"

"Oh, yeah. It was a doozy."

"Maybe we'll have to compare notes on our parents someday."

She ducked her head, suddenly serious. "I'd rather not."

"Tell me something," she asked, not meeting his eyes.

"Yes?"

"You said before that you and Jack didn't talk at all about me after we broke up."

Where was this all leading? Reid had no idea. He only knew that the reminder that she'd once been engaged to another man had his gut tightening. He really had no desire to talk about her ex-fiancé. "That's right."

"What about before the breakup? You two must have talked about the woman he was about to marry."

He shrugged, still confused about the direction this conversation had taken. He'd sat her down to try to convince her to accept payment for her hard work.

"What did he tell you about me, Reid? Did he say I was just after his money?"

He hadn't seen that question coming at all, wasn't sure how to answer. If he thought hard about it, Reid would have to admit that Jack had in fact insinuated that very thing. "Celeste, what's this all about?"

She took another sip from her straw, looked away toward the crystal-blue water of the pool. "See, he would have been right to say so if he did. It's the real reason he left me."

CHAPTER FIFTEEN

CELESTE COULDN'T REALLY say if her intention had been to shock Reid. But it sure looked like she'd done just that.

She hadn't had anything to eat all day, just that pot of coffee this morning. And the rum punch was so much stronger than any drink she was used to. Combined with the confusion that seeing Reid always seemed to bring forth within her, the alcohol had gone straight to her head and loosened her lips.

Reid suddenly stood. Dropping several bills onto the bar, he picked up his cell phone and the report. Then he gently nudged her up out of her stool.

"Let's go."

Celeste followed without question. The cat was out of the bag now. Might as well get everything out in the open.

He led her to a rental cabana that must not have been reserved for the day and pulled down the privacy flaps. A shiver of apprehension ran down Celeste's spine when he turned and fixed his gaze on her.

"Care to explain?" he demanded.

She dropped down onto the padded lounger and studied her toes. "I didn't grow up with any money, Reid. Unlike the way you and Jack grew up."

"Don't make assumptions, Celeste."

"What does that mean?"

But he wasn't going to allow the switch in topic. "Never mind. We're talking about you."

She let out a deep breath. "Why do you think Jack decided he couldn't go through with the wedding?"

"He got cold feet. It happens."

She laughed without any real mirth behind it. "He got cold feet because my mother and sister made no secret of the fact that they were very excited about how rich he was. They acted downright giddy."

Nausea roiled through her stomach at the memories. There'd been times when Momma had come right out and asked Jack about his net worth and how much he was willing to part with to help his future in-laws.

The humiliation had been unbearable.

She sucked in a deep breath. "Jack insisted we needed to get away from my mother and sister, starting with the wedding. Hence the desire to elope—so they wouldn't be there. He also suggested we consider living on the West Coast afterward. To stay far away from them."

"You said no."

"In no uncertain terms. I'm all the family Tara and my mother have. There is no one else. I couldn't just turn my back on them."

Reid remained silent, simply waited for her to continue.

"So Jack can't really be faulted for walking away, can he?" she asked. "I can't really blame him."

Reid crossed his arms in front of his chest as he analyzed her. "Is that what you really think?"

She could only nod silently, still staring at her toes.

"What about the fact that he waited until the last minute to do it? Or how cowardly it was to leave you waiting there with a church full of guests? Can you blame him for any of those things?"

"I'm not saying he's a saint. I'm not defending him. And I'm not defending my mother and sister. I'm just saying I understand why he did it."

"No, you're just finding ways to blame yourself. For the cowardly way he treated you. For the way your family members treated you. None of which had anything to do with *you*." He emphasized the last word with heavy inflection.

Suddenly, anger and frustration flooded her chest. She hadn't confided in him to be scrutinized or lectured to or somehow analyzed.

"Spare me the empty platitudes, Reid. I'm not telling you any of this to garner some sort of sympathy or for your pity."

"Then why did you tell me?"

"So that you know why I can't keep coming back here year after year. Seeing you again. That part of the deal is absolutely off the table."

She sucked in a labored breath. "And there's absolutely no way I'll take any money from you. I just wanted you to understand why."

She brushed past him and rushed through the canvas flap before he could see how close to breaking down she really was.

He didn't try to follow her.

Celeste hadn't stopped shaking by the time she reached her room and slammed the door shut. Her gaze immediately fell to the bed, bringing forth haunting and erotic images of all that she and Reid had shared the night before. How foolish she had been to fall in love with a man who was so terribly wrong for her. Her heart felt heavy and bruised in her chest. Like someone had struck a physical blow. She didn't know if the ache would ever heal.

Her breakup with Jack had been a hard hit to her ego. The loss she felt now felt like an open wound, one she might never recover from.

But now wasn't the time to dwell on any of that. She had a call to make. With shaky fingers, she reached for her phone and clicked on her mother's contact icon.

Wendy picked up after several rings. "Did you pay the bill?"

Not even a hello. Why was she even surprised?

"Momma. Listen to me. There's something very important I need to explain to you."

Celeste didn't give her mother a chance to protest. She just calmly and distinctly went over the decisions she'd recently made. Then she clearly explained the steps she planned to take in implementing them all.

Her determination must have rung through clearly in Celeste's voice because her mother didn't argue. In fact, Celeste thought she might even have heard a tinge of relief in Wendy's voice.

The perfect setting to fall in love...speaking from personal experience...

Reid reread the same passages from the file Celeste had turned in yet once more. He'd lost count how many times he'd already read them. As a marketing plan, she'd handed him pure gold. Her suggestions were sound, and many of her ideas could justifiably be described as brilliant. But those were the only lines he cared about.

She'd made it personal. And she was telling him she'd fallen in love with him. He was glad he'd made it back to his living quarters before taking the time to read her report. Something had told him he should be alone while looking at the file, someplace he wouldn't risk being interrupted. Finally putting the papers down, he walked over to the wet bar across the sitting area and poured himself a generous amount of aged dark rum.

She loved him. It said so in black and white. Written by her hand.

Lord knew he didn't deserve it. That he fell far short of the type of man someone like Celeste was worthy of. So now the only question was what was he going to do about it?

He downed the rum all at once, felt the satisfying burn of the spirit travel down his throat. It did nothing to ease his inner turmoil.

He'd called her ex a coward earlier today in the beach-side cabana when he'd pulled her in there after her so-called "admission." He had to examine whether he was the one being cowardly now. Was he going to let her walk off this island in a few short days and out of his life for good? Or was he going to be as brave as she was? The woman had fearlessly laid it all on the line by putting her feelings into words that the whole world was meant to see.

He wasn't worthy of such a selfless act done on his behalf. But he'd been bestowed with it nonetheless. He couldn't walk away. He would find her, and they would determine once and for all how to move forward. Together.

He had so much upheaval in his life right now, had no guarantee what the future held if this deal didn't work. His father was hell-bent on bleeding the company dry. He could only hope the board saw that fact and sided with him.

Because damned if he hadn't just realized that he'd fallen in love with her, too. He needed to tell her so. It was only right. He needed to follow her example and be as courageous as she was. He also needed to take her into his arms and make sure she understood that he was never going to let her go.

But first, a shower. It had been a long, grueling day that had left tension knotting in his shoulders and back.

Reid couldn't help the smile that tugged at his mouth as he walked to the bathroom and turned the water on. In a few short hours, if all went well and he could persuade Celeste to listen, he'd be holding her and kissing her again. That had to make him the luckiest man in the universe.

He realized all too soon that the universe had other plans.

Reid's phone lit up like a Christmas tree when he left the shower fifteen minutes later. With a chest full of trepidation, he returned the call to the number that had been trying to reach him for the entire time he'd been bathing.

One of his lawyers.

This was not a good sign.

The attorney answered on the first ring. "Bad news, Reid. We're going to need to do some damage control or you run the real risk of reverting all control back to Dale."

"I take it my father has managed to push through a vote?"

"You'd be right. You need to fly down to Boston first thing."

Reid disconnected the call and cursed the fates he'd been so sure were smiling on him just minutes before.

He tapped out Celeste's number on his screen but she didn't answer. His intended message wasn't the kind a man left on voice mail. He would have to try to get a hold of her later.

Right now, he had a flight to book and packing to do.

Celeste tried to focus on the same book she'd been try-ing to read ever since she'd arrived on the island. She'd barely gotten through the first couple of chapters. As gripping as the plot was, she couldn't seem to find herself immersed in the story.

She was much too distracted wondering whether Reid had read the file yet. There seemed to be no good conclusion. If he hadn't looked at it yet, what exactly was he waiting for? Why was he putting it off?

And if he had read it but wasn't reaching out to her... That scenario was the more heartbreaking possibility.

Well, she'd done all she could. She'd laid herself bare. Both with what she'd written and everything she'd told him in the cabana earlier. There was nothing more of her to expose to the man. Regardless of his ultimate reactions, she vowed to never regret her decision to do so.

She needed something to take her mind off him. The book wasn't cutting it. Celeste reached for her phone and dialed her sister's number. The gurgling, happy sounds of her baby niece would be like Uma's balm to her injured soul.

"Hey, Tara," she spoke into the phone when her sister answered. "How are you?"

"All right, putting up Nat's first Christmas tree. She's very confused about why there's a tree in the house. And why I'm hanging shiny things off its branches."

Celeste had to laugh at that. Maybe her little niece would be enough of a reason from now on to stay in New York for the holidays in the future. "I really miss the little tyke."

"She misses you, too."

"Can you put her on the phone? I just wanna hear her make noises for a bit. Maybe get her to say CeeCee again."

Her sister laughed. "I think you imagined that. She

is not trying to say your name already. She's only nine months old."

"I heard it loud and clear that day!" she exclaimed with a laugh.

"In any case, I'm afraid she's down for a nap right now."

"Oh. That's too bad." Celeste wasn't prepared for the depth of the disappointment she felt at the news. She really had missed the little girl, hadn't realized exactly how much until now.

Tara paused a beat before continuing. "You sound sad, sis. What is it?"

A sensation of warmth blossomed in her chest. She and Tara had their differences...what siblings didn't? But they somehow always knew how to read each other and tried to cheer each other up when it was called for.

"Nothing. And everything," she admitted.

"Does 'everything' include Ma?"

"So, you heard huh?"

"Yeah, she called here right after you told her. She knows it's the right thing to do. For what it's worth, I think you did the right thing, too."

Celeste sat upright on the bed. "You do?"

"Yeah. She's gotten bad. Doesn't pay attention to how much she's spending or what she's spending it on. She needs someone else to take charge of her finances. It might curb her drinking, too. Which also seems way out of hand lately."

"I set up an annuity for her," Celeste explained. "She'll get a certain amount every month as spending money. But I'll be the one in charge of her expenditures. And she has to agree to register for an addiction counseling service."

"I think that's wise." Tara hesitated before continuing. "Along those same lines, I've also been meaning to thank you. For setting up that trust for the baby. You know I appreciate it, right? And she will, too."

"I know, Tara."

This conversation was getting way too heavy. Celeste decided to change the subject. Though the next topic wasn't such a light one either. "How's the job search going?" she asked, knowing there couldn't be much of one.

Tara audibly sobbed into the phone. "Tara? Are you crying?" Not Tara, too! What was it with her family and all the waterworks today?

She heard a sniffle. "Maybe."

"What's wrong?"

"I just can't take it, sis. Those office buildings, sitting in those cubicles. It's not me. I feel stifled and caged. But office work is the only thing I'm qualified for."

Oh, dear. Celeste had no idea her sister felt that way. How had she never thought to ask? What kind of big sister did that make her?

None of which had anything to do with you.

Reid's words echoed in her head. He'd been right. This was about Tara, not about herself. She needed to find a way to separate herself from the needs of her family.

"What do you want to be qualified for?"

Another sniffle. "I don't know. But remember all those pictures I used to take before that camera Uncle Zed got us finally broke?"

The question invoked a vague memory in her mind. But apparently, the camera had meant a great deal to her sister. "Yes."

"I really enjoyed taking those pictures."

"You did?"

"Yeah, I did. And I was good at it, too. But you know how Ma is. She told me we didn't have the money to replace the camera. And that it was a stupid waste of time anyway."

That certainly sounded like their mother. Celeste had been so focused on her own treatment at her mother's hands, she'd completely missed the negativity that Tara had grown up with.

The answer came to her without question. "Then it's about time we replaced that camera, Tara." She told her sister. "And maybe we can find you a class that can show you how to take even better photos."

Her sister's gratitude came through loud and clear in her cheer of delight. "That's always been a dream of mine," Tara squealed into the phone. Again, Celeste had to wonder why she was first hearing this now.

"Careful," Celeste warned. "You'll wake up the baby."

Tara laughed. "I should probably go check on her. But just one more thing, sis."

"What's that?"

"I don't know why you sound so sad, you're on vacation in paradise, after all. But you deserve to have your dreams happen, too."

CHAPTER SIXTEEN

You deserve to have your dreams happen, too.

Tara's voice still echoed in her mind the following morning. Celeste showered quickly then quickly got dressed and threw on her sandals. She fled out the door before she could change her mind. Step one in pursuing a dream was to have the courage to ask for what you wanted.

She wanted Reid.

Unlike the previous days since her arrival, this morning's sky was cloudy and gray. The air was thick with muggy moisture. She would guess a rainstorm was headed their way soon. Hopefully, the weather wasn't any kind of ominous sign regarding what she was about to do. When she reached the concierge level, she made a beeline straight to Reid's door. She had to do this before she lost her nerve.

Her knock went unanswered. She tried again with the same result. A pleasant male voice sounded behind her. "Can I help you with something, Celeste?"

She turned to face Reid's smiling, handsome business partner, Alex.

"I, um, was looking for Reid."

"Maybe I can help you."

She quickly shook her head. "I don't think so. I did some work for him, I just wanted to get his feedback on it." She had to tell the lie. She couldn't exactly divulge to Alex the real reason she was here. Kind eyes or not.

"Ah, right."

She shifted awkwardly. "Do you happen to know when he'll be in today?" she asked, knowing she sounded anxious and impatient but unable to help it.

"I'm afraid he won't be in at all today. I actually don't know when he'll be back. He flew out to Boston earlier this morning."

Celeste would have sunk into the floor if she didn't have an audience. Reid had left. Without so much as a goodbye. He hadn't even tried to find her first.

Alex continued to speak. She barely heard him over the pounding in her ears. "But I know he's read your file," he told her. "I'm sure he'll email you his comments in due time."

Celeste felt as if the wind had been knocked out of her lungs. Reid was going to email his comments. She'd laid her heart out on those pages. And he didn't think enough of that to so much as try to talk to her about it. He'd run off. Just like Jack had done on the day of their wedding.

Ridiculous as it sounded, Reid's betrayal felt like the bigger one by far. She'd recovered from Jack's desertion. She knew the same wasn't going to be possible this time.

She did her best to summon a smile for Reid's friend. "Thank you. I'll look for it in my inbox."

She could do so on her way to the airport. Looked like she would be cutting her trip short. She no longer had any desire to stay.

Or to ever come back again.

In his anxiousness and relief to be back in Jamaica, Reid exited the town car almost before the vehicle had come to a complete stop in the circular driveway of the Baja Majestic.

This had to be the quickest trip he'd ever taken to Boston and back. He usually booked at least one night at the Evanson Premier Boston Harbor hotel before taking a morning flight the next day. But he'd had no intention of sticking around the city this time. Once the confrontation with his father was over, he was more than ready to fly back to the Caribbean. Back to the resort he'd called home for weeks now. Back to Celeste. They had quite a bit to work out between them.

Though confrontation wasn't exactly the correct term for the meeting he'd had with Dale. Reid had arrived at Evanson Properties headquarters just in time to head off a vote of the board of directors. The clear relief on the expressions of the twelve executives told him the vote could have gone either way.

After that, he'd made sure to finally have the one-to-one with his father that he'd been avoiding for so long. It had taken Celeste to help him discover his avoidance had been more personal than business. He had yet to thank her for that.

In the end, Dale had seen reason and agreed to a limited role as a company president. Another weight lifted off Reid's shoulders, though he and his father had a long way to go before their personal relationship could begin to mend.

All in due time.

Nodding to the doorman, he passed through the sliding doors into the Baja Majestic lobby, gratified that several guests were milling about, ready to check in. So far, the holiday season could officially be called a success. Celeste's marketing plan would only help once it was implemented. Yet another thank-you she was due.

He stopped at the counter and removed his sunglasses. "Sanya, please deliver a cart with our finest champagne and a variety of desserts to Room B717."

The woman behind the counter smiled and started clicking at the computer keyboard in front of her. "Right away, sir." Her smile suddenly flattened with confusion. "Is that the correct room, Mr. Evanson?"

"Yes. Is there a problem?"

She returned her gaze to the monitor screen. "Our system says the room is empty, housekeeping is in there now. The guest has already checked out."

Reid felt all the excitement he'd experienced only moments before extinguish like a blown-out flame, replaced with a pounding sense of disappointment and hurt.

She was gone.

If she kept busy enough, and took on enough projects, she could almost push Reid Evanson out of her mind for several minutes at a time. The only problem was, the days between Christmas and New Year's didn't exactly bring in a lot of business activity. Still, Celeste made it a point to go into her Upper East Side office in every morning to find ways to keep herself busy. Never mind that she was one of only a few people there. Most of the other employees were out preparing to celebrate New Year's Eve.

So far, she'd gone over all her deliverables for the new year, and then she'd gone over them again. She'd studied past successful campaigns to analyze what had worked and why.

She'd even cleared out her inbox and organized her paper files via a new method. Today she figured she might tackle cleaning out the break room.

Despite the relatively empty floor, a flurry of noise

drew her attention from outside her door. What was that all about?

The commotion drew closer to her door. "Ho-ho-ho!"

She stood from her desk and opened her door. Someone dressed as Santa appeared to be approaching her office. Celeste rubbed at her temples. How had this guy gotten past Security? There were no children's daycares or anything of the sort on this floor. Not to mention Christmas was already over, thankfully.

"I think you're lost, Santa," she addressed St. Nick, her phone in her hand ready to call Security if need be.

His response was to reach for his jaw and pull down the pretend beard and mustache—to reveal the face she'd been dreaming of since she'd left Jamaica all those days ago.

"Reid?"

"Hi, sweetheart."

Celeste had to brace herself against the wall at her back. She couldn't be seeing or hearing any of this. She must be having some kind of *A Christmas Carol* hallucination or dream. Tiny Tim would pop out any minute now.

She blinked and rubbed her eyes. But Reid still stood there. As real as the hammering of her heart.

"What are you doing here?" she stammered out.

"I had an emergency business trip to make right before the holiday. As soon as I successfully wrapped it up, I realized I didn't get a chance to wish my lady a Merry Christmas."

His lady?

"You flew out here just to wish me a Merry Christmas?"

They'd drawn the attention of the few other people who'd come into work. Her colleagues were staring at them in astonishment. Two of the women looked like they were dabbing at their eyes.

"I did," Reid answered her, walking closer until he stood mere inches away. How did the man manage to look sexy in a bulky Santa suit, for heaven's sake? It took all her will not to throw her arms around him and nuzzle her face into his neck. She'd missed him so much, still couldn't believe this wasn't some fantasy or dream she'd be waking up from any minute now.

"Oh, I also wanted to give your Christmas present. Didn't get a chance to do that, either."

He reached inside the pocket of his red fleece pants. Then shocked her to her core by pulling out a velvet box and dropping to one knee.

Flipping the top over, he revealed a sparkling diamond ring surrounded by dazzling ruby red stones. He'd been thinking of the black-and-red dress she'd worn the night of the dinner cruise. There was no doubt in her mind.

Celeste had to remind herself to breathe.

"Celeste Frajedi. You're unlike anyone else I've ever known."

Her voice shook as she tried to answer. "I am?"

"Without a doubt. I would call you the most generous person I've ever met. And I'd like to call you my wife." He took her shaking hand in his. "Will you marry me?"

She couldn't stand any more. Literally. Celeste felt her knees give out and Reid caught her as she dropped to the floor in front of him.

"Yes!" She'd barely gotten the word out when applause and cheers erupted all around them.

"I can't believe this is happening," she said over all the noise. "I can't believe that you're really here."

"I am, sweetheart. And I want to promise you that I'll

do everything I can to make sure each Christmas we celebrate together is more festive than the last."

That settled it. Her tears would not be contained any longer. The love she felt for this man overflowed through every part of her being. "Oh, Reid."

"It's like a wise newlywed once said…" He laughed, taking her in his arms and hugging her tight. "When you know you're with the right person, you just know."

Celeste knew. Just as she knew that the holidays would hold magic and happiness for her once again.

* * * * *

THEIR UNEXPECTED CHRISTMAS GIFT

SHIRLEY JUMP

To a Christmas I will never forget, with the man who makes every day better than the one before. Here's to many, many more!

Chapter One

Have a Holly Jolly Christmas!

Nick Jackson stood under the banner draped across the center of Main Street in Stone Gap, and debated sign sabotage. The entire town was in the process of getting decked out for Christmas. Elves—or rather, Department of Public Works employees in silly costumes festooned with bells—were on stepladders, draping garland over the street lamps. Shopkeepers were pasting images of fat Santas and fake snowflakes in their windows. Others were piping holiday tunes from their sound systems a full three days before the first day of December.

When Nick was young, he'd loved Christmas as much as any other kid, even though his parents hadn't been the traditional kind who woke up at dawn and had a pajamas-on-the-couch Christmas morning. They'd believed in dignified holidays, with practical gifts like suits and calculators. But for a kid of three, or five, or seven, the world still held magic and promise, and anything could happen. By the time he hit middle school, Nick had given up on miracles.

Until then, Nick had woken up at the crack of dawn every Christmas morning, then dragged his brothers Carson and Grady out of bed. He'd sat on the stool at the kitchen bar, fidgety and anxious and dreaming of finding something cool under the elegant, professionally decorated Christmas tree, like a race car or a skateboard. The three boys would wait through an interminable breakfast served by the cook, who shuffled around the kitchen and grumbled under her breath about being underpaid to make pancakes on a holiday morning.

Then their parents would wake, and there'd be a quiet, five-minute exchange of whatever sensible present had been chosen for the boys. Books, savings bonds, dress shoes. No Legos. No remote control cars. As holiday after holiday passed, and Nick began to realize there would never be one of those cozy family-by-the-fireplace scenes in the Jackson household, he'd told himself that when he was grown and out of his parents' house, his life would be different. He'd have the white picket fence, the Labrador and he'd flip pancakes for his kids himself every Sunday morning. He'd dreamed of that first Christmas, with all its perfection of a lazy morning by the tree. He'd even started filling in the image with his girlfriend, Ariel, and had been on the verge of proposing—up until she'd dumped him for his best friend.

The next day, Nick had hopped a plane to Stone Gap, North Carolina, to bury his grandmother and figure out what the hell to do next. After the funeral, he'd found out that Grandma Ida Mae had left Grady the house, and Nick and Carson each a nice sum of money. So he quit his job and stayed in Stone Gap, without a mustard seed of an idea of what he was going to do next. He had an inheritance to rely on once he decided, but that came with a few strings that Nick hadn't wanted to tackle yet.

After a month of scotch and self-pity. Della Barlow, owner and main chef at the Stone Gap Inn, got sick and left the kitchen understaffed. Nick had ended up taking her place temporarily, pinch hitting for Della and winning over the guests with his béchamel lasagna and lighter-than-air pancakes. By the end of that week, Nick had finally figured out what he wanted to do with his life at thirty.

He could have gone for another job in IT—he was certainly qualified for it, after several years working with his brother Carson at Tech Analysts. Somehow he'd slipped into a life of building computer security systems and analyzing hacker threats. Actually, it wasn't a somehow—Nick remembered the exact day he'd hung up his apron and toque and called Carson. The fight with his father, the confrontation when Richard Jackson found out his son had been lying about law school for over a semester.

The job with Carson was always supposed to be a

temporary measure, a stopgap, until Nick could save enough to go out on his own as a chef. One year had turned into two, had turned into four, and then he'd met Ariel, and leaving seemed like a bad idea. His cooking skills had gotten rusty, and he'd started to think he was too old to start over with a pipe dream. Until he'd found himself in the kitchen of the Stone Gap Inn. As the whisk turned wine and flour into a velvety sauce, his love of food returned. After she returned from being out sick, Della had offered him a job and Nick Jackson had had a purpose again, at least until he was done avoiding his life.

For now, he would be content to avoid the holiday season. He just wasn't quick enough.

"Hey, Nick! I forgot to say have a Merry Christmas!" Matty Gibson, the owner of Matty's Market, stepped out of the shop and gave Nick a wave. He was a tall guy, lean and lanky and with a balding dome hidden beneath a faded Atlanta Braves hat. Nick had heard that Matty had made it to the major leagues when he was only twenty, then tore his rotator cuff with a windup pitch that first spring training and had to leave before he played an actual pro game. He'd come back home to Stone Gap and eventually took over his father's grocery store downtown.

Nick worked up a smile of sorts. Could it at least be December before everyone started in on the holiday celebration? "Yeah, you too."

"So what are you making with all that stuff?" Matty nodded toward the paper sack. "I can't remember the last time anyone bought one of them jars of artichokes.

In fact, I don't think I've ever eaten an artichoke, jarred or otherwise. I only ordered them because Sadie down at the Clip 'n Curl said they're her favorite, and well, have you seen Sadie?"

Pretty much everyone in Stone Gap knew Matty had a crush on the owner of the hair salon. He'd asked her out twice, but she'd said no both times. As Matty told it, he had a bit of a reputation as a player, and Sadie wanted a steady man with a future. No amount of convincing had made Sadie change her mind so far about Matty's reliability as a boyfriend, but that didn't dissuade him one bit.

"I'm making a braised chicken with artichokes and cherry tomatoes," Nick said. "Nothing fancy."

Matty laughed. "Well, you use words like *braised*, and it sure sounds fancy. You have company coming or something?"

"Nope. Just me. There's no one staying at the inn tonight, so this is my dinner." He hadn't made any real friends in Stone Gap, just a lot of acquaintances. And that list included no one that he knew well enough to invite over to his room at the back of the inn. So tonight it was just him and the artichokes.

"Lot of work for one person." Matty shook his head. "Me, I usually just throw in a frozen pizza, kick my feet up and watch the game. These days, that's all I can do is watch the game." His gaze went to the distance, then he shook it off. "Anyway, you enjoy. See you around."

Nick said goodbye, then stuffed the bag of groceries in the cab of his truck. As he pulled away from downtown, he noticed the temperature had dropped since this morning, with winter taking as firm a hold as it could in North Carolina. It rarely got cold enough for snow, which was just fine with Nick. He'd had more than enough of below freezing temperatures when he lived up north. Plus, adding snow would just put the cap on *Holly Jolly* and he didn't need that.

Nick parked behind the inn, where a single door led into the kitchen, and his room, just to the left of the airy, sunny space. He supposed he could have texted and asked Grady, who had been the one to inherit the two-story, if he could live at their grandmother's now-empty house, but it had been easier to just stay here at the inn and settle into the small space that didn't hold any memories or connections to anyone else in his life. Bah humbug.

Okay, so yeah, maybe he sounded like Ebenezer Scrooge. All the more reason to just stick to his own company until at least January 1. Keep his head down, be alone and avoid human contact as much as possible.

Especially contact with his family. Grandma Ida Mae had left Nick a note in the package containing her will. A note he had read and set aside. What she wanted was too much to ask right now. Maybe ever.

An hour later, he'd stowed the groceries, done the few dishes from that morning and straightened the pillows in the front room. After a busy week for Thanksgiving, the renovated antebellum house was almost empty for the next two weeks, and then the Christmas rush began. Della had taken the opportunity to go away for a few days, leaving Mavis Beacham, her business partner, and Nick in charge of the inn.

As far as Nick knew, the only people currently staying at the inn were one elderly man who was visiting his daughter and grandchildren in town and two women who had shown up with a baby early yesterday. A blonde and a brunette, around his age. The brunette he'd only glimpsed a couple times, but she was one of those stunningly beautiful women whose presence lingered long after she left the room.

Nick hadn't talked to them, and they hadn't been social either, asking that their meals be left outside their door, and except for the occasional cry from the baby, the women had been pretty quiet. He made a mental note to ask the women if the baby needed any special foods. He assumed it was still drinking formula or whatever, but considering all that he knew about kids could be written on a grain of rice, Nick figured it didn't hurt to ask. There was some age when babies graduated to stuff like mashed bananas, right? Maybe the kid had already hit that milestone.

He had a couple hours until it was time to start his dinner. The women had asked for a late checkout today, and Mr. Grissom had already left to spend the afternoon and dinner with his family, which left Nick alone at the inn. Mavis would be in tomorrow morning, and they'd talk about the week's plan after breakfast. He liked that his life had settled into a routine of meals, cooking, cleaning, then rinse and repeat.

Nick stepped into the shower in the tiny bathroom attached to his room. The hot water eased the tension in his shoulders. By the time he turned off the tap, he was fit to be good company for himself. Just as he was stepping out of the shower, he heard a sound from the kitchen. It wasn't uncommon for guests to stop in and help themselves to a snack—free run of the kitchen was included in the price of the room—so the sound didn't worry him. He slipped on some jeans, threw on a T-shirt and thought he heard the front door of the inn shut with a soft snick, then the crunch of car tires on the crushed shell drive.

Nick took a few more minutes to comb his hair and tidy the bathroom before he ambled out to the kitchen. As he did, he heard a soft sound that began to grow louder by the second. It took him a moment to figure out that it was crying. And that the sound was coming from a small white basket sitting on the kitchen table, flanked by salt and pepper on one side and a cheery flower-patterned place mat on the other.

Correction—a white basket with a pink blanket and underneath the blanket…

A crying baby. An honest to God, miniature human. On the kitchen table. On a Sunday afternoon.

He hadn't seen the baby the women had checked in with yesterday—he had heard it cry only once in a while and had gotten a description secondhand from Mavis, who'd pronounced the baby the "cutest thing in the whole county," but he assumed it had to be that baby. It wasn't like babies rained down from the sky. At least, not in North Carolina.

But there was no one else in the kitchen. No one down the hall. No one at all.

He remembered the sound of the front door, the tires on the curved drive. He lingered in the kitchen, a few feet away, and waited. Surely they'd be right back.

But the door didn't open. The baby kept on crying. Not an ear-piercing wail, but more of a stunned, snarfling cry.

"Hey!" Nick called out to the emptiness. "Your baby is here!"

No answer. He grabbed the basket, holding it as delicately as a nuclear bomb, and dashed down the hall. He called up the stairs. "Hey, uh…ladies?" If Mavis had told him their names, he'd already forgotten them. "You forgot the kid."

Nick ran up the stairs, two at a time. His footsteps echoed in the empty house. He stopped at the Charlotte room, where he knew the women were staying, and knocked on the closed door. The door, which hadn't been shut entirely, swung open with a soft creak. "Um, just letting you know that your kid is downstairs. And seems…upset? Hungry? Wet? I don't know, but you should probably check on…um…her." Given the pink blanket, he figured "her" was probably a safe guess.

Silence. Nick peeked around the door, but saw nothing. Just the empty room. Which was pretty odd since he'd seen them check in with two sets of luggage.

It seemed pretty unlikely that they'd checked out and forgotten both a bag *and* a baby, no matter how much of a rush they were in. He returned downstairs, half expecting to see one of the women in the kitchen, apologizing and looking for the kid. But there was only the baby in the basket with him—crying louder now.

He bent down and tugged back the edge of the blanket. "Hey, there. What are you doing here?"

Even crying, she was a cute baby. Pink in her chubby cheeks, bright blue eyes and a flutter of blond curls on her head. Not that Nick had a lot of babies to compare this one to. In fact, the last time he'd been this close to a baby had been at his cousin Deanna's house three years ago on Easter, with his aunt Madge hovering over her "miracle" grandbaby like a helicopter. And even then, he hadn't gotten close enough to do much more than say congratulations, and back away before anyone got any ideas about making him do something like actually *hold* the baby.

"Stay here a sec," he said to the baby, who ignored him and kept on crying. Nick made a fast perimeter of the downstairs of the inn—living room, eat-in porch, dining room, den, then bathrooms one and two. No one else was inside the house. Just him and the baby.

"Where are your parents?" he asked the baby. No answer. Not that he really expected one. "Okay, then what am I supposed to do with you?"

Mavis's phone went straight to voice mail. Della didn't answer her phone either, but he didn't expect her to because she and her husband were on a cruise or something. The inn had a computer registry for guests—in Della's locked office. Mavis normally left the keys behind, but a quick glance at the hook in the pantry told him that she'd forgotten to do that today. So he moved on to his last resort. It took four rings before his mother picked up, her voice all breezy and cheery. The country club voice, as false as the Astroturf on the putting green of the back patio of the club. "Hello, Nicholas!"

"Mom, I...have a problem."

"I'm just heading into court. Can't it wait?" The friendly golf-course tones yielded to annoyance and impatience. Nick already regretted making the call, but it had seemed like the right choice. Find a baby on the kitchen table, call the woman who was biologically connected to you and therefore supposedly equipped for this kind of thing. Not that this was the kind of situation that had a guidebook.

He glanced down at the baby again. She'd stopped crying, thank goodness. But at some point she was going to start again, or need to be fed, or changed, or, well, raised into an adult. All things outside of Nick's capabilities. "Uh, no. This is kind of an urgent problem."

"Well, could you call your father or one of your brothers? Actually, your father is doing a deposition and I have this trial—"

"Mom, someone left a baby on my kitchen table and I don't know what to do with it." And his father wasn't talking to him, something his mother conveniently forgot whenever she wanted to pass the buck.

A long moment of silence. "Tell me this is a joke, Nicholas. What did you do? Did you impregnate some girl?"

He scowled. He should have known better. His mother lacked the maternal gene. The thought of her showing motherly concern for a stranger's baby was almost laughable, since the closest she could come to showing concern for her own son was to blame him for all of his problems. Some things never changed. She'd been the least maternal person he'd ever known, and had treated all three of her sons like mini-mes to their father, grooming the three of them to go into the family business of law. To achieve those goals, he and his brothers had been provided with nannies and maids and drivers and tutors, but when Nick had chosen a different path for himself, any hints of warmth or concern for him had vanished. What had made him think his mother would suddenly change in the course of a phone call? "I didn't do anything, Mom. Never mind. Sorry I interrupted you."

"Nick, if you truly have a baby there, call the fire department or something. Legally, you shouldn't touch that child because you could be sued if anything happens. The fire department will know what to do. There are safe haven laws—"

As always, Catherine Jackson went back to the comfort zone of the law. She was right, but that didn't mean he liked the option. "Yeah, thanks, Mom, I'll do that." Nick hung up, tucked his phone in his pocket, then paced his kitchen for a while. The baby stared up at him from her place in the basket, all wide-eyed and curious.

What was he going to do? He supposed he could call Colton Barlow down at the fire station and have him get the baby, the way his mother had instructed. But handing a baby off to someone he only sort of knew, especially at Christmas, seemed so wrong, so…cold.

Surely the whole thing had just been a mistake and the women would be back right away.

The baby's eyes began to water.

Oh God. She was going to start crying again. He poked around the blanket, careful not to disturb the infant, looking for a pacifier or a bottle—anything. All he saw in the basket was the baby and the blanket. The baby stared at him, ever closer to tears. "Hey, sorry. Just checking for a tag or something. Even Paddington Bear had one of those."

But the baby didn't. No supplies. No identification, at least not that he could see in his cursory look. No "if lost, return to" information. The baby started snarfling again and balled up her hands. *Don't cry, please don't cry.* "Kid, I don't have anything for you. I don't even know what to do with you."

The snarfle gave way to a hiccup, then a wail. She waved her hands and kicked her feet, dislodging the blanket, revealing pink socks over tiny feet and baby lambs marching across the baby's onesie.

"Oh, hell." He reached down and grabbed the baby. She was heavier than he'd expected, denser, and when he picked her up, she stopped crying and stared at him. "Well, hey there."

The baby blinked. Her eyes welled, and her cheeks reddened. Nick turned her to the right and did a sniff test. Nothing. Thank God. If there'd been a diaper situation, the kid would have been out of luck. She'd come with no instructions and no supplies. Maybe he should google baby care or something.

Then he saw the corner of a piece of paper, tucked

under the blanket at the bottom of the basket. With one hand, he fished it out and unfolded it. In neat, cursive script, the note said: "Please take care of Ellie as well as you took care of me. I know she'll have a good home with you. Love, Sammie."

Sammie. That was the name of one of the women, he remembered now. Who was the other one with her? Something with a *V.* Or maybe a *K.* Damn it. He couldn't remember.

"Ellie?" he said. The baby blinked at him. "Where's your mom or moms or aunt or whoever it was that brought you here?"

Ellie was holding her head up on her own, which was a good thing, he knew that much. It meant she wasn't brand-new, but also not old enough to make a peanut butter and jelly sandwich, so if he didn't figure something out soon, he was going to have to decide what—and how—to feed her.

"Kid, do you have teeth yet?"

The baby began to whimper. Nick brought her to his shoulder and began to rub her back in a circle. He'd seen someone do that in a movie once, and it seemed the kind of thing someone did to calm a baby down. Within seconds, it worked. The baby stopped crying, but then she did something worse.

She curled against Nick, fisted her hand in the collar of his shirt…and cooed.

"I'm not parent material, kid." Big blue eyes met his. Damn. He'd always been a sucker for blue eyes. "Don't get any ideas."

She kept on staring at him, nonplussed. As babies

went, she was pretty cool. And she smelled like strawberries and bananas, all sweet and innocent. Damn. "What am I going to do with you?"

Just then, the front door opened and the brunette who had checked in yesterday walked into the inn. About damned time.

Nick kept the baby against his chest, grabbed the basket with his other hand and hurried down the hall. With each step, his aggravation with the woman grew. It had been irresponsible as hell to leave a kid alone and drive off, even if she had come back just a few minutes later. At the last second, he put the baby back in the basket, then picked it up and carried it with him. If this woman was the kind of mother who forgot her kid on a kitchen table, maybe he shouldn't give her back without asking a few questions. Or calling the cops. "About time you came back, lady. You—"

"Why were *you* holding Ellie? Where's Sammie?"

Some of his anger derailed as soon as he was face-to-face with the woman. She was just that beautiful in her tailored navy suit and heels. She had her hair back in a bun at her nape, her eyes hidden by sunglasses. She had one fist on her hip, a circle of keys hanging from her finger and an oversize boxy purse in the other hand. For someone with a baby that he guesstimated wasn't more than a couple months old, this woman looked really, really great.

"Where is she? How am I supposed to know?"

Nick grabbed the basket and headed down the hall to the kitchen and set the baby back on the table. "If you're the kind of person who can't keep track of your girlfriend or sister or whoever Sammie is, not to mention your kid, I'm not giving the baby back to you."

The woman ignored him. She barreled past Nick and crossed to the basket before Nick could react. "Ellie! Are you okay?" She pulled back the blanket, counting fingers and toes, acting all concerned.

Nick wasn't buying it. He yanked the basket up and out of the woman's reach. "What kind of mother are you, anyway? And who said you can even touch her? I should call the cops. I found her abandoned on the kitchen table in this basket. Anyone could have walked in and taken her, you know."

The woman put her hands out. "Thank you for taking care of her. Now, if I could just have the basket—"

Nick should have slammed the door in the woman's face or something. But he'd been all discombobulated by the baby on the table, and the sneaking suspicion that he was missing part of the story here. "I'm not letting you leave here with this baby. In fact, I'm calling the cops right now." He unlocked the cell and started pressing numbers. "I've seen *Dateline*, you know."

"I'm not the baby's mother—"

"All the more reason for me to call the cops, babynapper."

"I'm her aunt. My sister, Sammie, is the irresponsible one." She gave the baby a smile, but stayed a solid three feet away. "Ellie knows, doesn't she? I'm your auntie Viv."

Nick tucked his phone away. The two women were sisters, and the baby was this woman's niece. Made sense, but still didn't explain why the baby got left on the kitchen table. "Well, I want to see some ID."

The woman smiled. Holy hell, she had a beautiful smile. Wide and with a slightly higher lift on one side than the other. There was a tiny gap between her front teeth that Nick might have found endearing under other circumstances. "An ID? For Ellie? I don't think they hand out licenses to three-month-olds."

Three months old. Barely a person, which caused a roar of protectiveness in Nick. "Not for her. For you. Prove you're this kid's aunt."

"I can't. I mean, it's not like I run around with an ID saying I've got a niece. A niece I have only known about for twenty-four hours." She sighed. "I checked in yesterday, and you saw me then. Mavis checked my license and took my credit card, and…" Her voice trailed off. She opened her purse, took out her wallet and cursed. "Damn it, Sammie. She must have taken my AmEx when I was in the shower."

"You still have to pay for the room." The words felt way too weak as soon as they left his mouth. *This* was his biggest threat? After Sammie or Viv—a nice name for a woman like her, as if it was short for vivacious— had left the baby behind?

"Of course I will." She sighed, tucked her wallet away, then put out her hands again. "Give me the baby."

So maybe she was the aunt. It all seemed plausible. Her sister was clearly an irresponsible parent. What assurance did he have that this woman would be a better caretaker? Viv looked like a responsible human, but then again…didn't most people? Either way, she was still a stranger, and this kid wasn't old enough to talk, so Nick felt like he had to do some kind of due diligence. "Well, I can't let you leave with her, not until I know for sure that you're her aunt and that you're capable of taking decent care of her."

Viv crossed her arms over her chest. "I'm not going anywhere without Ellie."

They were caught in a standoff. And Nick wasn't going to budge. He looked down at the baby, at those big blue eyes that were so trusting and innocent, and knew he couldn't let the kid down. He'd found her, after all, and like a lost puppy, he was tasked with making sure wherever she went from here was safe and warm and good. The kid—*Ellie*, he told himself—had started to grow on him, damn it, and until he could figure out the right thing to do—

He did the only thing he could think of. "Do you want to stay for dinner?"

Chapter Two

Vivian stood in a stranger's kitchen, sitting beside Sammie's biggest screw-up yet. Not Ellie, of course. The baby was precious and innocent, and smelled like bananas and everything that made Vivian uncomfortable.

If there were two people who shouldn't be mothers, it was either of the Winthrop girls. Viv, whose entire life revolved around her career, and Sammie, her irresponsible younger sister who had dropped out of high school and run away more times than Viv could count. Sammie considered laws to be nothing more than a loose guideline to life, didn't believe in self-control or apparently birth control, and had left her three-month-old on the kitchen table of the inn when Vivian drove to a meeting in Durham that afternoon, then told Vivian by text.

Stupidity of the highest degree.

Vivian shouldn't be surprised. Sammie had never been what people would consider accountable. For anything. She wasn't Vivian's half sister—the daughter of boyfriend number seven or eight, who took Sammie to his mother's house after they broke up, then brought her back and dropped her off when Sammie was nine and "too much of a handful." From that first day when she'd found Sammie crying and alone, clutching a well-worn stuffed bear, Vivian had vowed to protect the girl.

The two of them had huddled in Vivian's bed, clutching each other and made a solemn vow—they would never leave each other. Never. And when they grew up, they would be good moms to their children and pick good dads.

Vivian had tried her best to keep those promises for as long as she could. There had been no kids for her— there hadn't even been any potential baby daddies— but she'd tried to stick close to Sammie, even as the two of them had ended up shuffled through the system like they were candy bars in a snack machine. She'd tried to steer Sammie toward college, or at least a trade, but Sammie had balked at any restrictions, and at eighteen, jetted off on her own, popping in once in a while to drop a bombshell—or, in this case, a practically brand-new baby—into Vivian's lap.

There were days when Vivian was pretty sure she was from another planet. Unlike her mother and Sammie, Vivian had a degree, a career, an apartment and a predictable, responsible life. She'd made a conscious decision not to settle down, not to have kids and to stick to her comfort zone—the law. When she was fourteen, she'd made that crazy promise with Sammie to be a good mother, but at thirty, Vivian knew better. She wasn't mother material. Not even close. So best to avoid all that hearth and home stuff and stick to her career. Except now here she was in a town she hadn't lived in for at least fifteen years, with a baby she didn't know, wondering why she kept cleaning up after Sammie.

This weekend was supposed to be all about bonding, about spending time with Sammie after more than a year since the last time they'd seen each other. Then Sammie had showed up at the inn with a baby in a basket, and said, "Surprise!" to Vivian, and everything had changed.

Vivian knew she should be resentful. But all she had to do was take one look at Ellie's precious sweet face, and she knew why she'd dropped everything and broken the land-speed record this afternoon to rush back to Stone Gap when Sammie texted: I can't handle it. I'm sorry. I left Ellie at the inn. Please take care of her. The little girl hadn't done anything wrong except be born to a mother who wasn't ready.

Sammie's drop and disappear act had created a massive problem for Vivian, though. She couldn't take care of a baby. Not just because she had neither a single mothering instinct nor any practical experience. Vivian had a demanding job. The law firm where she worked called her the "Results Queen" for good reason. There was a trial to prepare for and an apartment in Durham in the middle of renovations. Meanwhile, a baby required around the clock care. Vivian would have to hire a nanny and find a place that wasn't swarming with construction workers for the nanny and Ellie to stay, which would mean one more stranger in Ellie's short life.

"Want some coffee?"

She'd almost forgotten the man was there until he spoke. On an ordinary day, Viv would have noticed a man who looked like that. Tall, lean, dark-haired, with a smile that went on for days, and dark eyes the color of a good espresso. He'd been terribly protective of Ellie, which had frustrated Viv but also kind of endeared him to her. Even now, he hovered over her and the baby, clearly worried and not at all sure that Vivian could be trusted.

"I'd love some." She'd had an emergency meeting this afternoon that she'd tried to get out of, because she'd promised Sammie a weekend together. So she'd zipped up to make a quick appearance at the office, and just as quickly turned around again when the text from her sister came in, and all hell broke loose. Now Viv was going to have to come up with a plan for Ellie between here and Monday morning. "And thanks for the dinner invitation, but I really need to get back on the road."

"With the kid?"

"Well, I obviously can't leave her here," Vivian said as she got to her feet. Maybe she could get an Uber with a car seat, then come back for her own car later. Or call a friend to pick her up. Except she had no friends who weren't as career-driven as she was, and all of them lived at least an hour away. And right now, she was feeling pretty lost about what to do, a position Vivian didn't like being in. The man across from her, though, seemed cool and collected, and good with Ellie. "I… I don't even know your name." Why had she even said that? She didn't need to know his name. It had nothing to do with her getting back to Durham. She should be leaving, now.

"My name is Nick," he said. "Nick Jackson. There. Now I'm not a stranger."

The joke made her smile a tiny bit. Inside, her confidence shook like a sapling in the wind. How was she going to handle Ellie and work? And how would she know what to do if Ellie cried or needed something? Vivian knew her way around a courtroom, but not around an infant.

"I'm Vivian Winthrop. I'm a civil litigator, and Sammie is my irresponsible sort-of-sister who abandoned her baby here. I invited her to the inn for a weekend away and to spend some time with her. Sammie showed up with a baby I didn't know she even had, and then disappeared. Which is typical for her. She's been doing it since she and I were in foster care together."

"Foster care?" He arched a brow. Clearly, those words had put her back in the *reluctant to trust her* column.

"Sammie and I had a…difficult childhood with a mother who was…unreliable at best. It's just been the two of us most of our lives." Vivian fiddled with the handle on her coffee cup, avoiding Nick's gaze. That was about all she wanted to say about that. The less she thought about her childhood, the better. "Anyway, didn't you say something about dinner?"

He grinned. "So you're staying now? I take it you trust me now a little?"

"Well, I'm kind of hungry." She returned his smile and realized it had been a long time since she'd smiled. Her entire career was about being serious, a determined and stubborn bobcat in the courtroom and a moneymaker for the office. She'd risen quickly at Veritas Law based on that reputation, and had won several multimillion-dollar judgments and settlements against major corporations.

Her latest case, though, was more personal. A chance meeting with a man who was working nights as a janitor in the building revealed an injury that had nearly cost him everything. Jerry Higgins used to be a machine operator in a cannery, until a new piece of equipment with a faulty release switch had crushed his arm. The equipment manufacturer refused to cover Jerry's medical bills after the cannery's insurance company decided the equipment was at fault, not the cannery, which had left Jerry bankrupt. It was a step outside the usual lawsuits she worked, where one behemoth sued another, but it was also the first case she'd had in a long time that made her feel good.

Ever since she'd met Jerry, Vivian had slept, ate and lived that lawsuit. Even now, she could feel the need to get back to work. To finish that brief she needed to file, and schedule the next few depositions. Jerry, his wife and his children were counting on her to make it right.

Then she glanced over at Ellie, so innocent, so helpless in that wicker basket, and knew she couldn't go anywhere, at least not until she figured something out for her niece. Vivian might not be mommy material, but she was going to make sure Ellie was cared for. She'd need to call the office day care program and figure out a way to live amid the current chaos of her apartment before she tracked Sammie down. Right now, on top of her already unwieldy and bloated to-do list, "calling the day care" seemed like a Herculean task.

And besides, it was Sunday. She had only a few hours before the clock ticked over to Monday and her life got crazy again. But first, there was dinner with this man who seemed calm and strong, two things Viv wasn't feeling at all. Surely she had enough time to eat.

"I haven't had a home-cooked meal in…forever," Vivian said. "My apartment is under construction right now, not that I ever get in the kitchen and cook. So whatever you were making sounds good to me."

"Well then let me show you what you've been missing." Nick got to his feet and started pulling ingredients out of the refrigerator and a paper bag on the counter. Just then, Ellie started to cry, her fists rising above the blanket and waving in the air. The cries pierced the quiet of the kitchen, demanding, insistent.

Vivian rose and paced the small kitchen. Ellie kept on crying. "Uh, what's wrong with her?"

Nick looked as clueless as Vivian felt. "I don't know. She probably needs a diaper change or some food or something," he said. "Do you have any of that?"

Vivian gave him an are-you-kidding-me look. "Yeah.

I have all of that in my briefcase in the car. Of course I don't have any of that stuff. I'm not a mom, and Sammie didn't send me a grocery list when she texted me. She just said Ellie was here and she had left."

And Vivian had come running, as always. Bailing Sammie out. Again.

"Didn't she have one of those bag things?"

Vivian brightened. "She did have a shopping bag with some formula and a couple diapers. Let me see what she left behind." She ran upstairs and returned a moment later with the nearly empty bag. "One diaper and a mostly empty can of formula. I'm no expert, but that doesn't seem like enough." She sighed. Once again, Sammie had left her older sister to pick up the pieces.

"I know someone who might have some extra baby stuff." Nick picked up his cell and dialed a number. He tucked the phone against his shoulder, started chopping some onions and gestured to Vivian to pick up the baby, whose cry had turned into a wail. "Hey, Mac, it's Nick Jackson. I was wondering if you had some diapers and what do you call it…?"

Damned if Vivian knew. She stood beside the table, hesitant, while Ellie kept on crying. Pick up the baby? What if she did it wrong? What if that only made the crying—which was reaching police siren levels—worse?

Vivian tried tucking the blanket tighter—wasn't there something about burritoing a baby that soothed them?—and it didn't work. She tried sh-sh-shushing Ellie, and the cries only got louder and stronger.

Nick put a finger in one ear. "Yeah, formula. Bottles. Whatever a…" He turned and raised a questioning eyebrow in Vivian's direction.

"Three-month-old," she reminded him. That answer she had, but not much else. Ask her stats—born at three twenty in the morning, six pounds, three ounces, twenty inches long—and she could fill in the blanks. But quiz her on what age a baby started real food or how to change a diaper, and she'd fail in an instant.

The closest she'd gotten to Ellie before this minute was admiring her as Sammie held her. And that was as close as Vivian had intended to get. Until Sammie screwed up again.

"…a three-month-old baby. No, not mine, Mac. It's a long story." Nick paused a minute, then gave Vivian another pick-up-the-baby nod. "Thanks, buddy. I appreciate it." He hung up and tucked the phone in his pocket. "Mac will be by in a little while."

"Mac?" Ellie kept on crying. Vivian kept on standing there, hesitating.

What was wrong with her? If this had been a court case, she wouldn't have paused for a breath. But then, in a courtroom, she always knew exactly what to do. In those wooden rooms, Vivian was at home. While Nick's comfort zone was the kitchen, hers was in that space between the judge's bench and the plaintiff's table. She could deliver a one-hour closing summary to a jury of twelve strangers, but when it came to a single three-month-old…

Well, that was different.

"Della Barlow's son. Della's the co-owner of this

place, along with Mavis—you haven't met Della because she's on vacation right now." Nick walked past her, picked up Ellie and swung her against his chest, as if he did this every day. A second later, Ellie plopped her thumb in her mouth and her cries dropped to whimpers.

Vivian decided to act as if a strange man calming her niece was not at all unusual. Except a part of Viv felt like a failure. Weren't aunts supposed to be able to handle this kind of thing?

"The Barlows are a great family, in case you're worried. I've been the chef at the inn for about a month now, and I've met all of them." Nick had started swaying, a movement that seemed unconscious, and Ellie's eyes began to shut.

"Really?" Vivian felt a little jealous of her niece. Right now, Vivian was in that odd place between uncomfortable and unconfident, and could sure use someone else to soothe her own worries.

"You're so good with her," Vivian said.

"This is about the extent of my parenting abilities. So don't ask me to change a diaper or make a bottle." He chuckled.

If he asked her how to do either of those things, she wouldn't have an answer either. So she changed the subject. "So what are you making me for dinner, Chef Nick?"

"Braised chicken with cherry tomatoes and artichokes." He kept on swaying with Ellie.

"That sounds amazing. You made the eggs benedict we had this morning, right? Those were incredible.

Most of the time I'm eating popcorn or a sandwich grabbed on the run."

"That's no way to live. I think food is one of the greatest pleasures in life."

The way he said that made her a little weak in the knees. Which was insane. Vivian was a practical woman, not one of those who swooned or got caught up in romantic notions. No, that was Sammie, who was the believer in fairy tales and Prince Charmings, no matter how many times she got burned by guys who were more frog than prince—unemployed scam artists who wanted a free ride and a few bedroom benefits.

"Oh my God. Ellie's asleep," Vivian whispered. "How did you do that so easily?"

"I don't know. I just went with my instincts."

Maybe Vivian was lacking the necessary strands of DNA because she had no instincts for babies. Not so much as a blip of an idea when it came to making Ellie happy. Late last night, after Sammie and Ellie had fallen asleep, Vivian had stayed up ordering from some baby website, shipping everything from the "new mom gift suggestions" list she'd found there straight to Sammie's apartment. Baby outfits, blankets and a stroller that cost more than a small bus—because buying things was the only way Vivian could handle being an aunt.

Nick headed toward the kitchen table. Ellie stirred and let out a whimper. "Damn. I have to put her down to cook, but I'm afraid of waking her up."

"We can put the basket in the living room, so the

noise from cooking doesn't bother her. She'll sleep better there."

"I don't know if we should leave her alone, though." Nick kept on swaying. He glanced at the chicken on the counter, then the basket, then his gaze swiveled back to Vivian. Damn, he had nice eyes. And a nice smile. "I'm good with having her in the living room, but I think you should stay with her. Just in case."

That would give Vivian some time to check her phone, go over some emails and maybe kick off her shoes for a second. Then, after dinner, she could call a car seat–equipped Uber, get on the road with Ellie, and come up with a plan.

Because standing in this handsome man's kitchen, mesmerized by the way he calmed a baby to sleep, was sending her mind down an entirely wrong path.

Chapter Three

Nick was not a softie. Nope. Not one bit. And the sight of Vivian curled against a pillow, asleep, did not affect him one bit.

She was a beautiful woman, with dark hair that had partly escaped the tight, complicated knot at the base of her neck, big blue eyes that reminded him of the Atlantic Ocean a few miles away, and legs that went on for days. Her black heels sat on the floor, twin soldiers nestled against each other. The basket with the baby was on the carpet below where Vivian's head rested, Ellie snoring lightly in the dim room, and one of Vivian's hands resting protectively on the top of the basket.

If the circumstances had been different, this would have been his image of a perfect family. Mom asleep on the sofa, baby nearby, dinner simmering on the stove. But all of this was an illusion—a very temporary one at that. They weren't his family. They weren't his anything. After the meal, she'd be gone, and so would the baby.

He wasn't going to lie. The thought disappointed him a little. Maybe it was all those years of growing up in a house as sterile and emotionless as a roll of paper towels. Or maybe it was the holiday season nipping at his emotions, with the added bit of sentimentality being back in Stone Gap with his grandmother's house and all its memories a couple miles away. But a part of him wanted this moment to last.

Vivian stirred, blinked, then jerked upright. A detailed list and pile of neatly labeled folders slid from her lap. He could see a planner open and marked with a dozen checkmarks and color-coded tasks. Earlier, he'd heard her making calls, each one devoid of small talk and focused only on whatever document or information she was requesting. It was only when she'd fallen asleep that he'd seen the vulnerable, soft side of the driven attorney. "I'm sorry I fell asleep. I didn't mean—"

"It's no big deal. You had a hell of a day. All three of us did." The kid was still asleep, tiny and angelic in the white basket. As far as kids went, he kind of liked this one. She was easy to hold, easy to care for and easy to fall for. "I didn't want to wake you, but Mac's going to be here in a minute."

"Oh, yes, good." She got to her feet, smoothed her skirt, then pressed a hand to her hair.

"That bun thing is pretty much done." Nick grinned. "Beyond repair."

Vivian pulled out the pins that held the remains of the complicated-looking knot in place, sending her hair tumbling past her shoulders. Holy hell. Letting her hair down gave Vivian an unfettered quality.

Sexy. Tempting.

She twisted the hair, then tucked it back into the bun and pinned it in place again. Nick tried not to let his disappointment show.

This woman had efficiency down to a science. He suspected if he told her *you can't do that*, she'd say *hold my martini and watch me*. If she even let loose enough to drink a martini. She was as locked up—literally— as a summer cottage in the winter.

Vivian had said she was a corporate lawyer. He should have guessed that, from the severe suit and the practical heels and the references to a briefcase. If there was any kind of woman he didn't want in his life, it was a lawyer. Didn't matter what she looked like with her hair down.

His parents thought their law degrees gave them license to argue everything to death, put their careers ahead of their children time and time again. They had been there for their firm more than for anyone who'd ever needed them. Their marriage had been strained, and even at its best, they'd acted more like roommates than lovers. If that was life with a lawyer, he didn't want any part of it.

A soft knock sounded on the door. Nick hesitated for a second, still caught in the thoughts of Vivian with her hair down, then jerked himself back to the present and opened the door. Mac stepped inside, followed by Savannah. Their baby was nestled in a thing that looked like a backpack, affixed to Savannah's chest.

Mac and Savannah had been married for a couple of years, but they were the kind of couple that still held hands in public and gave each other secret smiles. Nick had to admit that their tendency for PDA had grown on him.

"Oh my. Is that her? I just want a peek at your cutie, Nick," Savannah said as she hurried past him and beelined to the kid.

He raised his hands and backed up. "Her name's Ellie. And she's not my baby."

Savannah had already reached Ellie. She smiled at the sleeping baby, then looked at Nick, then Vivian. "Your daughter is lovely."

"Oh, she's not mine either," Vivian said.

Mac chuckled. "Don't tell me you stole a baby, Nick."

"It's complicated," he said. Explaining it would sound crazy, for sure. Woman leaves baby on kitchen table, her irate sister shows up and stays for dinner. "Did you bring the stuff?"

God, it sounded like he was making a drug deal, not a baby supplies pickup.

"Yep." Mac swung a padded bag off his shoulder and left it on the hall table. Bright yellow giraffes and zebras cavorted on the outside of the vinyl bag. "Savannah and I got an extra diaper bag thing at her shower, so we filled it up with stuff you might need. Diapers, wipes, rash cream, formula, bottles—"

"Whoa, whoa. We're not invading Normandy here. I just have the kid for a few hours."

Savannah shot her husband a confused look. "Are you babysitting? Why don't you have any stuff?"

"It's a long story," Vivian and Nick said at the same time.

"Okaaaayyy," Mac said. "Well, we have a Mommy and Me thing to get to. And yes, I have become that dad." Mac glanced at his wife, then his baby, with such obvious love it almost hurt Nick to see the emotion. "Let us know if you need anything else."

Mac and Savannah said goodbye, then headed back out the door. Nick supposed he should have invited them to stay for dinner, but considering his dinner for one had already morphed into dinner for two, he wasn't sure he had enough food.

Though there was something to be said for having a full house. Nick had been in a decidedly deep self-pity slump ever since the thing with his ex-girlfriend, and having people here—not just inn guests that he dodged, but people he actually interacted with—was… nice. Nicer than he'd expected.

Maybe he should do what his grandmother asked and go see his father. Bring him that box that Ida Mae had left for her son. *It'll do you good to work things out with your father*, his grandmother had written. *And for him to realize what's important before it's too late.*

Nick hadn't even gone to the house to find the box, never mind picked up the phone. His father had made a fast, almost silent appearance at the funeral, exchanging maybe a dozen words with Nick's brothers, and none with Nick. Which was par for the course for the last ten years. Ever since the day he realized Nick had blown half his law school tuition on cooking school. He could still see his father walking away in disgust. *Why you would try to make a living out of something as foolish as cooking, I'll never know. You're a disappointment to me.*

He turned away from the door, and pushed the thoughts of the past from his head. It might have taken him ten years, but he was finally making a living at his dream job. Albeit, not the kind of money he'd made working with Carson, but not chump change, either. And he was happy.

Wasn't he?

"What is all this stuff?" Vivian peered inside the bag. With just her and the sleeping baby in the house, the inn had never felt so intimate before. "It's just a baby, right? Aren't they supposed to be easy?"

Nick chuckled. "I may not know anything about kids, but one thing I'm sure of, is that babies are complicated. Not as complicated as women but close."

Vivian parked a fist on her hip. "Women are complicated?"

He liked seeing this spark in her. This, Nick suspected, was the Vivian with her hair down. Unrestricted. Spontaneous. Intriguing. "Not all women."

"Then what kind of women are you talking about?" Vivian arched a brow. A half smile played at the edge of her lips.

Damn, she was beautiful. Interesting. He moved closer to her. She was wearing a perfume that lured him in—dark, deep, sexy. Like a garden after the sunset. Ellie went on sleeping, and the house went on being quiet and a world of just the two of them. "Women like you. With your practical heels and your suit and your bun."

"That's how I dress for work. What's wrong with it?"

"It's very…businesslike. Why are you working so hard to hide that you're beautiful?"

"You…" She swallowed. Her eyes widened, and the tough bravado dropped away. "You think I'm beautiful?"

"Oh come on, I can't be the first man to say that to you." Surely a woman like her had dozens of men lined up and eager for a chance to spend time with her. She was smart, confident and gorgeous. A trifecta.

"I… I don't date much." For the first time since he'd met her, Vivian looked embarrassed, unsure. "Nor do the men I work with ever say anything like that. Probably because I'm winning more cases than them, but still."

He laughed. "I bet you're a barracuda in court. I saw the battle strategy you had on the legal pad back there. Clearly, that's your comfort zone."

"It's that obvious?" Her cheeks flushed.

"Yep. When Ellie was crying earlier, you looked like you'd rather have a stroke than pick her up."

Vivian laughed. Damn, she had a nice laugh, too. Too bad she worked in the one field he gave a wide berth to. In his experience, lawyers had a tendency to argue and control, two things that never really worked well with Nick.

"I really don't know what I'm doing when it comes to babies," she said.

The soft admission made him forget all his reservations for a moment. She looked so beautiful right now, with her hair once again escaping the restraints of the pins, and the questions in her face. He knew what it was like to doubt yourself, to wonder if you were doing the right thing. And maybe it was just the kindred spirit he saw in her, or maybe it was something more, but Nick shifted closer to Vivian. "There," he said. "Was that so hard?"

"Was what so hard?"

"Opening up. Letting that hyperconfident facade drop." He smiled at her. "You really should do that more often."

"Maybe..." Her gaze met his and held. "Maybe I will."

Nick leaned closer, almost close enough to touch... and then Viv leaned in the rest of the way, bringing their lips together. Slow, easy, sweet, his lips meeting hers with a gentle pressure that begged her to let him in, let him know her. His hand reached up to cup the back of her head, to capture the stray brown locks that had escaped the bun. He kissed her, tenderly, leisurely—

And Viv started to cry.

Chapter Four

Vivian never betrayed weakness. Doing that meant certain death in the courtroom. She prided herself on keeping her emotions on a tight leash. It was part of what made her a formidable opponent. But the second she and Nick kissed it was like a dam had burst, and the tears that rarely showed in her eyes began falling.

This man—a total stranger—had seen a part of her that no one ever saw. The unsure, hesitant, out of her element Vivian, who had to ask for help. And despite that, he'd called her beautiful and been drawn to her enough for them to kiss.

She broke away from Nick and took several steps back. He was still six feet of tall, dark, handsome and tempting as hell. She swiped at her eyes, and tried to still her hammering heart with a deep breath. *What is wrong with me?*

There was nothing wrong with the kiss—that had been phenomenal. Tender, slow and easy, as if she was a dessert he wanted to savor. The scent of the food he'd been cooking—buttery and as warm and comforting as an early-fall day—lingered in the space between them. She had the most insane urge to put her head on his chest.

"I'm sorry," she said, the words giving her a moment to center herself, bring her heart and mind back to the world of common sense. A world where she didn't feel completely overwhelmed by a three-month-old and a dark-haired man with espresso eyes who called her beautiful. "I don't normally cry."

"I'm the one who should be apologizing. I thought..." He shook his head and managed to look both embarrassed and contrite at the same time. "Argh. I'm sorry."

"No, no, it's not that. I didn't cry because we kissed. I cried because..." *Because you saw a side of me I never let anyone see. Because you reminded me of what I've put to the side time and time again in my life. Because for a brief second, I was caught in a different world.* She didn't say any of that out loud. Instead, she resorted to a half-truth. "I'm stressed. I just...for the first time in my life, I don't know what to do."

She sighed and dropped onto the sofa. Easier to do that than to look at Nick and wish he would kiss her again. Maybe she'd been working too much or maybe it had been the *you're beautiful*, or the fact that she was so far out of her comfort zone with Ellie it might as well be another planet, but right now, Vivian felt as vulnerable as a fawn in an open meadow. That was not a place she liked to be. The walls she had erected decades ago crumbled a little, and everything inside her was trying to shore them up again, but it was like bracing against a tidal wave with a piece of cardboard.

Ellie had woken and was staring up at Vivian with that "do something, Aunt Viv" look. What could Vivian do? She was in such deep water that she was sure she'd drown and screw this up. Ellie needed a mother, not an aunt who was more comfortable with a deposition than a diaper. "I have a new client who is depending on me to go after this shoddy equipment manufacturer. I need to prepare for a potential trial, which means hours and hours and late nights and weekends of work. My apartment is in the middle of a total renovation. I don't have room or time for a baby. But I don't want to hire a stranger to watch Ellie, because…" She shook her head. Where were all these tears coming from? What was wrong with her?

Nick sat beside her. "Because what?" he asked, his voice soft, gentle. And another chink in those walls opened.

"Because Sammie and I spent our lives with strangers and we swore that when we grew up, we would never do that to our kids." The words came out in a whisper, words that edged along the secrets Vivian had kept close to her heart all her life. The vulnerabilities she hid behind the suits and the heels and the attitude.

Her childhood had been spent moving from one house to another, as her mother got sober, fell off the wagon, got sober again, a hamster wheel of changes. Some foster homes had been great, others had bordered on nightmarish. There'd been people who had refused to feed her unless she finished an endless list of chores. Foster parents who believed a belt was the best means of communication. Families she loved and said goodbye to before she could spend more than a handful of weeks there, the happiness she'd had with them just a fleeting mirage. Living her life out of grocery sacks and someone's worn, discarded luggage. Long before the roller coaster of foster care began, Vivian had taken one look at Sammie, so thin and scared and frail, and vowed to be the one person her little sister could depend on, the one person who would never leave her. It had taken a lot of fighting with the system and the rules, but Viv had done her best to keep her promise, until she'd graduated high school and gone on to college. She'd made the mistake of thinking Sammie would be okay once she was out on her own. Viv had been wrong.

Maybe it was being in this town again, in the same place where Viv had learned to roller skate and where she'd found out she hated beets but loved pancakes for dinner on Thursday nights that had her emotions running high.

"Then don't do it. Don't hire a stranger."

She glanced at Nick. "What are you talking about? I have to do my job, and I can't just leave Ellie home alone with the cabinet installers. Yes, they're strangers, but there's a day care at the office. It's not like she's going to be alone."

"Stay here tonight. Let me help you."

Let me help you. Four words that Vivian had never

before admitted she needed to hear. She glanced at her niece, at the pile of baby things that could have been a pile of books written in Greek for all she knew about them, and then back at Nick. "What time is dinner?"

Nick had made a lot of meals in his lifetime. So many, he'd lost count a long time ago. There was something about being in the kitchen, measuring and stirring and tasting, that centered him. As soon as he started cooking the rest of the world dropped away. Every single time.

Until he'd invited Vivian to stay for dinner, in his space, at his table. She wasn't even in the kitchen right now—she'd kept the baby in the living room to feed the baby some formula—which meant Nick should have been able to concentrate on the artichoke and tomato sauce.

Instead, as the chicken cooked in the braising liquid of wine and broth, he found himself listening to the sounds of Vivian talking to the baby in the other room. Her soft voice, nearly a whisper, captivated him. His mind kept straying from the recipe—memorized because he had made the dish a thousand times—so much that he ended up searching the internet for the ingredients list and forgetting what he had just searched a minute later.

She distracted him. And that couldn't be a good thing.

"Smells good."

He damned near cut his thumb off when he swiveled at the sound of her voice. Vivian was standing in the doorway, with the baby back in the basket. When he'd peeked in earlier, he saw that she hadn't held Ellie to feed her; instead she'd sat beside the basket with the bottle. He vaguely knew that babies had to burp after they ate, but how to make that happen…he had no idea. And clearly neither did she. Given the amount of "yucks" he'd heard as she changed Ellie's diaper, she was clueless with that as he was, too. He got the feeling that Vivian was about as comfortable with a baby as she would be with a hand grenade. Not that he was much more of a parental figure, so he had no room to talk. "Thanks. It was one of my grandmother's recipes."

Yeah, all cool, no betraying the little hiccup in his chest just then.

Vivian came into the kitchen and gestured toward the maple table. "Mind if I work a little and watch you cook?"

"Sure." He rarely had company in the kitchen because when the inn was fully booked, both Della and Mavis were busy with the guests and general housekeeping. When the inn was empty, there was no one around to check in on him while he cooked. And the last time he'd had a beautiful woman in his kitchen—

Well, it had been a while.

His ex-girlfriend Ariel hadn't come to his place that often, and he hadn't offered to cook for her more than a handful of times. After a busy day at the office, it was easier just to stop at a restaurant, grab a bite, then go back to her place for a few hours. He rarely slept over, and Ariel had rarely invited him. Now that he thought about it, their relationship had seemed to be

more one of convenience than anything else. No fireworks, no surprises, nothing but moving from one expected step to the next.

Well, until he received the totally unexpected, blind-
siding news about Jason. But looking back now, after
the anger had dissipated, his strongest emotion was a
whole lot of relief that he hadn't created a messy, legal
mistake by marrying her. With his parents, he'd seen
firsthand what an unhappy marriage looked like—the
chill in every conversation, the tight lips, the great
pains to avoid physical contact. Not what Nick wanted
for his future at all.

Which reminded him yet again that lawyer Vivian wasn't someone for him to consider for anything
beyond dinner tonight. She'd already told him in no
uncertain terms that she placed a high priority on her
career. Like his parents, her job consumed her life.
*Hours and hours of work, weeks and weeks of prepa-
ration.* The kind of single-minded workaholic tendencies Nick steered clear of, especially when associated
with a law degree.

Vivian sat down at the table, with Ellie in her basket
on the seat beside her. As if to prove his thoughts true,
Vivian set the almost empty bottle on the table, then
pulled out her enormous black leather planner and her
laptop. For a long time, there was only the sound of her
fingers on the keyboard and the soft coos of the baby.

After a while, Vivian sat back, stretched and
glanced over at Nick. "So, how's the chicken coming along?"

He shrugged. "Since I'm making it for two after

buying ingredients for one, I added some fresh linguini I made yesterday." He scooped a ladleful of starchy pasta water out of the pot, then stirred it into the artichoke sauce, which began to thicken, velvety and rich.

"You make your own pasta? I can barely boil water."

He picked up the pasta pot and crossed to the sink to drain it, then set the cooked pasta aside. "It's not that hard. It's almost…therapeutic to make pasta and bread. All that kneading is very zen."

Now it was her turn to laugh. "If there's one thing I could use, it's a little zen."

She did seem very uptight, as if she was held together with steel wires. That had been him, two months ago, when he was working with Carson and hating his job. "Growing up as the child of two lawyers, I know that lawyering is stressful. My parents operated on short fuses, still do. My brother Grady runs his own company, and my other brother and I used to provide tech support. None of us went into the family business, so my dad thinks we're all failures, except Grady because he has a lot of zeros in his paycheck. I thought my job was stressful, but Grady's was ten times worse. He was a working advertisement for avoiding that kind of thing."

He hadn't strung together that many words at one time in weeks. What was wrong with him? Pouring out his life story to a woman—a lawyer—who he barely knew? In his experience, nothing warm and fuzzy ever came out of a lawyer.

"And now you're cooking?"

The lilt on the end of her voice made it sound like

she thought he'd taken a step down the career ladder. And yes, he had in terms of salary and benefits, but his days were far less tense and most mornings, he rolled out of bed, his mind whirring with menus and ingredients and purpose instead of dread and tension. "It's where I'm happy. I think."

"You think?"

He used metal tongs to toss the pasta and sauce together. A quick taste, and then a dash of salt, and the meal was done. He grabbed two white plates out of the cabinet and set a fat twirl of pasta in the center, topped it with slices of chicken and a smattering of vegetables, then added sliced homemade bread on the side.

All to avoid answering that question of whether he was happy or not. The answer was complicated, and Nick didn't feel like explaining anything complicated right now.

"Dinner is served." He laid the plate before her with a little flourish, then handed her a rolled napkin with silverware tucked inside. "I can carry the baby upstairs, if you want to eat in your room again."

A part of him hoped she'd say yes, and leave him to his kitchen and his solitude. And another crazy part hoped she stayed and ate with him.

"Oh, well, I wasn't planning to eat in my room. I know I did before, but that was so I could visit with my sister, which really meant working a lot while she napped." Vivian frowned, then the placid face was back, erasing any emotion. "If it's okay, I'd like to stay here. I could use some company. I so rarely have any while I eat, and it's been a hell of a day."

Nick didn't eat with the guests. He'd grown to pre-fer his meals alone, or occasionally taken with Della or Mavis. He'd flick on the television in his room and let some mindless sitcom or movie he'd seen a hun-dred times fill the silence. That way he could mope and stew, and not have to answer any questions about why he was or wasn't happy. Or dwell on why he was still avoiding his grandmother's last request.

"Uh, yeah, sure." He grabbed the second plate and sat down across from Vivian. The baby had fallen back asleep, which was both good and bad. Good because sleeping baby equaled some peace and quiet, and bad, because sleeping baby meant there was no distraction between them.

Vivian dug in, swirling thick pieces of linguine onto her fork, along with saucy chunks of chicken and veg-etables. As soon as she took the first bite, she smiled. "Oh my God, that's incredible," she said, the words coming out with a groan that sent Nick's mind down a path far from the kitchen.

"Uh, you have a little…" He reached toward her, then pulled back, with a reminder to himself that he wasn't supposed to be the guests' personal groomer. Even if said guest was beautiful and tasted like that first cup of coffee of the day. A little sweet, a little dark and a lot addicting.

Vivian wiped away the bit of sauce that had ended up on her chin. Without his help. Bummer.

"Sorry," she said. "I'm not usually such a mess when I eat. I'm just really hungry and this is really good."

"I'm glad you're enjoying it. I rarely have an audience for my food. Most of the time I'm in the kitchen cleaning up while the guests are eating."

In the space of time it took him to speak those few sentences, Vivian had wolfed down two more bites. "I haven't eaten since breakfast and didn't realize I was starving until now."

He chuckled. "You missed lunch? I would have gnawed off my arm by now."

She shrugged. "I very rarely eat during the day. When I do, it's a few quick bites at my desk. My days get so crazy busy that I forget."

He chuckled. "Honey, if you're forgetting to eat, then you're eating really boring food."

The *honey* hung in the air between them. It had slipped out of him, that Southern word that peppered almost every sentence down here in North Carolina and had invaded his own vocabulary now that he was back home. Vivian stared at him for a second, then dipped her head to take another bite. The memory of the feel of his lips against hers flitted through her mind, and she quickly changed the subject. "So, you're a chef instead of an IT guy. I get that. Sort of. More fulfilling and all that. But how did you end up here?"

"I grew up in Stone Gap, at least some of the time. My grandmother had a house in town, and my brothers and I were always pestering our parents to let us visit. We ended up here about once a month and if we were lucky, a week in the summer. Her house sits on Stone Gap Lake and was a thousand times better than the Mausoleum."

"The Mausoleum?"

"My parents have this monstrosity of a house with marble pillars and a lawn bigger than the state of Rhode Island, on a couple hundred acres up in Raleigh, where they work. The house was so damned big, we had to use an intercom system to find each other. My parents hated noise and so the house was almost always silent. Hence, the Mausoleum."

"We had very different childhoods," she said. "I don't think I lived anywhere quiet until I got a place on my own. Maybe that's why I still live alone."

Which implied no husband or live-in boyfriend. Why Nick cared, he couldn't say. Except that he couldn't forget kissing her or how much he wanted to do exactly that all over again. "I've lived with or near my brothers my entire life, until I came back to Stone Gap. Worked with them, ate dinner with them...we sort of became a tribe when we were younger, and that didn't change as adults."

"Until now." She speared a thick piece of chicken. "Why?"

"My life plans detoured." He took a sip of water and sat back, allowing the generous helping of food he'd just consumed to settle a bit. "I was dating this woman at work for a couple years. I planned to ask her to marry me, and to spend the week after Christmas in Jamaica to celebrate. Turns out she already had plans of her own—to dump me and go on vacation with my right-hand man and former best friend."

"Ouch."

"You can say that again. I was working so many hours, nose to the grindstone and all that, that I never even noticed the two of them had started hanging out more, finding reasons to talk to each other at work. The day after my would-be proposal turned into a breakup, my grandmother died. I came down here for the funeral and never went back."

"It's like a bad country song." A hint of a smile played on her lips. "Don't tell me you drive a pickup too?"

He laughed. "Actually, I do. But only because it's practical. Not because it carries my hunting rifles and Labrador."

A wider smile swung across her face. "This is good."

"You already said that. Twice."

"I meant the conversation. I forgot what it's like to talk to a normal person."

He wasn't sure whether to take that as a compliment or not. "Meaning someone other than a lawyer?"

She nodded. "All we do is argue."

So true. Nick had heard more hushed arguments between his parents in his house growing up than he'd heard conversations between them. On the upside, they were more interested in tearing into each other than yelling at their kids. On the downside, the reason seemed to be that they didn't much care about their kids at all. Not even enough to yell. His parents had rarely plugged in, hardly been a part of the boys' lives. Except for the time she'd worked, Vivian had surprised him by being far more engaged with him, dinner and the baby—more or less—than he'd expected. He'd held a firm no-dating-lawyers stance most of his life, but now, he considered easing that restriction.

Insane. She was only here for a couple days at the most. They weren't dating. This was just a shared meal in the kitchen. And there was a baby between them. Literally and figuratively.

"Tell that to my parents, will you?" Nick shook his head. "They never seemed to figure out how to talk to any of us boys, or each other, for that matter. Of course, we were also major disappointments because not a single one of us went into the law."

Nick almost had, being the one who'd tried the hardest to please his impossible-to-please parents. He'd lasted a little over a month in law school. One torturous, hellacious month of reading about tortes and case histories and evidentiary procedures before he bailed and lied to his parents for the next six months.

"I bet the guests at the Stone Gap Inn are really glad you didn't go into law. I know I am." She polished off her last bite, leaving the plate almost as clean as it had been when it came out of the dishwasher. "Is everything you make this delicious?"

He shrugged. "I think so. I mean, I just cook what I like to eat." That's how he'd always approached food— by instinct. He had the culinary degree, but he also regularly made it up as he went along. He seasoned by sense, rather than by exact measurements.

"Well, I'm eating whatever morsels are left in the pan and not being one bit shy about it." She rose.

At the same time, Nick got to his feet. "Let me," he said, putting his hand out for her plate. Their twin movements caused a quick, light collision. The plate wavered in her hands, almost toppled, before Nick caught it. Simultaneously, Vivian reached for his arm to steady herself.

Her lips parted in surprise and her eyes widened. "I... I'm sorry."

"It's my fault. Let me..." His voice trailed off as his mind went blank. It took a second for his hand to make the connection with his brain. "Uh, get you another helping."

"Thank you." Vivian dropped back into her chair, quickly, then whipped out her cell phone and busied herself with reading texts. The lightness disappeared from her features, replaced by the stern concentration of a workaholic.

If anything reminded Nick of what he didn't want, it was that.

Chapter Five

From the day she was born, Vivian Winthrop had spent every waking hour focused on excelling. When she was little, and living at home with a mother slipping deeper and deeper into an alcohol and pain-killer addiction, Vivian had worried over every single detail. Maybe if the beds were made and the house was clean and the dishes done, her mother wouldn't drink so often and yell so much. Maybe if she brought home perfect grades, her mother would notice and take her daughter to the park as a reward. Then maybe they could become a real family, like the ones she saw at school, with parents who scooped their kids into tight hugs in the parking lot after class let out. Maybe she could have a mom who marveled at the crafts and cookies from the Brownie meetings Vivian often had to miss because she had no way to get home afterward.

But the sparkling plates and hospital corners never earned a single word of praise. The A+ papers never got hung on the refrigerator. Every day, her mother retreated deeper and deeper into the shadows of her room and the solace she found in those wine bottles and the pills, until the state came in and decided Vivian and Sammie would be better off living with strangers. Every single time she and her sister were moved to another house, the cycle started all over again. *Let me be perfect*, she'd think, *and then maybe my mom will miss me enough to try harder, and she'll come get me.*

A psychologist would probably say she was trying to bring order to a chaotic life, but that quest for perfectionism had become an ingrained trait and made her a very successful lawyer. Vivian turned in every brief early, had the most organized office of any of the partners and dived into each case as if the fate of the world rested on the verdict. Meticulous, organized, perfect in every aspect of her life.

Until this weekend. Until Sammie up and ran away, leaving Ellie on the kitchen table. And leaving Vivian with the one thing she couldn't manage perfectly.

A baby.

And on top of that, the brief for the client she needed to write and file by Tuesday morning needed one more polish, the case law research was waiting on her review, and the emails she needed to return were multiplying like bunnies.

And Ellie was fussing and squirming, and on the verge of tears. She wasn't the only one.

"Come on, Ellie, please help me out. You know I suck at this," Vivian said to her niece as she tried to change diaper number two. "If you could just, say, not move for thirty seconds, maybe I can get this diaper on and then you'd be happy and I could work. Please?"

Ellie just twisted back and forth, her cries getting stronger by the second. She was much like her mother, all piss and vinegar, and anxious to see the world. Vivian thought babies this young slept all the time. Apparently, Ellie didn't get the memo.

Vivian slipped the new diaper back under the baby's butt for the fourth time, then taped one side in place and tried to quickly flick out and affix the other piece of tape. At the same time, Ellie moved, balling up her fists, crunching her legs to her stomach. The tape landed askew, and showed a gap between the diaper and Ellie's left leg. Vivian already knew—as did her pantsuit—what happened when the diaper wasn't firmly in place, so she unstuck the tape, tried again, darting past Ellie's complaining and twisting, and wham, fourth time was the close-enough charm.

"Phew. I need a vacation after that." Vivian dropped onto the bed and rolled Ellie toward her. She tried to give Ellie the rest of her bottle, but the baby just shook her head. She had her lips pressed together and the tears were starting again, dissolving into cries.

"Here, Ellie. Let's finish your supper." She nuzzled the bottle against Ellie's lips.

Again, no luck. Wasn't she supposed to be hungry?

Ellie hadn't finished the bottle earlier, and Vivian was pretty sure she was supposed to. Was Vivian feeding her wrong? Was there a wrong way to put a bottle in a baby's mouth?

"Ellie, come on, please." Again, Ellie refused and her cries yielded to screams. "Come on, honey. Take this, and we'll get your pj's on, then go to sleep." Vivian tried to say it all in the happy-mommy voice that Nick used. As soon as she said it, Vivian realized she should have saved herself some effort and put the borrowed baby pajamas on right after changing Ellie, instead of re-dressing her in today's pink onesie.

Ellie kept screaming, and as she did, her chubby fist waved, her fingers opening and closing around a hunk of Vivian's hair. Ellie pulled, and Vivian was sure she'd just earned a bald spot. "Ouch! Hey, honey, don't do that to Auntie Viv. Since you're not hungry, and I changed your diaper, you must be sleepy, right?"

The baby's blue eyes were wide open, without a hint of sleepiness. Vivian, on the other hand, felt like she could sleep for a week.

"Umm…let's go for a walk. Maybe that will calm you down." Vivian fastened her hair into a messy ponytail on top of her head, then picked up Ellie and paced the room. Holding the baby still felt weird and unnatural, and Vivian was pretty sure she was doing it wrong. When Sammie picked up Ellie, her daughter nestled into her neck. But when Vivian held her niece, Ellie remained stiff and separate.

Ellie's long, drawn-out wails were going to wake up the elderly man staying in the room down the hall, if they hadn't already. When Vivian booked the weekend away at the B and B, she'd been caught in some delusion about a drawn-out overnight party with her sister, the kind of late-night gabfest they'd had when they were young. Adding the surprise of Ellie into the mix had meant everything revolved around the baby. Which was okay, because Ellie was adorable—from a distance and to everyone else in the inn, it seemed—and Sammie seemed to be a good mother. But in the end, Viv had retreated to her comfort zone of working while Sammie took care of the baby.

Why Sammie had ever thought Vivian would make a better mother than her, she'd never know. Sammie had that natural connection—not to mention three months of experience. Sammie was the one who could intuit Ellie's every need. Whereas Vivian felt as lost as she had on her first day of law school. At least there, she'd had professors and books to consult. In this small room, she had only Ellie and some fumbled one-handed Google searches on her phone.

"How about this?" Vivian yanked the pacifier out of the diaper bag, pressed it to Ellie's lips, but again the baby squirmed and cried and refused to open her mouth. How terrible were Vivian's maternal instincts if she couldn't even get her niece to take a pacifier? Wasn't that basic stuff?

"What were you thinking, Sammie?" she said to the room, to the air, to all the miles between her and her irresponsible sister. Vivian sighed, tucked the pacifier into the pocket of her sweats, then grabbed the half-empty formula bottle and headed downstairs. Maybe in the kitchen, Ellie's cries would be muffled enough to not disturb the other guest.

Or Nick.

She'd been thinking about that man altogether too much when she should be thinking about work. Before, she could always keep work running in her mind while she did any other task. Maybe it was the quaint town or maybe it was the addition of the baby, or maybe, just maybe, it was that kiss she'd been unable to forget, but for the past few hours, Nick Jackson had lingered at the edge of her every thought.

A single light burned over the kitchen sink, casting a golden glow over the stove, the kitchen table, the white tile. Just a few hours ago, Vivian had been sitting at that same table, enjoying what might have been the best meal of her life, with one of the most handsome men she'd ever dined with. Nick had an easy comfortableness about him, in the way he moved and talked, and especially in the way he kissed.

Ellie buried her face in Vivian's shoulder and kept on crying. A reminder that Vivian would do well to focus on her niece and not on a man who was a temporary detour in a life that had been planned since she'd gone to college and decided the best way to avoid being disappointed by relationships was to not have them.

Vivian bounced Ellie in her arms, but the baby only got more upset, balling up her fists and waving them in her aunt's face. Vivian paced around the kitchen island, whispering *shh-shh* in Ellie's ear. She cried louder. Vivian offered the pacifier again; Ellie spit it back out. And cried more.

Vivian dropped onto one of the bar stools, clutched her niece to her chest and wondered if crying was contagious, because she was doing it now, too.

"Need some help?"

Nick was standing in the doorway at the other end of the kitchen, clad in a pair of flannel pajama pants and nothing else. His chest was bare, muscular and, even in the middle of her despair, Vivian noticed. "She won't stop crying," she said, swiping away her own tears before Nick got close enough to see them. "It took me seven hundred tries to get her diaper on right. Both times. I think I'm feeding her wrong, and I think she might starve, because she barely ate, and she isn't sleeping, and what if I'm screwing her up and—"

Nick crossed the room in three quick strides, and covered her hand with his. "Shh," he said, just as she had with Ellie a moment before. "She's three months old. It takes years to screw up a kid."

That made Vivian laugh a little. "True."

"Maybe it's just tough on Ellie to have all these changes in her life, and that's why she's so grumpy."

Vivian glanced down at her squirming, unhappy niece. She thought of her sister and herself, and how they'd acted out after yet another change, another home. They'd been much older than Ellie, but perhaps the feelings of disquiet, of frustration, were the same for babies. "You think so?"

"Babies like structure," Nick said. "They like schedules. It helps them learn that their world is predictable, and gives them a strong foundation."

Was this the same man who'd called her a babynapper earlier today? The same one who had seemed as clueless as she felt? "Where did you learn that?"

Nick shrugged. "I read a little tonight. I couldn't sleep, and I figured if I read some stuff about babies, maybe I could be more help to you. You know, if you wanted the help."

"That is—" she sniffled and tried not to show the wave of relief that filled her "—the sweetest thing anyone has ever done for me."

"Oh, honey, that's nothing."

There it was again, the word *honey*. It rolled off his tongue so easily, and melted her resolve to steer clear of this temporary man. It also made fresh tears well in her eyes. It had to be the hours of trying to be a mom to a child who wasn't hers, of struggling to succeed at something and failing so badly, or maybe just the holiday decorations all around town making her maudlin, but hearing that Nick had read up on baby care in his spare time just to help her made her cry even harder.

"Here, let me take her," he said, gently tugging Ellie out of her arms. "Looks like you might need the binkie more."

That made Vivian laugh again, and stopped the flow of tears. She swiped at her eyes and drew in a deep breath. It was a few seconds before she noticed that Ellie had stopped crying, too. "What did you do?"

"Nothing," Nick said. He was swaying left to right, as easy as a swing in a spring breeze, Ellie cradled in his arms. When he tried the bottle and she refused it, he set the bottle on the counter, hefted Ellie over one shoulder, and began to pat her back and rub it in circles at the same time. Ellie let out a loud, long burp, then settled into Nick's arm in contentment. When he tried the bottle again, she took it in with greedy slurps, and in minutes the bottle was drained.

Vivian stared. "You are like the baby whisperer."

"Seriously, it was all in this article for first-time moms that I found on the internet. When they don't want to eat in the middle of a feeding, sometimes they need to be burped. Or just calmed. So I tried both. I read some stuff because I knew nothing before that." Nick went back to that easy sway, and Ellie's eyes began to drift shut. "You know, I've been thinking..."

When he didn't finish, she prompted, "About what?"

He lowered his voice, nodding toward a sleepy Ellie. "Well, having a baby at the inn is kind of impractical. Because she's bound to cry, and guests are bound to complain. And you don't really have anything to take care of her besides this basket and the stuff Mac and Savannah brought over, which was really only for a temporary stay. You might think this is a crazy idea, but why don't you and Ellie come and stay at my grandmother's house with me? My brothers aren't going to care, I'm sure. Della is returning tomorrow from her vacation, so I don't have to stay at the inn every night anymore. My grandmother's house is on the lake, and the only neighbor is like a hundred years old, so the kid can scream at a hundred decibels and no one is going to complain."

Stay at his house? That was insane. She barely knew him. But then again, any man who researched baby care on the internet for a child he wasn't even related to had to be from pretty good beans, as one of her favorite foster dads used to say.

"I talked to Mavis earlier tonight, and she said she has an old crib and a car seat we could borrow. Her daughter's youngest is like three or four now, so she doesn't need it."

Cribs. Car seats. All things Vivian hadn't even thought about after Sammie left. She had some of those things being delivered to a Sammie who wasn't there to sign for the boxes. Damn it. Her mind had been on work, and when it wasn't on work, it was on getting Ellie to stop crying. And wondering when the hell Sammie was coming back to live up to her responsibilities.

Yet another sign that she was failing at temporary motherhood. Heck, even a half-decent aunt would have thought of all the things a baby might need and not just thrown a credit card at the list and forgotten about it. While Vivian had been trying to research case precedence in the state of North Carolina, Nick, a total stranger to both of them, had been rounding up stuff for a nursery.

"Maybe I should just call someone to take care of Ellie," Vivian said. "I'm clearly not cut out for this motherhood stuff."

"Who are you going to call? You said Sammie isn't answering your calls. Your mom is no longer alive." He gave her a lopsided grin. "And I don't think the Ghostbusters handle this kind of thing."

Vivian ignored the joke. "Well, there's nanny services and maybe Sammie has a relative... She is the legal mother, after all. I don't think the authorities will even let me keep her."

"You know where the authorities will make Ellie stay until they find that relative, right?"

Foster care. The exact fate Vivian wouldn't want her niece to suffer. Yes, there were some great foster homes—she'd been in two that were pretty good, out of the seven she'd stayed at—but there were also some terrible ones, and no one could predict what number the dice would land on.

The Langstons had been one of those families who hit seven and eleven. The Stone Gap family had been patient and kind, even though Vivian and Sammie had been dropped off in the middle of the night, with barely a bag of belongings between them. An emergency placement, the social worker said, but from the second they walked into the Langstons, it had never felt like anything other than home.

Ruth Langston opened her door and her arms to the girls, drawing them close and telling them it would all be okay. They'd woken up to cheesy scrambled eggs in the morning and fallen asleep to the sound of birds outside their windows. In between there were games of catch in the yard with John, trips to the ice cream parlor with Ruth, and one all-day shopping trip in Raleigh that had outfitted both girls for the new school year. Every one of the sixty-two days she had spent in the Langstons' home had been magical.

Then their mother had stayed sober long enough for the judge to return the girls to her care. The day they'd left the Langstons behind had been one of the hardest days of Vivian's life.

What would Ruth and John do? Would they pawn Ellie off or would they take her into their home and give her the love she so desperately needed?

Ellie had fallen asleep on Nick's shoulder. Her chest rose and fell in slow, even breaths. "Maybe I should pay you to be her temporary parent," Vivian said, only half-joking.

Nick chuckled. "For one, this was a fluke, her falling asleep on me. For another, I have a job, and for a third, I'd make a terrible parent."

"You're doing better than me." Which was depressing to admit.

Nick had a point—how *was* she going to do this alone? The Langstons had been a team, dividing and conquering everything from laundry to bedtime. But Vivian was only one person, who had a trial looming over her, a workload she would have to ignore to take care of Ellie, not to mention an apartment unfit for setting up a baby in right now. Maybe she could make room for Ellie in the second bedroom where she'd set up a futon for herself, but between the noise and the dust of construction…

"Were you serious about inviting us to stay with you at your grandmother's house?" The question popped out of Vivian's mouth before she could think it through.

"Completely."

She narrowed her eyes. "Why would you do that?"

"The kid has kind of grown on me. And…you look like you could use the help."

In her experience, few people did anything without expecting something in return. Especially a stranger. So if he didn't want a favor out of her, why make the offer? "Is this some kind of knight in shining armor complex or something?"

"Is this some kind of 'I'm too tough to accept help when it's dropped in my life' complex or something?"

For some reason, the retort made her laugh. She liked Nick, liked him a lot. And his kiss…well, that had been one of the best kisses she'd ever had, until she'd ruined it by crying. "Okay, maybe you're right. But that would be imposing too much. I can't possibly ask you to do that for free."

He grinned. "Oh, didn't I tell you my going rate for babysitting?"

She did a quick calculation of her bank account. The renovations were costing her a fortune, but a private nanny wouldn't be cheap if she went that route instead, and Nick was bound to charge less. "Whatever it is, I'm sure we can work out something equitable—"

He put his hand on hers and she stopped talking. Simply stopped. Maybe because every time Nick looked directly at her or touched her, she stopped thinking.

"I don't need money." He held her gaze and didn't say anything for a moment, as if weighing his words before they left his mouth. "Until today, my plan was to spend the holidays alone. Avoid people as much as possible, do a good job of Grinching it. But now…that idea doesn't sound as good as it did this morning. So why don't you and Ellie stay with me, keep me company with no complications, and we all get what we want."

"That's all?" She gave him a side-eye. "Then what was that kiss about?"

"Weakness." He grinned. "You're a beautiful woman, and I was mesmerized."

You're a beautiful woman. He'd said it twice now. And the way he looked at her… Well, that was no reason to agree to this crazy idea. But then she thought about the weeks she had ahead of her, the insanity of preparing for trial. Ellie did seem to like Nick, and Vivian could probably do a lot of her work from home. And during the hours when she was gone, maybe it would be okay with Mavis and Della for Nick to have Ellie around the inn—although Viv was leery of how that would work out. She didn't know this Della and Mavis, and didn't even really know Nick.

"This is going to sound nuts, but I've never had a traditional Christmas." He shrugged. "If you stay with me, it gives me an excuse to hang some lights and make some eggnog and cookies and have the kind of holiday normal people have."

Vivian had been prepared to say no. To do what she always did and handle the entire Ellie crisis alone. But the scent of the braised chicken from earlier tonight still filled the air, and the idea of a real Christmas, one with lights and presents and a tree, sounded insane… but nice. Like what she and Sammie had had that summer at the Langstons when she was fourteen. A brief peek into a normal life. A family. "On one condition."

"What's that?"

"I get to pick the tree." Then she put out her hand and shook with Nick, and told herself she wasn't making the most insane decision of her life because she was feeling overly sentimental.

The next afternoon, Nick loaded his pickup truck with the borrowed crib, car seat, enough diapers to cover a family of quintuplets, a bright pink playpen, a giant tub of baby clothes, and an equally giant container of toys, bottles, bibs and a lot of other things he couldn't have named if you paid him. Vivian had run into work long enough to file the brief, then stopped in at a Walmart and filled a cart with supplies before coming back to help Nick. Mavis shooed him out the door as soon as he finished making a chicken casserole for lunch, and told him she had the place under control for the rest of the day. "We've only got two guests checking in tonight. Della and I can take care of things for a few days, just like we did before you came along. You haven't had so much as an afternoon off since you got here. So go, shoo, and spend time with your baby."

"It's not my baby, Mavis."

"I know that. But the baby doesn't know." Mavis's trademark broad smile spread across her dark caramel face, then her features sobered. "And, if I remember right, you also have one other thing to take care of while you're at that house."

That's what he got for having a late-night conversation with Mavis after the reading of his grandmother's will. The comfort she'd offered at the time wasn't

worth the price of the ongoing guilt trip about not tending to Ida Mae's final wishes. "That can wait."

Mavis pursed her lips. She was a sturdy woman,
with a large heart and big arms that tended to hug about
everyone she met. "Well, y'all have a good time. And
remember, don't come back until Friday. Della and I
can handle things just fine."

Vivian came out to the porch just then, with Ellie in
the basket. She crossed to the truck, opened the back
door, then stared at the car seat. "Uh…"

Mavis laughed. "Sweetie, those things just look in-
timidating. Here, let me show you what to do." She
reached in the basket and picked up Ellie. "Aren't you
just the cutest thing? Next to my grandkids, of course.
We're gonna put you in the car seat, and then you can
go for a little ride, okay?"

A minute later, Mavis had buckled Ellie in, talking the whole time, alternating between high-pitched
baby talk for Ellie and stern car seat usage instructions
for the adults. Nick learned more than he'd imagined
there was to know about the hidden car seat latches in
his truck's backseat, crash force, proper buckling and
backward-facing baby seats. By the time he and Vivian were in the truck and on their way, facts and figures swam in his head.

"Who knew there was that much to know about a
seat?" Vivian said. "Or that they'd be that complicated
to operate? I think it's easier to replace a carburetor
than install a car seat."

"Your sister didn't own one?"

Vivian shook her head. "Sammie was unprepared

for Ellie, pretty much like she's been unprepared for everything in her life. When she arrived here for our weekend away, she was holding a baby I didn't even know she had. I don't even think the friend who dropped her off had a car seat in it. The least she could have done was be smart enough to travel in an Uber that had a car seat already installed."

"You can do that?"

"Apparently."

"Man, there's an app for everything these days." He took a left, leaving the Stone Gap Inn in the rearview mirror. It felt weird driving away from the place that had been home for the past few weeks.

He glanced across the front seat. The sun streaming through the windows danced off the waves in Vivian's hair. She had put the front part back with a barrette but left the rest down, and he had the most insane urge to reach out and touch her, to run his fingers through those tresses and draw her against his chest.

For a second, his mind imagined them as a family, heading home from a day at the lake or a trip to the store or whatever it was that normal families did. Then he shook off the feeling and concentrated on the road. They were not a family, and this whole arrangement was far from normal.

"So, changing out a carburetor. You have direct experience with that?" he asked.

She shrugged. "Foster father number five had an auto repair business. That foster mom had a lot of kids—I think there were six of us in a tiny little house—so he'd take some of us to work with him. I wasn't allowed to stand around useless, so I learned basic car mechanics."

He chuckled. "You surprise me. Uptight lawyer who can also change the oil and replace a spark plug."

"I'm not uptight. I'm…dedicated to my job. I have to be. People depend on me." Vivian buried her nose in her phone, which just solidified Nick's point, but he held back from saying so. As they drove, Vivian read emails, sent texts and made two phone calls, all during the short ride to Ida Mae's house. Work Vivian was completely different from barefoot in the kitchen in the middle of the night Vivian. The softness he'd seen last night disappeared, replaced by a harsher, more strident voice and rigid posture.

By the time they arrived, she had her laptop out and was back on the phone. When he parked, Vivian covered the mouthpiece. "Just give me a second. I need to finish this call."

"Sure." Nick unloaded the crib, playpen and baby supplies while Vivian stayed with Ellie in the truck. He dug the spare key out of the flowerpot, opened the windows to air out the house, lifted the blinds that had been closed for two months and set up the crib in the spare bedroom. Ida Mae had moved into a downstairs bedroom in the last few months of her life, leaving the upstairs rooms untouched, although as far as he could tell, she'd kept up with the dusting and general cleaning. Three bedrooms, one small enough to serve as the nursery for his father when he was born. The baby furniture was gone, but the pale blue paint had stayed, a perfect accompaniment to the white dresser, white twin bed and white borrowed crib.

After the crib was set up, Nick stepped back and took in the scene. The bright day outside cast dust motes into the air. He could almost hear his grandmother exclaiming about the visitors. About how good it was to have a baby in the house again. People sitting at her dining room table.

Ida Mae had provided the closest thing to a normal, loving home life that Nick and his brothers ever had. The big two-story house seemed deflated, empty, without her gregarious, giving personality. How his father, who was about as warm as a Popsicle, had come from someone so loving and homey, Nick never knew. Either way, he was certain his grandmother would have approved of him inviting Ellie and Vivian to stay. Grady hadn't minded. Nick had texted him a couple hours ago and asked if they could stay there. *Do what you want,* Grady had said, *I don't want the house.*

Grady had his own issues with the family to work out, while Nick had a few left untended himself. Nick could almost hear his grandmother's voice in his head. *Call your father. Work this out. Now that you're in the house, you have no excuse not to get that box.*

Damn that request. He supposed he could lie to the attorney who had handled the will and say he'd called his father, then the lawyer would cut the check for Nick's part of the inheritance. The idea tempted him, but the thought of one more lie didn't. Nick pulled out his cell and dialed the office number for his parents' firm. He debated calling his father's cell, but wasn't so sure Richard would answer.

The automated operator rattled off Richard's extension. Nick punched it in, took a deep breath and waited while the phone rang once, twice. "Richard Jackson."

The deep timbre of his father's voice surprised Nick. He'd expected voicemail. No, *hoped* for voice mail. "Dad, it's Nick."

Silence. "I'm in the middle of something. I'll call you back."

Nick already knew there'd be no return call. He'd been down that road before with his father. "Grandma left you something at the house. She wants me to give it to you."

"Just put it in the mail."

"Grandma said I have to do this in person." She'd mentioned that three times in her letter to Nick. "It's part of the terms of her inheritance."

Richard scoffed. "Leave it to my mother to put something stupid like that in her will. Listen, I'm not going to contest it. Just mail me the box, and we'll pretend we abided by her request." Before Nick could reply, his father added, "Is that all? I have work to do. I'm sure you have my address still."

Then the call ended. Nick stared at the black screen of his phone and cursed his grandmother's request. He loved Ida Mae, but what had she been thinking?

If his father wanted that box, he could come here. Nick was through doing Richard's bidding.

Nick went back out to the truck, to find Vivian still in the same place he left her. Working. Of course. Had he expected anything else? The sour mood brought about by the phone call with Richard deepened. He gestured toward the house. "I have the—"

Vivian held up a finger. "I want those files by the end of the day. Get a courier to bring them to me. Uh, the address?" She glanced at Nick.

"Thirty-two Lakefront Road," he said.

"Thirty-two Lakefront Road," she repeated. "In Stone Gap. I'll be in tomorrow morning to go over the new discovery."

She hung up and tucked the phone into her purse. "Sorry about that. We're in the middle of an important case, plus have another half dozen in various stages of development, and—" The phone rang again. She peeked at the screen and gave Nick an apologetic smile. "I have to get this. It's my co-counsel. Can you...?"

"Sure, sure," Nick said as if it didn't bother him at all that she was ignoring her flesh and blood for yet another phone call. Reason number 203 why he shouldn't kiss this woman again.

He walked around to the backseat to unbuckle Ellie. She squirmed against his chest when he lifted her out of the car seat. He grabbed the tiny blanket that had been on top of her legs in the truck and wrapped it around her, even though the walk from driveway to house was only a few seconds long. There was a decided nip in the air, a preview taste of the winter to come.

Once inside, he bumped up the heat a few degrees, glad that Grady had kept paying the utility bills, then set Ellie in the playpen with a couple of stuffed animals and large round plastic rings to play with. She lay on her back, taking more interest in her fingers than anything around her.

And Nick stood there, realizing that he had gone from helping-out babysitter to single parent in the space of a two-mile drive. If he'd known Vivian was going to be working this much, he would have gone along with the idea of hiring a nanny. Either way, this wasn't the holiday he had been envisioning when he proposed the two of them move in with him.

A feeling of dread chased up his spine. All his life, he'd avoided getting involved with workaholic women, because he had seen firsthand how that dedication to the job above everything else hurt a family. He'd seen how his own workaholic tendencies had caused his relationship with Ariel to crumble, and could only be grateful there had been no kids involved to be hurt by it. The endless hours he'd spent working with Carson, while good because he got to spend time with his brother, had almost completely precluded Nick from having a life, and kept him so busy he hadn't even noticed when his own began to fall apart.

No matter how beautiful or intriguing Vivian Winthrop was, he would do well to steer clear of falling for a woman who put work ahead of everything else.

Ten minutes later, Vivian finally came inside. "Gosh, it's cold outside. Thanks for taking care of all that stuff and getting it into the house. What do you need me to do?"

"It's all done." He scowled. "Ellie is happily playing in the big pink pen, and your bags are in the room upstairs, across from the nursery."

"You did it all? Wow. You work fast. I meant to help but—" Her phone rang again, and before she finished the sentence, she was already involved in another conversation. Vivian wandered off to the kitchen, pacing as she spoke.

Whatever was happening on the other end of the conversation didn't seem to be going well, which meant Vivian would be tied up for a while. Maybe he was wrong, and maybe her nose to the grindstone was a temporary byproduct of something going wrong in this particular lawsuit. He sure hoped so.

Nick did a quick assessment of the cabinets and freezer. The fridge had been emptied by a well-meaning neighbor after Ida Mae's death, but the freezer still held a quartered chicken. He did, however, find a bottle of wine in the cabinet. He set the chicken on the counter to defrost for dinner. He'd have to run to the market later for more supplies.

"What do you mean they filed a countersuit?" Vivian cursed under her breath. "They think Jerry was responsible? That's bull. I should have been there in court. Getting the judge to dismiss that would've been a slam dunk, Al, and you should have been able to handle it." She paced the ten feet from the stove to the back door. "No, I'll write the response tonight. Did you get the deposition yet? Never mind. I'll handle it myself." She ended the call and put the phone in her bag. She pulled out her laptop and turned to Nick. "I hate to ask but—"

Another phone call. Another work emergency. Of course. Red flags were waving in his face like a cape with a bull. "Go ahead, work. I'm good for a little while. I need to go to the grocery store at some point, and we need to get your car. We can do both later."

"Sure, sure, I'll be done by three." Vivian set up a temporary office at one end of the dining room table. Within an hour, it looked like a complete workplace, filled with files from her bag, notepads strewn with scribbled notes, and sheets she'd printed from Ida Mae's printer. Nick swore he barely heard her take a breath between phone calls.

As the clock ticked past three, he stood to the side of the room, holding Ellie as she drank her afternoon bottle, and Vivian kept on working despite her promise to be done by then. Transport all of this a few miles north and he could have been in the Mausoleum. Where everything outside the law ceased to exist to his parents, including their children.

"What have we gotten ourselves into?" he whispered to Ellie. She just blinked and kept eating.

Chapter Six

By Wednesday, they had all settled into a routine. Vivian got up at five and was on the road to the office by six, long before Nick and Ellie woke up. She texted him every day before she left the office at six thirty, and made any needed grocery runs on her way home. Meanwhile, Nick took care of Ellie, the house and made the meals. After dinner, more often than not, Vivian retreated to the dining room to work. If she got to bed before one in the morning, she considered it a good day. She knew she should help more with the household chores and Ellie, but Nick seemed to have it all under control, and she had a workload that seemed to grow by the minute.

Several times throughout the day, she called and texted Sammie. She'd received one *I'm okay, don't worry*, but no other replies. Sammie had dropped off the face of the earth. Vivian realized how little she knew about her sister—she had no idea where Sammie worked or who Sammie's friends were.

Maybe she hadn't been as good of a sister as she'd thought. That troubled her, and nosed at the insecurities Vivian did her best to bury every day.

She pulled into the driveway of Nick's grandmother's house on Wednesday night, and realized she hadn't been outside during daylight hours in days. She left before the sun rose, returned after the sun had set. The only time she'd spent outside had been going to and from her car in the parking lot. Vivian turned off the sedan and glanced up at the house.

Two stories tall with a wide front porch, his late grandmother's home was painted a pale gray with lilac shutters and white trim. Rosebushes sat beneath the windows, with a thick lawn rolling toward the driveway and sidewalk. Far in the background sat Stone Gap Lake, a deep, dark blue oasis ringed by a few year-round homes.

But it was the golden light framed by the living room windows that drew her attention. Inside the house, she could see Nick, holding Ellie. He'd captured one of her little hands between two fingers and was smiling down at her.

As Vivian stepped out of the car, she heard music. A country song, Thomas Rhett, maybe, coming from inside the house. She stood in the driveway in the cold air, clutching the box of papers she needed to go through tonight, ignoring the weight of the overstuffed bag on her shoulder and the pain of her heels after a long day, and watched Nick glide around the room with her niece in his arms.

And felt like a failure.

Nick made it look so easy. He had from the minute Ellie had dropped into his life. As far as she could tell, every time he picked Ellie up, she calmed down. Every time he changed her diaper, she looked up at him like he was the most adored human on the planet. And every time he held her, she placed her head on his chest and fisted his shirt in her palm, as if she never wanted to let go.

When Vivian picked up her niece, Ellie cried. When she changed Ellie's diaper, the baby squirmed and fussed and the tape went askew. When she held Ellie, her niece twisted away and pitched a fit.

Vivian glanced down at the box in her hands, the files and notes stuffed inside that needed to be looked over tonight. Maybe it was best if she just concentrated on her job. Jerry and his family were counting on her to make it right, to help them get back to normal lives. They needed her.

Ellie, clearly, did not.

Vivian turned, opened the rear door of her car and returned the box and her bag to the backseat. She dug out her keys and was about to open the driver's side door when Nick stepped onto the porch. He had Ellie wrapped in a blanket to keep out the cold. The country song floated in the air between them.

"Dinner's almost ready," he said.

"Actually... I'm not staying."

"You're leaving again already? Why? You just got here. If you want to hold Ellie for a minute—" he held her niece out to her, and as if on cue, Ellie began to scream and protest "—I can put the pasta in—"

"That's why I'm leaving, Nick. Because if I hold Ellie, she's going to scream. If I spend time with her, she's going to cry. And in the end, she's only going to want you anyway, so why should I even try?" She shook her head before her damned emotions got ahold of her. Nick had drawn Ellie back to his chest, and in an instant, the infant went back to being happy and content. Even the thought of being with her aunt upset Ellie. How could Vivian be any kind of parent to a kid who hated the sight of her? Nick was a thousand times better at this than she was. "I have a lot of work to do tonight—"

"You've had a lot of work to do every night, Vivian. And every morning. And all day."

"It's my job, Nick. That's what they pay me to do." It occurred to her that they sounded like a bickering married couple. When had that happened? When had they gone from strangers to friends to some sort of weird partners?

"Not to the exclusion of having a life, Vivian. If you ask me, you're just using the work as an excuse to avoid living. Your sister clearly isn't the only one who runs away." He turned on his heel and went back into the house.

Vivian stood there, fuming in the cold. How dare he tell her how to live her life? To imply she was missing out by being a workaholic? Or that she was running away? Okay, so maybe some of that was true, but as soon as this lawsuit was over…

She shut the car door, marched up the stairs and into the house, ready to tell Nick off. She stopped in the middle of the hallway. In the last few days, she'd come home, beelined to the kitchen for a quick bite to eat, then rushed to the dining room for a couple hours of work, then took the back staircase up to her room in the wee hours of the morning. She hadn't had a moment to pause and look at the rest of the house.

The living room she had been in on Monday, with the couch that was as comfortable as a slice of heaven, was in the process of being transformed. Evergreen garlands wove in and out of fat white pillar candles on the fireplace mantel, and beneath that, a fire burned, safely behind a wrought-iron grate she didn't remember seeing before. A ceramic miniature Christmas tree with hundreds of tiny lights sat on the end table, and the plain glass bowl on the coffee table was now overflowing with red ribbons and thick pine cones. A pillow-sized fat stuffed Santa sat on the sofa, against a thick afghan printed with a snowy mountain scene. The hallway rug beneath her feet had been switched out for a white-and-blue one imprinted with a holiday scene of children sledding down the long runner.

The words she'd planned to fling at Nick died in her throat. "When did you do all this?"

"Over the last couple of days. Whenever Ellie was napping, I'd go up to my grandmother's attic and unearth some more boxes. I had…something I was supposed to find up there, but then I came across the

Christmas decorations and figured it would be nice to put them up. So Ellie and I decorated."

Something he was supposed to find in his grandmother's attic? He didn't elaborate and she didn't ask. She did notice a lone box tucked away in the corner that was marked *Nick*, but didn't question it. This whole thing was temporary, a blip in her life, and getting more personal would be a mistake. "Ellie and you decorated?"

"Yep. I made her do all the heavy lifting while I watched." He grinned at the baby in his arms. "She's got quite the eye for mantel design."

"The room looks beautiful." She stowed her purse and keys on the end table, then stepped into the living room and did a slow spin. "It already looks like Christmas."

"Well, it will. We still need a tree. A real tree, not some plastic fake one that never sheds a needle." He waved toward the corner of the room. A few days ago, a small armchair had sat there. Now, the armchair had been moved to flank the sofa, leaving a blank space between the far left front windows and the wall. A stack of boxes labeled *Ornaments* was sitting on the floor beside the space. "I know this is a temporary situation with the three of us here, but I figured since it was Ellie's first Christmas, she might like the lights and stuff. She already thinks that Santa on the couch is a toy just for her."

Hard-nosed, dedicated, driven Vivian found herself tearing up for the third time in one week. Who was this man? And how did he happen to come into her life—and Ellie's life—exactly when they needed someone like him?

"So why don't you stay here tonight," Nick said, taking Vivian's hand and leading her farther into the living room, "and not work, and spend time with your niece and the man who made you fettuccini Alfredo for dinner?"

His hand felt nice on hers. Warm, safe, dependable. She curled her fingers over his. "You made fettuccini Alfredo? That's my favorite."

"I know. You mentioned it a couple days ago."

"And you remembered?" Damn it. Now her throat was thick, and her heart was full of some emotion she didn't recognize. She'd dated several men over the years, got sort of serious with a couple of them, but not a one could have named her favorite food, the flowers she loved best, or how she took her coffee in the morning. Nick paid attention to details—maybe that was part of the chef in him—and she'd already seen it pay dividends in the way he seemed to have an intuitive sense of what made Ellie happy.

And apparently, he also had a sense of what made Vivian choke up.

"Don't work tonight, Vivian," he said again, softer this time. "Let's eat and then go buy a tree, and decorate it tonight. I bet Ellie will love the lights."

She thought of the box in her car. Jerry sitting in the office conference room a few months ago and begged her to help them. The hours she and her team had put into this lawsuit already. She'd unearthed almost enough evidence of shoddy workmanship on the part of the manufacturer that she could go to them and hopefully negotiate a settlement and avoid a drawn-out lawsuit for that man and his family. Almost enough. A couple more days of work, and hopefully she'd have a solid argument for a hefty settlement.

"I have people depending on me," she said.

"You have a niece depending on you, too."

Vivian looked over at Nick. Ellie was nestled against his shoulder, her wide blue eyes fixed on his shirt. Her fist opened and closed over the soft cotton. "No, Nick. She's depending on you. And if you ask me, that's her best bet. Because I'm a lousy mother. And sister."

And I'm bailing just like Sammie did, bailing on Ellie, bailing on whatever this thing with Nick is.

Then she headed out of the house, got back in her car and drove to her apartment in Durham. At least there she wouldn't feel guilty staying up all night working and catching a nap on the futon in the spare room. And she wouldn't have to be reminded every time she turned around that she was letting down the one person she had sworn she'd never disappoint.

The next night, Nick tucked Ellie into bed, made sure her pink bunny footie pajamas were all snapped and that her room was warm enough. She had nodded off a few minutes earlier, about an hour before her regular bedtime, thanks to Nick skipping her usual late-afternoon nap and braving through the grumpiness that came after dinner. Nick headed back downstairs, set the table, then sat down to wait.

A week ago, he had scowled at the Christmas decorations going up around Stone Gap. He'd considered becoming a hermit until January 1, just to avoid all the cheery greetings and peppy Christmas carols. Then he'd found a baby on the kitchen table, and in the process of caring for her, he'd changed his mind about Christmas. Changed his mind about a lot of things, in fact.

Maybe he was more of a softie than he'd ever thought. Or maybe he didn't want to see another kid grow up in a Christmas void, like he had. Either way, he'd decided Ellie deserved a real Christmas—and he wasn't going to give it to her alone. Vivian had made a promise, and he intended to make sure she kept it.

Of course, all this was also a good way to avoid the request of his late grandmother. He'd found the box she'd mentioned in her letter, tucked in a corner of the attic. He'd done a cursory glance to find it filled with things from his father's childhood—baseball glove, stuffed bear, photo albums, a couple books. One of those leather-bound autograph books filled with signatures. *Build some common ground with him*, his grandmother had written. *You have more than you think*.

As far as Nick could see, he had no common ground with his father. He wasn't ready for another dismissive phone call, so the box sat in the corner of the living room, mocking his procrastination.

Ten minutes later, Vivian walked in. He heard the clatter of the giant bag she carried being set on the floor, the sigh that accompanied her kicking off her heels, then the soft patter of her bare feet down the hall. She stopped midstep when she saw him sitting at the dining room table. "Nick. You startled me. Sorry I'm so late."

"You're not late. You're coming home at the same time you've come home every day." He flicked out his wrist. "Just after seven."

She ignored the sarcasm in his tone. "Where's Ellie?"

"Asleep already."

"Already? Isn't that really early for her?"

"I'm surprised you know her bedtime." He sat back in the chair. The hallway clock ticked away the seconds.

Vivian scowled. "It's not like I haven't been here. Well, except for last night, but I had all this work to do—"

"What's the real story, Vivian?" Last night, when he'd confronted her and told her she was running away, she'd insisted he was wrong—just before she got in her car and, he presumed, went back to her Durham apartment for the night. He'd stayed up, staring at the ceiling above his bed, wondering why he had proposed this crazy idea of the two of them moving in together, and becoming a temporary family until Sammie returned. A few days at most, and then he had been sure Vivian's sister would show up. She'd left her baby behind, after all; surely she wouldn't do that on a permanent basis? But as day after day went by and Vivian's calls to Sammie went unanswered, Nick began to doubt the wisdom of agreeing to this arrangement. He'd had a different vision in his head than what it had become, that was for sure.

"Because you have avoided taking care of your niece since I met you," he said. "I offered to help you out, not become Mr. Mom. She's a great kid, really cute, and she's grown on me, but Ellie is not my daughter."

"She's not mine, either."

He got to his feet and crossed to Vivian. He paused a beat, holding her gaze before he spoke. "Well, she should be someone's, don't you think? She deserves a regular family."

"And why do you think I can offer that? I have no idea what a regular family is like." Vivian spun away and avoided Nick's gaze, just like she'd avoided this discussion for days. "I've got work to do."

"Not tonight." He got up and waved toward the seat across from him. "Tonight, we need to talk about this situation because it's got to change."

Vivian hesitated a moment longer, then dropped into her seat and took a sip of water from the glass on the table. "I can't believe Sammie left her daughter behind. I thought she loved Ellie."

"She does, if you ask me. 'Please take care of Ellie as well as you took care of me. I know she'll have a good home with you.'" He sat down, then slid the note that had been in the basket that first day across the table to Vivian. "Maybe Sammie left her with you *because* she loved her daughter, and because she remembered how you protected her when she was little, and thought you would make a better mom than the state, or some other stranger."

"I'm no good at it. I've seen how Ellie looks at you,

and how she falls asleep just like that for you." Vivian snapped her fingers. "Every time I try to pick her up or change her diaper or feed her, she cries and tries to get away. She hates me."

"You need to try more. Babies need consistency—"

"Thank you, Mr. Parenting Tips, for all your advice, but I don't need you to lecture me on raising my niece."

Her defensiveness was all barbs, a porcupine striking first to avoid an attack, but when she spoke, her eyes watered and her lips trembled, and he realized the capable, strong and smart Vivian was feeling completely unwanted and incompetent. Maybe it was all compounded by the fact that the world expected women to automatically know what to do with babies. Or maybe she truly was overwhelmed by the whole thing. He understood that—those first few hours with Ellie, he'd been convinced he was going to break her or something—but that didn't mean he was going to give Vivian a pass.

But it did mean he wasn't going to beat her up for struggling. If there was one thing that Nick understood, it was feeling like you were never going to measure up to some impossible standard.

He removed the foil covering the chicken parmigiana he'd made for dinner, then dished up a breaded cutlet and some sauce onto Vivian's plate. He topped it with freshly shredded Parmesan cheese. The time it took him to do that eased the tension in the room and gave Vivian a moment to collect herself. "So you mean to tell me that you can take on a multimillion-dollar company in court, but you're going to be bested by a kid who can't even hold a spoon?"

The joke eased the stress on Vivian's features, and she shot him a relieved smile. "Well, that's different. Clients don't need bottles, and multimillion-dollar companies don't need me to change their diapers." She settled her napkin in her lap. "In court, I know what I'm doing. When it comes to Ellie…I don't."

"Well, here's an idea," he said conversationally and easy as he dished up his own plate. "Why don't you take tomorrow off? Completely off. No work, no office, no phone calls. You can spend the time with Ellie—"

Vivian paused, her fork halfway to her mouth. "Alone?"

"Not completely. You'll have me, sort of. I have to go back to work tomorrow, but you and Ellie can come with me to the inn. You'll be in charge when I'm in the kitchen. That way you're not completely on your own, and I'm not missing that little munchkin, which I have to admit I never thought I'd say. Anyway, how's that sound?" He'd already talked to Della and Mavis, who hadn't hesitated to agree that he could bring Ellie to the inn. Both of them, he suspected, wanted to gush over and spoil the blue-eyed little girl. Nick couldn't blame them. Ellie was pretty cute. If he ever had kids of his own—

Well, that wasn't going to happen. But if he had, he would want one who looked like Ellie.

"Wait, you have to go back to work tomorrow?" Vivian said. "I thought we had until Friday."

"Today is Thursday. And in five short hours, it will be Friday."

She did the math, then shook her head. "Wow. The week flew by faster than I thought. I can't take the day off. We're in the middle of trial prep. If you're going back to work, then I'll have to find a nanny. I can't—"

"Try bonding with your niece?" He leaned closer. "She's your flesh and blood, not mine. And you act like she's got the plague."

"She's just not comfortable with me."

"You haven't given her much of a chance to learn to be. She needs a parent, Vivian. She needs someone who's going to plug in and be there for her for eighteen years, if necessary. That person isn't me. I'm a stopgap, not a father."

"I have work to do." She started to get to her feet.

He put a hand over hers and stopped her. He barely knew Vivian and Ellie, but he was damned if he'd let one more kid grow up with distant parents. Maybe all Vivian needed was a nudge in the right direction—and a jump into the deep end of parenting, like he'd had. "I can tell you firsthand that workaholic parents make for some pretty lonely kids who spend their birthdays alone, open Christmas presents alone, and spend all the time in between wondering what they did wrong to make their parents avoid them."

She bit her lip and sank back into the seat. "I get that. My mother was a 'holic' too. Just not a working one."

"Then don't do that to Ellie." *Or to me*, he wanted to add. But he'd already decided after last night that their relationship would be strictly about the baby. Nothing more. If anything proved Vivian's priorities, it was her going back to Durham last night. "Before Ellie got left on the kitchen table, I couldn't tell you the right end of a diaper or how to buckle a car seat. But I learned because that kid needed someone to."

"You're a natural, though." She waved at the dinner, then the decorations in the living room. "You're so domestic and homey, Nick, and I say that with envy. I wish I could be that way, but I'm just not. At all. My apartment was decorated by a woman I hired at the furniture store. And it shows. The entire space has this impersonal showroom feel to it, which is partly my fault because I'm barely there. I don't even own Christmas decorations or travel knickknacks or a set of dishes I inherited from my grandmother." She gestured at the plates and silverware on the table. "The only thing I can cook is spaghetti, and even then I overcook the pasta more often than not. I'm good at one thing, being a lawyer. I can't offer something to Ellie that I don't even understand myself, so how can I be her family when I don't have that foundation of a family, of a home? It's like I've lived on a different planet all my life, and now you're asking me to live on Earth. I'm no good at being a mother or being a housekeeper or even a—" her voice softened to a whisper "—good sister."

"You blame yourself for Sammie taking off."

It wasn't a question because he already knew the answer. He'd seen that guilt in Vivian's eyes from the second she realized Ellie had been left behind on purpose. "It's not your fault, Viv. Your sister made her own choices."

"And almost all of them have been bad, for years now, no matter what I did to try to help her sort herself out. I tried, Nick, I tried so hard to steer her onto the right path. But she dropped out of high school and ran off, and even after I set her up with a tutor to help her get her GED, she took off the day before the test. If she had passed that test, there was a place at a community college waiting for her, a college I would have paid for. I tried to give her a path to a life that was different than the one we grew up with. I swore to her, Nick, that I'd make sure our lives would be different. And now..."

"Your lives *are* different."

Vivian scoffed. "How? Ellie is living with strangers. Sammie is God knows where, doing God knows what, because she's not answering her phone, and all I can do is pray she isn't in jail or wrapped around a tree somewhere. I'm trying to juggle all of it, without anyone getting hurt in the process." She shook her head. "I failed her, Nick. I failed the one person I swore I wouldn't."

"You haven't failed anyone, Vivian." But she looked away and wouldn't meet his gaze, hearing the words but refusing to believe them.

Nick toyed with his fork, his gaze on the pale yellow tablecloth that had covered Ida Mae's dining room table for as long as he could remember. There were a few stains on it, from a splash of red wine, a dollop of spaghetti sauce, and the time that Nick had finger painted with a can of oil paint he found in the garage. Unlike the tablecloths at the Mausoleum, which were pressed and pristine, this one had memories imprinted in every crease. Ida Mae had been as proud of this blemished tablecloth as his mother was of the fourteenth century vase she bought at a Christie's auction. Ida Mae saw the wrinkles and marks as evidence that "the tablecloth had lived a good life," as she used to say.

And it had. Nick hadn't been here nearly enough, but as he looked down at the tablecloth and recalled the memories that included it, he realized he wanted to live a good life, too. He wanted to have the messes and the wear and tear and the memories. If he ever got married, he didn't want to spend more time in the office than he did with his family. Ida Mae had set an example that Nick intended to follow.

Even if it meant dealing with his father in person, as she had requested. Knowing his grandmother, she'd had a good reason behind the ask.

"My father would tell you I'm a failure too," he said. "In fact, he told me that of all his sons, he especially hoped I'd never have children because I was such a disappointment to him. He told me I would ruin the family name by breeding more laziness into the world."

Vivian gasped. "Your father said that to you? Why on earth?"

"Because I dropped out of law school. To him, that was an unforgivable failure. But I was on thin ice with him even before then—for most of my life, really. I've never been the super successful one, and my mother and my professors, would tell you that I'm a slow and stubborn learner, especially compared to my brothers, and especially when I'm studying something I don't like. I have to agree."

Vivian frowned. "I can understand what it means to pick things up slowly, but what do you mean you were a stubborn learner? Isn't stubborn a good thing when you're learning—to have that determination to stick with it?"

Nick chuckled. "For some people, maybe. But that's not how my stubbornness played out. In culinary school, one of the basic tests is to make a French omelet. They're different from regular omelets, softer in the middle, with a fluffy texture. They're one of those dishes that you can't walk away from, not for a second. It takes constant movement and attention and perfect timing to make a good French omelet."

"I don't know if I've ever had one. You'll have to make me one sometime."

That implied they'd have breakfast together. Something he had to admit that despite all his internal protests against involvement with Vivian, he would like very, very much, after a leisurely evening in bed. Because as much as he kept trying to resist this woman, the cold, hard-nosed, driven lawyer Vivian, another part of him kept falling for the barefoot, messy hair vulnerable Vivian from the other night. "I'd love to."

A flush filled her cheeks, then she dropped her gaze to her plate and took a bite. A moment extended between them before he cleared his throat and erased it. "Anyway, I didn't want to do it the same way the head chef did. I made up my own method. And time and time again, my omelet was subpar. The middle would be overcooked or the bottom too crispy. But I was sure I could come up with a better way, and prove my professor, and decades of other chefs, wrong."

"And did you?"

He scoffed. "Nope. But that didn't mean I gave up right away. I stubbornly persisted for way too long. Once I caved and began making an omelet the way I was taught to, though, mine turned out to be the best in the class. I had to fail before I could figure out how to be successful. I've done that all my life."

"That's just so…brave." She sipped her water. "I've never been that way. I've always taken the path of least resistance."

"I would say the opposite, Vivian. The childhood you went through—that's not something most kids survive, never mind thrive under. You went on to law school, and built a successful career. That's bravery. That's strength."

She lowered her gaze and focused on cutting a piece of chicken. "On paper, yes, but in my personal life… not so much."

"I think you are a very harsh self-critic." He covered her hand with his, and for a second, her blue eyes met his, and that barefoot, midnight Vivian flickered in her gaze, then disappeared just as quickly. She pulled her hand out of his and went back to her dinner.

"How did you end up in culinary school?"

A deft change of subject. He should be grateful. Hadn't he just resolved five minutes ago to be baby-business-only with Vivian? "The university where I went to law school also offered a culinary arts program. I went down to the dean's office and switched programs. One good thing about your father not paying attention to you is that it took him two semesters to realize what had happened."

"What did he do?"

"Cut me off financially. One hundred percent." He shrugged, as if the moment hadn't stung. "I started working after classes as a dishwasher and a busboy, and then I took out a loan for the rest to finish getting my degree. But the payments were too much for me to handle on a sous chef's salary, so I went to work for my brother in IT security. It was a job I hated every single minute I was there, but I got used to the steady paycheck and kept making excuses not to walk away. The truth was, I shouldn't have been there in the first place. My brothers are both megastars. Grady makes millions running his own company, and Carson just got promoted to VP. They were both at the top of their classes in school, and even though they didn't become lawyers, they have impressive business cards, you know? Me, I'm a law school dropout and now a chef at a tiny B and B in North Carolina. In many people's eyes, I'm a failure. But at least I'm a happy failure, and if you ask me, that's success."

She shook her head and laughed. "I've never heard success described as happy failure."

It wouldn't have been the way he would have described himself or his life just a few short days ago. But something about being around Ellie had restored his belief in himself. Maybe it was the whole new life thing, or maybe it was just realizing that he didn't have to be perfect, not with his omelets or his diapering skills, to bring the people around him joy. "You asked me that first day if I was happy."

"I remember. You said 'I think.'"

"At the time, I was still moping about the ex-girlfriend, and bah humbugging my way through the Christmas season. I'd been a hermit since I moved to Stone Gap, only coming out of my room to cook meals for the guests, and usually eating alone. Then you and Ellie dropped into my life—literally—and reminded me of what did make me happy."

"What is that?" Her eyes held a genuine question, as if she hoped he'd give her the answers she'd climbed the mountain to find.

"Family." He smoothed a hand across the tablecloth, erasing a wrinkle. When he lifted his hand, the wrinkle reappeared, as stubborn as the stains and history etched in every inch of Ida Mae's home. "This house and my grandmother were an incredibly important part of my family. My brothers and I would come here and be totally different people than we were in the Mausoleum. I think I'd forgotten all that until now.

"I came to Stone Gap a month ago, bitter and disillusioned. Which is pretty much how my life went when I lived with my parents. But here, in this town, at the inn with Della and Mavis, and in this house with that kid I swore I wouldn't even like, and the Christmas decorations on the table and you, I have to say I've got a family, sort of, and I like it."

The lightness disappeared from her features. Her blue eyes clouded, and a wall seemed to fill the space between them. Vivian pushed her plate away and got to her feet. "Family is the one thing I can't give you, Nick. So stop trying to make that happen."

Chapter Seven

Ellie was crying.

That was the first thing Vivian noticed the next morning. She was usually gone before Ellie woke up, and when Vivian rolled over to check the clock in her room, she realized it had been unplugged. Sunlight was just beginning to peek through the windows. Crap. That meant she was late for work. She still had the rest of those case studies to review and the research report to read. The worker she was representing had given her a number to work with—the amount that he felt he needed from the settlement to get his life back on track. But until she had all her ducks in a row, though, there wouldn't be much for ammunition in getting the manufacturer to agree to the number of zeros on the offer. It was a critical day. Heck, every day was critical.

Vivian sprung out of bed, tugged on her robe and hurried downstairs to grab her phone. In the nursery upstairs, Ellie kept on crying, the sound echoing through the silent house. Where the hell was Nick?

She headed for the counter, where her phone usually sat, attached to the charger at night. The space was empty, save for a sheet of paper.

Remember the whole "why don't you take a day off" idea? I called your office and said you were sick today. Al said he'll handle everything with the lawsuit, so don't worry about a thing. I loaded the car seat in your car and went to work. Bottle for Ellie is in the fridge. Take the day off. You need it. And Ellie needs to get to know her aunt. Nick

Clearly, he'd been serious about her taking the day off. That's what she got for leaving their conversation unfinished last night. All the fears, worries, inadequacies that their talk at dinner had unearthed were the kind of thing Vivian did her level best to avoid, and here was Nick Jackson, determined to make her face it all in broad daylight. Damn that man.

For the hundredth time, she questioned Sammie's thoughts in leaving Ellie here with Vivian, the least motherly person on the planet. She was so far out of her comfort zone with the baby, she might as well be in another stratosphere. Why couldn't Nick understand that?

Vivian stared at the sheet of paper, then spun toward the hall where she'd dumped her laptop bag last night. Upstairs, Ellie's cries had become full-on feed-me-and-change-me-this-instant wails. "Hang on, El," Vivian called up the stairs. "Let me just—"

Her bag wasn't there. Instead, another note, tacked to the wall.

I knew you'd try to work one way or the other.
Laptop and phone are at the inn. Breakfast is at
eight. Come join us.
Nick

Vivian was going to kill Nick when she saw him. He'd forced her into taking the day off, even though she'd told him she didn't have the time. Couldn't afford to take her eyes off the case. Now she was going to have to skip work, for at least another hour, until she could get to the inn and get her laptop and phone back.

Meanwhile, Ellie's cries had reached decibels normally reserved for rock concerts. Vivian stood there, trying to figure out which she should do first. Change her? Feed her? Both?

Maybe feed her while she changed her? Was that even possible?

Either way, it sounded like a good plan, and one that would hopefully ease the wailing coming from upstairs. She hurried back into the kitchen, pulled out the bottle that was filled and waiting in the fridge, and found a third note attached to the plastic.

Warm this in the pan of water on the stove. Remember, you want it to be body temperature.

Shake the bottle after you warm the formula, to make sure it's all evenly warm, and test the temperature by shaking a few drops on your wrist. And yes, change Ellie while you're waiting for the bottle. Diapers are next to the crib. You can do it, Viv. Babies aren't as complicated as lawsuits, believe me.

There's a French omelet waiting for you at the inn. With bacon. And blueberry muffins.
Nick

What was this man, a mind reader? And damned if the omelet, bacon and muffins didn't sound amazing. Her stomach growled, and if she'd been three months old, she might have cried and demanded the breakfast be brought to her.

A whisper of confidence trickled into Vivian. Maybe this wasn't all that hard. Maybe she could change Ellie and feed her, and get the two of them in the car and over to the inn for breakfast. It was, after all, the only way to get that deliciousness in her stomach and herself on her way to work. *Babies aren't as complicated as lawsuits.*

Vivian sure hoped Nick was right and that his belief in her wasn't misguided. She did as he instructed, setting the bottle in the pan of water that she started to heat before heading back upstairs and into Ellie's room. "Hey, sweetie. It's your Auntie Viv. Let's get your diaper changed, okay?"

Ellie stopped crying long enough to give Vivian a dubious stare. That was a good start, she hoped. Vivian grabbed a diaper and the box of wipes from the small table beside the crib, then reached for her niece. Ellie squirmed a little, but mostly looked curious and bewildered by the change in her morning routine.

"We've got this, right? We can handle it." The words had a lot more confidence in them than she felt. That whisper from before disappeared the minute she held her niece, still at arm's length, as if Ellie might explode at any second. She didn't have that easy casualness with Ellie that Nick had. Not ever...or maybe just not yet?

Since when have you accepted failure? she asked herself. She'd survived the nightmares of foster care, graduated near the top of her class in high school, then put herself through college followed by law school and risen to the top at Veritas Law in record time.

"Nick's right," she said to Ellie. "If I can argue with a multimillion-dollar company in court, I should be able to handle changing a three-month-old's diaper. It's not rocket science, right?"

Except the last time she'd attempted this, she had failed miserably. Nick made it look so simple. Maybe she was overthinking it.

She laid Ellie on the twin bed, then unsnapped the bottom of her niece's lilac-printed pajamas. Ellie's legs kicked and moved, and it took a couple tries to find and unfasten all the snaps, but a moment later, Vivian had the pajamas off and the wet diaper removed. A quick swipe with a couple of wipes and a clean bottom awaited a new diaper. "Success. Whoo! Wait, El. Don't pee on me, okay? I have to get the new one on.

Just give me a second. I've done this a couple times before—okay, really badly—but I can do it right this time."

She tried to think back to how she'd seen Nick do it, because he was definitely more adept at the diaper thing than Vivian had been—a diapering job which ultimately had to be fixed by Nick, because her bad taping job had fallen apart later. To his credit, Nick hadn't laughed at Vivian's lame diapering. Rather, he'd given her a few tips in that patient, calm way of his.

Center the diaper under Ellie's bottom, he'd said as he redid Ellie's diaper. *Make sure the front and back are evenly aligned. Set the tape across that top band, and fasten it tight enough so there's no gap in the legs.*

"Okay. We've got this." She said it more to herself than to Ellie. Before Vivian could keep puzzling over it anymore, she slipped the diaper under her niece, flipped out the tape on the left and then on the right, then pulled the sides tight as she pressed the tape down and over the marching monkeys on the front. The diaper miraculously stayed in place. She checked the left leg, then the right leg, and there didn't seem to be any gaps. "Wait. Did I actually do this?"

Ellie wiggled her legs, squirming against Vivian's hand of caution on her niece's chest. The diaper stayed put.

"Well, what do you know. Maybe I can handle this after all." She redid the snaps on the pajamas—changing Ellie into clothes seemed a little much for her first solo day—then picked the baby up and settled her against one hip. Ellie moved a millimeter closer than the last time Vivian had held her. A start, at least. "Let's try a bottle. Okay? Sound good?"

Ellie started to cry again, which Vivian took for *I don't care, I'm hungry*, and together, they headed downstairs and into the kitchen. For the first time in a long time, Vivian felt a tiny bit of optimism that maybe, just maybe, she could be the aunt Ellie deserved.

Mavis propped her fists on her hips and stood beside Nick while he mixed plump dark blueberries into fresh muffin batter. There were only a couple guests staying at the inn, both of whom had asked for a late breakfast, which gave Nick a little more time to prep a buffet in the dining room. Muffins first, then some bacon, waffles and eggs.

"Where is that baby, and why haven't you met with your father yet?" Mavis said.

Nick chuckled. "Well, good morning to you, too, Mavis."

"I know you're just avoiding the conversation your grandma asked you for, Mr. Nick Jackson. But it's got to be had. If there's one thing you should have learned from losing that sweet Ida Mae, it's that life is as short as an unlucky cat's tail."

He spooned the glistening batter into a paper-lined muffin tin, careful not to mash the fresh blueberries. "An unlucky cat? I don't think I've heard that phrase before."

Mavis ignored his attempts to shift the direction of the conversation. She handed him the jar of raw sugar, and watched while he sprinkled the muffin tops, then put the pan in the hot stove. In the oven, the sugar would harden, creating a sweet, crunchy topping. "I know you have your reasons why you don't talk to your father—"

"He chose to stop talking to me. And when I told him about Ida Mae's request, he said to just mail the box." Nick started some bacon sizzling in a cast iron pan.

"—but that doesn't mean you shouldn't reach out again and keep trying. Your grandmother, God rest her soul, was the kind of woman who forgave everyone, and just wanted her family to be happy and peaceful."

"Family" had never been a word he'd associated with his parents. It was as if Nick's childhood had happened on two different planets—the Mausoleum and Grandma's. Maybe it was because his father was an only child, or maybe it was part of his father's disdain for the small town where he grew up, but the elder Jackson had differentiated himself from his parents and his past as much as possible.

Nick cracked a couple eggs into a big bowl, added some buttermilk, then whisked in the dry ingredients for waffle batter. Once that was done, he set it aside and went back to the bacon. "That's never going to happen."

"Why do you have to be the thunderstorm on the picnic? You never know what's possible until you try, Nick." She put the empty mixing bowl from the muffins in the sink and ran some hot water over it. "Now, where's my temporary grandbaby?"

"Hopefully on her way over here." He was pretty sure Vivian was going to kill him when she saw him. But he stood by his actions. Even though he'd only known her a short while, he knew she would have found a way to work if he hadn't absconded with her laptop and cell phone. And as long as she put her work first, last and always, she was never going to truly bond with Ellie.

As if conjured up by the conversation, the front door to the inn opened and Vivian strode in, one hand carrying the baby carrier part of the car seat, the other holding Mac and Savannah's borrowed diaper bag. Instead of the severe suits she usually wore, Vivian was clad in a pair of butter-soft worn jeans, and a T-shirt with an image of one shark watching another trying to eat a plump lawyer under the words You're Gonna Need a Bigger Plate.

Her hair was out of its usual professional chignon, and loose around her shoulders. Her face was bare of makeup, which only highlighted her wide blue eyes and dark lashes.

Mavis nudged him. "Don't burn the bacon, Romeo."

He jerked his attention back to the stove. Reminded himself to play it cool. This whole thing was temporary, a deal for the holidays. She was a lawyer who clearly put her career ahead of everything else. If anything said Big Mistake, those two things did.

"Your evil plan worked," Vivian said to him. "I managed to successfully change Ellie, and feed her. She's even quiet right now. And dare I say it…happy."

He grinned. "I wouldn't call it an evil plan. But I'm glad you had a good morning with her."

"There's my little munchkin!" Mavis crossed the room, tugged Ellie out of her baby carrier and held her tight, covering Ellie's cheeks with kisses. "Oh, how I miss these baby days. I hope my daughter has at least two more little ones. There's nothing more fun than being a grandma, even a temporary one." She nuzzled Ellie's chest, and the baby's hand curled around Mavis's thumb. "Let's go visit Della, shall we? She's probably bored silly, paying bills in the office. Let's bring her some sunshine."

After they left the room, Vivian stowed the baby carrier in a kitchen chair, then leaned against the counter beside the stove. She let out a long breath. "Okay, I'm here. Now, where are my phone and laptop?"

"If I tell you, are you going to use them?"

"Of course I am. I have a job to do."

"Then I'm not going to tell you." He flipped the bacon strips. They sizzled and spattered in the hot pan. "Besides, you haven't even had breakfast. It's never good to work on an empty stomach."

"Come on, Nick, don't be childish. Let me do my job."

He avoided looking at her, and kept tending the bacon. In the other room, he could hear Mavis and Della exclaiming over Ellie's tiny feet and hands. "When was the last time you took a day off?" he asked Vivian.

She blew a lock of hair out of her face. "Two years ago. No, three."

"And did you actually take a vacation?"

She toed at the tile floor. "I had the flu."

"But you take off weekends and holidays, right?" He said the last with sarcasm. He already knew that answer, because he knew Vivian's type. He'd lived in that house, had watched that life. Even had a taste of it himself when he went to work with Carson. That job had been a constant, mind-numbing, soul-crushing hamster wheel that never stopped rolling. Just when you met one deadline, six more popped up in its place. It left almost no room for a personal life or anything outside of the office.

"What does that matter?" Vivian said. "I'm single, and I live alone. What is there for me to rush home to? I don't have a cat or a goldfish or so much as a potted plant. No one cares if I work a hundred hours a week."

"I care."

"Why? You hardly know me."

He stepped away from the bacon and shifted closer to her. Without makeup, he could see the dusting of freckles across her nose. Adorable. He softened, ignoring the ache to touch her. "Because I have seen where that path gets you. My parents are very good attorneys. Very busy and very wealthy. And very, very miserable."

"That doesn't mean I'll be the same."

He cocked his head and studied her. The defiant tilt of her jaw, the steely resolve in her eyes. "How happy are you, Vivian?"

She turned away and poured a cup of coffee for herself, adding a generous serving of cream. "I'm happy enough."

"And what kind of life is that?"

Instead of answering, she walked away, clutching the mug in both hands as if she was cold. She paused by the small window on the back door. Beyond the glass lay a long expanse of lawn, green grass rolling down to Stone Gap Lake, a similar view to the one from his grandmother's house a couple miles away.

Nick pulled the muffins out of the oven and set them on a waiting rack to cool. He turned off the bacon, lifting the crispy strips out of the grease and onto a thick stack of paper towels. He ladled waffle batter into the hot waffle iron, and worked his way through preparing two before Vivian spoke again.

"I don't think I know what it's like to be happy," she said softly. "Because just when I would think I was, or that I had found a place where I could bloom, it was all ripped away from me. I guess I've learned to never count on anything or anyone other than myself. I can control me. How much I work, how much money I make, how many people I let into my world. But I'm not sure that equates to happiness."

"If you ask me, that's kind of sad. Understandable, given your childhood, but still sad." He set the pile of hot waffles aside and covered them to keep them warm. Then he put the omelet pan over the heat and added some butter. While that melted, he whisked three eggs with a little water and salt until the mixture was frothy and light.

"It's my life, Nick. I don't know any other way to be."

"Then why don't you take today, and the opportunity Sammie dropped into your life, and see where it gets you?"

"It's not that easy." She watched out the window a little while longer, then sighed and crossed to the stove, watching him cook.

Every muscle in his body was attuned to her presence. To the soft swell of her breasts under the T-shirt and the way the jeans hugged her hips and legs. Her perfume wafted between them, and tempted him to move closer.

The butter foamed in the pan, and Nick poured in the eggs. He gripped the pan handle with one hand while he stirred with a silicone spatula with the other, moving the pan and the eggs at the same time. The cooked eggs moved to the center and the uncooked part rushed to the open edges. Over and over he repeated that step until the eggs were almost completely cooked. Then he shut off the heat, smoothed the top of the eggs and folded the omelet into thirds. He added a tiny pat of butter under the omelet, then tipped the pan toward one of the blue-and-white stoneware plates. The omelet slipped easily from the pan and onto the plate, looking like a pale yellow pillow of eggs. The whole process took maybe two minutes.

"Wow. That's almost a work of art."

"Well, taste it and see if it lives up to its appearance." He added two slices of bacon and a warm blueberry muffin to the plate, then handed it to Vivian. "Do you want a waffle too?"

"If I eat all of that, I might explode. Wait…is that real maple syrup?"

"Yep."

Vivian groaned. Nick would have paid a million dollars to be the reason she made that sound when he touched her. "That sounds good. Save me one." She stared toward the table, then paused and glanced at him. "Aren't you eating?"

"I have to serve breakfast to the guests first. I'm doing a buffet with an omelet station in the dining room. I'll eat later."

"That's no fun." She sat down at the table, spread a napkin across her lap and picked up her fork.

"Ah, but all the fun for me is in watching other people eat my creations." And even though he knew the guests were waiting for their breakfast, he turned and watched Vivian take her first bite.

A smile spread across her face, and she closed her eyes for a moment. "Wow. That's amazing. Velvety and buttery and not at all like I expected."

"A good French omelet will make you forget all other omelets. Sort of like a good man." What was he saying? Where the hell had that come from? Was he volunteering for the job?

"I wouldn't know." Her cheeks flushed. "I mean about the omelets. My breakfast is normally a granola bar eaten on the run—or just a cup of coffee if I'm really in a rush. And if I do a business breakfast, I'm too busy working and talking to eat more than a couple bites of anything."

"That's no fun," he said, repeating her words. He

really needed to get back to work, but he was enjoying this rare moment of being alone with Vivian more than he wanted to admit. Mavis and Della were still cooing over the baby, their voices carrying down the hall from the office. He could hear the guests milling about the dining room. And still he stayed.

"I've always looked at food as a means to an end, you know?" Vivian said. She paused to eat the rest of her omelet, and let out a little moan of satisfaction at the end.

Damn. Nick was never going to be able to concentrate on cooking if she kept doing that. All he wanted to do was hear her make those sounds in his bedroom. "You, uh—" he cleared his throat, refocused his attention "—enjoyed your breakfast?"

She nodded. "Very much. I never realized what an experience a meal could be if I just slowed down and appreciated every bite."

She had finished the eggs and bacon, and was slathering butter on her muffin. If only to stop thinking about kissing her, Nick grabbed the pot of coffee, topped off Vivian's mug and set the creamer on the table. The waffles, muffins and bacon waited for him to bring them to the dining room. "I...should get back to work."

A soft smile curved across her face, and her blue eyes held his. "That's no fun."

He stepped away from the stove, his focus narrowing to only Vivian. Just as he moved to cross the kitchen toward her, Mavis marched into the kitchen with Ellie in her arms. An interruption both welcome and frustrating. In an instant, the sexual tension between Vivian and Nick evaporated.

"We have decided we are going to kidnap this little munchkin tonight!" Mavis exclaimed. "Because Della and I think you two need to go out and have a date."

"Oh, we're not..." Vivian looked at Nick. Her cheeks flushed, as if they'd been caught kissing by her father. "We aren't..."

Dating Vivian would be a huge mistake. He already knew where this path ended. He'd had a taste of it for the past week. His parents' relationship was bad enough, but at least they shared similar goals. Selfish goals that meant neglecting their kids, but shared goals all the same. He and Vivian didn't want the same things at all. He wanted a family. She wanted a career, to the exclusion of everything else. They'd never be happy together in the long run. If he was smart, he'd say thanks but no thanks to Mavis and get back to work.

Instead, he poured another ladle of waffle mix into the iron, then turned to Vivian and said, "We should."

"We should...?" The question trailed off, and a flicker of mischief lit her eyes, maybe started by the decadence of blowing off work and indulging in real maple syrup. "That would be a full day of playing hooky for me. I don't think I've ever done that."

He wondered what else Vivian had yet to do. And how he could figure into that. "Then let's do it. We can grab some dinner and then go pick out that Christmas tree. Together."

"I'd like that, Nick." The whispered words were almost buried under the beep of the waffle iron, but he heard them. And told himself that the warmth he felt from them was just the steam from the iron. It couldn't be anything more.

Chapter Eight

When Ellie napped, Vivian was finally able to work. She'd opted to hole up for the day in Della's office with her laptop, because being in that kitchen with Nick this morning had been way too tempting. Not just to eat ten more omelets, the entire stack of waffles and every last blueberry muffin, but to touch him, kiss him and find out why he'd agreed to that crazy plan of a date tonight. The initial plan of a full day of playing hooky had been replaced by a full day of working and an evening off. Anything else was too distracting and awoke a craving inside her she'd never known before.

An insane part of her was looking forward to the whole thing. She hadn't been on a date in over a year, and had never picked out a Christmas tree. The few holidays that she'd had when she was in foster care had been half-hearted at best, with overwhelmed temporary parents and houses full of kids. Every year, her mother had promised. *I'm gonna get you girls back, and we're gonna have the best Christmas you've ever seen. I'm just waiting on a paycheck*—or the courts or a man or whatever the excuse was that year—*and then I'm gonna get you and we'll be a family again.*

Even before foster care, there had been broken promises and empty dinner tables. Vivian stopped believing in her mother a lot sooner than she stopped believing in Santa Claus. There were no Christmas miracles, just a lot of empty promises.

But maybe this year she could create a little Christmas magic for Ellie. Her niece wouldn't remember it, but years down the road, Vivian could show her pictures, and tell her that for her first Christmas, there had been a tree and a Santa.

Vivian took a sip of lemonade—yet another homey touch from Della and Mavis—then got back to work on an email reply to the equipment manufacturer's legal team. They wanted to avoid the lengthy court trial and millions it would likely cost them by settling out of court. The settlement they offered, however, wasn't enough, not without an admission of guilt and a recall of all other similar machines in use in factories across the country. Vivian didn't just want justice— she wanted to protect anyone else from suffering as Jerry and his family had.

She glanced over at Ellie, who had just nodded off. The day with Ellie had gone smoother than Vivian expected, mostly because there were plenty of hands on deck whenever Ellie was awake. It hadn't been the trial by fire that Vivian had expected, thank God. Nick had popped into the office between shifts in the kitchen, but a guest who asked for a last-minute birthday cake kept him busy most of the day. Between chores around the inn, Mavis and Della hovered around the office, ready to offer advice when Vivian was feeding or changing her, and to pick up Ellie the second she let out so much as a squeak.

Vivian had researched the Stone Gap Inn before making the reservation for her and Sammie, so she'd known that the place would be comfortable and well-maintained, but the surprise—during her stay, and then during this unexpected day visiting the inn—was how big a role the owners played in making the inn such a wonderful place.

Della Barlow and Mavis Beacham welcomed every guest at the Stone Gap Inn with a Southern drawl, a warm hug and a friendly smile. Their gracious Southern hospitality matched the rooms at the inn, with their big, fluffy comforters and deep, floral-patterned armchairs. Wicker baskets overflowing with local goodies—jams, cookies, candles—waited in every guestroom for new arrivals. If there was ever a place that could be called a home away from home, it was the Stone Gap Inn.

Little wonder, then, that Ellie responded well to both the environment and the women fussing over her. All the attention wore Ellie out, and she napped without complaint, twice in the morning and once already this afternoon.

Della rapped lightly on the open door. "Care for some company with your lunch?"

Normally, Vivian would say no because she often worked while she nibbled. But today was technically a day off, as Al reminded her in a stern voice every time she called him, and Ellie was asleep in the playpen set up in the corner of the office, so it might be nice to have some girl time with one of the inn's owners. A few minutes of that wouldn't make a big difference in her workday. She could always make up the time after five.

Except there was that "date" with Nick tonight that she'd agreed to. Dinner alone, before Christmas tree shopping. A part of her kept getting distracted by the idea of being alone with Nick. Of the possibility of him kissing her again.

"Sure, come on in," Vivian said. She caught the scents of toasted bread and something fruity, and her stomach rumbled.

Vivian cleared a space at the desk for Della, then took her plate. "Thank you for bringing me this."

"Nick's in the kitchen, whipping up some buttercream frosting. He says baking is not his thing, but I tasted the cake batter and it was delicious. Who knew such a simple thing as a white cake with buttercream frosting could taste like heaven?" Della had a friendly face, eyes that seemed to dance every time she talked and deep red hair that spoke of a lively spark in her personality. She loved her boys, her husband and her town with a fierceness that Vivian envied.

"Just like the muffins this morning," Vivian replied.

"Nick is an incredible chef. He made something as simple as eggs, bacon and muffins into something that could rival any five-star restaurant. And this…" She glanced down at her plate. "Is this a panini?"

Della nodded. "Turkey and Swiss with homemade raspberry jam and watercress on rye bread. With a side of sweet potato fries and a cinnamon dipping sauce."

Vivian's mouth watered. The sandwich was perfectly toasted, glistening with warm butter. A dollop of raspberry jam slowly oozed out from between the slices of pressed bread. A towering bonfire of crispy fries was stacked beside the sandwich.

"God, that looks good. If I keep letting Nick cook for me, I'm going to gain a hundred pounds," Vivian said. "Nick is an incredible chef."

"You said that already." Della grinned, then took a bite of her sandwich, chewed and swallowed. "He's also a pretty incredible man. Any woman would be lucky to have him, if you ask me. Mavis and I have gotten to know him pretty well since he started working here."

Vivian avoided the obvious sell of Nick as a romantic prospect. This whole thing was a bump in the road, a short detour. As soon as possible, Vivian had to go back to the real world and that meant leaving that "incredible man" here in Stone Gap. The renovations on her apartment would be done soon, and then she could go back there. Get Ellie set up in the day care program at work, maybe hire a nanny for when she had to work late, and essentially go back to her normal life. Even if the idea of that sounded awfully stale right now. "Mavis knew his grandmother, she said."

Della nodded again. "Pretty much everyone in town knew Ida Mae. She was a big part of the Stone Gap community. Always organizing one thing or another, or helping out at things like the town picnic and the garden club. She's going to be sorely missed."

Despite Vivian's vow a second earlier to forget about Nick, curiosity nudged at her. "Did you know Nick when he was growing up?"

"No, not really. The Jackson boys lived in Raleigh, so they weren't in school with my three." Della grabbed a fry, dipped it in the cinnamon sauce, then popped it in her mouth. "I saw the boys with Ida Mae a few times when they visited her, and she'd take them down to the lake or over to the ice cream shop, but from what I gather, they liked to stay close to home during their visits. And with three of them, they could play together, so they didn't worry about making friends in the neighborhood. I did, however, get to know Nick's father. Regrettably."

"Why do you say that?"

"I know you're a lawyer, dear, and I'm sure you're a wonderful one. But Nick's father is...well, a bulldog. If he was fighting for the underdog then I'd be fine with it, but he doesn't care who he's fighting for or against—he just wants to fight. He sued my husband's auto repair business for something that didn't need to go to court. Nearly bankrupted us, until Bobby went to the guy who filed the suit and worked it out in person. Those lawyers who go after businesses without knowing the whole story..." Della shook her head. "Well, I don't have anything nice to say about them."

Vivian nudged her trial paperwork to the side of the desk. She liked to think that she *did* fight for the underdog—Jerry certainly fit that description—but she knew she could be as ruthless as anyone in the courtroom, although Vivian's job was to make cold monolithic corporations pay for their mistakes and shortcuts. She wasn't trying to wipe out the neighbor's business. "I worked in an auto repair shop for a few months when I was young, doing little jobs mostly. One of my foster fathers owned a business like your husband's." Vivian had seen the sign for Gator's Garage on her way into town last week. She'd heard that Bobby Barlow was partially retired, and one of his sons was running the business now.

A business passed down from one generation to the next. If she'd had a child, would her son or daughter follow in her footsteps and go into law? Maybe come to work at the firm with Vivian some day? Or would her child be a rebel chef like Nick, carving out his or her own path?

"Well, should you ever need a job, Luke's always looking for extra hands at the garage." Della grinned.

"I'll keep that in mind." Vivian took a bite of her sandwich and swallowed. The flavors melted against her tongue, sweet and savory, all in one. "This is really good."

"Nick's amazing. We've had so many recent Yelp reviews raving about the cooking at the inn that we can hardly keep up with bookings. December's going to be crazy busy. Mavis and I never expected this little inn to take off so fast."

"I'm happy for both of you. It's a lovely place to stay."

"That's because Stone Gap is a lovely town to live in." Della dipped another fry in the cinnamon sauce. "Nick says you lived here briefly?"

Vivian had already finished off most of the sandwich and made a serious dent in the fries. No wonder people raved in reviews about the meals here. "I was only here for a couple months one summer, with my sister Sammie, Ellie's mother. We lived with a foster family. The Langstons."

"Oh, Ruth and John," Della said. "Lovely people. They must have fostered a hundred kids over the years. Opened their hearts and home to so many youngsters. They retired and moved to Arizona a couple years ago."

A regrettable fact that Vivian had learned after she booked the stay here, and looked up her former foster family. They'd had a pleasant phone conversation and made vague plans to meet up another time.

"It was the best foster home I ever stayed in." The only home where Vivian had imagined a real future, with family dinners around the dining room table and sleepovers with friends from school. From the day the girls stepped across the threshold of that blue-and-white ranch house, the Langstons had been warm and loving and had treated both girls like family. "I only wished I could have stayed longer."

"What happened that made you leave the Langstons? If you don't mind my asking." Della's eyes softened with true caring, and her hand covered Vivian's for a moment.

"The same story that happened over and over again in our lives." Vivian sighed. "Us girls were like a boomerang that pinged between my mother's house and wherever the state could find space for us. That summer, my mother got her act together enough to get custody of us again. We went back, but all her promises not to drink and to hold on to a job lasted about two weeks, and then we were taken away from her again and sent to the next home, and the one after that. Rinse and repeat. We bounced all over North Carolina. Sometimes Sammie and I were separated—not all homes want two teenage girls at the same time—but I managed to keep in touch with her, and sometimes got to go to the same school."

Sympathy shimmered in Della's eyes. "You poor things. All kids should have a proper home to grow up in. I just don't understand parents who can't put their children first."

Parents like Sammie, who had abandoned her daughter. Or like Vivian, who kept abdicating all the responsibilities to Nick, when Sammie had left her to be Ellie's parent. Did Della put them in that same category?

"So you and your sister are close?" Della asked. "She looked like a lovely girl when the two of you checked in. I'm sure being a single mom has been tough on her. I remember how overwhelming it was when I had my first son."

Vivian picked at the fries, her appetite gone. "Sammie and I grew apart after I turned eighteen and started living on my own. I booked the weekend here because I hoped it would be a chance for us to reconnect, in the one place where we both were happy for a short while. I didn't even know she'd had a baby until she showed up. And within twenty-four hours, she was gone again."

"And left her baby with you."

Vivian nodded.

"Poor girl must have been so desperate to do something like that," Della said. "Being a new mother is not an easy job. When my boys were little, there were many days when I thought about running away and joining the circus. Kids are a lot of work, and when you're a brand-new momma, you're always sure you are doing it wrong."

Or a brand-new aunt who had a thimbleful of parenting skills. "Maybe. But Sammie has never been super responsible anyway."

"Well, maybe she got scared when she realized little Ellie was counting on her to be responsible, and Sammie didn't quite know how to do that. Did I ever tell you about my early days with Jack?" Della shook her head and let out a little laugh. "Of course I haven't. We've only just met. But pretty much everyone around here knows what happened."

Vivian took a sip of her lemonade. "I can't imagine you ever being overwhelmed, Mrs. Barlow. You just seem so...capable of anything."

"Smoke and mirrors, sweetie, smoke and mirrors." Della pushed her plate to the side. "Jack was a fussy baby from the start, and I was a terribly nervous momma. My own mother was a good mother, but a little…distant. Not cold, just not warm, you know?"

Vivian nodded. She thought of Nick's parents. If Della had become a person who embraced everyone and made mothering look easy, then maybe Vivian would be able to do the same. Someday. Someday she would be somewhere else. And someday Nick would, too. Maybe he'd be with his own family with another woman. The thought made a sharp pain sear her chest.

"Anyway, there was one day when Jack just wouldn't stop crying. I'd gone maybe three, four days without sleep. That little booger was up all night, and both Bobby and I were exhausted. Jack was probably colicky, but I was so headstrong, I was sure I could handle this on my own, and that I didn't need to go to the doctor. Anyway, Bobby went to work, and I was home alone with little Jack. I tried everything. Blankets, bottles, binkies, walks, singing, rocking, offering him bribes—"

Vivian laughed. "I take it those didn't work?"

"Nothing worked. I felt like such a failure. So I decided I was going to just find someone else who could take care of Jack. I wasn't thinking of giving him away exactly…honestly, I'm not sure what I was thinking in my sleep-deprived mind. I was so convinced I was a terrible mother. I bundled Jack up and put him in the stroller and headed downtown. I was either going to find Mary Poppins or go see Bobby and have him help me somehow. I didn't even make it to the garage before Jack started crying so hard, I was worried he might choke. I stopped, sat down on a bench and just broke down."

"What happened?"

"Ida Mae, of all people, happened by. She sat down beside me and told me that her Richard had been the same way. A real pain in the butt, she said. That made me laugh, but I still couldn't stop crying." Della smiled at the memory. "I'm sitting there, holding my crying baby, and crying just as hard as he is. Sweet Ida Mae said, *here, let me*, in that soft, sweet way she had. She took that screaming little boy and rewrapped his blankets around him like a burrito."

"Swaddling." Nick had mentioned something about that the other day when he was holding Ellie. He had clearly inherited that soft, sweet way from his grandmother. "It calms the baby, right?"

"Yep. Makes them think they're all snug and happy in the womb again. Wouldn't you know, my little Jack stopped crying quick as a minute, and took his bottle like nothing had ever happened." Della pressed a hand to her heart. "Made me so happy. But then one second later, I felt like a failure all over again. I was his mom. I was supposed to know what he needed."

"I've felt the same way." The admission took a weight off Vivian's shoulders. If this capable, kind, smart woman had felt the same way with a new baby in her life, maybe it was more common than Vivian thought? "I'm a woman—aren't I supposed to be a natural mother?"

"I don't know if anyone is a natural mother. It's natural to love our kids the second they're born, of course, but we're also all scared to death we're going to screw them up. Most moms get past that, and realize that all they can do is their best and pray the good Lord directs their hand and watches over their kids."

"And some moms just keep on screwing up." Like her own mother.

Della gave a sad, slow nod. "They do, and they sometimes hurt their kids in the process. Not by intention, I don't believe, but like a car accident on the highway. A chain reaction. If you ask me, those moms are the ones who need the most love and understanding. They're struggling so very hard, and they still keep falling down."

"Like my sister. And my mother."

"Exactly. Just before she went on her way, Ida Mae said something to me that day that I've never forgotten. Something that got me through mothering three very active, very boisterous boys." Della leaned across the desk. "You can either choose to believe in yourself the way your baby does, or choose to believe the doubts that are whispering in your ear. From the day they were born, all my boys looked up at me and Bobby with love and trust. They believed we could take care of them and love them the way they deserved. It was up to us to rise to that challenge."

Undoubtedly, Vivian had looked at her own mother that way. There were days when her mother had been good—Vivian had spotty memories of doing puzzles and making sandwiches together—but then her mother would sink back into depression and self-medicating, and those days would end. Could it be that her mother had felt the same as Vivian and Della? Like a failure?

And every day she let her girls down again, she just proved her worst fears about herself?

"All your sister is hearing in her head are all those doubts," Della went on, "all those whispers that say she's not a good enough momma for Ellie. She's got to choose to believe differently." Della's concern and soft voice made it all sound so simple and clear. "Maybe Sammie truly isn't ready to be a parent right now and that's why Ellie is with you. Because it wouldn't be good for her to be a…what did you call it? Boomerang baby."

Vivian shook her head, and tried to ignore the flicker of guilt that she'd come very close to finding another home for Ellie. *Boomerang baby.* Just like she'd been and Sammie, too. "I'm no good at being a mother. I don't have the instincts for it."

"Oh, sweetie, you do too. We all do, if we choose to open our hearts." Della rose and picked up both plates. "Being a good mother starts with love. I've seen how you look at that baby. You have love in abundance. Start there. The rest will come. And give that little girl the kind of home and childhood you dreamed of having."

Then she left the office, leaving Vivian alone with Ellie, who had started to stir. No matter what Della Barlow said—or how cleverly she tried to convince Vivian to stay by mentioning jobs and what a wonderful place Stone Gap was to live in—Vivian knew the best option, for herself and for Ellie, was to stick with what she did best.

Being an island unto themselves.

* * *

The afternoon passed in a blur of emails, files, phone calls, diaper changes, bottles and visitors. The inn was a busy place during the day, guests in and out, meals served, housework done. The dining room was transformed for the impromptu birthday party for one of the guests, and the scent of cake fresh from the oven kept tempting Vivian out of the office. She tried to avoid Nick, but she found at least a half a dozen excuses to go into the kitchen. A glass of water. A paper towel to wipe up a spill. A new bottle for Ellie.

Every time, he greeted her with a smile that made her heart flip. As if he was genuinely glad for the interruption. They chatted a little, mostly small talk, then Vivian used the work excuse to duck back into the office.

She buried herself in the pages before her, the documents she was supposed to read. But it wasn't enough to forget Nick—

Or the big decisions that were waiting for her soon. Al had been the first to ask when she'd be back in the office full-time. "That court date is going to be here before you know it, Viv. We're going to need all hands on deck if any of this goes south before then."

She'd mumbled something vague, then hung up. Ellie, on her back in the playpen, was watching her hands wave back and forth. Happy, content, warm, fed. Looking up at her aunt with trust and belief. *You can either choose to believe in yourself the way your baby does, or choose to believe the doubts that are whispering in your ear.*

How could Vivian leave her? With the state, with a nanny, with anyone?

But how could she keep her? And do it all herself? Or manage to juggle motherhood and a busy career?

Vivian was just about to call the client with a status update when her phone rang. Sammie's number lit up the screen. Vivian nearly dropped the phone, fumbling to answer it. "Sammie. Where are you? Are you okay?"

"I'm fine." There was the sound of passing traffic behind Sammie's voice. "How's Ellie?"

Was her sister on a freeway? Hitchhiking? Frustration and anger trumped Vivian's concern in that moment, though. "She's fine. We've been watching her. What were you thinking, leaving her here?"

"Who's we?"

"Me and Nick, the chef at the inn. He's the one who found her in the kitchen. It's a long story. But she's fine." Then Vivian's anger ebbed, and her worry for her little sister returned. For so many years, it had been the two of them against a world that was always upside down. Outside, the air held a December chill, and Vivian wondered if her sister was cold, alone, hungry. "And you, you're okay?"

A horn blared. A beat passed. "Yes. I just…needed some time to clear my head."

Vivian bit off the first comment about being a responsible parent that came to mind. If she kept lashing out at her sister, it would only make Sammie more distant. "Where are you? Tell me, and I'll come get you."

"I'm okay," Sammie said. "I'm glad Ellie is with you. I…" Her voice caught. "I miss her so much, Viv."

"I know you do. I know you love her." Vivian pressed the phone tighter to her ear, as if she could transport through it to Sammie's side. "When are you coming back?"

"Soon. I promise." The traffic whipped by with a steady *vroom-vroom* sound. It had to be a highway. Vivian prayed Sammie wouldn't be stupid enough to hitchhike.

"I'll send you some money. Give me the address of where you're staying." Vivian readied a pen and dug through the pile on the desk for a blank sheet of paper.

But Sammie was already refusing. "I can't. Not yet. I... I wasn't ready to be a mom, and that's why I left. I've been going to counseling and working, and just trying to get my act together so I can be there for Ellie. I don't want to fail her like Mom did, you know? But I still don't know if I'm ready."

"You don't get a choice in that, Sammie. You have to grow up sometime. Ellie is here and she needs a mother."

"Who can be you until I'm ready."

"Sammie, I have a demanding job and a life in Durham. I can't be a mom, too." Vivian softened her tone. She thought of Nick's notes, of his soft, calm words that guided her through the simplest tasks with Ellie. "You can do this, I know you can."

"I'm not like you, Viv. I work as a waitress, and I barely pay my rent. I can't afford Ellie. And I sure can't afford day care while I work. You...you have money and a nice apartment and I'm sure you're so much better than I am with her. You were so good with me, Viv. A better mom than ours."

"Sammie, Ellie loves you. I've seen the two of you together. You're her mother, through and through. I'll help you with the money. Just come back. Please?"

"Take care of her for me, will you?" Sammie's voice broke. "I hate not being with her. But…I didn't know what else to do."

Damn it. Why wasn't Sammie listening? "Come back to Stone Gap. Ellie misses you."

Sammie's words caught on a sob. "I swore I'd never do this to my kids. Not after Mom did it to us."

In the space between them, a dozen memories flowed. The two girls, huddled together, sobbing, while strangers invaded their house yet again, piling their belongings into garbage bags while their mother ranted about the government. Being hungry, dirty, scared, but not wanting to leave. Not again. And then their mother, packing the rest of their things in the bags and shoving them out the door and turning her back on her daughters, a drink in her hand. Always a drink in her hand. "Then don't, Sammie. Please don't."

"You make it sound so easy. It's not, Viv. Babies need food and diapers and cribs and car seats, and all these things I can't afford."

"I'll buy all that. Call it early Christmas presents. I already shipped a bunch of things to your apartment a couple days ago." Vivian could hear the desperation in her voice, the hope that some money could smooth all these bumps for Sammie. She knew that was impractical, and a panacea for an unwieldly problem. But it was the best Vivian could offer.

There was a long moment of silence. "Do you really think I can be a good mom?"

"Yes, Sammie, I do."

"Maybe if I can get a better job, and find a better place to live—"

"Let me help you with that. I can pay—"

"I need to do those things on my own, Viv. I appreciate it, but like you said, I have to grow up sometime. And now is the time." Sammie sighed. "Just a few more days, okay?"

Vivian thought of the work week ahead of her. Nick was back at the inn during the days, which meant he wasn't going to be babysitting full-time anymore. He'd forced her to take a day off, which had been a nice break, she'd give him that, but it had put her even more behind. She needed to be in the office, not working from home. Otherwise, details got missed.

She was just going to have to contact her work's day care and find a nanny for after-hours. Go back to Durham this weekend, interview some caregivers and get a plan in place before Monday. Talk to her contractors and see if they could put a halt to the renovations and make the place livable by Monday. Staying here much longer only put her more behind at work. Maybe with the help of a nanny, she could at least leave the office at a reasonable time every day so she could spend time with her niece on a daily basis until Sammie returned.

"Yeah, sure. That'll be fine," Vivian said.

"Thanks, Viv. You're the best. I knew I could count on you."

As she hung up with her irresponsible little sister, Vivian realized she had just done the same thing she'd always done for Sammie—made escaping reality easier by taking away the pressures of real life.

Chapter Nine

Nick hadn't been this nervous in a long time. He finished the dinner shift at the inn, with Mavis and Della practically shoving him out the door so he could go home and get ready for his date that may or may not be a real date. He'd decided to treat it as a real date, regardless. Vivian might be all wrong for him, this always-working lawyer who had no interest in a family life, but the little glimpses he'd had of another side to her intrigued Nick. And as much as he tried to repress it, he couldn't deny that he was interested in her. Vivian had left a few minutes earlier, leaving Ellie with the two women. Della had Ellie in her arms, and was waiting for a bottle to warm.

"Don't you worry about a thing," Mavis said. "We are going to spoil this little girl rotten, and keep her up well past her bedtime."

Nick chuckled and gathered up his bag. "I have no doubt you will. All right. We'll be back by nine to pick her up."

When he pulled in the driveway of Ida Mae's, he did a double take. The lights were on, drenching the windows with a soft golden glow, and the soft strains of the radio could be heard when he stepped out of the pickup. Some Frank Sinatra song. Nick could see the Christmas decorations he'd put up in the days before, looking bright and festive and homey. Welcoming.

For a second, he was ten years old and running into his grandmother's house, rushing toward the sight of warm cookies and even warmer hugs. This house, with its lilac shutters and ring of rosebushes, was home, Nick realized, more than any home he'd ever known.

He pulled out his cell and called Grady. "Hey, big brother. When are you coming down here to see your inheritance?"

"Work is crazy," Grady said into the phone, then he gave directions to someone driving. "I'm heading into a meeting in a minute. I thought you said you were staying in the house. The electric and gas are all paid. And I'll send a maintenance guy by every month to check on any necessary repairs."

In other words, Grady was going to be as hands-off about his inheritance as Nick was about the box. He wondered what that said about the two of them. "I am staying here. But the house is technically yours. Which means I think I'll have to look for one of my own."

"What, down there? In Stone Gap?" Grady scoffed.

"I know you loved that place but the only good thing about it to me was Grandma."

"There's more good here than you know." Was Nick talking about the weather? The inn? Or maybe a certain woman he was seeing tonight?

"Well, feel free to stay there as long as you like," Grady said. "I miss you, brother."

"Miss you too. Come down and visit sometime."

Grady scoffed. "Chances of that are slim. Talk to you later."

Grady hung up and Nick realized that telling his brother to come and visit sometime implied he wasn't going anywhere. He'd thought his move to Stone Gap was temporary, but as he stood there in Ida Mae's driveway, he realized he didn't want to leave this place, a town that held all his best memories. The job at the inn might not be glamorous or even pay all that well, but it was a job where he felt content, where he created things that made people happy. And that was something he'd been seeking all his life. He was going to take Grady up on his offer, and stay in the house until he found one of his own.

Nick got out of the car, took the porch stairs two at a time, then walked inside. "Honey, I'm home!"

The joke echoed into an empty space. He checked the living room, then the kitchen. No Vivian. As he returned to the hallway, he heard the sound of her heels on the wooden staircase. He watched Vivian descend, giving him a slow reveal of long, long, amazing legs, a sleek black dress and sexy shoulders bared by her upswept hair.

"Holy cow. You look…" He turned to the small bookcase in the hall and feigned grabbing a book. "Wait, let me get the thesaurus, because amazing isn't a good enough word for how you look."

She laughed and stopped on the last step. A faint blush filled her cheeks. He liked that blush. And loved that he was the one who caused it.

"This is probably too much for dinner and tree shopping," she said, "but my wardrobe consists mainly of the things I've brought back from my apartment over the past few days, and the things I brought with me for the weekend with Sammie—so basically, court suits, jeans and this one dress in case Sammie and I went out."

"It's perfect." He leaned over and kissed her cheek, drawing in a whisper of her fragrance, a bit of her warmth. He wanted to draw her close, to touch all the enticing parts bared by the dress. Later, he hoped, there would be time for that. "Give me five minutes and let me see if I can find something that does that dress justice."

A tease quirked her lips. "Should I time you?"

He slipped off his watch and pressed it into her hands. "If I don't make it in time, then how about… I owe you another night on the town?"

She parked a fist on her hip. "And how is that a prize for me?"

"Hopefully, you'll see tonight." He gave her a quick kiss, then took the stairs two at a time, peeling off his shirt as he headed for the shower, and getting ready in record time. He opted for a pale blue button-down shirt and a dark patterned tie under the suit he'd worn for Ida Mae's funeral. Like Vivian, he hadn't packed much beyond the essentials. At the inn, he didn't have to get any fancier than jeans and a polo shirt. The few extra pieces he'd needed in the last month, he'd bought locally. At some point he had to go back to his apartment and clean it out, he supposed. The thought didn't depress him anymore and in fact, he was looking forward to finding a little house of his own here in town. Except to have the money to do that, he had to fulfill Ida Mae's request. That thought *did* depress him. Maybe he should just put the damned box in the mail and be done with it. Until then, there was tonight. And Vivian. And that sexy black dress.

He charged down the stairs and feigned panting, his hands on his knees. "Whew! That was tough. Did I make it?"

"Five minutes and twenty-seven seconds." She gave him back his watch. "I think you did that on purpose."

"I may have." He grinned, then put out his arm. "Your dinner awaits, milady." He took her out to the pickup, held the door and helped her up into the seat. She'd put a long coat over the dress, and the suede slid across his leather seat with a slight whoosh. "Sorry we aren't riding in something fancier, but the truck is the most practical for Christmas tree shopping."

"I'm not a fancy kind of girl, Nick," she said. "I like a simple life. I really do."

He was counting on that tonight, and had wagered his idea for a date would be perfect for the Vivian he knew. Not harsh, commanding courtroom Vivian, but the barefoot in the dark Vivian he liked very, very much. He put the truck in gear, swung out of the driveway, then took a left on Lakeshore Road.

"We aren't going into town?"

"Later, when we get the tree. But for now, I wanted to take you somewhere special." The road curved around the perimeter of the lake, winding down past the Sea Shanty, which was lit but sparsely populated on this early winter night, and then came to an end at a park that had seen better days. The town still decorated it for the holidays, though, and dozens of white lights greeted them as Nick pulled into the parking lot and shut the truck off. The engine ticked as it cooled, the only sound in the quiet night.

Vivian drew in a breath. "Wow. This looks so beautiful."

There were lights all over, but a particularly large concentration had been woven along the posts and between the rafters of a white-and-dark-green gazebo, as if God had dropped a constellation in the middle of the park. The reflection of the decorations twinkled on the dark lake, undisturbed save for the occasional splash of a rushing fish. Swags of evergreens looped around the railings, caught with giant red bows at each pillar.

Nick got out of the truck, came around, opened the passenger door, and extended a hand for Vivian. "You can leave your coat in the truck."

"It's cold out, though."

"Trust me, Vivian."

She shrugged out of the long garment and set it on the seat. "I rarely trust anyone."

"I know. Come see for yourself." As she stepped down, he grabbed the basket he'd packed earlier. She gave him an inquisitive glance, but didn't say anything as he led her up the crushed shell walkway, one arm around her, supposedly to block the faint breeze off the lake, but considering it was warm, he knew, as she probably did too, that he was using the kiss of wind as an excuse to touch her. Three steps up to the gazebo's entrance, and Vivian paused.

"Oh, Nick." She turned to him, a hand to her lips, her eyes shimmering. "That is the sweetest thing anyone has ever done."

His heart jumped and he had the craziest urge to cry. The joy and surprise in her face could have knocked him over. He cleared his throat. "Now don't go getting all emotional on me. It's just some blankets and a ceramic heater." He led her to the cushions he'd borrowed from the inn's outdoor furniture, then fished a lighter and a big candle out of the basket and lit it.

"How did you…where did you…?"

"I borrowed the heater from Jack Barlow when I got this crazy idea this afternoon. Ran up here and set all this up on my way home from the inn. It wasn't much. Really." Because the way she was looking at him made Nick feel like he could have done so much more to earn the tears brimming in her eyes.

Vivian shook her head. "No, it's perfect. It's truly perfect. And warm, like you said."

He uncorked a bottle of white wine he'd kept chilled in the basket, then poured them each a glass. "I'm glad you like it. We could have gone to a restaurant, but I thought we both could use a night…"

"Alone."

He shrugged, because that one word held connotations Nick wasn't sure either of them was ready to address. Instead, he sat down on the opposite cushion and began unloading the basket. "Chicken marsala, with whipped Parmesan potatoes and Italian peas with roasted pearl onions. And…homemade Parker House rolls."

"You know my weaknesses well, Mr. Jackson."

"I hope that one of them is me." He tucked a lock of hair behind her ear and allowed his hand to linger on her jaw. "And that is, without a doubt, the corniest thing I've ever said."

"I didn't think it was corny." Deep blue pools met his gaze, as dark and mysterious as the depths of Stone Gap Lake. "Not at all."

She leaned forward, and the shifting of her weight on the cushion made her slide into him. He didn't complain. Nick slipped an arm around Vivian and lifted her onto his lap. She laughed and wrapped her arms around his neck. "What are we doing?"

"Enjoying our appetizer." He nibbled at her neck, then down the curve of her dress to the swell of her breasts. She arched into him, her hands tangling in his hair. Their breath was short, their hearts racing, and everything within him wanted to lay her down on those cushions and make love to her until the sun came up. Instead, Nick drew back and pressed his forehead to hers. "If we keep that up, we'll never have dinner."

"Or dessert."

"So, do we eat first? Then make out?"

She laughed and slid off his lap, then settled on the cushion, in prim and proper form. "Yes. I do think that's wise."

He did, too, but not because he was hungry. Because he knew that he wasn't just falling for this town, and thinking about something more permanent here. He was falling for Vivian, too. The vulnerability she struggled so hard to contain, the strength and smarts that had gotten her from foster homes to multimillion-dollar lawsuits. The fierce love and loyalty she felt for her family, her sister.

And the way she kissed him. For the first time in a long time, Nick realized what it was like to be with someone who had no other someones in mind. Whose sole attention was on him, with a warmth and connection that he hadn't realized he'd been missing until he had it.

If he was going to make this work, then he had to do it right, and that meant not rushing headlong into a relationship. That was the kind of thing that would make Vivian bolt. And besides, there were questions he had to answer for himself, too. Like how much he was willing to compromise when it came to her work situation.

He put his phone on some soft jazz background music, dished up the food and for a while they exchanged small talk about Ellie, the inn, the town, the weather. The words flowed between them on a companionable river, light and easy as leaves skimming the surface.

"So, what's your plan for this Christmas tree we are buying later?" she asked.

"I don't have a plan. It can be whatever we want. I'm not one of those 'everything must match and look like it came out of *Architectural Digest*' kind of people. I'm pretty much a go-with-my-gut guy. Which works well in cooking, not so well in designing security code for computers."

She laughed. "I can see that. That's a job where everything has to follow precise directions, I'm sure. As for me, I've had everything mapped out for my life for so long, I'm not sure I have the ability to go with my gut."

He mixed some chicken with the potatoes and swallowed the morsel. "Isn't that exactly what you have to do when you're raising a kid who can't speak yet?"

"I'd say I'm just following your lead and hoping I don't screw up." She took a sip of wine, then set the glass on the wooden floor of the gazebo. The twinkling lights woven into the rafters bounced off the goblet. "Although today went much better than I expected. It helped that Mavis and Della were in the office every five minutes to hold Ellie."

"You're better with Ellie than you think," Nick said. "When you loosen up the bun and the rules, you're calm and that's contagious to everyone around you."

"Loosen up the bun?" She laughed a little, then sat back on her elbows. "What does that mean?"

"Well, there are two Vivians. Courtroom Vivian,

with the bun and the suits, and late at night home Vivian, when you quit working and take a breath. The Vivian with the bright red nail polish and the smile that lights up a room." He toyed with a lock of her hair. The easy updo she had tonight meant a few tendrils framed her face, dusted her neck. "That's the beautiful Vivian I can't resist."

"You can't?" she asked, the words breathless and hushed.

"Not from the minute you came storming into the inn."

"And you threatened to call the police on me."

"Well, I thought you were a babynapper."

"Do I look like a babynapper?"

He pretended to study her, tilting his head left, right, tapping a finger on his chin, until she laughed. "Nope. You look like a woman I would enjoy spending time with."

"Well, when you find that woman, you might want to spend some time with her."

That earned a laugh out of Nick. "Touché. I think I've met my match. You are pretty damned smart, Vivian." He shifted closer to her. The scent of her perfume warmed the space between them. "In case you're keeping track, that's two compliments in the space of five minutes."

That flush filled her cheeks again. "I noticed."

"I must say, I'm feeling quite unappreciated." He feigned outrage and put a hand on his chest. "Every night this week, you have come home to dinner made, kid bathed and ready for bed, and a bevy of compliments—"

"I'd hardly call two a bevy."

"And what do I receive for my efforts? An 'I noticed.' Humph."

She laughed. "You do know that you sound like a nagging wife, right now, don't you?"

"Considering I've never had a wife, I wouldn't know."

"Why not?" She put a little distance between them and took another bite of dinner. "Why haven't you been married?"

"I could ask you the same thing. You're a beautiful woman, and I can't imagine why you're still single."

"Will you quit calling me beautiful?" She ducked her head, and he swore he saw another blush on her face. "Besides, I asked you first."

He paused a moment, thinking about his answer. He'd never really given the subject much thought. Even the decision to propose to Ariel had been a more of a this-is-the-logical-next-step thing "I avoided anything that had the potential to become a long-term relationship most of my life. My parents had such an awful marriage, and I didn't want to end up like them. From what I heard, my grandparents had a perfect marriage, but after my grandpa died when my dad was a teenager, people said Ida Mae was never quite the same again." Grandma Ida Mae had kept her late Henry's portrait on the mantel, and hanging in the hallway. She'd stop and talk to it sometimes, her undying love clear in her voice. Even as a kid, Nick had understood that pain, that deep, abiding emotion, and the fragility of it all. "I guess I didn't want to take a chance on having something that good and losing it."

"I understand that." She sighed and took another sip of wine, then waved off his offer of a refill. "I've spent my entire life not counting on good things. Every time my life seemed to be on track, I'd end up yanked out of that house and sent to another, or I'd be moved to another school or Sammie would get in trouble and I'd have to go run and help her."

"And you learned not to rely on anyone but yourself?"

"Exactly."

"Sounds like we're two peas in a pod," he said. He set down his half-empty wineglass. "And maybe I should do the same, considering the first woman I thought about marrying ran off with my supposed best friend."

"But you seem to fit into the two-point-five kids, dog in the yard life and all of this—" she waved a hand around the gazebo, past the lake, toward the town and the life that existed just around that bend "—so easily. You created a home in a vacant house in a few days, Nick. I haven't been able to do that in thirty years."

"All I did was build on the home my grandmother had. She was the one who did all these things—set up the Christmas tree, baked the cookies, read us stories at bedtime. My parents hired nannies and chauffeurs and paid people to raise us, essentially." He had, indeed, re-created his memories in the way he'd decorated the house for Christmas. The stuffed Santa was in the same place on the sofa, the candles and evergreen bows displayed as they always had been. Grady, he knew, wouldn't have cared if Nick redecorated the whole house. Grady clearly had no intentions of living there, and no intentions of returning to Stone Gap. Grady would keep up the maintenance of Ida Mae's house, but otherwise ignore his inheritance. Nick wanted to have one last holiday there, even if the rooms echoed a little too much now.

"So you spent your childhood with strangers, too, in a way," Vivian said.

Strangers. That was a good word for the paid help who'd raised him, and for his parents, especially his father. They'd never seen eye to eye, never had a single thing in common. Why Ida Mae had tasked Nick with reconnecting with Richard, Nick had no idea. Of the three Jackson boys, he was the least likely candidate. Even though none of them had become lawyers, at least his older brothers were both successful, driven, hard-chargers like their father. Nick was far more content with his low-stress, low-ambition chef's life in Stone Gap. The direct opposite of his father. Maybe that was part of Ida Mae's thinking. "Guess that whole living with strangers thing might be another part of the reason neither one of us have settled down."

She scoffed. "Boy, we'd make some therapist rich if we ever decided to unpack our emotional baggage."

"That's very true. Here's to us." He raised his wineglass, and she did the same. A merry clink sounded in the quiet night. "Now all that aside, we have yet to settle our debate."

"What debate is that?" She took another bite, and he could tell by the smile on her face that the dinner was a hit. He'd made hundreds of dinners, but never had he been so committed to making a diner happy as he had with Vivian.

"Whether or not you appreciate me, especially after my bevy of compliments." Nick grinned.

She rolled her eyes and laughed. "Okay, you want a compliment?"

"Why yes, I do."

Vivian glanced around the space. Her gaze skipped over the thick blankets, the ceramic heater, the basket and the spread of food, now almost entirely gone. "You...cook very well."

"Well now there, Ms. Winthrop, be careful because you're getting awful personal."

She pursed her lips but her eyes danced with merriment, and Nick decided this was his favorite Vivian, the one who laughed and teased. "Okay, so you're also...pretty good-looking."

"Be still, my heart." He put a hand on his chest. "I may have to put that in my next online dating profile. Should bring the ladies running. Cooks well and is pretty good-looking."

"And you know it. So there, that's the end of my compliments." She raised her chin and met his gaze.

"Too bad. Because now I'll never know..." He raised up on his knees and leaned toward her.

She watched him, her eyes wide. A breath passed between them. The lights sparkled on her face, danced golden dust on her eyelashes. "Never know what?"

"If you want me to kiss you again."

A loon called across the lake in the distance. A soft splash spoke of a fish being chased. Clouds drifted past the moon, casting a hazy veil over the world.

"Well, I...well..." She swallowed, then let out a breath, and one whispered word. "Yes."

Instead of kissing her right away, Nick got to his feet, put out his hands, then drew Vivian up and into his arms. The radio shifted to a slow song, as if the DJ was in on some kind of a conspiracy to bring them together. Nick put one hand on Vivian's waist, took her opposite hand with his, then began to waltz her away from the blankets and the heater and into the center of the gazebo. She kicked off her heels, and danced barefoot on the painted wood.

With her shoes off, she was a few inches shorter than him, but she fit against him as if she had been made for the space between his arms. A couple of missteps, and then their rhythms synced. He leaned closer, inhaling the dark scent of her perfume. Like Vivian herself, even her perfume had layers and surprises.

A few more renegade tendrils had escaped the updo and skated along the edge of her neck. He whispered a kiss just below them, as light as a breeze. Then another and another, dancing down her neck with his lips. She let out a soft gasp, and her hand tightened in his. Her eyes widened in the low interior light. "What are we doing?"

"Dancing. Kissing. Mostly dancing."

"It feels a lot like something more."

"Yes, it does." What more, he didn't want to voice,

afraid the moment was as fragile as a soap bubble. Instead, he stopped moving, cupped her face in his hands, and kissed Vivian good and proper. The way he'd wanted to since the day he met her.

She leaned into him, her hold tightening. The music shifted to something else, but neither of them noticed. They had this moment, and neither wanted to let it go.

Chapter Ten

Dozens of Christmas trees lined the tarred parking lot of the white Presbyterian church in downtown Stone Gap. One wizened old man in a Charlotte Hornets ball cap and a flannel shirt manned the lot. A bright orange pair of work gloves waved from the back pocket of his worn jeans. "Merry Christmas! Can I help you two lovebirds find a tree?"

Lovebirds?

Then Vivian realized she'd been holding hands with Nick ever since she'd gotten out of the truck. Actually she hadn't stopped touching him ever since they left the gazebo. They'd danced and kissed until the air got too cold, and they had to pack up the food and leave. She could blame it all on the wine, but she'd only had one glass, and Nick hadn't even finished his. The dancing, the kissing, the hand-holding, had all been...

Wonderful.

If she was honest with herself, that's what she'd say. Wonderful and sweet and temporary. She'd expected Nick to be like every other man she'd dated—men who took her to nice restaurants and said nice things, but left as much of an impression as a drop of water on a sponge. The romantic gazebo setting, the thoughtfulness of the heater, the amazing meal and ambiance had all been the kind of moments she would hold on to long after she left Stone Gap.

And that's what she needed to remember. No matter how wonderful their date had been, no matter how much she wished they'd done more than kiss and dance tonight, this was a single date that was coming to its inevitable end. She had yet to tell Nick she planned to go back to Durham this weekend because she kept getting distracted from her job and her situation with Ellie by this man. She had maybe twenty-four hours left in this fantasy bubble of Stone Gap and Nick Jackson before her real life returned. Selfishly, she didn't want their time together to end yet, but she also knew the sooner she stopped being so attached, the easier leaving would be.

She released his hand and stepped away, drawing her coat tighter as an excuse to let go of Nick. A chill chased along her empty palm. "Just a simple tree," she said to the man. "Nothing fancy."

The older man thrust out his hand. "Name's Cutler Shay. Welcome to Stone Gap."

"How do you know I'm from out of town?" Vivian asked.

"I've been around Stone Gap long enough to know pretty much every man, woman, child and grandchild in these parts. You don't look one bit familiar, so I'm guessing you're an out-of-towner. But you…" He stepped toward Nick and studied his face for a moment. "You're… one of Ida Mae's grandsons, aren't you? You've got her nose and her eyes, my boy."

"I am. I'm Nick. The youngest of the three." Nick shook his head. "Wow. I'm surprised you'd recognize me."

"Oh, I'm not that good." Cutler waved off the words. "Just joshing with you. I saw you moving into your grandmother's house. I live across the street. And scuttlebutt around town is that you've been settling in here, working at the Stone Gap Inn."

Nick grinned. "Of course. The Stone Gap gossip chain. Nice to see you again, Mr. Shay."

"Cutler will do just fine. Any relative of Ida Mae's is a friend of mine." He gave each of them a grin, then made a sweeping gesture of the lot. Trees lined either side of a pathway that extended from the front of the church to the back, all along the side driveway. Three-inch white Christmas bulbs strung between the trees to separate them somewhat into aisles provided decent enough lighting to see the trees, and hand-lettered bright red and white tags showed the pricing up front. "You might want to look at one of the Douglas firs. Ida Mae was always partial to them, and they look mighty nice in that corner of her living room. How long are you living there? Might want to get a watering system if you're staying past the holidays."

Vivian glanced at Nick, then back at Cutler. "It's just a temporary thing."

"Uh-huh. I've heard that before." Cutler started walking through the tree lot, passing the squat blue spruces, the plump Norway spruces and the skinny traditional pines as he spoke. "You know, your grandmother and grandfather, God rest their souls, said the same thing when they first bought that house."

"I thought my grandmother always lived here in town."

"She did. Like me, she grew up in Stone Gap, and like most of us when we hit eighteen, she said she was going to move to somewhere bigger and fancier after we graduated. Living in Stone Gap was only a 'temporary thing.'" Cutler's wrinkled hands fashioned air quotes around his words. He paused by a selection of Douglas firs and raised a caterpillar brow in Vivian's direction. "But this town has a way of growing on you when you're not looking."

Why was everyone trying to sell her on Stone Gap as a home? She had a life elsewhere, a job, an apartment. Her time here was all going to be done and over in a day or two. "Yeah, like moss on a tree."

Cutler laughed. "Yeah, like moss. But you know, moss serves a purpose. It helps the tree retain water, save it up for those days that are dry and hot as Hades. At first, the tree might be annoyed by the moss, but after a while, it realizes the moss gives the tree a better life."

Vivian didn't quite see how that equated to moving to a tiny town in North Carolina, but she wasn't about to argue. Cutler seemed to be full of homilies, and right now, she just wanted to get the tree and go. This night with Nick was making her want things she couldn't have. Best to end it quick, with this one last memory. "All these trees look great. Can you just wrap one up for us?"

"Now, now, you can't just pick a tree like that. A Christmas tree is special. It needs to be chosen by the people who are putting it up. It's going to be a part of your home—" Cutler put up a hand "—temporary or not, doesn't matter a whit. You should always make sure the tree feels like part of your family."

A part of their family? It was just a tree. And they were not a family. Not even close. Even if Nick saw it that way. The words panicked her because a part of her had long ago stopped believing she could have the very thing that she'd lacked all her life.

Vivian looked at Nick. He shrugged and gave her a grin, unfazed.

"Now, the Douglas fir isn't exactly a fir. You see these cones here?" Cutler reached in between the branches to point out one of the long brown cones. "They're distinctive just to the Douglas firs. This French botanist some years back—and his name is all Frenchie, so I can't pronounce it—named the Douglas fir a 'false hemlock,' because it looks like one of those trees. But don't worry, it's not the kind of hemlock that Socrates used to poison himself. Or was it Plato?"

Cutler shook his head. "That's neither here nor there. What's important is which of these trees feels right?"

To Vivian, every one of the bright green trees with their dark brown cones looked exactly the same. Okay, yes, she could tell that a few sat wide and short, others were taller and leaner. But tree for tree, they were nearly indistinguishable. Cutler was staring at her, though, with a grin on his face that was half-knowing and half-expectant, so she pointed to the tree on her right. "That one." She turned to Nick. "Does that work for you?"

"Yep. Seems like the perfect tree for us. A little lop-sided and in need of a good home."

Lopsided? She hadn't noticed that. But as Cutler pulled the tree out from among the others, she saw that the one she'd chosen did, indeed, lean a bit to the left. "Are you sure you want a tree that's not perfect?" she asked Nick.

"None of us are perfect, Vivian," he said. "You can look at that tree, or that one, and you'll find a flaw. The flaws are what make the trees interesting, though. And people, for that matter."

Good Lord. Cutler was rubbing off on Nick. But why was it that when Nick talked, all Vivian could do was stare into his dark brown eyes and listen to the cadence of his words? The wine. It had to be the wine.

A single glass of a fruity chardonnay affecting her that deeply? Unlikely. More that she'd grown to like Nick. Very much. That was all. He was a good friend. An interesting man.

An interesting man who could kiss her and make her forget everything and everyone else. An interesting man who touched her and made her melt. An interesting man who wasn't going to be so easy to leave behind.

Cutler cleared his throat. "All right, kids, let me wrap her up and get her ready for you. Then you can go home, put on the Christmas carols and get decorating." Cutler took the tree with him as Nick and Vivian followed, then he laid it on a wrapping machine and pushed a button. Orange netting slipped around the tree, pressing it into a more easily transportable shape. "After we finished decorating the tree, my wife and I, God rest her soul, would sit on the couch and watch the lights twinkle. I used to think she was a sentimental fool, but now that she's gone, I realized I was the fool for not paying more attention."

A brisk breeze whistled through the lot, as if in answer to his words. Love and devotion weighted the ends of Cutler's words, and shimmered in his eyes. He raised his gaze to the sky for a moment, then gave a little cough and bent to tie some twine around the base of the tree. "Damn, I miss her. Should have appreciated her more when she was by my side."

"I'm so sorry about your wife," Vivian said. What would it be like to be loved that much? Or to give that kind of love to another? The kind of love that transcended life and death, and lingered in your veins?

"Aw, thank you, miss. My Sarah was a saint for putting up with me. And when you find a keeper like that, you don't let go." Cutler straightened and took the cash from Nick. "Doesn't matter where you live or what you live in. The right woman is the one who makes it a home. Remember that, son."

"I will," Nick said. "You have a good Christmas, Cutler." He hoisted the tree onto one shoulder and headed back to the pickup truck, sliding the tree into the bed in one smooth move. He opened the door for Vivian and helped her up.

Their touch extended a few seconds longer than necessary. His hand warmed hers, and his gaze filled her with a comfortable joy she had never known. If only a bottle existed that could hold this moment, so that when she returned to Durham she could revisit Nick's touch from time to time. "We, uh, should pick up Ellie and get that tree set up before it gets too late."

Nick dropped her hand and stepped back. "You're right. We should." Then he closed the door and walked around to the driver's side. The drive to the Stone Gap Inn only took a few minutes, but the bubble that had wrapped around them from the minute she'd come down the stairs in her dress had popped, and they were back to being simply strangers who'd formed a temporary alliance to help one little baby feel safe and protected.

Mavis and Della almost didn't want to give Ellie back. "She is just the cutest thing," Mavis said, with Ellie in her arms, swaddled in a pink blanket and already dressed in her pajamas. "Such a good baby."

Della ran her finger over Ellie's tiny hand and gave the baby a smile. "My boys were never that sweet.

They cried so much, I've always told them I would have given them back if they weren't so darn cute."

Nick laughed. "If I promise to bring her back, will you let us take her home and put her to bed?"

Mavis made a face of discontent, but handed Ellie over. "You make sure to tell her that her aunties Mavis and Della can't wait to spoil her again."

"And that we'll bake her cookies soon as she starts getting a couple teeth." Della tapped Ellie's chin. "Isn't that right? Any kind of cookies you want, sugar pie."

"We better get out of here before they build her a swing set in the yard," Nick muttered to Vivian. She'd said maybe three words to him on the short ride from the church to the inn, and had found ways to avoid his touch. After the wonderful time they'd had in the ga-zebo—most of all, the way she had responded when he kissed her—Nick wondered where things had gone left instead of right. Had he said something that made her mad? Things had changed after the Christmas tree purchase, and he was damned if he knew why.

"Thank you so much for watching her." Vivian gathered up the diaper bag while Nick put Ellie in the baby carrier. Vivian headed out the door first, but Della pulled Nick aside just before he left.

"How did it go tonight?" she whispered.

Della had helped him coordinate the heater with Jack, and had lent him the insulated basket for the food and wine. Probably out of some misguided plan to make Nick and Vivian fall in love and settle down in Stone Gap with Ellie, the newly adopted granddaughter of the Stone Gap Inn. He couldn't bear to tell Della that the evening was ending on a flat note. "Pretty good."

Della smiled. "She seems like a very sweet woman when you get her away from working. I had a lovely conversation with her this afternoon, you know. About babies, motherhood, and you."

About him? Nick wanted to ask what Vivian had said, but that would have been obvious and needy, and he was neither.

"I agree," Mavis said. "I've seen how that girl looks at you, Nick. She's more smitten than she realizes."

The two women couldn't have been more blatant matchmakers if they'd been holding up signs. Nick bit back a groan. "I'll see you tomorrow morning, ladies. Thanks again."

"No worries. It was our pleasure." Della gave Ellie a quick kiss on the forehead. "See you tomorrow."

Nick started out the door again, but Mavis stopped him with a touch on his shoulder. "One more thing." Cold air was coming through the open door, and he could see Vivian sitting in the truck, but Mavis paid neither any attention. "I heard your father will be in town tomorrow."

"Why? And how did you hear that?"

"I have a little birdie down at the town hall. He said your dad is coming into town to meet with a client about a new building project that's getting some pushback from the commissioners."

"That's a lot of words for a little birdie." There had been talk about a small outdoor mall going up in Stone Gap, something many people in the town opposed because they believed it would ruin the character and charm of the area. Some corporation had apparently looked at Stone Gap's location off of Route 95 and decided it was perfect for more tourism. Nick wasn't surprised his bulldog father was involved in the legal battle over that.

"Just call him. Meet him for lunch. Like Ida Mae asked you to." Mavis's features softened. "Your grandmother wouldn't have asked if she didn't think it was important. For you *and* her only son."

Ida Mae's only son had barely stayed to the end of his own mother's funeral. He'd let her grandsons handle the arrangements, contributing only by handing Grady a check. *Just tell me the time and date,* their father had said. Ida Mae leaving the house to Grady rather than Richard wasn't a big surprise—over the years the Jacksons had made millions from their law firm. They hardly needed more property when they already owned the Mausoleum and multiple vacation homes all over the world. Instead, she'd left her son and daughter-in-law some stocks, her other grandsons money equal to the house she'd left Grady, and then that damnable box that Nick had yet to deal with. And a not-so-simple request for Nick.

"I'll…think about it." Then he said goodbye for the hundredth time and stepped out into the chilly air.

Ellie was completely worn out by her adventurous day at the inn, and fell asleep as soon as the truck started. Vivian had hoped for some baby distraction tonight, but Ellie went straight to bed, barely stirring when they got home and Nick carried her upstairs.

Vivian followed him up to the nursery. Ellie's tiny head was nestled into Nick's shoulder, and soft baby snores escaped with her breaths. Nick paused by the crib, cupping Ellie's head as he lowered her onto the mattress. Every move he made with the baby held tenderness.

It almost made Vivian jealous. What would it be like for Nick to touch her that way?

He stood beside the crib and smiled down at Ellie. "She really is a beautiful baby," he said quietly. "And so well behaved. Not that I have any other babies to compare her to."

Vivian shifted to stand by Nick. She held the railing, her hands close enough to touch his. Ellie's eyelashes fluttered, and every once in a while one of her hands would clench and unclench, as if she was holding something in her dreams.

A beam of moonlight speared into the carpet, reflecting off Ellie's delicate features and then the dancing horses mobile above her head. On the scarred maple dresser, the short night-light matched the moon with a silvery pool of light. The carpet beneath their feet was soft and thick.

All across America, new parents were doing this same thing. Standing in a dim nursery, watching their sleeping baby, a little universe of just the three of them. If she and Nick were married, she could, for a split second, imagine that this was their life. Their family.

Her heart filled, a rush of emotion so strong, tears

threatened her eyes and her throat thickened. Vivian Winthrop had gone most of her life trying not to make connections, because she'd learned early on that the love of others could disappear as quickly as a storm cloud. She didn't get attached, didn't start to care, didn't let her heart open. Until this week with Nick and Ellie.

He'd made her believe in things she'd convinced herself were fictional. And worse, he'd made her want those very things for herself.

"She really is beautiful," Vivian whispered. "And impossible not to love."

"If she were ours…" Nick began, then shook his head, as if speaking the words aloud would create something he didn't want to breathe to life.

"Yeah," Vivian said. "But she isn't."

His hand slid over to cover hers. His fingers were warm, strong. "I never realized how much I was missing out on until you and Ellie came into my life."

"I was thinking the same thing just now." She turned to face him. Maybe it was the dim light, or the moment, or the dinner date, but for just tonight, Vivian didn't want to be her usual cautious, closed-off self. *If you stay with me, it gives me an excuse to hang some lights and make some eggnog and cookies and have the kind of holiday normal people have*, Nick had said a week ago. She had gone along with the plan then, mostly out of desperation. Now, they had a tree in the back of the truck and a box of decorations to hang, and the rest of the wine to drink while Christmas carols played in the background. "Tonight, Nick, let's just pretend."

"Pretend what?"

"That…this is our baby, and our first Christmas and…that there's an us." That he wasn't with her out of an agreement or because of Ellie, but because he wanted her and wanted to be with her forever.

"I think that's a great idea because I really want there to be an us right now," he said. Nick leaned over and kissed her, then took her hand, and the two of them headed downstairs. While she put on the radio and poured the wine, Nick brought in the tree.

She held the door for him, ushering in a chilly breeze. Vivian had yet to change out of her dress, and she stood in the doorway, shivering. "Hurry up. It's cold out here."

"I can't believe that because you're looking mighty hot."

She rolled her eyes. "Okay, now *that's* the corniest thing you've ever said." But she laughed anyway, as the tree spearheaded the way down the hall, and Nick pressed another quick kiss to her lips as he passed by.

Bing Crosby was singing "White Christmas" on the radio as Nick set the tree into the stand in the living room, then pulled out a pocketknife and cut off the netting. The branches sprung out, casting a spray of needles on the floor. Nick adjusted the stand, pulling it away from the wall to give the tree more room. "Do you want me to straighten it so it doesn't look so lopsided?"

Vivian shook her head. "You're right. It's better because it's not perfect." This entire week with Ellie had been imperfect, filled with a couple bumps and detours, and yet, right now, Vivian wouldn't change a thing. The forced day off and the time with the baby had begun to loosen the bonds and expectations that had guided her life for nearly thirty years, and it hadn't been as bad as she'd expected. The world hadn't imploded, and she hadn't ended up heartbroken. At least, not yet. She handed Nick a glass of wine. "Where do we start?"

"Here," he said, then kissed her again. This time, he lingered, his kiss deep and true and tasting of chardonnay. She curved into his arms, arching into his chest, wanting more, wanting him, wanting whatever this was. In the background, Bing gave way to Burl Ives's peppier "Holly Jolly Christmas."

Nick stepped back. "We're never going to get this tree decorated if we keep doing that."

"Nothing wrong with a naked tree."

He laughed. "I do like your train of thought, Viv. But let's at least get some lights on there. Ellie will love that."

A part of her heart melted at the thoughtfulness in Nick's words. The tree, the lights, were about making a three-month-old happy. A baby who would never remember this moment, or this tree. Nevertheless, Nick had slipped fully into the role of surrogate father—protective, considerate and sweet.

Those were good qualities in a man. The kind of qualities a smart woman hung on to and treasured. Except some smart women had careers in another city, and lives too cramped to have room for a child and a husband. Some smart women had never dared to dream of a man like Nick.

As she crossed to the decorations box, she saw the other box with Nick's name on the outside, still sitting in the corner. "What's that?"

"A request." Nick sighed and dropped into the arm-chair. "My grandmother left it for me to give to my father. She actually listed it in her will as a condition of me receiving my inheritance. She wants us to go through the box together. Why, I have no idea. I looked in there, and it's just a bunch of stuff from his childhood."

"The same father who doesn't talk to you?" Vivian sat on the ottoman across from him.

Nick nodded. "I called him and told him about it, and his words were, 'drop it in the mail.' Even this final request from his mother wasn't worth him coming around to see his own son."

"His name sounds familiar. I'm sure he is doing all that because he's probably a very stubborn man." She paused, thinking of the lawyers she knew, the ones who would argue to the death for a small point, the ones who had been divorced many times or were on the outs with their families. Time and again, she'd seen the same common thread. "Or a very hurt one."

"What makes you say that?"

As the words coalesced in Vivian's mind, she saw the connections, the echoes between her childhood and Nick's. Perhaps that was what had brought them together, these shared wounds. "My mom hardly visited Sammie and I when we were placed in foster care. She messed up so many times that I stopped counting on her, although it took Sammie a lot longer to do that.

When I was fifteen or sixteen, Sammie and I waited all afternoon at a playground for her to show up. Sammie was only eleven or so, and still so optimistic and sure that our mother would be there. She'd worn her best dress, and had our foster mother braid her hair. She'd drawn a picture of the three of us to give to Mom when we saw her."

"And she didn't show up?"

"She did. Two hours late. By then, Sammie's dress was dirty, her braids were loose and the picture was crinkled." Vivian shook her head. She could still see the defeat in Sammie's eyes, the tears that trickled through the dirt on her cheeks. "Then I saw my mom, standing at the edge of the park and marched over to her. I read her the riot act for five minutes straight."

Nick smiled. "That I can imagine you doing."

"My argument skills have always been pretty strong." Vivian took a sip of wine, and in her mind she was that teenager again, trying to put all those hurts from her childhood together, and drag answers out of the one person who had never given her any. "I asked her why she even bothered to set up visitations if all she was going to do was bail at the last minute. And she said…"

When Vivian didn't continue, Nick reached out and touched her hand. "She said what?"

"That she felt so guilty about being such a bad mom that she couldn't bring herself to face us. She knew she'd screwed up. Knew she'd said things and done things that had hurt us, and it was easier for her to ignore us than to apologize. Or show up and deal with how much she had let us down." Vivian leaned toward Nick. "Some people just don't know how to deal with the pain they've caused. Maybe your dad is one of them."

"Maybe. Or maybe he's just a stubborn man who can't admit he's wrong."

"Kinda the same thing, don't you think?" Vivian gave him a soft smile.

"You may be right." He got to his feet and pulled an extension cord from one of the boxes. "Do you think that's part of why your sister has stayed away? She knows she let you and Ellie down and she can't face that right now?"

Vivian thought of the conversation with Della, the challenges of being a new mom and the sense of failure when things went awry. "Maybe."

The heavy conversation was making Vivian far too self-reflective. Her mind pulled at threads of her own avoidance of relationships and connections. But that was a knot she was nowhere near ready to untangle. She'd much rather be hanging plastic Santas on the tree. "Well, let's get this tree decorated before it gets too late." Vivian dug in the box marked Decorations, and pulled out two strings of multicolored lights. "I hope they still work."

"They do. I tested them the other day." Nick started at the top, wrapping the tree with the lights, weaving them in and out of the branches, then adding the second string and a third that she discovered under a container of ornaments. "Turn off the lights," he said.

"Why?"

"Because the first time we light this tree, I want to get the full effect."

She did as he requested, and the room plunged into darkness. "Silent Night" began to play on the radio. A second later, Nick had plugged in the lights, and a bloom of red, green, blue and yellow filled the living room. The soft strains of the Christmas carol made the room feel hushed, almost sacred.

Nick came to stand beside her. "It's beautiful."

"It is." Vivian had seen hundreds of Christmas trees over the years—mostly on TV or in magazine ads— but none seemed as precious as this tilted, barely decorated one. Maybe because she'd chosen the tree, this part of the family as Cutler had called it. She turned to Nick. "This is going to sound crazy, but one of the things I've always wanted to do is lie under a Christmas tree and look up at the lights."

He considered her for a moment, a quirk of amusement in his features. "I don't think it's crazy at all. Let's do it."

Like two ten-year-olds, they lay on their backs and shimmied under the tree. Their heads pressed together, and a dusting of needles scattered across their faces and chests. Vivian giggled. Actually giggled. She couldn't remember the last time she'd done that, if ever. Above her head, the lights blinked on-off, on-off, a constellation of colors nestled among the branches. "It's like fireworks. So cool."

"It is." Nick's hand covered hers. They lay there for a while, silent, while Christmas carols played in the background and the lights twinkled.

Nick kept holding her hand. He was close enough that she could feel the warmth from his body, inhale the scent of his cologne. She could get used to this. Very used to it.

At the same time, they turned to look at each other. Neither said a word, but their hands tightened and they drew closer. Nick cupped her face, then kissed her, and before she knew it, she was pressed up against him and he was devouring her, and Vivian Winthrop finally stopped overthinking the whole thing.

Chapter Eleven

Nick had told himself—very firmly and many, many times—that he was not going to do anything more than kiss Vivian. Then she'd worn that dress, and his resolve had melted a little. But what tipped the scales from no to yes had been that moment under the tree when she'd turned to him, the look in her eyes both sultry and vulnerable, and all those arguments in his head disappeared. Whatever reservations he'd had about Vivian vanished in light of that vulnerable conversation and that moment under the tree.

He took her hand, pulled her to her feet. She swayed into his arms. "What are we doing?" he asked, repeating her question from earlier.

"I don't know. I just know…" Her blue eyes met his, and in them, a dark storm brewed. "I don't want to stop."

"Neither do I." His voice was a hoarse rasp. Blood raced through his veins, thudded in his heart. Her hair had come undone, and the combination of the loose tangles and the sexiness of her bare shoulders nearly undid him. "I want to take you up to my room and—"

"Then do it, Nick. Please."

It was the *please* that erased the last of his resistance. He'd wanted Vivian almost from the second he met her, but she'd made it clear she wasn't a long-term girl. Maybe he was blind or a fool, but all he saw when he looked at her was long-term. She had committed to her sister, to her career, and in a fierce, deep way that he admired. She had passion, and he wanted to explore every inch of that.

He took her hand and they went upstairs, passing the nursery where Ellie still slept, and turning left to Nick's room, at the end of the hall. He started to shut the door, then left it slightly ajar. "Just in case Ellie wakes up."

"And that," she said, tangling her hands in his hair, "is why I want you."

"Because I'm leaving the door open?"

"Because you are thoughtful…" She pressed a kiss to his neck. "Considerate…" Another kiss. "Kind…" A third. "And gentle."

The desire that had simmered all day inside him flamed into an overpowering need. It was all he could do to stand still, while she kissed and teased him. "Is that what you want me to be, Vivian? Gentle?"

She drew back and met his gaze head-on. "I want

you to love me, Nick. Just for tonight. We'll worry about gentle later."

Good Lord. Did this woman know what she did to him when she said things like that? He scooped her up and laid her on the bed, then kicked off his shoes. She started to do the same, but he put a hand on her bare leg. "Leave the heels on. Please."

Her brows arched. A devilish smile lit her face. "My, my, Nick Jackson. You do surprise me."

"Good." He undid his shirt and tie, tossing them to the side. "Because you're the kind of woman who deserves to be surprised. And loved. No, not just loved, but loved well."

He climbed onto the bed beside her. She rolled toward him, and he reached for the zipper on the back of her dress, then stopped. Tears shimmered in her eyes. "Did I say something wrong? Did you change your mind?"

"No. Not at all." She cupped his face and kissed him. "I want you more than I've ever wanted anyone and…it scares me."

"To want something you can lose?"

"Something I *will* say goodbye to." She let out a long breath. "I don't want to give you a forever impression, Nick. Let's just have tonight, and tomorrow will sort itself out."

Something I will say goodbye to.

When he heard the words, he realized how much he'd hoped Vivian would stay in Stone Gap. That this little temporary family could become permanent and real. The truth was, none of this was real. Ellie wasn't theirs, they weren't each other's, and very soon their lives would diverge in two radically different directions.

He would have tonight, and that would be it. Would that be enough?

For the first time in his life, Nick was afraid, too, of losing someone he'd begun to care very deeply about. It had taken Ariel walking out of his life for him to see how shallow his feelings for her had been. Losing her had smarted, of course, but only for few weeks. But the thought of never seeing Vivian again—

If he thought about it long enough, it would damned near make him stop breathing.

"Tonight, Nick. Let's just pretend," she said. Then she kissed him again, curving against him as she did, her hands roving over his bare back, lingering along his waistband, and Nick stopped thinking. The zipper on the back of Vivian's dress slid down with a soft snick, and a second later, she'd kicked it to the floor.

"Damn, you're beautiful." He kissed a trail from her jaw to the valley between her breasts, then over the cleavage that spilled out of the black strapless bra. She shifted up on the bed as he kept moving down, kissing, licking, teasing. He tugged off her panties, then slid between her legs.

The easy softness in her disappeared, and her body stiffened. "I've, uh...never..."

He shifted back to lie beside her again. He danced an easy caress across her belly. "I'm not going to lie, that makes me pretty damned happy to hear."

"I just don't know if I can..." Her cheeks flushed,

"well, you know. I don't want you to feel like you're doing something wrong if I don't...get there. I don't usually in general. Most of the guys I've been with have been kind of...fast and well... Anyway, I don't want you to be disappointed."

He cupped her face. "Vivian, *nothing* about you disappoints me. You are strong and fierce and gorgeous. And any man who didn't appreciate that, appreciate every inch of you, is the wrong man to be with."

That adorable blush appeared in her cheeks again, then she danced a tentative hand down his pants to cup him. The sensation of her soft, warm hand against him instantly made him even harder. The desire raging inside him urged to take her, hard and fast, but tonight, it was all about making Vivian feel good. "As much as I want you to do that forever," he said, "I think it's your turn."

She nodded, then smiled as he kissed his way down her breasts, across her belly and back to her legs. She laid back, propping her feet on the bed, the black spiked heels digging into the comforter while he tasted her. He went slow at first, teasing her, dancing around the outer edges, before coming back to the center.

She moaned, writhing against his tongue. Her hands tangled in his hair, and when he moved deeper, faster, and harder, she gasped, arched against the bed, and a moment later, shouted his name. "Oh my...that was... unbelievable."

He grinned, and slid back up her body. "Well, let's see if we can make you do that again. And again."

That devilish look flashed in her eyes again. "You think you're up to the challenge?"

"I'll take whatever challenge you throw at me, Vivian." And when he finally slipped inside Vivian's body, he made sure to appreciate her very, very much. She was fiery and sweet, passionate and tender.

And somewhere along the way between the gazebo and the bedroom, Nick Jackson fell head over heels in love.

The sun had just started to crest when Vivian opened her eyes. Nick's chest rose and fell in steady, even breaths. She had her head on the valley beneath his shoulder, her hand on his abdomen and one leg wrapped around his body.

She moved back, out from under his arm, as carefully and quietly as she could. What had she been thinking? Making love with him—and yes, holy hell, that had been amazing, both the first and the second time—and then sleeping beside him? She never spent the night with men. Never let them stay at her place. That kind of thing led to too many misconceptions about what she could offer them.

It had been sex, plain and simple. Just sex.

Right?

Even in sleep, Nick had a hint of a smile on his face. She sat back on her knees and watched him for a moment. He was a handsome man, with a chiseled jaw and one lock of hair that often fell across his brows. He clearly worked out—given the muscular planes of his chest and abs. But it was the heart of the man that she was most attracted to. The man she had slept beside, and the man she knew she should leave.

When she thought of last night, of his tenderness and consideration, her resolve softened. Nick had done more than just make her orgasm—he had shown her there were men who cared enough to put her needs first. All her life, she had avoided long-term relationships—and not once had she ever regretted it or even had a second thought. Maybe she'd chosen poorly, but most of the men she'd dated had been selfish and emotionally closed off. Not Nick. He wore his emotions on his chef's apron, and was as open as a prairie.

That was dangerous. Because it was the kind of thing she could fall for.

Or maybe already had. Something about him had her seriously considering staying in Stone Gap. Staying meant going all in with what he wanted—a family, a forever. Despite her speech about her mother that night, a part of Vivian had always been afraid that she would turn out to be just as bad of a mother. Emotionally unavailable to her husband, her children, and basically addicted to work, instead of her family. Work was her comfort zone, the one place where she felt sure and confident.

She started to slip off the bed when Nick stirred. "Hey, don't get up yet. Ellie's still sleeping." He patted the mattress beside him. "Come back to bed with me."

The thick white comforter and soft sheets beckoned her. She could easily slide back into that bed with Nick and pretend, just a little longer, that this was her life. Her man. Her family.

Outside the window, the Saturday-morning sun continued ascending. Yesterday she'd called her contractor and made sure the apartment was near enough to done to be habitable. Which meant tomorrow, she would go home to Durham with Ellie, then hire someone to take care of the baby for the hours after the day care closed. And all of this, whatever this was, with Nick would be over. That was for the best. Before she hurt him, or disappointed him too.

"You sleep in. I have some work to do," she said, then hurried out of the room before she changed her mind.

She took a quick shower, dressed in jeans and a T-shirt, then settled in at the dining room table with her laptop and a stack of files and briefs to read. She could hear Ellie beginning to stir, and the patter of Nick's feet as he headed into the nursery.

"Good morning, sunshine," he said to Ellie, the words happy and sweet, and just the kind of words every little girl should hear when she woke up. "You hungry?"

The words on the page in front of Vivian swam. She closed her eyes and pinched the bridge of her nose, but when she opened her eyes again, everything was a teary blur. Did she really have to leave this weekend? Couldn't she wrangle a few more days in Stone Gap?

She got to her feet and was halfway down the hall to go talk to him when the doorbell rang. At six thirty in the morning? Who on earth would be coming by that early? Vivian pulled open the door to find Sammie standing on the doorstep, wearing the same jeans and T-shirt she'd been wearing the day she left, with a backpack slung over one shoulder and a brand-new stuffed white bear under her other arm.

"Hi, Viv! I'm back!" Sammie grinned. Her sister looked healthy and happy, better than she'd looked in years. Maybe the time on her own had been a good thing after all. "The people at the inn told me where you were staying. For a second, I thought you'd left town. Where's my little girl? I can't wait to hold her again."

Vivian glanced up the staircase and saw Nick, holding Ellie, with her favorite pink bunny blanket clutched between them. An unreadable expression filled his face. In that instant, Vivian realized that once again, her world had imploded. But this time, the implosion would be affecting Nick and Ellie, too.

"She just got up," Nick said.

Sammie's gaze shot to Nick. As soon as she spied the baby, Sammie barreled up the stairs, her arms out and reaching for her daughter. "Ellie! Oh my God, I've missed you so much!"

Nick glanced at Vivian. She gave him a small nod of assent, and he handed Ellie over to her mother. Sammie drew the baby tight to her chest, covering her with kisses, talking nonstop. The bear squished between them. Ellie stared at Sammie, but didn't cry. "You got so big! I swear, you've gained five pounds. Oh, Momma has been so sad without her Ellie girl."

"I was just about to change her," Nick said to Sammie. He still had his hands halfway between them, ready to take the baby back at any second. "Do you want me to—"

"I can do it. Then I can spend time with my little Ellie Boo." Sammie nuzzled Ellie's stomach which made Ellie let out a little giggle, then turned into the nursery. She kept on talking to Ellie as she changed her.

Nick came down the stairs, his steps heavy and slow. Vivian waited in the foyer, her heart a riot of mixed emotions. Joy, loss, regret, sadness. "She's back," she said to Nick. "For Ellie."

Gratitude for Sammie's safe return was quickly chased by frustration with the entire chain of events. Sammie had just walked out, assuming Vivian would take care of everything for her, like she always did. If Vivian hadn't been here, what would have happened to Ellie? And now, Sammie expected to waltz back into their lives as if nothing happened? How did Vivian know for sure that Sammie wouldn't do this again? There wasn't going to be a Nick standing in the kitchen the next time.

"I'm sure that's best," Nick said, but his words were edged with concern. "Ellie should be with her mother. Not her aunt and a…stranger, or whatever I am…or was." He shook his head and let out a little cough. For a second, he stared at the hardwood floor, looking lost and distracted. "Since you don't need me here, I, uh, should probably get to the inn. It's almost time for breakfast. Will you be by today?"

"Actually…" Now was as good a time as any to tell him her plans. If there was one thing Vivian had learned in law, it was that dealing with the facts was a lot easier once they were all on the table. She had no reason to delay her departure, now that Sammie had returned. And maybe it would be easier if she just told Nick now, while her heart was already hurting. "I'm going to go back to Durham today."

He wheeled back to her. "What? Now?"

"I was going to go tomorrow but now that Sammie's here, I don't have any reason to stay." Nick winced, and Vivian wished she could take the words back. "I meant, I have a job—"

"I know what you meant." He scowled. "By all means, run back to Durham."

"I'm not running. I have a court case and work, and that renovation to oversee—"

"And what about us?" Even though Sammie was still in the nursery with Ellie, Nick lowered his voice.

Vivian raised her chin. "What about it? We had a great time, and made some memories. And got a Christmas tree. I call that a successful evening."

He scoffed. "A successful *evening*? Is that code for—" he lowered his voice even more "'—thanks for the sex, Nick, I'll send you a postcard once in a while'?"

The harsh words made her recoil. Last night had been wonderful, yes, so why couldn't Nick understand that one night, one date, would have to be enough? That even if she wanted to try to take this further, she also knew that they didn't have what it took to make this anything more? Or rather, that she didn't? The last thing she wanted to do was make him think she could be that family woman he kept seeing her as. "That wasn't what that was, and you know it."

"Oh yeah? Then what was it? For you? Because it was a lot more than one night for me," he said, as if he'd just read her mind. Nick took a step closer to her, placing one hand on her waist. She wanted to lean into the warmth of his hand, into him, into this. "I want you, Vivian. Not for one night. Forever."

Forever. The word alternately terrified and thrilled her. Nick wanted something permanent. Pretty ironic that the very thing she'd always craved was right before her, and she was throwing it aside. But she knew that life wasn't for her. And trying to make it work would only hurt them both even more in the long run.

"I'm not a forever kind of girl, Nick," she said. "I'll just let you down in the end. You should know that by now."

"Honey, you have forever written all over you. The problem is, you're too damned scared to take it when it's right in front of you. You're like your mother, standing at the edge of the playground, afraid to go in and visit with your daughters. Take the leap, Vivian."

Damn it. Why did he keep calling her *honey*? It was all she could do not to kiss him right there. An insane thought because she was in the middle of telling him they were done. "It's not that. I can't just up and leave my job. You make it sound like I can settle down here and be your sous chef or something."

"I never said that. You want to live in Durham? Fine, we'll live in Durham. You want to live here? We'll live here. They need chefs pretty much everywhere in the world, so I'm good with wherever you need to be. What's more important to me, Vivian, than where I work, is who I come home to. And that I have a home. Not just a room in the back of a B and B."

Or an apartment in Durham as sterile as a hospital room. Ida Mae's house, with all its memories and mementos, felt more like home than any place Vivian had ever lived. The tree in the corner, its lights muted for now, was hers. Well, hers and Nick's. They'd bought it, set it in the stand, hung it with lights. Turned this place into a home in just a few days.

He wanted to build a home with her. Come home to her. Make something that would last, beyond this week and this holiday season. She should have been elated, should have leaped into his arms and said yes, yes, yes. Instead, fear tightened her chest and shortened her breath, and she backed away from him.

"I can't do that, Nick. I'm sorry." She tore her gaze away from his because if she looked at the hurt in his eyes one more time, she'd lose her resolve. "I'm just going to see if Sammie needs anything, and then I'll start packing. Say goodbye to Della and Mavis for me, will you?"

She headed upstairs. Even as she loaded her clothes into her suitcase and her files into her briefcase, she couldn't shake the feeling that she was leaving something very important behind.

Chapter Twelve

After the breakfast shift, Nick mixed up a quick chicken salad for the guests for lunch, adding a bowl of washed fruit and a hearty potato salad he'd made the day before. Once the food was laid out and the beef stew he'd made for dinner was simmering, Nick stood in the kitchen, with nothing to do, and knew he'd put the decision off long enough.

Vivian was leaving. Sammie had Ellie. The little charade of a life they'd been living had come to an end. And that meant Nick had no excuse to keep him from the conversation he'd been dreading for months.

"Mavis, I'll be back this afternoon." He hung his apron on the hook by the pantry, grabbed his keys from the shelf by the door, then headed out to his truck.

When he got inside, he noticed a forgotten pacifier from Ellie on the backseat.

Damn.

Nick turned it over in his hand. His chest ached, and damned if he wasn't half close to tears for a kid that wasn't even his. Maybe it wasn't the baby so much as the potential she had awakened in him. A dream of a forever with Vivian and him. A child of their own someday. More nights on the couch and dances in the gazebo.

Bah humbug. Nick tossed the pacifier into the glove box, put the truck in gear, then headed back to Ida Mae's. His grandmother's house echoed with emptiness. Sammie had taken Ellie with her. Where they'd gone, Nick had no idea. Rather than sticking around to ask, he had ducked out of there as soon as Vivian said she was leaving.

Vivian's car was gone, and so was her suitcase. The dining room table held no files, the bathroom held no makeup. All that was left was a crib and diaper bag in a nursery that would never be used again.

Nick picked up the box he'd pulled out of the attic last week and set it on the kitchen table. Then he picked up his cell phone and dialed his father's number. It took four rings before Richard answered. Had he been standing there, debating whether to pick up?

"Nicholas. What did you need?"

Nick sighed. "I know you're in Stone Gap today. Thought you might want to come by and get the box Grandma left for you."

"You can drop it off at my office. I'm about to head back there."

Nick bit back his first, instinctive response. And his second. He thought of Vivian's words, about how his father's distance was more about fear than disappointment. He found that hard to equate with the cold man who had raised him.

Had his father held Nick when he was an infant and marveled at his fingers and toes? Laughed when his tiny hand gripped one finger? Paced the halls when Nick's cries wouldn't stop? Had he ever, for a second, loved his sons the way Nick had begun to love Ellie?

"It's Christmas, Dad. Can we just pretend we're a family for a couple hours? Swing by Grandma's and I'll give you the box in person, like she wanted." There was more to his grandmother's request, but Nick kept it simple for now. His father would be less likely to come if he knew it would be more complicated than just accepting the box.

Like his father had said, Grandma wouldn't know if Nick didn't abide by every part of her letter, which had asked him to sit with his father and go through the contents. Except, Nick would know. And he owed the woman who had been more of a parent than anyone in his life this one last request.

His father sighed. "I have a meeting—"

"Screw the meeting. You have a son who wants to see you, and I think that takes precedence, don't you?"

A long pause. A sigh. "I'll be there in ten minutes."

"See you then." But the phone call had already ended and Nick was talking to the air.

His father pulled into the driveway fifteen minutes later. He locked the Mercedes with a double beep, then climbed the stairs. Nick pulled open the door before Richard knocked. "I have to say, I'm surprised you came."

Richard scowled. "It was out of my way."

Good to see his father was his regular warm and cuddly self. "Come on in."

His father entered the house and paused in the foyer. His gaze went to the Christmas tree, the decorations. For a moment, his features were unreadable, then he cleared his throat and strode into the kitchen. Nick had left Ida Mae's letter on the table beside the box. His father began to reach for the box.

"I think you need to read the letter first," Nick said.

His father shot him a look of annoyance, but sat down at the table to read the letter. It was short, just a single sheet of paper, but Richard seemed to take forever to read it. When he put the letter back on the table, his hand shook. "She always did see me with different eyes than I saw myself with."

"Grandma was good at that. She saw the best in everyone she met."

"I've always been more like my father. He was a loner. Hardly ever showed any emotion unless he was with my mother. He was a stoic man, but a marshmallow with her." Richard cleared his throat. "I see you, uh, decorated the house."

"Yeah. I wanted one more holiday here." Nick left out the rest, because it was far too painful to tell anyone that the holiday he'd dreamed of had walked out the door a few hours ago.

"It looks like it did when I was a kid. That's nice, Nicholas." His father fiddled with the letter. "Your grandmother said she wants us to go through the box together."

"Yeah. I have no idea why."

"I think I do." Richard pulled open the lid, then took out the first few things and set them on the table, talking as he did. "She wanted me to remember what I used to be like. When I was a kid, I was more like you than Grady or Carson."

Nick scoffed. "I find that hard to believe."

"This glove," his father said, "was pretty much welded onto my hand most of my childhood. I played on every Little League team I could find. I thought someday I'd end up in the major leagues. Me and Matty."

Nick had forgotten that his father had grown up with Matty Gibson, the owner of the grocery store downtown. "He did go on to the major leagues, didn't he?"

His father nodded. "He got signed by the Braves but barely started the season. Tore his rotator cuff, he ended up coming back here, taking over his father's market, and never living his dream again." His father reached in the box and pulled out the autograph book. "My dad would take me to ball games sometimes. I'd wait outside the stadium afterward and get the players to sign my book. I told them all I'd grow up to be like them someday."

Nick couldn't imagine his suit-wearing, stern father as a kid, sitting outside a baseball stadium, an eager fan seeing his heroes. "But you went into law instead."

"Yeah." His father sighed. He pushed the box aside and picked up the letter again. "My mother, God bless her, thought she was doing the right thing."

"What do you mean?"

"My dad died when I was seventeen. I had a chance that summer to play for a travel team, sort of a year-round thing for the best players. Matty was going, and I'd been selected to be the shortstop. Everyone knew that college and major league scouts came by to watch this particular team because they only picked kids who'd had pretty knockout high school careers. That's how Matty ended up getting signed later. A scout saw him, and offered him a major league position. Matty's dad insisted he get a couple years of college first, but then he went to the big leagues."

"And you didn't."

"I didn't because I didn't go with the team. I turned down the opportunity." His father let out a long breath. "I haven't thought about any of this in a long damned time. And didn't want to. But after you called the other day, I started wondering what my mother could possibly have held onto all these years and I realized it had to be my baseball stuff. I guess this is her way of apologizing."

"Apologizing? For what?" The grandmother he remembered had been kind and loving, and probably the best person Nick had ever met.

"For talking me out of going with the team. I stayed

home that summer to help my mother. She was a wreck after my dad died. She could barely function. To help make ends meet, I went to work in a law office, as a gofer of sorts, and she told me I should bet on the sure thing and let the rest go. So I did."

Nick thought of his own career. How he'd worked for so long in a career he hated because it was a sure thing. If his life hadn't imploded, he never would have come here and taken the chef job. Security. It was what Sammie had been seeking for her daughter, what Vivian retreated to whenever she got scared and what he had banked on for a lot of unhappy years.

"I watched Matty's career take off as the years passed, and I was angry. Resentful. Jealous. I blamed my mom for my choice to give up the career I wanted, so I guess I thought I was punishing her by staying away and being the most successful lawyer I could be. Turns out—" his father let out a long breath "—I was punishing myself. I could barely stand in that funeral home that day. I felt like such a terrible son for not being here. For her. For you."

Vivian had been right. His father had been overcome by his regrets, and so sure he couldn't earn forgiveness. Richard had been harsh and cold to his boys—there was no disputing that—but he had also been a man in pain for a long, long time. A man who could argue for hours in a courtroom but couldn't bring himself to say anything that came from his heart.

"I didn't stop talking to you because I hated you, Nick. None of that crap I said about you being a disappointment was true. I stopped talking because…" His stoic, pressed, severe father's face began to crumple. "I didn't know how to say what I needed to say. That I was envious that you took the risks I was afraid to take. That you went after what you wanted, what you were passionate about. While I sat in my office day after day, making a paycheck and counting my regrets."

The kitchen clocked ticked past the hour. A tree rattled against the windows. The scent of the glove oil hung in the air. Here was the moment Nick had wanted. A chance to tell his father what he thought of all those years of silence. The missed father-son opportunities. The resentments that had built and built.

Instead, Nick opened his heart and let all that go. What was the point, really? They'd each made their own mistakes to get to this point.

Nick reached in the box and pulled out a worn baseball, the leather cover grayed by age and years of use. It sat smooth and heavy in his palm. He tossed it up and down a couple times. "Dad, now that you're here, why don't you finally teach me how to catch?"

Richard got to his feet, grabbed Nick and hauled his son to his chest. The two of them stood there for a long, long time. Then they went into the yard and tossed the ball back and forth until the sun began to go down. Anyone going by wouldn't have seen two grown men working out decades of issues. They'd have heard and seen exactly what it was—a father and son bonding.

The day before Christmas, Vivian sat in the conference room at the office and faced the man who she had taken on pro bono almost a year ago. She'd been home for two weeks and poured herself into her work, sometimes sleeping at the office. Winter was definitely in the North Carolina air, and most of her office had already left for the holidays.

But here she was, on a Sunday, working, as she had last Sunday and all the ones before that. Ellie sat in her car seat beside Vivian's chair, content and recently fed. When she stirred, Vivian reached in and picked her up. The baby sat on Vivian's lap and watched her tiny hands press into the wood table. Sammie was supposed to drop by soon, to pick up Ellie on her way home from work and give Vivian some time to stay late at work.

Ellie had become a frequent companion at the office. Vivian couldn't spend all day here with the baby because it threw Ellie off her schedule, but a couple hours a day worked out pretty well and meshed with Sammie's flexible waitressing schedule. Still, a part of Vivian ached every time she saw her niece. Sammie had her life together now, more or less. She had found a better paying job, but was still struggling financially, so Vivian had offered to let her and Ellie move in with her now that the apartment renovations had been completed. For the first time since Vivian had moved into the building, the apartment felt like a home. Not because of the new granite countertops or hardwood floors, but because of the stuffed animals on the floor and baby bottles in the sink. At the same time, every one of those things reminded Vivian of Nick. She found her mind wandering during the day, pondering what he was doing.

The hole in Vivian's life only widened when day after day went by without a word from Nick. A part of her had thought he'd chase after her in some grand romantic gesture. But there'd been nothing, not a word. Maybe he'd accepted the same facts that she had—they wanted different lives. Or maybe her bailing on him had made him give up.

Jerry sat at the huge mahogany table, flanked by his wife, who gave Ellie a little wave and a smile. The papers Vivian had drawn up sat in front of the couple. Legally, she was compelled to present the settlement offer to her client, even if she thought it was a paltry sum that was far less than he deserved. For a long moment, no one said a word.

"This is quite a sizable offer," Jerry said. His right arm rested on the table, a little smaller and weaker than his left. Long steel rods had replaced the shattered bones, and months of physical therapy had brought him back to 80 percent. He'd never be 100 percent again, and never go back to his assembly job. "It will help out a lot. And they offered an apology and are recalling the rest of those machines."

"I think we can fight for more," Vivian said. "I have enough documentation here to prove that this equipment manufacturer has a long list of shop violations, and shoddy workmanship with their machinery. You won't be able to work the same job again, and you still have years of therapy ahead of you. For all that, you deserve at least three times that in compensation."

"How long will a lawsuit like that take?"

"If they refuse to make a new offer and insist on a trial, it could be three, four years. Unfortunately, these kinds of cases drag out. The lawyers for the other side will file everything they can, and ask for extensions at every step of the process. They want to drag it out so that hopefully you'll give up. But I'm here to fight for all of you. I know what this has done to your family and your life." She nodded toward Jerry. "You've lost your home and your car, and had to depend on your family members for charity when you were out of work for six months, recuperating. But if you can just hold on a little—"

"No." Jerry glanced at his wife. She took his hand and gave him a slight nod. "Me and the wife, we talked this morning. And we decided that no matter what the offer was, we were going to take it."

"But you could have so much more—"

"No offense, Ms. Winthrop, but I don't think you know what it's like to get up in the morning and look in your wife's eyes or your kids' and see their fear and disappointment because you lost their home. It takes a toll on a man, on a family. This might not be as much money as we could have if we held out, but the wife and I don't care about that. This will be enough money to pay the medical bills and get us back on our feet and under our own roof." He pulled out a pen and clicked the top.

"Wait, before you sign." Vivian bounced Ellie on her lap. The baby clutched at Vivian's shirt. "Is there nothing I can do to convince you to pursue this further? I have a strong case and no doubt that we will prevail."

"We appreciate how hard you've worked on this, but you gotta understand something." Jerry cleared his throat. "The morning after we lost our home, I woke up in the basement of my cousin's house, all four of us cramped in one sofa bed, with our belongings stacked up around us like a wall. I spent fifteen years saving for the down payment on that house, another five years fixing it up and making it into the kind of place where Marie and I could raise our kids. And just like that, it was gone. I should have been depressed. Should have been mad as hell, or something. But instead, I was... and you're going to think I'm crazy for saying this, but I was happy."

Vivian stared at him. This man, who had undergone three surgeries, months of painful rehabilitation and suffered devastating losses had been happy? "How is that possible after all you and your family went through?"

"I had what mattered with me. My wife under my arm, my son under the other arm and our fierce and stubborn little girl sleeping on the end of the bed." Jerry chuckled. "She's the kind of kid who goes left when you say right. Drives me crazy, but I wouldn't trade her for all the kids in the world. Anyway, I looked at all of them, and yes, I felt like I had let them down, but I was also grateful as hell to have the only thing that would break me if I lost it—my family. This is enough money to let me take care of them the way I should—to get our lives back on track, and for me, that's good enough."

"I'm…surprised. I don't think I've ever had a client who said they didn't want to fight for more money." She was used to being the lawyer who dug in her heels, who fought—and won—against impossible odds.

"It's Christmas," Jerry said. "I just want to go home and enjoy the holiday and hug my kids." His wife nodded. "And I'm sure you'd rather be anywhere but in this office this time of year, especially since it's that little one's first holiday. So go home and enjoy the people you love. We're very grateful to you for taking on our case, Ms. Winthrop. But if it's okay with you, I'm just going to sign this and go. I promised the kids I'd help decorate the tree tonight." He swooped his signature across the settlement offer, then slid the paper across the table.

Vivian stared at them both, stunned. "When I met you that night, you were so broke, Jerry. All I wanted to do was change your life."

"You did." Jerry smiled. "And what's better, because those machines are being recalled, you're saving other people the pain we went through. I'd say that's enough of a Christmas present for everyone." He rose and handed her the document. "Go home to your family, Ms. Winthrop. Me and mine will be just fine. Merry Christmas."

Nick stood in the glass-and-marble foyer, and wondered if he was a fool. He'd shown up here without calling, without texting, without even checking to see if Vivian would talk to him. It was a crazy idea.

He'd spent two miserable weeks in Stone Gap, a misery compounded by several meals at the inn going awry because Nick's mind was here in Durham, and not in the kitchen. It got so bad that Mavis pulled him aside and told him to *either go get that girl, or go back to culinary school.*

So here he was, on Christmas Eve, in the lobby of the towering building that housed the Veritas Law firm. He'd taken a chance coming here on a weekend before a holiday. He almost turned around, then saw Vivian's car in the parking lot. Only a handful of cars sat in the lot, which made hers stick out even more. He wasn't surprised to find her here, even on Christmas Eve.

He scanned the sign mounted beside the elevator. Veritas Law took up four floors in the building. No indication of which floor held Vivian's office. He picked a number at random and pushed the button. The screen above the car counted down the elevator's approach to the lobby: 12, 11, 10.

A few seconds later, the elevator dinged and the doors opened. Nick moved forward, putting out a hand to stop the doors from closing. As he did, Vivian stepped out and into the foyer. For a solid five seconds, he couldn't think. She was holding Ellie against her chest and had a diaper bag over one shoulder. "Nick. What are you doing here?"

"Looking for you." Now that Vivian was standing before him, all those pretty words he'd composed in his head on the trip up here disappeared. Damn, she looked good. A dark blue dress hugged her curves. Black heels showed off those incredible legs. The long hair he loved was pinned up. And Ellie—she looked like she'd grown three inches. Her big blue eyes stared at him and as recognition dawned, they lit up and she reached for him.

"Seems like she remembers you." Vivian laughed, gave Ellie a kiss on her cheek, then handed the baby to Nick in one fluid movement. Vivian's ease with the baby surprised him almost as much as finding her behind the elevator doors.

"Did Sammie leave again?" Nick gave Ellie a grin, then nuzzled her cheek. In answer, she grabbed his shirt. Damn, she smelled of freshness and hope, and he hadn't realized until just now how much he'd missed this little booger.

"No. She'll be here in a minute to get Ellie. She's just getting off work now."

As if on cue, there was a beep behind him. He turned and watched Sammie pull into the lot and park her beat-up Toyota. Vivian headed out to the lot and greeted her sister with a hug. Nick trailed along behind, surprised as hell. "I just fed her. But I think her diaper will need to be changed," Vivian said. "I think she's teething so don't forget to put the teething ring in the freezer for a few minutes."

Nick stared at Vivian as if she was speaking a foreign language.

"Thanks." Sammie turned to Nick. Vivian's sister

looked happier and brighter than the last time he'd seen her. "Hi, Nick."

"Hi, Sammie." He didn't know what else to do or say so he handed Ellie over. His arms felt too empty already. "Uh, Merry Christmas."

Sammie just grinned. She slipped the diaper bag off Vivian's arm and onto her own. "Did you tell him yet?"

"No."

"Okay. Well, I'll meet you there. See you soon, Nick!" Sammie grinned again, then turned on her heel and hurried to her car. A few minutes later, she was gone.

Meet her there? See him soon?

"What was that about?" Nick asked.

"Nothing." A breeze kicked up, scattering leaves across the tarred lot. Vivian drew her coat tighter.

He swallowed his disappointment. What had he expected? That she'd jump into his arms and they'd have some kind of Nicholas Sparks ending? He'd shown up unannounced, without much of a plan. "I was hoping we could talk."

"Okay," she said. "I know it's a little chilly out, but what do you say to a walk?"

Considering how much he'd moped around the rooms at the inn, being outside would probably do him some good. Although half of him was convinced she was just going to tell him to give up already. "Sure."

When she slipped into place beside him, the scent of her perfume teased him. Reminded him of that single night they'd shared. Damn. What kind of glutton for punishment was he, anyway?

"Are you sure you want to walk?" he asked. "You have on heels."

"Where I want to go isn't very far away." She reached for his hand, and led him through the parking lot to a paved path that circled the back of the building.

Okay, so she was holding his hand. He'd take that as a good sign. A sign of what, he still wasn't sure.

"How are you?" he asked, then rolled his eyes. That's what he came up with after all those miles, all this time? Small talk for the win.

"I'm fine. Busy, of course. I've been working a lot."

She didn't say "miserable without you," or "sobbing into my coffee cup every morning." Maybe coming up here had been a mistake. "That's good."

She stopped walking and stared at him. "No, it's not."

"You're right, it's not." It meant she was still the same woman who had bailed on him and Ellie to work over and over again. The same woman who had escaped into emails and phone calls when she didn't want to face her fears. "I was just being polite."

"I should have more of a life. I should have hours in my day where I hang out with my girlfriends or go on a date or just go shopping. Instead, I have this office." She waved at the behemoth of a building behind them. "And I decided, well, cemented my decision after the meeting I just had, that… I don't want to go home to an empty house anymore."

Go on a date. Empty house. Sounded like she wanted to move on. Except she was holding his hand

and looking into his eyes, and he was still trying to figure out what the hell was going on.

"What are you saying, Vivian? Because I didn't come here to hear that you want to date someone else."

A smile he couldn't read curved across her face. "Just walk with me, a little longer. Please?"

A slight breeze kicked up and rattled through the trees. The rest of the world was quiet, the traffic behind this woods-lined path almost nonexistent.

The sun had begun its descent, oranges and mauves washing over the world. A bit of bright orange light peeked through the trees for a moment, then disappeared. They rounded a bend, and the path curved farther into the woods.

"I walk this path almost every day," she said. "Or at least, I do now. I've tried to get out in the sunshine and air more often since I came back to Durham. Sometimes I walk alone, sometimes I take Ellie with me, in that stroller I bought her that cost a mint, and I had to have redelivered here." She laughed. "Anyway, I like this path because it reminds me of Stone Gap."

It did have that leafy green, quiet peace about it that Nick had found in Stone Gap. Almost as if they'd discovered an unsung corner of the world. Did she miss the town? Or him? "It's a lot like the road that runs beside the lake. Except for the lack of a lake."

"It also has one other thing that we had in Stone Gap." They turned again, and from here the path spilled into a park. A playground sat to the left, built on a rubber surface designed to be soft when little ones slipped and fell. A small pond lay in the far distance, a dock jutting to the center. A heron picked his way among the grassy shore. But it was the circular building on the right that drew Nick's eye.

A gazebo. Like the one in Stone Gap, this one had been decorated for the holidays. Similar white lights were twined among the railings and rafters, and giant red bows hung on each of the side panels. As they approached, the lights blinked on, glowing softly in the gathering dusk.

"I come here every night at this time. I never even knew the gazebo existed until I started walking the path. But then I found this and...well, some nights it's hard to leave it and go home."

"Why?" He prayed she'd say what he wanted to hear, that she came to remember the night they shared—that it meant as much to her as it did to him.

"Because it reminds me of our gazebo," she said.

The words *our gazebo* made that hope spring to life in his chest again. "Vivian—"

"But then I realize nothing has changed. I'm still here, you're still there." She drew in a breath and raised her chin. "And even though I told you it was over... I kind of hoped you'd reach out anyway."

Yeah, there was that. Every day that passed, he'd wanted to call, but he'd either caved to fear or stubbornness or some kind of convoluted male pride. "It's not like I haven't thought about contacting you. I have. A thousand times. It wasn't until I screwed up a French omelet that I realized I was avoiding talking to you because I was afraid." He shook his head. He had driven all the way up here, maybe because he was feeling sentimental, maybe because he was a fool, but if he didn't say what he'd come here to say, he knew he'd regret it the rest of his life. "I don't want to end up like my father, letting the words go unsaid for years. So here I am, and I'm going to say them." He took a deep breath. "I love you, Vivian. I want to be with you. I should have gone after you when you left two weeks ago, but I was afraid."

"Afraid that I'd say no again?"

"You did kinda run out the door when I said I wanted forever." But so far, she was still here. Still looking at him with those big blue eyes and still holding his hand.

Her laughter was merry and light. "I did. You scared me, too, Nick. I was afraid to have the one thing that I had convinced myself I could live without. A family." She led him up the gazebo steps and into the magic spot in the center where the lights above formed a halo on the floor. She shifted into his arms. She felt good there, really good. "All my life, I've focused on being smart, strong, successful. That turned into pouring everything I had into my career. That was my safety net. If I could keep succeeding there… It's just like when I was a little girl and thought if only I was smart enough or neat enough or polite enough, my mother would step up, stop drinking and be a real mom. Instead, I was so busy being perfect and successful that I forgot to connect with the people I love. To build relationships. I was the one who wasn't taking risks with other people. People like you. And yet, you know what? My sister still loved me and thought I would be a better mother than her."

"Maybe she saw something in you that you didn't see. Like I do." Damn, Vivian was beautiful and smart. The day she'd walked into his life had made him one of the luckiest men on earth. It had just taken him a while to realize that.

"Maybe," Vivian said. "But Sammie is also far smarter than I give her credit for. She asked for help when she was overwhelmed. Granted, running away and leaving Ellie in the kitchen unsupervised wasn't the best way to do that, but she wasn't afraid to admit she couldn't be a mom on her own. Since we got back here, she's been living with me. And I've been taking Ellie to work for the couple hours a day when my schedule overlaps Sammie's at the diner."

"Really? That's great." That explained the ease with Ellie, the conversation about bottles and teething. Vivian had changed, in a lot of good ways, since that day in the kitchen of the inn.

"And in doing that, I realized I could do all those things I had been afraid of before. Raise a child. Fall in love. Create a home. Have a merry Christmas."

He thought of his grandmother's house. The tree still sat in the living room, with only the lights on the branches. Since Vivian left, he hadn't been able to bring himself to finish the decorating or to turn the lights on again. Nothing in that house felt right, not without her. "Wait. Did you just say fall in love?"

She nodded, her smile wide and unmistakable. "I fell in love with you, Nick, the night we had that date in the gazebo. It was because of how considerate you were. With the heater, the lights for Ellie in the tree. I just took a while to admit it to myself. And to you."

"That's okay. It took me a while to come after you and tell you that you are the best thing that's ever happened to me." He brushed away an errant tendril of her hair. "I want to spend Christmas with you, Vivian. This Christmas and next Christmas and all the ones after that."

She shook her head. "We can't do that here."

His heart dropped. Damn it. Had he wasted all this time? Misunderstood what she just said?

"I won't be here for Christmas, because…" Vivian said, "I want Ellie's first Christmas to be special, even if she is very unlikely to remember it. And I wanted to give Sammie a real holiday too. So I took a week off, and called the inn. Except there's one problem."

"The inn is closed for Christmas." A smile began to tease at the edges of his mouth.

"Yep. So I'm going to need another place to stay. You see, I really want Ellie's first Christmas to be in Stone Gap. And sadly, there's no other B and B in town. I do hear, however, that there is a mostly empty house that already has a very special lopsided tree."

The smile spread across his face and felt like it reached all the way to his toes. "That house also has a nursery already set up." He couldn't bring himself to walk in that room since they left, never mind bring the crib back to Mavis.

The tease he loved lit her eyes. "Are you accepting reservations? Otherwise, my plan was to just show up on your doorstep, sort of like a baby showing up on your kitchen table."

Damn, she felt good in his arms. He never wanted to let go of her again. "I'm sorry, but you have to be a part of the family to stay at 32 Lakeshore Drive."

She raised her gaze to his. "And am I? Part of the family?"

"Honey, you are all the family I want." He leaned down and kissed her then, slow and sweet and tender. She raised on her toes and wrapped her arms around his neck, and when Vivian kissed him back, Nick's heart soared. They stayed there, until the sun went down and the air chilled, and then they went home.

The next morning, Vivian woke up in Nick's arms. The sun had yet to rise, but she couldn't wait. All her life, she'd dreamed of this moment, this exact kind of day, and now she had it, with her sister sleeping in the next room and Ellie in the crib across the hall. And the man she loved right beside her, still tangled up with her. "It's Christmas, Nick," she whispered. "Wake up so we can go downstairs and open presents."

He opened his eyes and gave her a smile. "I already opened mine."

She laughed. "That was last night. Today, I want a Christmas to remember. For all of us."

For the first time in his life, Nick Jackson was up at dawn on Christmas morning. There were no servants to make breakfast or butlers to hand out the presents. There was just them, in the house that held all of Nick's best memories.

They went downstairs, still in their pajamas, followed a moment later by Sammie and Ellie, and the four of them sat around that lopsided tree, with its lights and the dozens of decorations they'd hung together the night before. Later, there would be pancakes and presents, but in that moment, watching the rainbow of lights dance across the features of the woman he loved, Nick realized even Santa couldn't top this gift.

* * * * *

MILLS & BOON

Coming next month

SNOWBOUND WITH THE HEIR
Sophie Pembroke

'Tori, sweetheart.' Jasper whispered the words against her hair, kissing her head softly as her cries lessened. 'Wake up, love.'

And she did.

Lifting her head, she blinked up at him, tears still glistening in the half-light. 'I was dreaming…' She shuddered at the memory.

'About Tyler?' he asked gently. She nodded. 'Would it help to talk about it?'

This time, she shook her head, her hair whipping around in defiance. 'I just want to forget.' She looked up at him again, and there were no tears this time. Just a new fierceness to replace the armour she'd lost. Her body shifted, and suddenly every inch of her seemed to be pressed up against him, tempting and hot and everything he'd never even dreamed of.

That was a lie. He'd dreamed about it. Often. Especially since the night they'd spent together.

But he'd never imagined it could actually happen again, not here and now.

She raised her mouth, pressing it firmly to his, her tongue sweeping out across his lower lip, and his whole body shuddered with want and desire as he kissed her back. The kiss was deep and desperate and everything he remembered about their other night together. When she pulled back, just far enough to kiss her way along his jawline, Jasper could barely remember his own name.

'Help me forget?' she murmured against his ear.

And suddenly the heat faded.

Not completely, of course. The lust she'd inspired was still coursing through his blood, and certain parts of his anatomy were absolutely on board with her plan—right now, preferably.

But his brain, that frustrating, overthinking part of him—the part that had come up with a dream of a frozen river and this woman's hand in his—had other ideas.

'Tori...' He pulled away, as far as he could without falling out of the narrow single bed. 'Tori, not like this.'

God, he wanted her. But he wanted her to want him, too. Not just forgetfulness, not just oblivion. He'd had enough of that sort of relationship himself, when he'd first moved away from Flaxstone. The kind of sex that just blocked out the world for a time, that helped him pass out and sleep without dreaming of the life he'd thought he'd had and the lies that had lurked behind it.

He didn't want that with Tori. Not this time.

Continue reading
SNOWBOUND WITH THE HEIR
Sophie Pembroke

Available next month
www.millsandboon.co.uk

COMING SOON!

We really hope you enjoyed reading this book. If you're looking for more romance, be sure to head to the shops when new books are available on

Thursday 28th November

MILLS & BOON

THE HEART OF ROMANCE

A ROMANCE FOR EVERY KIND OF READER

MODERN

Prepare to be swept off your feet by sophisticated, sexy and seductive heroes, in some of the world's most glamourous and romantic locations, where power and passion collide.
8 stories per month.

HISTORICAL

Escape with historical heroes from time gone by. Whether your passion is for wicked Regency Rakes, muscled Vikings or rugged Highlanders, awaken the romance of the past.
6 stories per month.

MEDICAL

Set your pulse racing with dedicated, delectable doctors in the high-pressure world of medicine, where emotions run high and passion, comfort and love are the best medicine.
6 stories per month.

True Love

Celebrate true love with tender stories of heartfelt romance, fro the rush of falling in love to the joy a new baby can bring, and a focus on the emotional heart of a relationship.
8 stories per month.

Desire

Indulge in secrets and scandal, intense drama and plenty of siz hot action with powerful and passionate heroes who have it all: wealth, status, good looks…everything but the right woman.
6 stories per month.

HEROES

Experience all the excitement of a gripping thriller, with an int romance at its heart. Resourceful, true-to-life women and stron fearless men face danger and desire - a killer combination!
8 stories per month.

DARE

Sensual love stories featuring smart, sassy heroines you'd want a best friend, and compelling intense heroes who are worthy of t
4 stories per month.

To see which titles are coming soon, please visit

millsandboon.co.uk/nextmonth

MILLS & BOON

HISTORICAL

Awaken the romance of the past

Escape with historical heroes from time gone by. Whether your passion is for wicked Regency Rakes, muscled Viking warriors or rugged Highlanders, indulge your fantasies and awaken the romance of the past.